Also by Adriana Trigiani
available from Random House Large Print

The Queen of the Big Time

Rococo

Rococo

A NOVEL

Adriana Trigiani

R A N D O M   H O U S E
L A R G E   P R I N T

Copyright © 2005 by
The Glory of Everything Company

All rights reserved.
Published in the United States of America by
Random House Large Print in association with
Random House, New York.
Distributed by Random House, Inc., New York.

**The Library of Congress has established a
Cataloging-in-Publication record for this title.**

0-375-43529-8

www.randomlargeprint.com

FIRST LARGE PRINT EDITION

10 9 8 7 6 5 4 3 2 1

This Large Print edition published in accord with
the standards of the N.A.V.H.

For my husband,
who can fix anything

Contents

Rococo

CHAPTER ONE

The Duke of Décor on the Jersey Shore

1970

I want you to imagine my house. It's a classic English country cottage, nestled on an inlet overlooking the Atlantic Ocean in the borough of Our Lady of Fatima, New Jersey, about five miles north of Interlaken. The fieldstone exterior gives the illusion of a small fortress, so I softened the overall effect with white hyacinth shrubs and a blanket of sky-blue morning glories cascading over the dormers like loose curls on a cherub. After all, a man's home must first be inviting.

Every morning at sunrise a honeyed pink light fills the front room, throwing a rosy glaze on the walls that cannot be achieved with paint. Believe me, I've tried. I settled instead for a neutral shade on the walls, a delicate beige I call flan.

When the walls are tame, the furnishings need to pop. So I found the perfect chintz, with giant jewel-toned flowers of turquoise, coral, and jade bursting on a butter-yellow background, to cover my Louis Quatorze sofa and chairs. The upholstery soaks up the light and warms the room better than a fire blazing in the hearth. Anyone who says you will tire of a bold pattern on your furniture is a fool. The right fabric will give you years of joy; it can become your signature. Scalamandré's Triomphe #26301 has my name on it.

My day begins at dawn as I take my cup of strong black espresso outside to watch the sunrise. I learned this ritual from my mother, who worked in a bread shop. Bakers are the great philosophers of the world, mostly because they have to get up early. When the world is quiet, great art is created—or, at the very least, conceptualized. Now is the moment to sketch, make notes, and dream.

From my front porch, a dignified, simple portal with a slate floor (I laid the charcoal-gray, dusty-mauve, and smoky-blue slabs myself), I watch the colors of the sky and sea change at the whims of the wind. Sometimes the ocean crashes in foamy white waves that look like ruffles. Then, suddenly, the light is gone and everything turns to gray satin. When the sun returns, the charcoal clouds lift away and the world becomes as tranquil as a library, the water as flat as a page in a book, Venetian glass under a blue cloudless sky.

What a boon to live on the water! Such delicious shades and hues! This is a template worthy of the greatest painters. The textures of sand and stone could inspire incomparable sculptures, and the sounds—the steady lapping of the waves, the sweet chirping of the birds—make this a sanctuary. I soak up the view in all its detail and translate this glorious palette to the interiors of local homes. You see, I am the Town Decorator.

Many have compared our little borough to the village my family emigrated from, the enchanting Santa Margherita nestled in the Gulf of Genoa on the Mediterranean coast of Italy. I've been there, but I favor my hometown over the original. Italy, despite its earthiness and charm, can never be New Jersey. Here we value evolution and change; Italy, while it warms the heart, is a monument to the past. In America we change our rooms as often as our fashions. In Italy you're likely to find throw pillows older than the Shroud of Turin. It's just a different way to live.

Part of my job is to convince my clients that change is good, then guide them to the right choices. I remember when I installed a velvet headboard on my cousin Tiki Matera's double bed (she was plagued by insomnia from the cradle) and she told me that, for the first time in her life, she felt so secure that she slept through the night. That Art Deco touch changed her room and her life—not a small thing. That's the business I'm really in: creating appropriate surroundings to provide comfort and that essential touch of glamour. I built my company, the House of B, and my reputation on it. HOB stands for the eye of Bartolomeo di Crespi and the guts of beauty itself: truth, color, and dramatic sweep, from slipcover to oven mitt. I don't fool around.

My work can't be defined by one particular style. The rococo period where French design and Italian flair came together make my heart leap for joy in my chest. But, I love them all: Chinese Modern, Regency English, French Norman, Prairie Nouveau, Victorian (without the precious), Early American (with the precious), all the Louises from I through V (Vuitton, of course), postwar, prewar, bungalow, foxhole, and even the occasional log cabin. I can go big and I can do small.

I work from the inside out. Truly great interior design includes the rooms you live in and everything your eye can see from your windows. I often bring the colors from outside indoors, which soothes the soul and creates harmony. I may install a reflecting pool outside your living room to catch the moonlight, or plant a garden of wildflowers with a rose arbor anchored over a flowing fountain beyond your kitchen window, or perhaps place a wrought-iron loveseat surrounded by lilac bushes outside your bedroom for a midnight rendezvous.

Your home should inspire you to greater heights of emotion. It should crackle with color and pizzazz. Every detail is important; every tassel, tieback, and sheer should say something. Under my trained eye, stale corners become Roman baths, while bland entryways become magnificent foyers and crappy pasteboard ceilings become frescoes. Let's face it, I can take a ranch and turn it into a villa. In fact, I did that very thing right on Vittorio Drive, three blocks away.

My life as a decorator began not with a sudden flash of inspiration, but with a problem. I was born without symmetry. This is not my real nose. As soon as I was old enough to pull myself up onto the stool in front of my mother's dressing table (an Art Deco red enamel vanity with a pink velvet seat circa 1920), where I could pull the side mirrors in to study my face from three angles, I realized that something had to be done. From the east, my nose looked like the fin on a Cadillac, from the west, a wedge of pie, and dead on, a frightening pair of black caverns, two nostrils so wide and deep you could lose your luggage in them. It had to go.

As an Italian American, I was born into a family of prominent noses. The di Crespi clan was known for their fish (Pop had a dinghy for clamming and crabbing, and a storefront in town to sell his catch) and their profiles. We were not alone. Our neighbors were also of Italian descent, many from the same village, and they too had versions of The Beak. The variations included all possible shapes, angles, and appointments, all with the same result: too large.

I was raised to be proud of my cultural and nasal heritage, so it wasn't shame that brought me to the surgeon, it was a desire for perfection. My instinct is to create balance. Faces, like buildings, require good bones.

As soon as I could save up enough money (I worked after school and for five summers in the Mandelbaums' bank as a coin sorter and roller), I took the bus from Our Lady of Fatima (OLOF) to the office of Dr. Jonas Berman on East Eighty-sixth Street in Manhattan. I was eighteen years old with a spiral-bound sketch pad under my arm and a checkbook in my pocket.

First, I'd drawn a self-portrait in charcoal, showing my original nose. Then, in a series of detailed drawings, I fashioned the nose I wanted from every angle. Dr. Berman flipped through the pad. Amazed at my artistic skill, he cited Leonardo da Vinci's pencil sketches of early flying machines as being substandard to my talent.

If I was going to have rhinoplasty, I wanted to make sure I had the nose of my dreams. I didn't want a hatchet job that would leave me with a Hollywood pug. I wanted regal, straight, and classic. In short, Italianate without the size. I got exactly what I wanted.

My sister, Toot (as in the song "Toot, Toot, Tootsie," not the toot of a horn), who is eleven years older than me, was the first person to see my new nose when the swelling went down. She was so thrilled at the result that she convinced my father to sell his car so she could have the same surgery. My father, never one to tell a woman no, paid for her to have The Operation (as my mother came to call it). Never mind that I had worked like a farmer to earn my new profile. But I don't hold a grudge.

Toot elected to have her nose done not in New York City by my capable surgeon, but by a doctor in Jersey City who was rumored to have given Vic Damone his signature tilt. (I am

the only person in my family who does not believe in medical bargains.) When Dr. Mavro-
dontis peeled Toot's bandages off, Mom, Pop,
and I were there for the unveiling. Mama
clapped her hands joyfully as Papa got a tear in
his eye. Talk about change. Her new nose had a
sharp tip with an upturn so steep you could
hang a Christmas stocking off it. Gone was her
old nose, which had looked like an elbow; but
was this delicate Ann Miller version an improvement?

To be fair, the new nose gave my sister the
dose of self-confidence she needed. She suddenly believed she was beautiful, so she went on
a spartan diet of well-done steak and raw tomatoes and lost a good thirty pounds, tweezed her
eyebrows and straightened her hair (by sleeping
on wet orange-juice cans every night for a year),
and, shortly thereafter, in the right pair of black
clam diggers and a tight angora sweater, fell in
love with Alonzo "Lonnie" Falcone, a jeweler, at
a Knights of Columbus weenie roast in Belmar.
Six months later they had a big church wedding
at Our Lady of Fatima Church and three sons
followed in short order. Her nose may not be
perfect, but it was lucky.

817 Corinne Way has been Toot's address for
eighteen years. After they lived for a couple of

hardscrabble years in a row house in Bayonne, Lonnie's business took off, so they bought a home in OLOF to be near my folks. When Toot and Lonnie divorced, she got the house, a lovely Georgian with grand Palladian columns anchoring a polished oak door trimmed in squares of leaded glass.

I pull up in the driveway next to my sister's chartreuse Cadillac. I get out of the car, taking a small footstool that I reupholstered for Toot with me. The lawn is freshly mowed and green. The boxwood hedges are trimmed and tidy. Everything about the exterior of the house is appropriate except for one glaring design misfire: My sister mucked up the entrance with a countrified porch swing she found at a tag sale in Maine. I tell her that a Georgian with a porch swing is like a hooker in a girdle, but she keeps the swing and I keep my mouth shut. The truth is, I'm a little afraid of her. Toot has always been a second mother to me, and any Italian son will tell you that two Italian mothers in a lifetime is a handful. I'm not complaining, because we adore each other; I defer to her on family matters, and she to me on aesthetic ones (most of the time; after all, she kept the swing).

"I'm here!" I holler cheerfully. Toot's house always smells of anisette and fresh-perked coffee, the lovely bouquet of our mother's home.

"Back here, B," she yells.

Carrying the footstool I'd re-covered in pale blue wool for her boudoir, I make my way down the long hallway, which is papered in a Schumacher pale-yellow-and-white paisley print. I decorated the entire house, but my favorite room is her kitchen. I did a real number on it.

First, I sent my sister to Las Vegas to visit Cousin Iggy With The Asthma for three months. Then I gutted the old kitchen. I installed a bay window on the back wall to maximize the light and designed a Roman shade of pure white muslin to let in the sun but keep out the nosy neighbors. Underneath I built a window seat with cushions covered in a practical red cotton twill (Duralee Hot Red #429). I believe that any fabrics used in a kitchen should be washable.

For fun, I used oversized zippers on the seat cushions to pick up the metal accents of the appliances. To bring nature indoors, I used rustic white birch paneling on the wall around the window. I papered the remaining walls with a bold Colefax and Fowler red-and-white stripe and installed white Formica cabinets with red ceramic pulls. The result is peppermint-candy delish!

The countertop, in white marble, has an extension that swings out in an L shape to make a breakfast nook, with sleek bar stools covered in white patent leather with brass-stud trim. The studs are an excellent accent to the shimmering copper pots that hang over the sink area like charms on a bracelet. The refrigerator (side-by-side) and stove (gas) were purchased in white, but I had them delivered to Chubby's Garage, where they were jet-spray-painted a bright, shiny, fiery red. I'm forever thinking of ways to give design that extra kick, using unlikely sources. Take note.

The kitchen table is topped with wide white ceramic tiles. Beneath the table, I installed a cutting board that pulls out for additional workspace. It comes in handy when Toot makes pasta. The table is surrounded by cozy booth seating in a cheerful red gingham. The palette works. It's vibrant! It's up! When you stand in this kitchen, you feel as though you are on the inside of a tomato, the exact effect I wanted.

"You like my pants set? It's new." Toot does her version of a model's twirl, pointing her right foot out in front of the left and holding her arms out waist-high like a milkmaid. The sweater is a disaster, an enormous white pilgrim collar on a cable-knit orange cardigan. (I can see that the wool is a fine cashmere, but what good is it? The eye sees round, round, round instead of sleek. My sister needs length, not width.) The brown slacks have a wide bell hem. She looks like a piece of candy corn. "It's a St. John knit," she says, giving me an in-the-know wink.

"Only a saint could get away with such a color combination," I say.

Like all Mediterranean girls, my sister is aging well. By soft candlelight or with the help of a dimmer switch, she has the look of a plump Natalie Wood. In broad daylight, she's a dead ringer for our great-grandmother, the pleasantly pudgy Bartolomea Farfanfiglia, whom we never knew, but who stares at us with disgust from a sepia photograph on the television set.

"I'm going to get my teeth capped," my sister announces.

Keep in mind, it is always something with Toot. Self-improvement is her Holy Grail. If she isn't going on a diet of Metrecal shakes or installing an in-ground pool (inspired by the Summer Olympics), there's some other project under way that, alas, she never sees through to completion. I've learned to play along. "Why would you touch your teeth? You have a lovely smile."

"Only when clenched. In repose, I'm a knockout." Toot looks at her reflection in the oven window. "But when I throw my head back and laugh, it looks like I've been eating black jelly beans for a living."

"So get the caps."

"Darn right. I'm fifty-one years old and I've been grinding my teeth all my life. That's how I work off my nervous energy, and now I'm biting my tongue all the time. See?" Toot pulls the sides of her mouth open with her forefingers. "I'm afraid the constant gnashing is gonna give me mouth cancer. Not my fault, though. I use the Waterpik. My oral surgeon said everything shifts when you go through The Change." Toot motions for me to sit down. "Another reason to throw myself out the attic window and not look down."

Toot goes to the sink and washes her hands while I display the re-covered boudoir stool on the window seat for her appraisal. "Well, do you like it?"

"It's cute," she says. "I'll put it next to the chaise lounge."

"Toot, how many times do I have to tell you, it's chaise **longue,** not lounge. **Longue** means 'long' in French."

"When I'm lying on it, I'm lounging. What's the damn difference what we call it?"

"Because it's **wrong.** I don't make these things up." I try not to snap. "These are historical terms we use in the design field. Please respect them. Make an effort."

Toot shrugs as she pries open a large Tupper-

ware cookie saver and carefully lifts iced coconut cookies out onto a plate. "I've got so
much on me, B." She breaks off a corner of a
blue frosted cookie and eats it, then hands me
a pink cookie. Soon our blood sugar reaches a
comfortable high and we relax into the soft
booth like spoons in cake batter. Toot pours hot
coffee into two red-and-white polka-dot mugs.
She scoots the sugar bowl and creamer toward
me and places a small silver spoon on a red-and-
white gingham napkin next to the mug.

The crease between her eyes relaxes as she
takes a larger piece of cookie and dunks it into
her coffee. I can't count the number of times in
my life I have sat at my sister's kitchen table
and dunked something sweet into a mug of
something hot. The ritual always brings me
great comfort. Toot picks up the cookie like it's
the Sacred Host at Mass and says, "After the
new year, I'm giving these up for good."

"It's April."

Toot chews. "I need a few months to practice."

My sister has delicate hands for her size. Her
given name, Nicolina, means "Little Nicky,"
but I don't remember her ever being small. I remember my mother taking us shopping for
bathing suits when I was little, and Toot weeping behind a muslin curtain, saying, "The size
sixteen is too tight." Of course, I was young

during the final sputtering of the Great Depression. The girls wore one-piece black wool bathing suits to the shore, and the only embellishments were buttons. Toot had her heart set on a boat-neck maillot she'd seen Myrna Loy wearing poolside in **Modern Screen** magazine. No one had the heart to tell her that the only thing she had in common with Myrna Loy was the occasional freckle. My mother, God bless her, kept steering her toward the old-lady styles and away from the Young Sophisticates, knowing that Toot wouldn't fit into the fashionable suits. Toot kept arguing, telling Ma, "I'm young! I want a girlish suit!" Finally my mama lost patience and said, "**Non puoi uccidere una mosca con un cannone**," which, loosely translated, means, "You can't stuff an olive with a drumstick."

"Good, huh?" Toot watches me chew. I give her an okay sign with my fingers so as not to choke on the crumbs. "So are you with me on the teeth?"

"Whatever you want to do is fine."

"It's not just cosmetic, B. Though, at my age, you look for little avenues of self-improvement even if they lead you up a blind alley of ugly. I wish it were just naturalism—"

"Narcissism."

"Uh-huh. But it's medical. I can't chew. I have

to chop my salad so fine it's like soup. What the hell, maybe I'll lose a couple of pounds."

It occurs to me that my sister has grown larger over the years out of necessity. Without a man around, she had to stay the size of her sons to keep order in this crazy home. I did all I could to help, but it wasn't enough. My nephews, Nicholas and Anthony, are, sadly, **gavones.** Yet there's a ray of hope: Her youngest son, my namesake, Bartolomeo the Second (whom we call Two), seems to have my artistic eye. He's a theater major at Villanova.

"Well, who are you going to?"

"Dr. Pomerance. The man is a genius. They say he did Hubert Humphrey's teeth."

"He had his teeth capped? It doesn't look it."

"Old pictures." She shrugs. "Listen. I need a flavor."

"Uh-huh." My sister, who doesn't know "longue" from "lounge," has always said "flavor" instead of "favor," and I'm not about to start correcting her now.

"It's my Nicky. He's moved into a house in Freehold with . . . her."

"The girlfriend?"

"Ondine Doyle. Sounds cheap, doesn't it?"

"Actually it sounds like a flounder special at the Mayfair."

"That's not even slightly funny." Toot fans herself. "It makes me sick. Rosemary Callabuono has loved my son since high school, and he won't give her a tumble."

"Rosemary With The Lupus?"

"Yeah, but it's in remission. Better a woman with lupus than a woman with no virtue. Of all the girls in the world, he chooses **that**. Please."

I try to picture Ondine. It's not easy, since my nephew changes girlfriends as often as he changes pants. I recall a curvy, petite blonde with short legs and an upturned nose. "Is she the one who sat in his lap at the Feast party?" I ask, remembering her grinding into my nephew like a drill bit while the band played "Louie, Louie."

"That's the one! She hooked him with sex. They're not kidding me. Nicky said, 'I love her, Ma.' I said to him, 'You love your ass!' "

"Why is it fast girls always have French names?"

"How the hell would I know?" Toots's eyebrows weave together, the lines quizzically forming the shape of a bird in flight.

"If Nicky's moved out, that means you have an empty room."

"Don't get any ideas," she warns. "I'm not ready to redecorate. I think I'm going to put an exercise bike in there."

"Wonderful!"

"Maybe I can build up a little muscle tone."

"Good idea." I am nothing if not supportive.

"What? I look flabby?"

"No, no, it's just that exercise gives you pep. And who couldn't use a little extra pep?"

"You have a point." Toot smiles.

I've learned over the years to stay mum with my sister on the subject of physical fitness. She's never broken a sweat in her life, yet the basement is filled with every new piece of exercise equipment that comes on the market. A couple of years ago Woolworth's carried the revolutionary Tummy Chummy, a small wheel with two handles for toning stomach muscles. Toot bought it, took it home, got down on her knees, and commenced rolling; but her abdominal muscles were so weak she collapsed on the wheel, hit her head on a chair, and gave herself a black eye. **Ciao, ciao,** Tummy Chummy.

"I'm so ashamed of my son. Shacking up in Freehold like he was raised in a barn. They live in the nicer section, but still . . . it looks like a rat hole." Toot holds her nose. "Everything about it is **stashad.** Mark my words. Nineteen seventy is the beginning of the end of civilization. Morality has gone right out the window." Toot sips her coffee. "They need curtains—"

"Draperies," I correct her.

"Draperies. Furniture. Lonnie said he'd pay."

"Good. Because I'm busy. I don't have time to run around shopping for deals."

"Believe me, if she was a quality individual, I could trust her to do the decorating, but she's from the side of the tracks where the houses shake when the trains go by, so she doesn't know from nice. She doesn't own foundation garments. I know for a fact she doesn't own a slip, because I saw France when she climbed into Nicky's car after we visited Aunt Mary Mix-Up at the home."

"At least she visits the infirm."

"Nicky dragged her. Oh, I could cry. No class. She wears open-toed sandals in December without stockings. You get the picture. Everything about her clings."

"She's young."

"Seven years older than Nicky. No prize there, I'm telling you. She's well on her way to wizened. You don't know. You don't have children. How could you know the disappointment, so deep I get a shooting pain in my pelvis—"

"Stop," I interrupt. Toot has a terrible habit of getting pains in places men would prefer never to hear about.

"My pelvic bone. Right here." She points south. I don't look. "No wonder it became inflamed when Nicky passed through the birth canal. It was like an omen. Nine pounds of him dragged through me like a wagon wheel. And didn't the little bastard bring me pain for the rest of my life?"

"Come on. You adore him."

"I know. I hate him and I love him so much I could kill him. Why would my firstborn son waste himself on **that?**"

"Maybe he loves her."

Toot gives me a look as though the stench from the Carbone paper factory in Hazlet were right here in Peppermint Candy Land. "If only Ma was here."

"If Ma were here, what? She'd commiserate, but neither of you would say or do one damn thing to fix it, because you're Italian mothers." I feel my face flush as I raise my voice. Toot looks startled. "That's right, Toot, you're all talk. You have these sons—you treat them like kings, waiting on them hand and foot, spoiling them, coddling them, worshipping them, never expecting them to lift a finger to help you in any way—then you're surprised when they fall for these come-hither French maids instead of nice Catholic girls. You want to know why they end up with harlots? Because your boys know **easy,** that's why!"

"I suppose it's all **my** fault!" Toot says, banging the table and beginning to weep. Her mascara runs. Big navy blue tears roll down her face like ink from a dropper. She wipes the streaks away with a white **moppeen.**

"Partly!" I yell back. "But not all! Mama raised me like you raised your boys, with one difference. I knew better! I wanted to take care of myself. I took pride in my surroundings. I tried to build upon what our parents taught us. When I watched Ma iron, I thought, **I can do that collar better,** and I'd show her how. When she made soup, I thought, **I can chop the celery finer,** and I'd take the knife from her hands. When she decorated the Christmas wreath, I thought, **That bow is too big,** and I'd fix it. Mama was never my maid."

Toot wearily opens a cabinet neatly filled with extra utensils from Chinese takeout, a stack of paper plates from last summer's Fourth of July party, and plastic cups that say HAPPY EASTER. She pulls out a Santa-and-the-reindeer paper plate and stacks cookies on it. "What can I do now? They're men. The ship has failed."

"**Sailed,** sis. Sailed."

"I want you to take these over to Nicky. God knows if he gets enough to eat over there. Of course, that's probably my fault too."

"Probably. If your Mother Guilt was paint, I'd have enough to put a coat on Yankee Stadium. You did the best you could. **Fini.**"

A buzzer blasts from the laundry room.

"That's the dryer." Toot wipes away her tears, then gets up and goes into the next room. She returns with a basket of freshly laundered whites. She pulls a pristine undershirt from the pile and folds it.

"Whose laundry is that?"

"What?" she asks innocently.

"Whose is it?"

"Nicky's," she says softly.

"He's living in his own home and you're still doing his laundry? What kind of nonsense is that?"

Toot ignores the question and tilts her chin toward heaven. "Do you think Ma knows her favorite grandson is living in sin?"

"Of course she knows, and she doesn't care. She's flying around up there like an angel, probably at the speed of sound to avoid running into Pop."

"That's where all this started. It started with their sick marriage. I didn't have a good example."

"We've been through this," I tell her firmly. "Don't start."

Toot grows pensive. Despite my eagerness to change the subject, she goes on a diatribe about our immigrant parents and their arranged marriage and how that scarred her for life, and I'm not excluded because "Look at you, you're almost forty and you're not married." I let her talk while I have another cookie.

I never feel the need to defend my bachelor-hood. In fact, when I look over the landscape of my life, it's the best choice I ever made. I love living alone—knowing there's exactly enough milk in the fridge for cereal, always knowing where the roll of Scotch tape is, sleeping in the buff, waking up to **silencio** instead of bells and yells. I don't miss a thing about living with fam-ily. I had eighteen years of it with my parents and my sister, and that cured me of any desire to repeat the experience.

"This is the crux." Toot thumps her chest in the vicinity of her heart. "We're a couple of love cripples, you and me. We can't shake the past. I had a good marriage that went sour, and now look at me; I can't move on. Everybody in the world seems to move on but me. Lonnie's had two wives since he left me, and I've barely had a date. A little dinner and a show, is that too much to ask?"

"No, it's not too much to ask." But even agreeing with her can't stop the onslaught.

"I'm besmirched." She takes a stack of Nicky's briefs and smooths them flat with her hand be-fore returning them to the laundry basket. "No one wants besmirched. Ma married a lousy cheater, and I did the same. Shame on me for being sucked into the flume of infidelity and spit out the other end like charred rubble. Why couldn't I see what was happening under my nose? I shoulda known better. Or, at the very least, I should've known something. If my ex-husband walked through the door right now, I'd throw a chair at him."

"Which is probably why he doesn't visit." And probably why he left, but I won't say that out loud. Why pile on?

"Maybe it's the end of the road for me, but not for you. You should marry Capri Mandelbaum." Toot places the laundry basket on the window seat.

"I do not like the word **should**."

"You can afford to be cavalier. If you want to marry"—she snaps her fingers—"you can. A man can always find a woman, but a woman after a certain age can only find heartache. Lucky you. You don't know what it's like when loneliness is thrown on you like a burlap tarp and you can't breathe some nights from the regret." Toot refills my coffee mug.

"I doubt I'll regret anything."

"I'm older than you. I know all about it. The day comes when your youth leaves you like a dying whiff of Jean Naté. You still have your hair and your waistline, B. Look at Capri, she's turning forty. God knows she's lonely too, with that myopia so bad she can't even see her own hand without glasses. She needs you, you need her."

"I know what I need," I say quietly.

"Take Capri away for a weekend. It'll be like throwing two old cats in a closet—something will happen. You'll either kill each other or mate." Toot burps the Tupperware cookie saver.

"What a lovely proposition either way."

"Go on, joke. I don't understand you. She's rich! The Mandelbaums have more money than Onassis, and it's even better because it's American dough. Can't you see? You could redecorate the entire state of New Jersey; the old lady would write the check. You could be hanging chandeliers in the men's room at the Shell station on Route 9, for godsakes."

"That's not my goal. I want to make the world elegant. Decorating homes is satisfying, but I have a bigger dream." The moment I say it aloud, I'm sorry I did.

"What?"

"It's bigger than just being rich or decorating gas stations."

Toot sits down. "You don't want to move out of town, do you? 'Cause if you moved, I'd kill myself."

"I'm not moving."

"Thank God." Toot exhales. "What is it, then?"

"I want to renovate and redesign the Fatima church."

Toot waves me away like a gnat. "You've spent your whole life there. I don't see why Father Porporino wouldn't give you the job. You're the only decorator in town." She cups her hand at the edge of the table and scoots a couple of crumbs off the tiles.

"I should get the job because I have a vision for the church, not because there are no other candidates."

"You and your megamania."

I don't bother to correct her. This time, she's close enough.

She continues, "Relax. I've never seen a room of yours that I didn't love. You may be the only decorator in town, but you're also the best."

My sister makes no sense, but I'm in no mood to explain and the cookies are giving me a sugar drop that makes me feel like I'm plummeting in an elevator shaft. I hold my head. Toot gets up and leans against the sink. She surveys her backyard as she folds her hands, looking eerily like the Saint Theresa statue on the window ledge. "What's going to become of us?" she says. "I'm gonna wind up all alone like Aunt Teeney, who went to sleep sucking on a sourball and choked to death after it lodged in her throat like a pinball, creating a dry socket that paralyzed her larynx and killed her dead. Who'll be there for me?"

I feel a rush of pity for my sister, but I resist it. Her Miriam Hopkins act isn't going to wash with me. "Oh, please, you are not alone. Who comes when you call?"

She takes a moment to think about it. "You do."

"Who papered your living room and hung your sconces?"

"You did."

"Look at this kitchen! It's a triumph of design! It could be in **House and Garden**! Brand-new everything from stove to cassoulet pot." I get up and join her at the sink.

"I love what you did in here. I do." She reaches up and runs her hands over the copper pots. They tinkle like chimes.

"Who helped you buy your new car and took you into the city for toe surgery—"

"That hurt worse than the pelvic bone," she says quietly.

"I've always been here for you." I put my arms around her. "And I always will be. So knock it off."

"Every man I've ever known has let me down . . . except you. Three vaginal births, and you drove me to the hospital every single time."

"That's right. I did."

"You even cut little Two's cord. Lonnie was in Miami. He was always in Miami." Toot pulls a handkerchief from under her bra strap; she unfolds it and blows her nose. "You know, I've never been to Miami."

"You want to go to Florida? I'll take you."

"No thanks. Too much humidity. My hair goes to Brillo in that heat. But you're a prince to invite me." Toot takes my hand. "I want to thank you for everything you've done for me. So I'm going to make you a birthday party."

"No you're not."

"Yes I am. I've already planned the whole thing with cousin Christina. Poor thing. She's so depressed. I was hoping a party would help her through her grief."

I yank my hand away. "I can't believe you're guilting me like this."

"What guilt?" Toot looks off in the middle distance innocently.

"No party!"

"I know you hate surprises—"

"Detest them!" I rap my fist on the counter to make the point.

"So I'm telling you all about it beforehand. The guests, of course, will think it's a surprise, because I have to have something for them to do."

"No!"

"I want to give back. Let me do this. Forty is a millstone."

"Milestone," I correct her.

"Whatever. All the cousins want to come."

"I can't stand those people."

"All these years you gave them gifts. Let them buy **you** a present for a change."

"I still have fifteen wallets from my thirtieth birthday party."

"You should have returned them."

"And gotten what?"

"A professional man like you can always use ties and handkerchiefs."

"Have you seen how they dress? I'll choose my own accessories, thank you. No party! Do you understand plain English? No!"

Toot checks her manicure and then looks at me. "Too late. I already cleaned out the garage."

As I drive to Freehold I'm tempted to get out of the car and throw myself into the manmade lake outside the industrial park to cleanse myself of my sister's bitterness. I don't know what she's complaining about. Her ex set her up for life. To this day, Lonnie sends her jewelry; in return, my sister makes a pot of gravy and meatballs and sends it over on the first Sunday of the month. Granted, it's not a fair exchange—the pieces Lonnie sends are samples, and half the time the bales are flimsy and the clasps don't catch—but perhaps it's the thought that should count.

My nephew Nicky resides **con inammorata** (there's a handwritten card that says "Doyle/ Falcone" on the mailbox) in a ranch on Main Street in Freehold. It's a pleasant neighborhood with houses facing one another in the cul-de-sac like triangular wedges of cheesecake on a platter.

The ranch has a faux-brick front, a two-car garage, and the bane of any decorator's existence, cheesy Florida windows, the kind that open out in flaps. I ring the bell. When no one answers, I knock on the door.

"Hey, stop beatin' the door, you're scarin' the cat!" I hear Ondine's muffled voice through the door's small rectangular windows, which are lined with stick-um-stained glass. She opens the door and smiles. "Oh, hi." She's busty, with a fading tan, wearing an Empire-waist smock dress. Her long blond hair is hoisted into a fountain ponytail on top. In the bright sun she looks a solid thirty-five, which is why I don't like to know chronological ages—once you know, the person looks every day of the number. Her eyes are as powdery blue as Toot's frosting. She squints as she takes a drag off a cigarette. I hand her the paper plate of cookies. "For you and my nephew."

"Bar-toe-low-may-oh." It rolls off her tongue slowly as she exhales a puff of smoke. I cough.

"Your mother-in . . . rather, my sister, Toot, sent me over."

"She tole me all about it. She thinks I don't know how to decorate a house. For her information, I've lived in one since the day I was born." Ondine reaches down and picks up the cat. "This is Pierre." The cat looks like an oversized fuzzy slipper with eyes.

I look around the living room, a postcollege mishmash of donations: a plaid couch, a green velvet lounger, and a glass coffee table with four wrought-iron owls holding it up along the edges.

"Ignore this room," she says, and motions for me to follow her.

"With pleasure," I tell her cheerfully.

"This is my dilemma." Ondine puts the cat down on the shag carpet. For a moment I can't tell where the salt-and-pepper shag ends and Pierre begins. "The dining room."

I give it a quick survey. The room has one solid wall; the opposite wall is lined with the long, thin Florida windows. It might as well be a tunnel, it's so narrow. It reminds me of Captain Kirk's time-travel capsule on **Star Trek.**

"What would you do in here?" She stands too close to me as I examine the room.

"I'd move."

Ondine throws her head back and laughs. "No. Seriously."

"You need draperies, floor-length, to give the illusion of height."

"I like draperies," she coos.

"You need a long server on this wall."

"Okay."

"That"—I point to the ugly dining room table and chairs—"must go."

"But it was my grandmother's."

"She gave it away for a reason."

"She died."

"Oh, you inherited it. Do you know the value of sentimental is zero?"

"Not to me! I could never part with it. It's all I got from her. That, and these"—she points to her décolletage—"for which I am grateful."

"I see." Ondine does have a great figure, and her bustline is surely something to be proud of. I look at the walls. "What I would recommend is mirrors on the far wall, to open up the room.

"That's what I thought!" she squeals. "It needs to feel wider. More light! Yeah, I love mirrors!" She winks at me inappropriately.

"Right. And then you need a new dining room suite, one with a circular glass-top table.

The chairs should be open, with polished-cotton seats." I turn around, trying to determine the dominant color scheme in the house. There is none. I go with a classic. "A bold white-and-chocolate-brown stripe. Polished cotton is best because it repels stains; you know, spaghetti sauce and kitty accidents."

"But I want to keep the suite. Can't you paint it or something?" She runs her hand over the heavy dark brown Regency table like she's massaging a sore thigh muscle. Her affection for the furniture doesn't make it any more attractive. This clunky repro looks like an operating table you'd find in Dr. Frankenstein's laboratory. The claw feet are particularly obtrusive and ugly, but not to be outdone, the chairs have hideous bishop-hat finials.

"If you insist on keeping this furniture, there's no point in mirroring the wall."

"Why?"

"Because, Ondine"—I feel myself losing patience—"you should never look at shit twice."

Ondine follows me to the front door and opens it. "I'll think about selling it," she says quietly.

"You do that."

"What do you think I could get for it?"

"I'm not an antiquarian."

"Oh, okay." Ondine looks confused, then she

smiles brightly. "Well, thank you for coming over." She leans over and gives me a quick kiss on the cheek. Then she steps out onto the stoop. "You're a gentleman with fine taste. I trust you with my domicile." She does a slow inventory of me, starting at my feet (in black suede Gucci loafers), moving on to my gray Paul Stuart wool trousers and finally my black V-neck cashmere sweater. She gazes through me like she's wearing X-Ray Specs, those magic eyeglasses they sell in the back of comic books that claim you'll be able to see people without their clothes on. "I wish Nicky had one thimbleful of the class you got."

I don't know what to say, so I smile politely and turn to go. She grabs me around the neck, pulls my face toward hers, and kisses me again. This time she drags her tongue over my upper lip. I pull away when I feel the wet warmth.

"Ondine, I am almost technically your uncle!" I look around to see if anyone has witnessed us. I fish my handkerchief out of my trouser pocket and purse my lips to discourage any further activity.

"I'm in charge of the decorations for your birthday party. I'm thinking balloons." She gives me that wink again.

After a strenuous day of meeting clients, plowing through paneling samples at the lumberyard, and mixing paint at the hardware store, I am starving and ready for a martini. I pull into the Mandelbaums' driveway in Deal with a coconut-cream pie I picked up at Delicious Orchards on Route 34 in Colts Neck. I went out of my way for the pie, not only because it's Aurelia's favorite, but because I need her support. There are rumblings that Father Porporino is finally prepared to renovate our church, and I need my good friend Aurelia to put my name at the top of the list for the big job.

Capri, my friend since I had a memory, meets me at the front door. She is a petite five feet tall, which has always made me feel protective of her. When we were babies, our mothers hatched a scheme that we would someday marry. Mama said, "They're rich and we have taste. That's a perfect match." Here we are, thirty-nine years later, and the scheme is still in full swing, at least in Aurelia's mind. A doting mother with a firm hand on the control switch, she has always handpicked everything for Capri, from her socks to her college curriculum to me. Aurelia Castone Mandelbaum is a local Italian girl who married so well she never looked back. To her credit, she never forgot where she came from, but she sure liked the other side once she got there.

"I just got over a bad cold." Capri is always

getting over something. Her hair, skin, and wool cardigan are the color of a peanut shell. Though not officially sickly, she has the look of someone who is battling an infirmity, which gives her the blackest under-eye circles I've ever seen on someone who doesn't live in a tree. She has been this way all her life. In fact, in all of high school she never took phys ed. The hand-written excuse notes from her doctor were legendary. He started with diseases that begin with an **A** (asthma) when Capri was in eighth grade, and by senior year she hit the **Z's** (zinc deficiency). Capri has never lived outside her parents' home, so she seems much younger than she is. It's like when you keep a banana out of the sun—it doesn't ripen. Capri is a forty-year-old green banana.

Capri has a heart-shaped face and a short neck (an unfortunate combination—it's like an egg cradled in a spoon). On the plus side, she has long sensuous fingers and a plush caboose. She's so nearsighted that she is legally blind without her glasses. Even though she wears fashionable frames (in our youth Capri wore cat-eye glasses with real diamond chips on the wings), there's only so much a doctor can do with lenses as thick as ashtrays. Poor Capri always looks as though she is peering through the wall of an aquarium. She tried contact lenses, but she has recessive tear ducts (a painful condition, her mother is always quick to remind me), so she can't wear them. I am one of the rare people who has seen Capri without her eyeglasses, and while she is no Claudia Cardinale, it's an improvement. I kiss her on the cheek.

"Mom made shepherd's pie," Capri says by way of greeting.

"Great. I need some nutritional gravitas."

"Well, as casseroles go, it has it." Capri takes my jacket and hangs it in the hall closet, whose door has an artful trompe l'oeil column painted on it.

I started coming to dinner at the Mandelbaums' once a week after Capri's father died, and like all small-town habits, this one stuck, and now it's a standing engagement. I never call ahead of time; if it's Monday, I'm at the Mandelbaums' for supper.

No matter how many times I stand in this foyer, with its winding staircase covered in beige Berber carpeting, hemmed by the banister lacquered to a shiny black, lit by the Baccarat crystal chandelier, and with a round needlepoint area rug in pale peach and soft gray silk and wool, I always see something new. The lighting is soft and golden; all the chandeliers have dimmer switches and bulbs that twinkle like actual candlelight. A chandelier is to a room what diamond-drop earrings are to a beautiful woman—the perfect accessory.

"If I had to choose one thing that makes or breaks a room, it's the chandelier. It's the crowning glory of good design." I catch myself pontificating. "I'm sorry. I sound like a windbag, but if you had seen some of the crap I saw today—"

"I don't mind." Capri threads her arm through mine as we walk to the back of the house.

Capri's father, the late Sy Mandelbaum, was like a second father to me. Following my graduation from Parsons School of Design, he hired me to do the window treatments and carpets in all his banks (by that time he had several). He not only trusted me with his commercial properties, he hired me to do his home. When the Mandelbaums entertained, Sy would brag about my work. Suddenly, I had more jobs than I could handle with clients who could afford the very best. This house became my own Kips Bay Bazaar. Luckily, Aurelia loves change, so I've never really stopped decorating this house. I'm still futzing with it; I'm about to redecorate the solarium, which overlooks the pool out back.

Castle Mandelbaum, as I call it, was built in 1960 in the French Norman style. It sits atop a hill on five acres of manicured lawn. The imposing limestone tower and cupola can be seen from several miles away. I encouraged Sy to put in a gate and a circular drive to conjure the carriage stop of the past, thus adding to the house's old world charm. I found an iron-worker from Germany who made an imposing gate using the letter **M** as a motif. Sy watched the installation in awe. "I love an expert," he used to say. We even had the contractor install heated pipes under the concrete in the driveway, which was treated to look like brick. No nasty falls when you come to visit **this** house in the winter. The driveway is always clear of ice and snow.

Inside, the rooms are well proportioned, with tall, wide windows and vaulted ceilings, creating a feeling of openness. This is the perfect home for Aurelia, the leading art collector in New Jersey, who can afford the Monet and Cy Twombly paintings that adorn her walls, and has the space and light to display them properly.

I survey the rooms as we pass them. Damn, I'm good. Pastel colors wash through this house like brushstrokes on a Degas. As far as the eye can see, it's a celebration of all things **français;** they are cleverly tucked in corners or displayed boldly front and center.

There is a delicate hand-painted **armoire de**

mariage in the sitting room, filled with glorious linens embroidered with the Mandelbaum family crest. In the kitchen a set of hand-carved cherrywood **buffet a deux corps** is filled with pottery from Marseille.

The taffeta window treatments are so chic you could wear them to a fancy dress ball. Room to room you will find Austrian-style shades, floor-length balloon draperies in shimmering silks of pewter gray, soft rose, and mauve. I sewed panels of off-white silk onto either end of the draperies; these mirror the window panes, giving a crisp look and definition to the billowing silk. The draperies look like fluted ribbon candy when they're down and become jazzy ruffles when raised to let the sun in.

The mantels throughout the house are carved white marble, and we hunted down oversized antique mirrors to place over them. One of the most delightful pieces I found was from the going-out-of-business sale at Hess's department store in Philadelphia. If you look closely at the smoky blond glass, you can see the words "Milady Chapeaux" written in swirly letters. How lovely the mirror looks as it reflects Aurelia's grand **lit à l'impériale,** with the handmade lace canopy and matching duvet. Sy was claustrophobic, so there were no canopy beds allowed prior to his death; Aurelia enjoys this one now without guilt.

What fun we had placing the **objets artisanaux:** lovely miniature botanical prints displayed on wooden easels on the mantels, and glistening ceramic urns, most from Saint-Rémy-de-Provence, with quirky French sayings on them. My favorite? **Une poule qui marche de travers ne pondra jamais d'oeufs,** which means "A chicken that walks sideways has no eggs."

Going French is all about regal touches set against antique wood grains and fabrics. Touches of gold leaf and polished silver are used sparingly but with great effect throughout the house. We placed the occasional silver flask with a silk tassel dangling from the handle on a side table. A silver bookmark denotes a favorite poem in a leather-bound collection by Rimbaud. It's the small details that bring warmth and not simply ornamentation to a room: a **salière** filled with pungent lavender seeds or a **verrier** full of Renaissance pie plates provides elegance and whimsy.

The kitchen is done in cherrywood (the farm table and chairs were imported) with a tile-lined hearth that is deep enough to bake bread in—Aurelia loves to cook pizza in it. When there's a party, we always wind up in the kitchen. Aurelia stands at the sink. She turns and smiles when we enter the kitchen.

"B, sit down and put your feet up. Capri, please toss the salad."

"Your favorite," I say, handing Aurelia the pie.

"You're a doll," she replies, greeting me with a big hug.

Aurelia Castone Mandelbaum has all the stature her daughter does not. She is around five feet eight with an hourglass figure that is holding firm—a feat for a woman in her seventies, she will be the first to tell you. Her red hair (which used to be chestnut brown) also keeps her looking youthful. She has been the organist at the Fatima church since she was a girl; her size-eleven feet come in handy when she pumps the giant pedals to send sound through the bellows.

Aurelia is the richest woman in the state of New Jersey. By the end of his life, Sy owned a string of banks, which Aurelia eventually sold to Chase Manhattan, retaining control as a major stockholder. Folks were skeptical, but Aurelia proved that she wasn't just serving tea at the board meetings all those years; she was listening intently to the proceedings. The stock for the company has split so many times the smallest shareholder has walked away with a bucket of cash from the dividends. I know Sy would be proud of his bubola.

"I hope you're both hungry." Aurelia lifts an enormous Pyrex dish from the oven with her Toile de Jouy oven mitts. "I heard Arlene Francis talking on television about a dish she serves to guests at her New York penthouse on opening nights, and it sounded divine. I thought I'd give it a try."

ARLENE FRANCIS'S SHEPHERD'S PIE
Serves 48

Two 28-ounce cans crushed tomatoes
½ cup Worcestershire sauce
1 cup flour
1 cup water
½ cup shortening
2 cups chopped onions
1 cup diced red pepper
5 cloves garlic, minced
6 pounds ground beef
Salt and pepper to taste
1 cup sliced mushrooms
10 pounds white potatoes, peeled
1 pint hot milk
Butter
Paprika

In a large pot, mix the tomatoes and Worcester-shire sauce and bring to a boil. Make a paste with the flour and water in a small bowl, and add to the pot. Stir until thickened at medium heat. In a skillet, heat the shortening, then lightly brown the onions, pepper, garlic, and meat at medium to high heat. Add salt and pepper. Add the meat mixture to the pot and cook over medium heat until browned. Stir in the mushrooms and cook over low heat. Meanwhile, boil the potatoes in salted water about 20 minutes. Drain. Using a mixer or by hand, whip the potatoes with hot milk and butter until fluffy. Spoon the meat mixture into two 9 × 13-inch pans, greased with a little shortening. Spread the whipped potatoes over the meat. Sprinkle with paprika. Bake in a 350°F. oven for 20 minutes, until the potatoes are lightly browned.

"I made so much I brought a pan over to the rectory," Aurelia continues.

"It would have been cheaper to take Father out to dinner," Capri says, pouring wine into our glasses.

"Why's that?" I ask pleasantly.

"When Ma dropped off the shepherd's pie, she left a check for one hundred thousand dollars for the church renovation."

"Who came up with that figure?" I hear my

voice break. There has been lots of talk about renovating the church, including a big article in the diocesan newspaper, **Feel the Spirit,** in which Father Porp was quoted as saying that the people of Our Lady of Fatima Church needed renewal in their surroundings and their souls. I couldn't sleep after I read it. I've been bursting with ideas about how to redo the church since I was a boy. I love my dusty old church, but the Gothic design with its heavy pediments, scrollwork, and stiff pews have never matched the spiritual heights I feel during the Mass. I want a crack at giving the interior a fresh, new design that will draw people in and lift their weary souls.

"Father says it's a gut renovation. That's pricey." Aurelia shrugs.

I take a deep breath. "It's my dream to re-design the church." This is not easy for me, to admit my highest dream to Toot, and now to Aurelia and Capri. I feel as exposed as I did when I lost my swim trunks in the diving con-test at OLOF Park in 1941. The opportunity to renovate my church would mean everything to me. It means so much to me my voice squeaks.

"Oh, Father knows that." Aurelia smiles. "I made sure he knew my feelings. You are the Billy Baldwin of OLOF; the arbiter of taste. If not you . . . who?" Aurelia reaches across the table and squeezes my hand. "Don't worry."

"Thank you, Aurelia."

Aurelia spoons the shepherd's pie onto a plate and sets it before me. "Go ahead, taste."

I take a bite. "Delicious," I pronounce to her great delight. Perhaps it tastes so good because it comes on the heels of such good news. "Arlene Francis triumphs!"

"Hmm. I hope it wasn't Dinah Shore. You know, when the television is on, I'm knitting or baking or something and I don't really pay attention."

"To Dinah Shore, then!" I raise my glass, and we toast Dinah.

"Wherever it came from, I'll make a batch for your birthday party."

"You're all in cahoots, and I want it to end right here," I say politely. "There is not going to be a party."

"Oh, why not, B? Your sister throws the best parties." Capri butters a roll.

"Toot said it's planned down to the rose soap petals in the guest powder room," Aurelia says. "I just don't know what to give you. Hmm." She taps her chin mischievously.

"Nothing. And I really don't need a wallet."

"No, it's a big year. And in a couple of months Capri will also be turning forty."

"Mom." Capri blushes.

"I know, it's a number to choke on. But be-

lieve me, when you're seventy-three, you remember forty as an age when you could still do
backbends. I'm going to do a joint gift for you
two. I'd love to throw a wedding."

Capri and I look at each other, horrified.

"Did you have anything else in mind?" I ask
softly.

"I was thinking of sending you two kids to
Italy."

Capri's eyes widen, and the thick lenses of
her glasses make her pupils look like black golf
balls. "I'd love that."

"Well . . ." I feel cornered, but I don't want to be
rude. Capri and I both know we've tried to rub the
wooden sticks of passion together, but all we got
were splinters. We've tried here at home and even
on the road, thinking a change of venue might ig-
nite mutual ardor. We went to Toronto for the
Our Lady of Mount Carmel Festival, to New York
City for the 1964 World's Fair, we even took a
bus trip to Colonial Williamsburg with the Sons
of Italy. We've gone near and far hoping the
backdrop would change the facts. But no box
lunch, carnival ride, or glassblowing demonstra-
tion could bring us together in the romantic sense.

"You can't say no." Aurelia smiles. "I'm sending you to the capital of romance. My goodness, if sparks don't fly there, then we really do
have a problem."

Capri raises her glass. I raise mine to tap it, then do the same to her mother's. We sip. I look around the table, and for a fleeting moment I feel like the three of us are a little family, which causes me to choke on my wine.

"Are you all right?" Capri asks.

How do I tell her that my throat snapped shut at the thought of entrapment, cutting off my oxygen like the door of a safe? "I'm fine," I lie. I can't believe I have to dream up a way to break off an engagement with a girl I never asked to marry in the first place! There isn't a bachelor in the world who isn't walking around with his eyes to the sky, waiting for the big net to drop on him—like the ones the police use to trap mad grizzly bears wandering loose in suburbia. Things have gotten out of hand. Sometimes the borders of this lovely town can close in like prison walls. I fish in my jacket pocket for my cigarettes. I allow myself one a week. Usually I wait for the espresso after dessert, but something tells me to have one right now.

"Let me tell you kids a little story. It's got it all, tension, romance, and a denouement that John Ford could not invent," Aurelia says.

Cripes, I'm thinking, if the wind-up is any indication, this story is going to last longer than a John Ford epic.

"I'd like to share it with you," she continues.

"It's a love story. The only one I know. Mine. I was in college at St. Elizabeth's in Convent Station, as a literature and composition major, where I contemplated life as a teacher."

"You'd have been excellent, Ma. You're **good** with rules." Capri stabs her iceberg lettuce.

"Thank you. What is life without discipline? We'd all be fat, drunk and—"

"Happy?" Capri smiles.

"Don't interrupt, dear. Anyhow, I met this handsome young man in a navy blue suit with a red tie at the Latin Quarter in New York City."

"There was a rumba contest." Capri helps the story along patiently.

"Right. **Heavens,** could he dance. And this fellow was so funny, sparks flew, and we agreed to see each other again. After a year of meeting at Schrafft's on Fifty-sixth Street for lunch during the week, and at the Sailor's Lake Pavillion on the weekends, he asked me to marry him."

"You couldn't have done better than Sy Mandelbaum," I tell her.

"I know that. But our families were horrified that a Roman Catholic girl and a Jewish boy would fall in love and want to get married. But it was 1929 and no one was paying attention to anything once the stock market crashed. We had our window of opportunity. It wasn't easy, though. I had to go to Florida to find a priest. I found a Capuchin monk half in the bag who agreed to do the ceremony, since I couldn't get my parish priest to perform a wedding with a rabbi. The rabbi wasn't too thrilled either, but he was a cousin of Sy's and owed him a favor. We did it, though. We found a way. Look at the obstacles I had in my road to happiness. And here you are, with more in common than any couple I know, with more going for you than any two people I've ever met, and look—no wedding."

Poor Aurelia. Doesn't she know her Depression-era love affair is full of moth holes and sounds like a ghastly black-and-white B movie? This is 1970 on the East Coast of the United States in the Age of Aquarius in the Land of Free Love, where we let it all hang out. No one cares about marriage the way they used to. It is hardly the building block of civilized society that it once was. No, the Celebration of Self is the new cornerstone of culture. But this lady is not going to give up. I tap my cigarette on the ledge of the lead-crystal ashtray.

"Everything in its time," I say pleasantly. But I don't think Aurelia has any idea how much time I'm talking about.

CHAPTER TWO

A Tudor in Tumult

Besides the Villa di Crespi, the place where I feel most at home is the church of Our Lady of Fatima, a glorious Gothic structure that sits on top of the hill above town. Every Saturday afternoon I can be found here, dressing the altar with linens and flowers for the weekend services. My church was built in 1899 with monies raised by the first wave of Italian immigrants, shepherded by the Diocese of Trenton, which has always been known for its ambitious building projects and deep pockets.

The church, with an exterior of marble (imported from Italy) and sandstone (strictly local), has always been a mecca to me. When I was a boy waiting for Mama to pick me up from school, I would stand across the street and study the details of the façade, thrilled by the gargoyles nestled in the spires and mesmerized by the rose window, which seemed to spin in the light like a bejeweled wheel.

Whenever I enter its cool, dark interior, I feel an overwhelming sense of peace; it has always been this way for me. More than a few people in my family thought that I would become a priest, since I served nearly every Mass as an altar boy and never missed a holy day of obligation. What boy misses basketball practice to make a novena? Since 1962, I've been the only male voice in the choir. I have also been volunteer chair of the Altar and Flower Committee for nineteen years. I believe in giving back.

While the bachelor aspect of the priesthood was appealing, the poverty requirement seemed impossible. I love my suits and china too much to give them up. Also, my mother threatened to kill herself if I became a priest, and when you're the only son and a change-of-life baby, you try to add to your mother's longevity, not cut it short. I abided by her wishes, and she lived to be eighty-five and died in her sleep. I attribute this to my having done my best to make her happy. Sacrifice never hurt anybody—certainly not me.

As I push open the heavy brass door, I am met with the buttery perfume of beeswax candles, sweet smoke, and Lemon Pledge—an elixir that brings me back to the 1940s, pagan babies, and velvet knee pants (mine) with one whiff. I straighten the church bulletins on the entry table. When I notice they are last week's, I take the stack with me. I enter the nave, then dip my fingers into the cold, clear holy-water font, blessing myself and then kissing my hand, remembering my parents, grandparents, favorite aunts and uncles, all dead.

The clerestory windows fill the pews with afternoon light that turns to streams of pale blue around the altar. I become calm in God's house, and it has always been this way for me. The place is filled with soft light and sweet silence, much as I imagine heaven to be.

Behind the choir loft, the rose window makes a runner of pink light down the aisle that disappears at the gold-leafed Communion railing. Stained-glass windows, depicting scenes of miracles performed by saints, line the church walls like giant playing cards. Some of the windows are propped open at the bottom, leaving the occasional saint without feet.

A fresco behind the main altar, painted by local amateur Michael Menecola during the 1920s, peels with age. It depicts the miracle at Fatima, where three village children in rural Portugal were said to have seen Mary, the Mother of

God. The mural dramatizes the precise moment on May 13, 1917, when the Blessed Virgin appeared to little Lucia, Francisco, and Jacinta in the sky over a field where they were tending sheep.

I know many boys who fell in love with the face and form of this rendition of the Blessed Mother, hovering overhead like an angelic movie star. There were plenty of girls who tried to model themselves after her. The Holy Mother's clear, creamy golden skin and wet blue eyes look up to heaven in complete supplication. There is something almost dreamy about her. My mother told me that the Blessed Lady's pencil-thin eyebrows had all the girls in OLOF plucking to match them. The girls would light a wooden match, blow out the flame, and, with the charred end of the stick, draw thin arches over their own brows. Instant glamour.

I walk down the aisle and genuflect before the altar, then make my way to the sacristy, the small room where the priest and servers dress. I check the vestments first.

The priest's white cassock with billowing sleeves and fat hems hangs next to the smaller versions, surplice robes for the altar boys. On separate pegs, braided white satin belts hang in a row like nooses. When I was a boy, I made three knots in my belt in honor of the Holy Trinity. I remember another altar boy, Vinnie de Franco, a real cut-up, who used to make two knots in his belt, one for Martin and the other for Lewis.

The OLOF sodality does a good job with the spiritual laundry; the heavy cotton vestments are bleached to a bright white and pressed to a crisp. The smell of starch fills the tiny room like a vapor. Hanging to the side of the vestment closet, in a dress bag, are the altar cloths. Attached to the bag is a scrawled note from Nellie Fanelli, laundress to the church. It says: "**B: the purificator is in the baggie. N.**"

I reach into the bottom of the dress bag, and there, just as she promised, is the pressed purificator, the official **moppeen** of the Mass celebration. The priest uses this starched dish towel to buff the chalice clean at the end of Communion. I take it out and place it on the credence table next to the cruets (for water and wine) and paten, a gold disc with a polished wooden handle held under the chin of the communicant by the altar boy to catch any fragments of the holy wafer that might drop during distribution.

I return to the sacristy and take the rest of the linens to the altar, where I kneel, then rise and carefully dress the marble slab with the snow-white cloth. It takes a touch of maneuvering, just as it does when you set a formal dinner table at home. I return to the sacristy and take a second cloth off the hanger, the smaller one known as the corporal, which is like a place mat on the altar for the chalice and paten.

I move the squat candles on their flat brass holders from the credence table to the altar. One candle has burned down haphazardly, probably from a draft, so I trim it with my pocketknife so it matches its mate. I walk around to the front of the altar to check the hems and placement. There is a large spray of pink gladioli and waxy green leaves behind the altar. I trim off a few dead leaves and arrange the flowers. Much better.

"Bartolomeo?" Father Porporino's gravelly voice says from the doorway.

"Yes, Father?" My voice squeaks. I was raised to be in awe of priests, and therefore was always scared of them. After all, they held the keys to my salvation. The last thing I wanted them to do was drop those keys down a sewer hole, so I always did my best to be perfect in their eyes. Still do.

"Father, I noticed the church bulletins are old." I hand him the stack from last week. Father Porp looks like a slim Mario Lanza with his full head of wavy gray hair and nice teeth.

"I haven't put the new ones out yet."

"Is there a problem? Marie Cascario said we need a new mimeograph machine."

"Marie needs to learn how to operate the thing. I'll put them out later."

I smooth the hem of the altar cloth. "Father, I was having dinner at Aurelia Mandelbaum's, and she told me about the renovation of the church."

"And?" He looks at me.

"Well, I'd like to come and talk to you about it sometime." Father does not respond, just looks at me, so I fill up the silence with babble. "You see, I have a lot of ideas, and I've already spoken to some of the members of the parish council. I could make this holy place dazzle." I think I see Father raise an eyebrow, but it's hard to tell in the slowly vanishing light. "I could come by next week, if that's all right. If that's not good, you can call me and we'll set up another time." Father Porp looks down the main aisle as though he's searching for something. I feel the creeping warmth of humiliation overtake me. I do what I always do when someone makes me feel uncomfortable. I chirp. "Well, see you at Mass, Father." I close my hand around the wax shards and rotten leaf stems I've collected and genuflect a final time. Father goes back into the sacristy. I shiver.

A beam of bright white light fills the foyer as Zetta Montagna pushes the brass door open. She wears a chapel veil studded with jet beads, even though head coverings for women went out with Vatican II. Once the chapel veils came off, the guitar Masses came in. No more Latin, no more fish on Fridays, and bareheaded women are no longer an affront to God.

Zetta's slim frame casts a long pencil-like shadow down the aisle. She is probably the most important person in our church besides Father Porp. Zetta is president of the sodality, the women's group that maintains the church, plans all the receptions, and sponsors the annual Cadillac Dinner, the fund-raiser for the Fatima elementary and middle schools. She is also the widowed mother of nine children, all of them grown, two of them doctors, and one, alas, a drug addict somewhere out west. Her beloved husband keeled over of a heart attack at the age of thirty-four, leaving her to raise all those children on her own. She is a woman who does not wear the tragedy of her life in any way; she always looks fresh and stylish. She might be sixty but looks fifteen years younger. She genuflects at the Communion rail.

"Hello, B. The altar looks lovely."

"Thank you."

"Who did the glads?"

"Fleurs of Fatima." I make a face.

"Awful," she agrees.

"I know. I trimmed them up. But you can't really balance glads and waxy leaves and wind up with a decent arrangement."

"Were the vestments all right?"

"Perfect."

"I worry. Nellie's eyesight is going."

"Well, she can still handle a hot iron," I reassure her. "Zetta, I hope you don't think this is bold of me . . ."

"What is it, B?"

"Father is going through with the renovation of the church, and I wondered if you could put a good word in for me."

"To do the design?"

"Yes."

"Of course I will."

"I'd appreciate it," I tell her.

"You're a devoted parishioner. I can't imagine a better choice for the job," she says.

With Aurelia Mandelbaum and Zetta Montagna on my side, I'm certain I can overcome Father Porp's unexpected silence on the subject.

Zetta walks over to the alcove next to the side altar and kneels before the statue of Saint Michael. What a saint he was, with his silver doublet and sword hoisted high in the air, his big feet planted firmly on the ground, and his mighty thighs lunging forward to defend the faith. Michael is our Superman, while Saint Theresa of the Little Flower, who hovers on a stand close by in her chocolate-brown nun's habit holding a spray of pink roses, is our Lois Lane. Pray to Saint Michael to save you from harm, and to Saint Theresa for what you want. They have never failed me in either department.

As Zetta makes the sign of the cross and kneels at the statue's feet, I remember that her husband's name was Michael. I feel the tip of my nose heat up, but I take a deep breath, swallowing the tears.

Whenever I see people humble themselves in prayer, I feel something deep within me stir, a sort of charismatic empathy that makes me want to sit down next to them and cry. You can imagine what a minefield of emotion Sunday Mass is for me, with all the kneeling and genuflecting. Perhaps it's best that I became an interior decorator instead of a priest. Who needs to call on Father Weepy when they have a problem? I want my religious leaders strong and at the ready. My temperament is better suited to making art than saving souls.

My first cousin Christina Menecola (related by marriage to Michael Menecola, who painted the church's fresco of the dreamy Virgin Mary) is my favorite relative, which is no small feat, as there are hundreds of di Crespis, not to mention the Crespys, who are related but, after some medieval falling-out, dropped the "di" and later replaced the "i" with a "y," probably because it Americanized them, giving them a leg up in business or when applying to fancy country clubs.

Christina and I have always been close. I was nearly five years old and allowed to be present at the hospital when she was born prematurely. (Not because I was ready to be around childbirth, but because Toot had a date and couldn't be bothered to babysit me, and Daddy had pressing business out of town.) I was ultimately glad for the experience because it gave me my first window into the power of prayer. I remember my mother on her knees in front of the incubator praying for Christina to survive. I also remember the nasty look the nurse shot at me when I asked if they could give the baby a blanket instead of a lightbulb for warmth.

Christina just turned thirty-five. I have a basket of childhood memories with her: collecting shells after the clambake at the Legion Hall, and taking them home, washing them up, and drawing lips on them to create a shell choir; rides on the Scrambler at Asbury Park, where we held hands (afterward, I would throw up and she would laugh); watching the fireworks at the St. Rocco picnic and being hustled back to the station wagon by my mother when the two of us accidentally discovered two teenagers having sex behind the security fence; swimming at the shore; and even starting up an imaginary business in her basement where we sold cement (her father was a bricklayer, so the materials were handy). We called ourselves the Mixmasters.

Christina's mother, Auntie Carmella, was a statuesque knockout who made cheese at the Hodgins dairy in Bradley Beach. She twisted glorious Italian love knots that looked like white satin bows out of fresh mozzarella. She died shortly after my mother, of a massive stroke following a terrible argument with her husband—who has since married Aunt Carmella's hairdresser, a portly blonde named Cha Cha Cerami. The word is they're very happy.

I decorated Christina's home on Cheshire Lane shortly after she married. English Tudors are, by nature, a design challenge because they're so dark and dreary. Most people are tempted to cheer them up with modern furniture, but it's a mistake. Contemporary just winds up looking ridiculous. (Always suit the interiors to the architectural style of the home. It's an obvious concept, but you'd be surprised how many people put a flokati rug in a Victorian or hang Renaissance tapestries in a split-level.) A Tudor with low-slung dormers, wrought-iron details, dark alcoves, and tiny nooks can feel like a claustrophobic dungeon, made creepier by the stucco plaster walls, rounded doorways, and menacing coffered ceilings. Why did Romeo and Juliet kill themselves? Because they lived in depressing English Tudors and couldn't take it another minute!

I brightened up Christina's house with pin lights, paint, and a color scheme of soft corals and earthy greens. Botanicals succeeded in giving it a garden feel. I bleached the dark brown wood floors a sandy off-white and painted the floorboard trims a light, toasty cinnamon color, which perked up the place considerably. You feel like you're entering Sherwood Forest when you walk into this house. I challenge any decorator here or abroad to do better than me with classic English. I may have the soul of an Italian and the joie de vivre of a Frenchman, but I have the classical eye of a Brit.

I went traditional with the fabrics—an array of calicoes in golden yellow (Greeff is the best with fine English prints) and sturdy linen in pale green (Rose Cummings has a knockout Fresh Meadow, #15677)—to offset the coral.

Christina's kitchen was so gloomy you would swear you had just missed the mutton-chop lunch following the guillotine matinee. I yanked all the dark cabinets out and put in a lime-green-and-white hutch, a bright matching dish rack on the wall to display all that wedding china (Haddon Hall by Minton), and lots of shelves covered in natural grass paper. I opened up the room with lots of low, warm, glowing brass lamps placed down the center of a long, rustic farm table. I painted the low-backed benches antique white and put a rocking chair in the corner with a crazy Pucci green paisley cushion and a standing brass lamp. The result is fizzy and fun. My inspiration: a crème de menthe cocktail.

As I pull into the driveway, I see Christina's daughter, Amalia, sitting under the maple tree with books spread around her, paper and scissors in her hands. I love to visit the houses I've decorated unannounced and see my work shining amid the grind of daily life. Amalia hears my car and looks up. She doesn't run to me like she used to; instead, she just looks at me with boredom. Of course, she has hit that age where droll is in and warmth is out. She is twelve.

"You look busy," I call to her as I get out of the car.

Amalia is slender with freckles and long coppery braids. She puts down her scissors and examines a leaf. Her coloring might be Irish, but her black eyes are Italian. "I have a science project. I'm doing a report on indigenous trees of New Jersey. I'm bringing in examples."

"Well, you don't have much of a selection here. You only have maple in your yard."

"I know. I'll copy the shapes in the book and cut the leaves to look like they're from all different trees." She holds up the butchered maple leaves. "See? Elm. Chestnut. Birch."

"Your teacher might notice that the leaves are doctored."

"I don't think so."

"But that's cheating."

"So?"

"Do they still have an honor code at St. Ambrose's Middle School?"

"No one checks."

"Then do what you will," I tell her pleasantly. It's not my problem if my second cousin gets punished by the heinous nuns of St. Ambrose. I did my bit in that POW camp of a school for twelve years. She's on her own.

"You got a new car," she says, looking at my new navy blue Dodge station wagon, fully loaded. The gold family crest underscored with my business's name is painted on the driver's side door. It looks impressive, if I do say so myself. "Why do you call your company the House of B?"

"Because everybody calls me B."

"You should have a flashy name, not just a letter. How about the Prince of Chintz."

"That's taken." New York designer Mario Buatta was lucky that someone anointed him with a catchy title. He's in more magazines than Pat Nixon. "Who died and left you in charge of **BusinessWeek**?" I ask a little testily. Honestly, if I have to start taking advice from a pipsqueak, I'll quit.

She ignores the comment. "Did you bring me M&M's?"

"Of course." I reach into my portfolio and give Amalia a sack of M&M's. "Where's your mother?"

"Inside." Amalia says. "She's still depressed." She pitches her long braids onto her back. "She's always gonna be depressed."

"Nonsense! Your mother will be back, I promise you. You must have faith."

"Faith? What's that?" She snorts. "God sits up there on a cloud and picks people to die. What a job."

I don't know whether to smack this kid or hug her. I haven't had this kind of philosophical discourse since I studied the essays of Montaigne under Father Otterbacher in the OLOF Catholic-college prep course I took my senior year of high school.

"It's not God's job to make sure everything goes your way," I remind her gently. "I know how hard it is to lose a father—"

"But your dad was old," she interrupts.

"That doesn't mean it didn't hurt."

"Yeah, but you had him around for a long time. Years longer than me. And my dad went fast. A car crash is instant. You can't even compare it." Amalia tries to sound defiant, but she comes off like a scared kid.

I would like to inform her that my father might have had dinner with our family every night, but he never said much to me. I recall no ball throwing, no trips to the movies, and no collecting fabric swatches to help me make uniforms for my iron soldiers.

On Saturday nights, Daddy had a mysterious ritual of getting all dressed up in his best suit. On his way out, smelling of citrus and patchouli, he'd give me a quarter, followed by a kiss on the head. After a quick wave to my mother, he'd climb into his freshly washed (by me) Buick, roll down the window, and say, "I have business up on Blue Mountain. I'll see you in the morning for Mass."

Toot, a teenager at that point, would simply shake her head when I told her Dad went up to Blue Mountain. When I pressed her repeatedly to find out exactly what went on up there in the Poconos, she would say, "You're just a boy. Someday you'll do dirty things like Daddy." That was hardly the explanation I was looking for. Eventually I understood that Blue Mountain was code for "Dad's got a girlfriend."

I loved my father, I just didn't know him very well. When he died, his **comare** (translation: girlfriend—I notice we use Italian words when we are ashamed, uncomfortable, or exhilarated—let's put Daddy's **comare** under the shame banner) showed up at the wake with a lily plant and wept into his casket. When my mother realized who she was, she grabbed the plastic pot out of her hands and threw it on the floor. No one said a word, we just went on saying our rosary aloud (sorrowful mystery, of course) while Dutch Schiavone, the funeral director, cleaned up the mess with a whisk broom. Evidently it wasn't the first potted plant that had been tossed during a wake.

I studied the plant lady for the brief moment she was in my presence before Dutch showed her the door. She had shiny lacquered red hair in a chignon that didn't move (even when Ma lunged at her), and no hips. That's how I knew she wasn't Italian. Italian women always have plump, peachy rear ends. My mother did and Toot used to (until it sank), not to mention all my girl cousins who had The Hips. For me, one of the characteristics of ideal feminine beauty is a plush caboose. This lady had none. You could have tucked her ass into the back of her boots.

Her red hair didn't make her a non-Italian, by the way, because all the brunettes in my family go red as they age. You'll never see an Italian woman with gray hair until the lid of her husband's casket is snapped shut. That's the moment she stops dyeing her hair. "What's the use?" my mother said to me when I was shocked to see her black hair turn white so soon after we buried Pop.

"Okay, Amalia, you got me. Your father's death was much worse than mine; you win the Sweepstakes of Suffering. Saint Amalia of the Maple Leaves." Finally she smiles.

"What are you two talking about?" Christina pushes open the screen door and joins us in the yard.

"Death," Amalia says.

"Oh, that." Christina looks at me and rolls her eyes. Christina is a whisper of a thing, but her chestnut-brown hair and black eyes indicate she's one of our tribe. Luckily her nose is razor straight, with no bulb on the tip. She is classically beautiful in every detail. Her lush eyebrows accentuate her almond-shaped eyes like black velvet piping on silk. "Toot called.

I'm in charge of stuffed artichokes for your birthday party."

I can't respond, I'm so annoyed.

"Sorry, was it a surprise?"

"No, no surprise. I don't want a party, that's all. And my sister never gives me what I want. Now, if I wanted a party, you can bet I'd be sitting home twiddling my thumbs come May thirteenth."

Christina smiles. "You know what she calls me now? Honest to God, she called and said, Cousin Christina The Widow! As if that's my name!"

"Better to be Christina The Widow than Rosemary With The Lupus. Now, that's a nickname a girl can never shake, short of a cure. I'm taking a ride into the city. You want to go?"

"No, thanks."

There was a time when Christina would grab her purse, jump into the car, and come into Manhattan to shop for clients with me. She'd leave baby Amalia with her husband and we'd go. She was so spontaneous, we'd laugh all the way through the Holland Tunnel, have a quick bite in Little Italy, then head up the East Side to Scalamandré's to find the perfect taffeta. I can't tell you how much I miss our day trips. "I'm losing patience with you!" I say, trying to lighten the mood but not succeeding.

"Oh, B, I've lost patience with me." Christina

kneels and helps Amalia pick up her Picasso-esque maple leaves. Amalia juggles her pile of books and supplies and climbs the porch steps to go inside. I help Christina up.

"You know last week I told you I was getting better?" Christina plucks at a maple leaf. "Well, I got worse again."

"I wish you'd go and see Father Porporino."

"Oh, please."

"No, you really should. He's a mean bastard, but he's good with grief and fund-raising."

Christina laughs. "You're crazy. You're the only guy I know who still prays."

"It can't hurt."

"Now, **there's** a philosophy I can embrace wholeheartedly."

"Do it for Amalia."

"Everything I'm doing, I do for her. I get up in the morning, don't I?"

There is nothing I can say. Since Charlie died eleven months ago, there is nothing I can do either. The shock hasn't fully worn off, and if you had to name Christina's stage of grief, it would be the one before acceptance. All her dreams are shot, the one where she would grow old with her true love, have a second baby, enjoy the fertile valley of her youth with a guy who made her laugh. Now she's just another lonely woman, and it's killing her.

"Try me again next week." She smiles.

"I will." I give her a hug. She holds on like a drowning woman. "You aren't going to drag your tongue over my upper lip, are you?"

"Who did that?" Christina lets go of me, and for a second, she's her old self again.

"Nicky's girl. Ondine Doyle. She's a gold band away from being my legal niece and she licks me."

"Yuck!"

"You're telling me. She's like diesel fuel, that one—all over the highway. You know what I mean?"

Christina throws her head back and laughs, just like the old days, just like we were before everything changed.

Everyone has a place that calls to them, a place where they flourish, where their best self emerges and they remember true happiness. For some, it's a college reunion under a beer tent being groped by an old flame. For others, it's a summer share outside Atlantic City with an all-night poker game and cold pizza. For me, it's the Scalamandré townhouse, home of the greatest hand-woven silks in the world, on East Fifty-seventh Street and Third Avenue in noisy, dirty, delicious Manhattan.

I try to get into town at least once a week.

Tonight I make several stops before reaching the townhouse. I pick up samples of ceramic tiles at Kovack's and wool rug squares at Roubini. I photograph a Grange settee at the furniture mart. I duck into Scalamandré's just before closing time.

When I come to the city, I call friends, most of them in the design business, and we swap stories over a glass of wine and baked chicken at the Cattleman West Restaurant. I have had these friends since my days at Parsons, where I majored in fibers. I went on to take graduate courses, focusing on interiors. As the only designer in OLOF, I crave a peer group, fellow designers and artists with whom I can consult, share ideas, and discuss trends. Just because I live in a small town in Jersey doesn't mean I can't stay cosmopolitan.

New York City is the place where all art comes home to roost. This is certainly true in my trade, as there is not a fabric woven anywhere in the world that cannot be had in one of the showrooms here. When I earned my full ASID (American Society of Interior Designers) credentials, the first thing I did was push open the doors of Scalamandré's. The words painted in gold leaf on the door say TO THE TRADE, but they might as well have said BARTOLOMEO DI CRESPI, COME ON IN! I felt like I joined the best club on earth. I may pray in Our Lady of Fatima Church, but I do my worshipping in the House of Scalamandré.

The windows are showstoppers. They combine classic elements with a touch of humor—usually there's a chair covered in a signature pattern, backed by the latest wallpaper, with a chest, mirrors, and decorative boxes as accents. Once it was a moss-green velvet tuffet trimmed in a Medici floral print with a fringe knotted with crystals. On a plump canvas mushroom sat a bowl of porridge. A black velvet spider on a silver cord hung from the ceiling. Little Miss Muffet on Third Avenue.

Franco Scalamandré is not only a great weaver, he's a serious historian in the field of fibers. His research of Italian antiquities often inspires his designs. He reissued silkscreen prints of velvets woven with metallic accents that were used in the Medici palaces in the 1500s. The collection was so luscious, there was a time when I used a touch of Medici in every house I decorated.

Scali's is a typical Upper East Side townhouse, long and thin like the women who live in the neighborhood, and beautifully maintained. There is never a streak on the polished tables, a curl in the seam of the wallpaper, or a nick in the floorboards. It has the feel of a private home, with its round Roman foyer featuring fresh dahlias in a silver pitcher on the Biedermeier entry table. Over the table hangs a chandelier of smoked Venetian glass with bobeches so delicate they look like spun sugar. At the foot of a grand staircase is a bust of Marie Antoinette. The carpet runner is a kicky tan leopard print. Instead of a banister on the inside wall going up the stairs, they draped a wide silk satin cord attached with brass grommets. The spiral steps twist like a swizzle stick up to the fourth floor.

A sign at the foot of the stairs directs you through the building. The first floor is fabrics, the second, wall treatments (paneling, paper, and fabric murals), the third, trims and fringe, and the fourth, private offices. No decorator worth his salt ever takes the small service elevator for fear of missing a new display.

In the back room of the first floor, the fabric samples are hung on racks in billowing streams from ceiling to floor. Each sample has its own clamp and hanger, so you can see the fabric at full height and width. I love the sound the fabric makes when I flip through the racks— **whoosh, clink. Whoosh, clink.** Imagine the waves of color, sumptuous silks, glossy taffetas, crisp plisses, and stiff organzas. Even the sturdier fabrics—wools, linens, and cottons—are displayed with imagination in every possible color combination and weave. On the hem of each sample is an identification card with a name and style number, crucial for sampling, ordering, and pricing.

An assistant joins me instantly, greets me by name, and hands me a small clipboard and pencil. A decorator is asked to write down the item numbers he's chosen and give them to the assistant, who goes to the dumbwaiter in the foyer and sends the list of selections down to the basement.

We call the kids in the basement who sort swatches "the elves" because, while the work may be drudgery, it definitely has its magic. Imagine handling fabric samples for ten hours a day when you love raw silk more than life itself! Such history in those little squares—some fabric designs as old as ancient Rome. When your stack of swatches appears in a crisp envelope on the shelf of the dumbwaiter, you can take it home and dream. I have several corkboards that become my template for a job. I arrange the swatches, paint chips, sample tiles, and photographs (for inspiration) that become the components of my design. When the board is filled, it's a vibrant collage that becomes a work of art in its own right.

"B?" I hear the singsongy voice of Mary Kate

Fitzsimmons, the young yet seasoned expert in Trims. "The bullion fringe arrived." Mary Kate knows my weakness for the hand-braided silk fringe I use to trim my ottomans and draperies.

"What colors?" I try not to sound too excited.

"Get ready! There's a dark blue, almost black, that shimmers like licorice. And a gold. I've never seen such a buttery gold in my life! But the best is a pumpkin color; it looks magnificent against ruby red. This batch is French."

"No one does fine hand knotting like the French." I sigh.

"Nope. They are the best." She smiles at me while gently caressing a sheer voile with tone-on-tone embroidered accents. Mary Kate is a classic Irish lass with her oval face, small nose, delicate pale skin, the regulation smattering of adorable freckles, and a bow-shaped, sensual smile. Her teeth aren't quite perfect, but the slight overbite is sexy. "The Italians are pretty good, though," she says, flirting.

"It's so hard to find the right fringe for an ottoman. I like my ottomans to be focal points, and if the fringe is stringy, it ruins the design completely." I find myself falling into the deep blue, almost turquoise, of her eyes.

"I could listen to you talk about ottomans all day," she purrs. "If you need anything, you know where to find me." She turns to go up the stairs. For an Irish girl, she has a very Italian rear end. Funny the things you notice when you're in the thrall of creativity.

By the time I work my way up to Trims, I am the last customer in the store. Even the assistants on the main floor have left, leaving me with my clipboard and pencil to make notes. This is when I love Scalamandré the most—it's quiet and I can think. I compare colors and prints, choose gimps for chair details and fringes for draperies, and use my color wheel against the chroma of various wallpapers. Mary Kate looks up from her desk as I peruse some new silk tassels with hand-painted ceramic beads over the knots. Very Marrakesh.

"What are you working on these days?" she asks pleasantly.

"Several homes. You know how it is—when the spring comes, people see their rooms in bright sunlight, and suddenly everything looks shabby. I can't work fast enough."

"Not everyone is as busy as you are. Of course, you're a superb decorator."

"Thank you. I try."

"You're the real article. Not like the dilettantes who call themselves decorators because somebody told them they have a **flair**. That's the first sign of a no-talent—they use the word 'flair.' "

"Now, Mary Kate, I'm not going to compare myself to the competition."

"Sorry. I have to deal with them all day, and they don't know brocade from burlap. I get tired of it."

Because I was hoping cousin Christina would come with me, I didn't call any of my city friends in advance, and I'm hungry. "What are you doing for dinner?" I ask Mary Kate.

"Nothing." She smiles.

"How about a plate of spaghetti?"

"Mmm. With a nice red wine and hot bread?" She opens her desk drawer and pulls out her purse.

We head to Le Chantilly, a cozy joint where designers lunch or sup between appointments. The chef is Italian, and though the place is better known for chops and chicken salad, he makes a hearty Bolognese sauce. Mary Kate has me order for both of us, and she proceeds to regale me with stories of the name designers who frequent Scali's: Carleton Varney, Sister Parrish, Mario Buatta, Chessy Rayner, Mica Ertegun, Albert Hadley, David Hicks, and Mark Hampton—all the biggies.

As we swap stories, I notice that Mary Kate slides closer and closer to me in the booth. By the time we're eating dessert—vanilla ice cream with hot-fudge sauce—I'm wedged in the

curve of the banquette with Mary Kate pressing so close I can smell her hair.

"What's your dream?"

"What do you mean?" In thirty-nine years, I
don't believe anyone has ever asked me that
question.

"The decorators who come into Scali's always have a big dream. It's that one property
they want to get their mitts on because they believe they're the only decorator in the world
who could do it justice. I've heard them all.
The duplex penthouse of the Beresford on
Central Park West is a big one. The Pabst mansion in Milwaukee. The White House. What's
your dream?"

"It's a church."

"Saint Patrick's Cathedral?"

"No, no, the one in my hometown."

"That's so sweet." Mary Kate, genuinely
touched, puts her hand on my arm and nuzzles
my ear with her nose.

"We should be going," I tell her. Mary Kate
goes off to the ladies' room while I pay the bill.
She meets me at the coat check.

"Are you seeing anyone?" Mary Kate asks as I
help her into her coat.

"I'm a free bird," I tell her. As soon as I say it,
I feel a rush of guilt. I am, after all, slightly engaged to be married, even though it is more of

an arrangement than a betrothal. After all, I rationalize, our mothers schemed for us to marry. The plan seems intact only because we're both still single. But I could never explain Capri, Aurelia, and The Match to Mary Kate. We've had a good wine, great food, and scintillating conversation; why drag the evening down with details?

"Good news for me." Mary Kate takes my arm, then snuggles her hand into my pocket. "You always smell so good. Clean, like cedar."

"I was just thinking the same thing about you."

"Do you find me attractive?" Mary Kate asks nonchalantly as we cross Third Avenue.

"You remind me of a Capodimonte rose," I answer. "Whimsical, yet perfectly lovely."

When we reach the corner, Mary Kate stops and faces me without taking her hand out of my pocket. She puts her free hand behind my neck, pulls me close, and kisses me. I have to say, the girl can kiss. It's very sweet, not like getting swabbed by Ondine Doyle.

"I never showed you the bullion fringe," she says with a smile.

"Scali's is closed."

"I have a key."

The thought of being alone in Scalamandre's, just Mary Kate and me and all that fabric, is irresistible. "What are we waiting for?" Mary Kate giggles as we run back to the townhouse. I feel delightfully conspiratorial. As a young man, I never rebelled or did anything to upset my parents, so sneaking into a locked professional building feels downright thrilling. Once we reach the front doors of the townhouse, Mary Kate looks up and down the street. When she sees no one familiar, she opens the front door with her key, lets me in, then locks the door behind us. She flips on the recessed lights over the staircase. I take her hand as we go up the stairs two at a time until we are in her department.

"Wait till you see it!" She slides a wall festooned with trims to the side, revealing rows of bullion fringe. "They used this at the Met on the fire curtain," she says proudly. "I helped them choose. Go ahead. Feel."

Mary Kate takes my hand and runs it over the long fringe, three feet of twisted silk braids hand-stitched to a matching embroidered gimp. The top knots and twists are as sensual as fingers; they slip through my hands like Christmas tinsel. I am mesmerized by the way the streetlight plays on the pulls of the fringe. Suddenly I'm William Powell, Mary Kate is Myrna Loy, and Manhattan twinkles in the backdrop like candlelight on crystal. Oh, the ambience!

I am lost in the moment as I caress the soft fringe and imagine it under low lighting, swinging from the draperies of the bay window of the Shumans' living room in Spring Lake. What a perfect accent to the rococo fantasia I'm creating for them!

Mary Kate grabs me from behind, running her hands from my waist to my lapels. She pulls off my jacket. "Mary Kate, darling, what are you doing?" I ask.

"Don't talk," she says softly. I hear buttons pop and zippers rip and the low whisk of her breath, rhythmic at first, then turning to a pant as though she is running to catch a train. She rubs furiously against my back and then climbs onto me like I'm Pikes Peak. I grip the fringe like a trapeze artist waiting to swing over the crowd in the circus tent and let Mary Kate take the lead. I feel as though I am waiting my turn, or perhaps awaiting instruction.

Mary Kate sucks on my neck in the same way she slurped down the Clams Casino appetizer at Le Chantilly. Then she peels off my shirt from behind. "God, your back!" she moans. I am proud of my shoulders and neck, and it has been said, when I was being fitted for custom shirts, that a hostess could serve dinner for eight on my back—it is **that** broad and toned, leading to a tight thirty-inch waist, of which I am equally proud. I seem to have broken the mold of box-shaped di Crespi men. Of course, I work at my musculature with a combination of brisk walks, light weights, and small portions.

Mary Kate thrusts against me, and I grip the silk-weave gimp for traction, like a lifeline, as she has her way with me. The girl is everywhere! Like a hairy spider in a horror movie, she moves over and under me, around and behind. This little speck of a thing works me over like pie dough, hitting pulse points and tender spots with precision. This is a woman who worships at the altar of the male form! She compliments every muscle and ripple as she goes.

And yet, for me, with all its hoopla and mystery, the sex act boils down to an exercise in friction. I never feel very much emotionally when in the throes of it, and I often wonder why. I know for most of the world making love really means something, but to me it has never been the ultimate human experience. Yes, it can be relaxing and pleasant, but as the great minds point out, pleasure is simply pleasure, it is in no way joy. Creativity is bliss to me. I find the exchange of an idea, the collaboration over a common goal, and the art of conversation far more satisfying than the huff and puff of The Act. "I'm sorry, did you say something?" I ask Mary Kate.

"I said, you're fantastic!" she whispers, then goes back to the job at hand.

I have been told that I'm a great lover, but I don't do anything in particular, I simply hold on. I play captain of the ship, keeping the boat steady with a firm hand on the tiller when the motion gets intense. In any event, Mary Kate Fitzsimmons seems so completely satisfied when she's had her fill that she collapses in a clump, the tassels forming a canopy over her sweet head.

"Oh, B," she whispers.

"Well?" I vamp, never knowing what to say to a naked woman who is looking at me as though I could change the weather.

She laughs. "I don't know what happened to me. The wine. The spaghetti. The fringe."

"The hot-fudge sauce!" I snap my fingers as though I just found the answer.

"No, no. It's you." She smiles.

"Thank you." What else can I say? She's giving me too much credit.

Mary Kate loops her red hair into a bun on the nape of her neck. "I really like Italian men. It's the way you look at a woman."

I think of my father, who used to look at my mother's face as though it was a beanbag. "What do you mean?"

"It's awe," she says earnestly as she puts on

her blouse and buttons it up. "You look at women like we know something." She stands without a shred of modesty or shame and looks for her skirt. Her pink skin, saturated in gold streetlight, looks like polished marble.

I don't know what to say, so I simply smile and step back into my pants.

"But you know what I really, really like about you in particular, Bartolomeo?" She takes my hand. "You don't ruin it with a lot of talk."

We return the fringe to the display wall, she turns out the lights, and we walk arm in arm down the winding staircase, which gives me a slight case of vertigo. I hold on to her on one side and the rope railing on the other. "Wait. I have to give you something." What an odd thing for a girl to say after sex. Mary Kate disappears into the back showroom, leaving me in the foyer. She returns quickly with a book.

"Here." She gives me the book **An Outline of European Architecture** by Nikolaus Pevsner. "This will give you lots of ideas for your church."

"Thank you." I kiss her and tuck the book under my arm.

Once outside, I hail a cab, help Mary Kate into the backseat, and stuff some money into the driver's hand, instructing him to wait until she is safely inside her building in Sunnyside, Queens. She rolls down the window and leans out. The wisps of her red hair flutter against the yellow taxi like feathers.

"The bullion you liked," she says.

"Yes?"

"It's number 1217." She smiles sweetly.

The taxi drives away, its red brake lights disappearing as it moves toward the East River Drive. I button my coat against the chill of the night air. I miss Mary Kate for a moment. I miss her creamy skin that smells like vanilla saltwater taffy. But the pang of sadness quickly fades as I walk up Third Avenue. Let's face it, the best part of sex is when it's over. I like to make love, say good-bye, and then be alone to reflect. Of course I always say a prayer that I won't rot in hell for having done the deed in the first place. Guilt after sex is the espresso after dessert.

I don't know what kind of Catholic Mary Kate is, but somehow she avoided the modesty and shame pill the rest of us took. Good for her. Perhaps Mary Kate has the right idea—making love is absolutely ordinary and as delicious as a bowl of ice cream. Why can't I let it be that? Why can't I learn from a bright girl with legs so strong she could crack walnuts between her knees? Something more to think about on the drive home, but first I need a nightcap.

I walk over to Gino's, a decorator hangout near Bloomingdale's, for one of their Manhattans, heavy on the sweet vermouth, just the way I like them. I feel a twinge in my left calf, similar to the tug one feels after riding a horse. I slip onto a bar stool and place my order, propping my foot on the brass rail to relax my leg. I open Pevsner's book, falling into the glorious illustrations of baroque architecture.

"Somebody has a charley horse," a voice says from behind me.

"Too much walking," I lie.

"If you say so."

I turn to this nosy yet perceptive stranger. How exotic she is, and how familiar she looks! Her jet-black hair reaches to her waist like the lushest silk fringe. She wears a midnight-blue sari wrapped close to her trim waist, bound by intersecting streamers (!) of gold lamé. Her shoes are flat gold sandals, the same color as her enormous hoop earrings and bangle bracelets, which take up most of her forearms. While she is formidably bold in her fashion choices, she has a charm to her that is completely accessible.

"Do I know you?" she asks.

"I'm Bartolomeo di Crespi."

"Don't know the name. Are you ASID?"

"Yep. How could you tell?"

"Eydie Von Gunne." The beautiful woman extends her hand. I take it, admiring her firm grip. Then she does a delightful thing. She shakes her wrist so the many gold bangles fall over her hand like gold lassos. Her arms are long and thin and remind me of one of those fertility goddesses with many arms you see in Tibetan art. "Your suit is a dead giveaway. Charcoal-gray with magenta pinstripe. Only a decorator would go for such a daring choice. What are you working on?"

"A church." Why am I telling her this? I don't even have the job yet; why am I trying to impress her?

Eydie smiles. "Europe or America?"

"New Jersey."

"Gothic, Romanesque, or modern?"

"Gothic."

"My specialty is churches. I know them like the back of my hand."

"You don't look like a cloistered nun."

"Nope, I never took the veil. Unless it was in a harem, of course." She snaps open her evening bag, a velvet clutch covered in peacock feathers, and hands me her card:

Eydie Von Gunne—Architect & Historian
17 Park Avenue
555-1127

"If you ever want to talk church, give me a call."

"I'll do it," I promise her.

"Any guy who reads Pevsner at a bar is my kind of guy." She smiles.

"You know what I love the most about New York City?"

"Let me guess. The lake at Central Park, the grand staircase at the Met, or the Milbank Mansion on West Tenth Street?"

I stop her. "No, although that's a fantastic list."

"What, then?" She seems truly interested in my answer.

"I love that I'm sitting here alone reading a book and you said hello."

She shrugs. "I like that suit."

A tall, chiseled Cary Grant type with white hair comes up to the bar and puts his arm around her. "Ready, hon?" he says in her ear.

"Uh-huh." She tilts her head and nuzzles his cheek. The maître d' pulls Mr. Chiseled away for a moment, so I am not formally introduced.

"That fellow is Hollywood handsome," I tell her.

"Oh, he knows it." She smiles and turns her head in profile to look at him.

Now I realize why Eydie looks so familiar. Against the forest-green walls, her head and neck are outlined like a tintype. That's it! She has my old nose! Except on her, with her height, long face, and heavy-lidded Egyptian eyes, it works. "Nice to meet you, Bartolomeo."

"Good night, Eydie."

As her companion holds the door open for her, Eydie steps out into the night like a blue bird sailing up into a dark sky. For a second, I want to follow her. She took one look at me and seemed to know who I was. How ridiculous! I just met the woman! What is it with me? Whenever I'm with a woman, I want to escape, and once she's gone, I miss the trap.

CHAPTER THREE

The Ottoman Empire

I take the steps two at a time as I climb to the choir loft for Sunday Mass. My rendezvous with Mary Kate has turned out to be a tonic. I have a pep in my step that wasn't there last week. My postcoital regret has turned to a warm glow, almost like a shot of Fernet Branca after a rare steak. My chance meeting with Eydie Von Gunne has also given me a boost. I keep looking at her business card as though it's a diamond. I'm going to sing my lungs out in Mass this morning.

I'm also feeling good because I've decided to have a serious sit-down with Capri and end our betrothal charade. After my night of love in Scalamandré, I said two rosaries begging the Blessed Lady for forgiveness—not for the act but for lying about being unencumbered. The phrase "free bird" keeps ringing in my ears like a fire alarm. I can't be part of this ongoing deception anymore. Capri is a wonderful girl, and she deserves to find happiness on her own. After all, if she was attracted to me, we would have had a little more contact than the one time she grazed my thigh with her left breast when I was on a stepladder hanging a valance in the Mandelbaum den in 1968.

Every Sunday, Capri sits in the first row of the choir loft wearing her prescription sunglasses, resting her chin on the railing, watching the action below like she's spending the afternoon at Brandywine Raceway betting on the horses. As I observe her from the back row of the choir loft, I realize that we've never broken up because there was never a reason to. She never pushed me to marry, and I never pushed back. Our relationship was like a brown overcoat. It works with everything, so why change it?

Aurelia is at the organ, going over the choir selections with Zetta. I slip into the seat next to Capri.

"How are you?" Capri looks at me and smiles. She is not even slightly suspicious that I went to New York and made love with Mary Kate Fitzsimmons, which is another reason to break up. "You're not going to like this," she whispers. She opens the church bulletin and points to an announcement.

> *Father Porporino has retained the design firm of Patton & Persky of Philadelphia, Penn., to renovate our church. Patton & Persky are world-renowned interior designers with clients as diverse as the Liberty Rose Hotel in Philadelphia and the Crestview nursing home in Frenchtown . . .*

I feel as though I've been stabbed.

My stomach begins to churn so loudly I grab my belt buckle as though it's a volume-control panel. I blink several times and read the last line of the announcement:

> *The diocese has approved the selection. The renovation will begin this fall after the Feast of Our Lady of Fatima.*

"I can't believe he did this to you." Capri takes my hand and squeezes it. "Are you okay?"

Shaking my head, I make an excuse and peel down the stairs, push open the side doors of the church, and suck in fresh air. That explains the smirk on Father's face when I came to dress the altar, the sudden cancellation of the parish council meeting, and the church bulletins he hid until he knew I was long gone. It all makes sense now. He didn't want to lower the boom in person. He wanted it to crash down around me once it was too late for me to object. I cannot believe that he went outside his own parish to find a decorator. Not only have I served this church faithfully **all my life,** from altar boy to altar dresser, but he knew what this renovation meant to me. I've been sandbagged!

"B! Don't go!" Capri says from the door. She races down the steps. The plush vibrato of the organ sails out the windows sounding like the chug of a train going uphill. The congregation belts out "They Will Know We Are Christians by Our Love."

"Did Father mention anything to you?" she asks when she catches up to me.

"Not a word." My face heats up with embarrassment over having bared my creative soul to him. No wonder he looked at me like I smelled of rotten meat.

"Mom will talk to him."

"No!" I nearly shout. "If this is how he feels, and this is what he thinks of my talent, let it go," I sputter. Capri takes a step back. For the first time in forty years, she is afraid of me. The last thing I want is for her mother to fix this.

"Okay." She raises her hands in the air like she's under arrest. "I'm just trying to help. I know how much this means to you, that's all." She turns and goes up the stairs. She stops at the door, slips her glasses off, and puts her face in her hands.

"Capri, are you crying?" I feel terrible. I've never yelled at her before. I go up the stairs, stopping her before she goes back inside. "I didn't mean to snap at you." I take her in my arms. She wipes her tears on her sleeve and looks up at me. Her expression is like Saint Rose of Lima's (the third stained-glass window on the right), filled with disappointment and hurt. I feel like I'm seeing her for the first time. "You have beautiful eyes," I say quietly. I make a mental note that whenever I see something lovely, it pulls me out of whatever suffering I endure in the moment. "I never noticed before."

"How can you even see them behind my glasses?" Capri sniffles as she pushes her hair behind her ear. She puts her prescription sunglasses back on.

"It's not easy."

Capri smiles. "You have a knack for saying the wrong thing."

"I know," I say apologetically.

"Mom is going to wonder where I went. I'd better go back in. Are you coming?"

"No . . . I can't."

Capri goes back into the church, and I catch

my breath. The years of service to my parish spin through my head like confetti. I had such plans! I wanted to ditch the heavy eighteenth-century stuff and replace it with a modern, open field, thus creating a sense of space. I wanted to use soothing colors, like eggplant and nut-brown, on the walls and trim, to invoke nature and serenity. I imagined a sleek modern Communion railing, a simple Quaker-style altar, and the priest's chair refurbished in a plum cut velvet with gold trim to pick up the veins of the marble statuary. I had mentally designed a shrine to the Blessed Mother—a contemporary white marble Madonna and child by Pizzo—that would replace the hand-painted cement statue. I planned to construct a simple backdrop for the statue, studded with pin lights and votive candles in a field below, creating an indoor grotto. I try to erase the pictures that have lived in my mind's eye for so long, but they won't disappear.

Oh, what I would have done with the opportunity! Our Lady of Fatima would have been a point of interest for the ecumenical tour buses that come through New Jersey during the jubilee years. Who knows? Perhaps, given the right circumstances, the church might have been the site of a miracle or two.

I can hear the murmur of the congregation as

they plod through the Nicene Creed. Tears sting my eyes as I remember the joy this church has brought me through the years, starting with the All Saints Day parade on All Hallows' Eve when I was six and wore a Saint Bartholomew costume and brandished an actual sword (on loan from Anthony Cappozolo, a generous member of the Knights of Columbus), to Toot's brutally hot July wedding when I keeled over in the heat in my white gloves and tails and had to be carried out of the sacristy like a slab of plywood after repeated attempts to revive me with sips of holy water from the font, to every single confession I made in Lucky Booth Number Two since I was ten years old. I never made up sins like my peers did; I always told the truth—and this is how I'm thanked.

For the first time in thirty-three years I will miss my Sunday Communion, but I cannot bear to face the crowd of people who will know that I have been passed over like Clemmie Valentini's stale cannolis on Bingo Night. How could Father do this to me? There is not a family in this parish whose home I have not decorated! Every chandelier, sconce, and drapes in this town was hung by my own hands! As for the diocese, this slight reverberates all the way to Bishop Kilcullen's mansion in Rumson. How dare they!

As I park in the lot of the Weis Market in Wall Township, the only twenty-four-hour seven-day-a-week supermarket in the county, the shock of Father's rejection has turned to anger, coupled with the guilt I feel about missing Sunday Mass. After all, I am a devout Catholic. I've never understood parishioners who left their church because the priest had wronged them. After all, it's not the priest who knows our souls, it's God. But now I understand. Evidently I'm not as devout as I thought I was, because I didn't drive to Saint Catharine's in Spring Lake for the noon Mass to fulfill my obligation, and I could have. No, this morning I feel finished with RC Incorporated.

One of the reasons I started my company in OLOF was to bring beauty to the town I grew up in. I could have easily gotten an apartment in New York City and swum with the big fish, vying to decorate Park Avenue apartments, Fifth Avenue penthouses, and Turtle Bay brownstones. Instead, I brought my education and gifts to the place where I was first inspired to do something wonderful with my life. Now I see that everything I believed in was a veneer. A local boy could never be good enough to redo the House of God.

When I was small and had a particularly rough go of things, Mama would make me a consolation cake called Our Lady of (Drown Your) Sorrows, with Heavenly Frosting. Current wisdom is that one must never reward or congratulate with food, or use it to soothe sadness. My mother disagreed, which might be why, when Toot and I are upset, agitated, or hurt, we like nothing better than whipping up a bowl of frosting. We used to take a box of confectioner's sugar, a stick of soft sweet butter, a thimbleful of vanilla, and a shot of half-and-half, beat it into a creamy frosting, then grab spoons and take turns eating it out of the bowl. When we got old enough to enhance food with alcohol, we replaced the vanilla with a shot of Amaretto. Buttercream frosting is our family Valium, and boy do I need it now.

When I think about Eydie Von Gunne and how I bragged that I was doing a church renovation, I feel like I could crack open a bottle of cooking sherry and guzzle it before I reach the checkout. Instead, I throw the ingredients for Heavenly Frosting into the cart and envision an afternoon at home finding solace in a bottomless pan of sheet cake.

OUR LADY OF (Drown Your) SORROWS CAKE WITH HEAVENLY FROSTING
Yield: Enough for an army

CAKE

3 Milky Way bars, cut into small pieces
3 Three Musketeers bars, cut into small pieces
3 Snickers bars, cut into small pieces
½ cup butter
2 cups flour
½ teaspoon baking soda
½ teaspoon baking powder
1 cup sugar
½ cup shortening
3 eggs
1 cup buttermilk
1 teaspoon vanilla extract

Preheat the oven to 325°F. Grease and flour a 9 by 13-inch baking pan. Melt the candy bars and butter in a saucepan. Blend. In a large bowl, mix the flour, baking soda, baking powder, and sugar. Then mix in the shortening and eggs. Beat well. Slowly add the buttermilk, beating until fluffy. Then add the vanilla and the candy-bar mixture from the saucepan. Beat well. Pour into the pan, and bake 60 minutes until done. When the cake is still hot, ice with:

HEAVENLY FROSTING
1 bag marshmallows, cut in half
1 cup chopped pecans
2 cups shredded coconut
1 box confectioner's sugar
4 tablespoons cocoa
8 tablespoons heavy cream
4 tablespoons butter, softened

Place the marshmallow halves, sticky side down, on top of the hot cake. Scatter the nuts over the marshmallows, then a layer of coconut. In a bowl, whip the confectioner's sugar, cocoa, cream, and butter. Pour over the hot cake. Serve when cool.

After I ice the cake, I lick the spoons, then wash the pans and straighten the kitchen. My head is throbbing, so I decide to take a nap. I go to my bedroom, climb into bed, and pull my silk wool afghan up to my chin. It's the last thing I remember when I wake up an hour later. A cool breeze wafts through my bedroom doorway, and I sit up. I must've left the garage door open.

"Uncle B?"

I hear my nephew Two's voice in the hallway.

"I'm in here," I call out.

Two appears in the doorway of my bedroom.

"Thank God," he says when he sees me. "You didn't answer the phone."

"I was taking a nap." In our family, if someone is missing for five minutes, we assume they are dead. No one has ever forgotten the day that Aunt Mirella Bontempo was scheduled to work the zeppole fryer at the OLOF Feast and didn't show up. My cousin Mona Lisa instantly formed a search party. We found Auntie in her basement with her arm stuck in the agitator of the washing machine. She had been washing her bras and one of the straps had choked the main water pipe and broken the machine. When she reached in to yank the bra loose, her hand got stuck. We got there in the nick of time, as the water was up to her midcalf. It would have meant certain death, as Auntie was a poor swimmer.

"We were worried. Nellie Fanelli called Mom and said that she saw you go into church for Mass and then she didn't see you in the Communion line." Two goes to the window and yanks the pulley that opens the drapes.

"It's a relief to know that besides her job ironing vestments, she has now become my Orwellian Big Brother."

Two laughs. "Nellie's always looking for dirt."

It's a sin to have favorites, but Two is special and not just because he's my namesake. He has always been reasonable and steady, a cool head in a crisis. He was with Toot when she caught Lonnie at an American Legion clambake with a date after they'd just returned from a marital retreat in the Catskills for Catholic couples in crisis. It was quick-thinking Two who got Toot out of there before she poured a pitcher of beer on Lonnie's head. The woman did not fare as well. Toot yanked off her pillbox hat and filled it with empty clamshells before throwing it against the wall.

Two doesn't look like the rest of the di Crespis, which may be why he commands a certain amount of attention. He has light brown hair in loose curls to his shoulders, green eyes, and the demeanor of a benevolent king. At six feet two, he is the tallest di Crespi of his generation.

"Ma said the parish is buzzing about the announcement in the bulletin."

"Let them buzz. Father signed a contract with Patton and Persky, so it's over."

"I can't believe you're not going to fight."

"No one has ever fought the Holy Roman Church and won. Look at Martin Luther—they almost killed him before he started his own church. And now what's he got? A paltry worldwide membership compared to the Baptists, who could take the Lutherans two to one in a softball tournament any day."

"But you've done so much for that church."

"Remember this always, Two. Put out your hand to help someone, and when you pull it back you've got no fingers. I told Father Porp I had ideas about the renovation, and he was completely dismissive. Of course, now I realize that he had already made his decision. He played me like a rube."

"Screw him," Toot says from the doorway. "I can't stand that guy, even if he is a priest. I remember when he came to me and asked me to annul my marriage to Lonnie. He told me I couldn't have the sacraments if I didn't get the annulment. Little did he know that Father Wiffnell over in Brielle gives me Communion and confession whenever I want it, no questions asked. He's the same guy that let our cousin Connie With The Curvature have birth control pills because with her back, if she had a sixth baby, she would have wound up in a wheelchair, and then who would have taken care of those kids? I told Porp when he pressed me to file the paperwork. 'Annul **this**, Father.' "

"I had no idea."

"Oh, yes. I grew golden gottz after Ma and Pop died. I might have played along when they were living, but trust me, I've had it with the rules and the regulations and the hypocrisy. Out of respect for you, my devout brother, I've kept my mouth shut about all things Roman Catholic. Now I can say what's in my heart. You're too good for those people. You don't need Father Phoney to talk to the man upstairs. Pray direct. With no entreaties—"

I stop and think before correcting her. "You mean encumbrances?"

"All I'm saying is, talk to God whenever you want. That's what I do. And I know my god-damn sins are forgiven. Where's the cake?"

"How did you know I made it?"

Toot looks at me. "You gonna go through a trauma of this magnitude without cake? What home did you grow up in?"

"It's in the kitchen under Ma's server."

"I'll be right back." Toot disappears down the hallway.

"I had to beg her not to go to the rectory," Two says quietly.

"It won't do a bit of good. Remember when our cousin Finola Franco wanted to marry that Methodist from Pennsylvania? Father Porp had him investigated and found out he was di-vorced. Finola knew, but she didn't care. Porp told her she'd fry in the bowels of hell if she married the guy. Her life was ruined. She got that disease where she never left her house again. Dried up in there like an orange peel."

"Why do you put up with this?" Two asks.

"Why don't you write to the bishop and get Porporino moved?"

"Oh, there have been letters and calls and meetings for years. But Porp is untouchable."

"That's ridiculous." Two stretches out on my chaise longue. "This is really comfortable."

"It's stuffed with goose down and lined in Lee Jofa's silk chamois number seventeen."

"Okay, waitress coming through." Toot puts a tray of coffee and cake on the bed. She gives me a slice, then serves Two. She fixes my coffee and puts it on the nightstand, gives Two a mug, and pulls my straight-backed chair from the desk to sit down. We eat the cake and don't say much.

I look around my bedroom, decorated in serene white with silver accents. I pulled a real Elsie de Wolfe in here. It is spare, simple, and sleek. There's a bed, a desk, a chaise longue, and that's it. There's never clutter—this is my haven. I can hear the ocean from my window, and even in winter, I sleep with it cracked to let in the fresh air. I look at my sister and my nephew eating their cake with the intensity of scientists sampling atoms in search of radium. The looks on their faces make me smile.

Whenever I've felt sadness or despair, I've always turned to my work for solace. The rituals of my craft help me keep my mind on what's important. Since my rejection at church a few days ago I've put together several corkboards with swatches and samples for my clients. I'm keeping busy.

As I drive to the Baronogans', I think about the House of B.

Every decorator has a signature piece, something that he can place in any house, in any period, in any style that somehow defines who he is to the creative community. While I am known for my overall design (authentic historical) and point of view (freewheeling fun), my signature piece is The Ottoman.

I hate coffee tables. If you find a decent one, please let me know. In twenty years and in hundreds of homes, I've never seen one that I thought was artful. But they perform a necessary function. You need them for drinks, books, magazines, feet, what have you. In desperation, I once sawed the legs off a Shaker dining table for an Early American home I was doing in Shrewsbury because I couldn't find one that suited the room. Determined to never ruin another gorgeous room with a substandard table, I came up with an alternative. Why not take a traditional ottoman and give it a new purpose?

I select an ottoman (or settee or upholstered stool) in a shape that works with the furniture configuration. I like a large piece with a good-sized surface, and a circular shape creates a better flow. Then I deal with the legs; black lacquer on the feet works in any decor, it makes the legs disappear. Then I let my imagination go wild. I upholster the ottoman with whimsical fabrics, adding wild trim (fringe, gimp, covered buttons, dangling crystals). After festooning, I have a piece of thick glass made to go on top, creating an instant multipurpose coffee table. When you need extra seating, simply remove the glass.

I park outside the Baronogans'. I pull their final bill out of my file folder and go to the front door. Midge Baronogan greets me at the entrance with a kiss. I follow her inside. The living room looks lovely but needs some adjusting in the placement.

So, I push the sofa in the Baronagans' living room back about two feet, then take the floor lamps and anchor them at either end of the couch. I scoot the ottoman closer to the sofa.

"Oh, B. I am cuckoo nuts for the ottoman!" Midge Baronagan, a tawny Filipina around seventy years old, steps back as I rearrange the pillows on the sofa. She is Geoffrey Beene chic in her simple pantsuit, a flowing white chiffon blouse over stovepipe white chino pants. A chain belt grazes her hip, then dangles to her knee. She wears delectable jeweled slippers in pale silver with a demi heel. "I love what you do! Such an artist!" Midge claps her hands. Her husband is a quiet man, chief surgeon at the best hospital in Trenton. I've met him only once, and he said whatever makes Midge happy makes him happy, including the ultra-expensive Japanese waterfall and goldfish pond I installed outside the dining room. This house is the jewel of Spring Lake.

"I'm glad you like it." I adjust the glass top to fit perfectly over the seams of the ottoman. I had a ball with this one, oval with simple wooden legs. I covered it with a deep blue satin brocade embroidered with a multicolored bird-of-paradise design. I used a six-inch silk fringe in pale blue from the base to the floor, then added a kicky ball fringe in gold around the top seam to give the piece movement. I covered forty-seven large buttons in cornflower-blue velvet and staggered them on the sides, giving texture to the satin. It's a triumph.

Midge puts her arm around my waist; her head fits into the crook of my arm. "Look at this room. It's a masterpiece."

I have to agree. Midge loves blue. People who tend to decorate with blue as their base color are usually very upbeat, while clients who choose rosy reds are first in line for the strait-jacket. Here I used shades of azure throughout the house and in the artwork. I found some casement fabric samples from Dorothy Liebes through a friend who had seen them in San Francisco. I took these squares woven with raffi and set them in rough-hewn frames, filling an entire wall.

The home is an architectural wonder, a Modern Prairie style with movable inside walls (which I covered in a cornflower-blue toile chinoiserie wallpaper depicting the ancient healing arts I found at Houles) and glass-brick room separators that give an icy twist to the cool blues.

Since the house gets so much sun, I made simple eggshell-colored muslin draperies, double-sided. The filmy muslin feels modern and young and gives the home a layer of softness and movement against the knotted-pine floors and stainless-steel accents.

The walls are a shade of white I call "Movie Star Teeth," so white it's blue. I mixed the color myself using a flat white enamel, adding deep blue with an eyedropper until I achieved the perfect shade.

I covered Midge's twenty-foot L-shaped sofa in a cuddly navy blue chenille, her pillows in a Stroheim & Roman pale-green-and-midnight-blue stripe, a lovely combination in a woodsy setting. I found area rugs at Saxony, large squares of off-white and moss green with ribbon etching in a pale salmon. My pal Helen McNeill had to twist arms to find what I was looking for; we wound up sewing smaller area rugs together because we couldn't find ones large enough.

"Now we're done," I say to Midge. My voice breaks a little—I've enjoyed this job so much I hate to see it end.

"But I don't want to be done!" Midge swats my arm affectionately. "I want to start all over again."

"Now you know how I feel. If I could decorate every house in New Jersey, I would. And then I'd start over. There are millions of possibilities for every home, and in a lifetime we only get to try a few."

"It's a shame." Midge shakes her head.

"Ah, well. As my dear mother used to say, our homes on earth are just hotel rooms until we get to our permanent home in the promised land." I place my bill on the side table.

"No, I mean, it's a shame what happened at Our Lady of Fatima." Midge gestures for me to sit down. "Shame on them! Here, right under Father Porporino's nose, is the best interior decorator in New Jersey. The old saying goes, a king is never a king on his own island. They don't appreciate you!"

"It's all right. I've come to terms with it."

"It's wrong." Midge looks at me with a steely gaze, the likes of which I haven't seen since I recommended a pink dining room in her otherwise blue house.

"I appreciate your concern."

She puts her hand on her heart. "I've been a Catholic all my life. The priest always has too much power! It was the same in the Philippines. Priests are nothing but little potentates, ruling over their kingdoms with God as their judge. Sometimes they go too far." Midge pats me on the back. "This time he blew it."

I wonder if people know how painful it is for me to be reminded that I was passed over to renovate Our Lady of Fatima Church. I would never go into a bank and say to the teller, "Did you ever find that nine dollars you were short yesterday?" Or tell the guy at the gas station after he cleans my windshield, "Hey, you missed a spot." Nor would I say to Dr. Wallace, "Hey, sorry about those four cancer cells you missed that cost Aunt Snooky that additional four feet of colon." No, I would never hurt someone who was doing his or her best.

The problem is, I'm a **stewer**. I can hold a grudge longer than a lifetime (an incentive to embrace reincarnation now that I'm stepping back from Catholicism). I'm certain I'll be taking several grudges with me into the next world, with matching axes to grind them. It's like that peach pit I swallowed when I was six. I'm sure it's still sitting in my gut like a stone and will be there on the day I die. I hold on to things!

After a week of chronic anger, which led to sleepless nights, daytime dyspepsia, and a gassy, distended abdomen, I decide to take the bull by the horns. Sometimes there has to be a reckoning before one can move forward. Father's day of reckoning is here.

The red light is on outside my Lucky Confessional Booth Number Two, which means some sinner is in there, so I slip into the back pew to wait my turn. It's funny how the place has changed in my perception. In just a few days, the church I've loved all my life now seems old and tired.

I've spent years making this place beautiful in the details: well-placed altar linens and seasonal flower sprays made special with offbeat accents like grapes during Advent and cotton pods in the summer. If I didn't do the flowers myself, I'd often stand behind the florist, giving instructions. Now all I see from font to altar are the flaws, the design missteps (like the cheap brass-toned light fixtures that replaced the old crystal ones), and the neglect (the peeling paint over the radiators and the toddler teeth marks on the backs of the pews). But these are no longer my problems. Let Patton & Persky figure out how to make this place look regal again.

When Mr. Fonti, the bulbous town tree surgeon, exits my confessional, he heads directly for the altar of the Blessed Lady, where he kneels with his head in his hands. He must have committed a doozy of a sin to get what looks like a major penance. I heard he likes go-go dancers, a bad habit for a married father of nine.

Taking a deep breath I approach the booth, yank the heavy velvet curtain back, close it behind me, and kneel down.

"Bless me, Father, for I have sinned," I begin. "You know what? Forget that. These words of penance that have meant so much to me all of my life suddenly sound like a lie. I am not here to ask for forgiveness. **You** have sinned."

"I beg your pardon?" a stunned Father Porporino whispers back.

"What do you take me for?"

"Bartolomeo?"

"How dare you hire Patton and Persky, those . . . those preppy Main Line Presbyterians! This is **my** church, **my** community. I worship here! I was baptized in the marble font, took my First Communion kneeling at the railing, took my confirmation and the holy oil from the bishop. I've been here all my life—twenty years longer than you!"

"I'm sorry if you feel bad—"

"Bad? I don't feel bad, I am humiliated. Do you know the Latin root of the word 'humiliation,' Father?" He tries to interrupt again, but I steamroll right over him. "The root is 'humility.' The ability to be humble in the eyes of God. What do you think my devotion to this church meant to me? Everything!"

"You should do good works for the satisfaction it brings others, not for acclaim."

"I'm not asking for fame, Father. I'm not Joey Heatherton looking to headline at the Sands after years of being an opening act. I deserved the job! Nobody has loved this church more than me. You took away my dream and handed it off to some second-rate Philly talent like it never mattered in the first place."

"They've won awards," Father says meekly.

"What does **that** mean to the heart and soul of this congregation? Most of them have never heard of Philadelphia outside of cheesesteaks and football—it is hardly the epicenter of interior design." I begin to feel better and stronger, not afraid of Father Porporino anymore. My self-confidence rises like a tidal wave. "It would be one thing if you had democratically opened up the job to bids. Then at least I could believe that you were watching the purse strings. But to simply ignore, to deliberately insult, any local talent—"

"But you **are** the local talent. You are the **only** decorator in town."

"Then your job was even easier! All you had to do was give me a call, or stop me on the steps after Mass and give me the heads-up that you were going elsewhere. Instead, I read about it in the bulletin! You seem to find time to single me out when you need me to raise money for the Bishop's Annual Appeal. That's what I'm good for—going door-to-door like a Fuller Brush man, can in hand, begging for the diocese. Well, listen to this, Padre, and listen hard; I am done with you and your cans and your fiefdom. You run your church with arrogance. A local boy is not good enough for your grand visions. No, you have to go to the big city to find a big name. You're buying for the label, not the craftsmanship."

"They're quite good, and I liked their portfolio." Father bristles.

"We'll see if Patton and Persky support this church as I have all these years. Will they come at dawn on Saint Lucy's feast day in the freezing cold and haul out the man-sized crèche figurines and string lights in the outdoor manger until their fingers bleed? Will they organize the pancake breakfast for the retarded and set the tables with festive linens because even retarded people deserve ambience? Tell me: Will they give up four weekends in a row to make gravy to freeze for the spaghetti supper to finance the new roof for the rectory so you won't sleep in a draft and die of consumption? I think we know the answer. You've got a lot of crust, Father. A lot of crust!"

"Are you finished?" Father Porporino seethes.

I press my nose so close to the screen I taste metal. "In more ways than you can ever know." I push the velvet curtain aside and stumble out. I've gone my whole life without disagreeing with authority of any kind: not a priest or a nun or a meter maid (I even spelled my name for one who was writing me a ticket once). It was always "Yes, Father," "Of course, Sister," "Give me the ticket, Officer." Now I'm dizzy with anger.

As I turn to go, I almost trip over Nellie Fanelli's feet as she kneels before the pietà shrine. Then I swivel and poke my head into Lucky Booth Number Two.

"And one more thing, Father. I had big plans for this church. Marble inlays and sumptuous fabrics and crystals and lights and an eternity font that would spit holy water well into the next century! You think about **that** when you're meeting with Patton and Persky."

I take a deep breath and yank the curtain closed again. Nellie stands in the corner by the door waiting for me. Her white lace chapel veil, studded with small pink chiffon butterflies, is pinned to her gray-blue bouffant, holding it like saran wrap on leftovers. She looks me straight in the eye and with her gnarled fingers makes an "okay" sign. "I heard everything," she whispers. **"Va bene."**

Nellie goes into the confessional and winks at me before she pulls the curtain shut. If I felt slightly guilty about telling Father Porporino off, I certainly don't now. The Little People, in the form of pastoral laundress Nellie Fanelli, have given me their imprimatur. The House of B still carries some clout around here, maybe not enough to get me the Big Job, but it clearly means something to the people who **really** count.

Despite the liberation of telling Father Porporino what I really think of him, by the night of my surprise birthday party, it's all I can do to pull myself together. I'm blue, plain and simple, down in the dumps. During the day I function just fine, but the nights hit me like a trash-can lid. There's no worse punishment than having to go out at night when you feel pitch-black inside. As I lock the front door behind me, I plaster a smile to my face. I inhale deeply to calm my nerves before I climb into Toot's Cadillac.

"Hey, Unc. Are you ready for your party?" Two, my chauffeur, grins.

"I'll give you five dollars to drive me in the other direction."

"Sorry. Ma already gave me a ten to get you there." Two steps on the gas.

"See, even my own sister sandbags me." I pinch the crease in my slacks from thigh to knee. "How many people are there?"

"About a hundred."

"Dear God," I moan. I think about all the years and all the parties that have come before this one. It's like watching a slide show in my emotional ViewMaster. I remember my sixth birthday, when Daddy rented a pony that ended up having a mental condition and bucked Rosemary With The Lupus into the cherry tree, where she hung like a Wallenda until the mothers found a tall ladder to help her down. Rosemary was fine, but the pony was banished to Ohio to live on a farm. When I was fifteen, Toot and Lonnie took me and six of my friends into New York City for a floor show at the Copa. One of my best pals, Cookie Francesci, disappeared during a Carmen Miranda send-up. We couldn't find him for three hours. It turned out that he hired a hooker and had sex standing up in the men's room at Luchow's. Then there was my thirty-fourth birthday, when I went into the hospital with a kidney stone and Father Porp gave me last rites. I'm sure my fortieth is going to be a doozy.

"Unc?" Two grips the steering wheel and checks the rearview mirror.

"Yes?"

"I'm going to take a year off from college."

"Does your mother know?"

"Not yet. I plan on going back. I just need some time. I'm having a problem fitting in. I don't know what it is, exactly. I get along fine with everybody, but I don't feel like I'm making progress in the theater department like I should. I'm missing something."

"I thought you were directing a play."

"I was. It got to be too much."

"Two, you know I think you're brilliant, but you can't start out your life quitting school because you don't like it. Look, I have clients I can't abide, but I go into their homes radiating joy and filled to the brim with good taste. I bring them swatches and paint chips and samples, and I endure their small minds, bad breath, and tight wallets because I'm a businessman. An artist, yes, but a businessman also."

"I don't feel like an artist yet."

"It doesn't happen overnight. It takes years to know what you like and then to fight for it. I was a pushover at first, but I learned that people were hiring me for my eye. It's the same thing in the theater. You have to train your eye."

"I don't relate to the other students."

"Why? Villanova has nice people. After all, they're Catholic, aren't they?" I sound like such a square. So I change my tone. "You're serious about this?"

"You know I always tell you the truth."

"I know." Maybe it's because I've been there for every major event of Two's life—and every play, recital, and party—that I don't do him the injustice of behaving like a parent. Who am I to tell him what to do? "Then . . . you should do what's right for you."

"Thanks, Unc." Two smiles. "Do you have some work for me?"

"You want my blessing **and** a job?"

"Well, like you said, otherwise Ma will kill—"

"Okay, okay. I'll talk to my drapery guy. He might need someone in the studio."

Two thanks me profusely. Toot is going to make mincemeat out of me. As we turn onto Corinne Way, cars are parked bumper to bumper as far as I can see. Toot's garage is aglow like a federal prison, the driveway ablaze with tiki lamps stuck into the ground. Two pulls the Cadillac onto the lawn, where a place has been saved for the guest of honor.

At the entrance to the garage, the crowd lunges at me. "Surprise!" they shout, joyful anticipation on their faces. Italians, who plan their parties down to the fantail arrangement of silver teaspoons on the Venetian table, need to pretend that every detail just happened to come together casually to create **la Festa**.

The Nite Caps, my cousin Dom Ruggiero's swing band, is perched on risers in the space normally reserved for the Caddy. They launch into a high-voltage rendition of "Oh Marie," and the guests swarm onto the rented parquet wood dance floor like the crowd at St. Peter's Square when the Pope gives the Easter benediction. I am kissed and slapped and squeezed by my cousins (a few "y" Crespys have come down from Boston), my inner-circle clientele (the Baronagans, Aurelia Mandelbaum, the Schumans, Hagans, Kuglers, and Rabinskis), and dear friends from the trade in New York City (Helen McNeill, Susan Friedman, Norbert Ratliff).

More lightbulbs flash in my face than when I keeled over in the heat at Toot's wedding. Despite my walking depression, I feel loved and treasured, and younger than the enormous number printed in gold on the napkins alongside my initials. My sister is nothing if not subtle. My family loves to celebrate, and nothing tops a party in honor of a birthday ending in a zero.

To commemorate the year of my birth, 1930, Toot looked to Hollywood. Festive blowups of icons Charlie Chaplin, Tom Mix, Deanna Durbin, and me—posed nude at age one on a leopard rug at Atlantic City's Steel Pier—hang from the ceiling amid colorful crepe-paper streamers.

The portable tables are covered in red, with multicolored tulips for centerpieces. Toot took my twelve years of school pictures, glued them to a wire, and stuck them in the vases amid the flowers. She covered the floor with green Astro-turf, except for the wooden dance floor, where the riding lawn mower usually sits. The windows are propped open and a fresh spring breeze wafts through the well-scrubbed garage, carrying a faint smell of motor oil mixed with the heady floral tones of Youth Dew perfume worn by every lady in the joint.

The walls are decorated (obscured, really) with a row of orange-and-white helium balloons suspended on multicolored ribbons and attached to weighted flowerpots on the floor. There are funny quips printed on them: THIRTY-NINE AND COUNTING, 40 AND FANTAS-TIC, and I'M SO OLD I CAN'T TELL MY KNEES FROM MY ANKLES.

The cake, a replica of the Villa di Crespi, is lit by a spotlight on a round table covered in lace doilies. It is a wonder. The architectural details are exactly right, from the slope of the roof to the arch of the doors, all re-created in vividly colored buttercream icing (even the garden and lawn are done to scale). The dormers are outlined with licorice whips, the stonework fence is made with gumdrops, and the windows are Necco wafers. There's a little man—me?—in the yard. (It looks as though the baker ripped a groom off a wedding topper. I would never wear a white tie and tails around the house.)

"Bartolomeo, happy birthday from the Salesian sisters!" Sister Theresa Kelly, my favorite nun, gives me a small package.

"Let me guess, Sister." I shake the box. It gurgles. "Lourdes water."

"How did you know?" She smiles, and it's as if an aura of good temper suddenly surrounds me. Or maybe it's the pulsating strobe light and the up-tempo version of "After the Lovin'." Sister Theresa is a striking presence, with her green eyes and porcelain skin set against the stark black-and-white habit. What a color scheme that would make for a room!

"We can't stay." Sister Theresa points to the other nuns sitting at a table for eight eating an early supper. "Nicolina told us to go ahead and have a bite. I hope you don't mind."

"Of course not. Who's driving back?" North Haledon, where the convent is located, is pretty far, and the highway is busy on weekends.

"Sister Ercolina. She just got new eyeglasses."

"That's a good thing. I saw her at the Fatima sidewalk sale, and she almost plowed into the bingo tent when she was parking."

"I heard." Sister Theresa lowers her voice. "That's why the new glasses." She gives me a hug as we join Sister Lead Foot and the rest of the nuns at the table for a photograph. They gather round me like chorus girls. I ask Sister Theresa to make devil horns behind my head while the rest of the nuns fold their hands in prayer and look up to heaven. What a shot for next year's Christmas card.

"Did I go all out or what?" Toot comes up behind me, gives me a kiss on the cheek, then takes my hand to show me the decorations.

"Thank you, sis. What a party. And the cake!"

"Well, you love your house more than anything."

"Not more than you," I tell her sincerely. "You look lovely, Toot."

"Think so?" My sister wears a black chiffon

cocktail dress with peekaboo nude lace inserts over much of the bodice. Her hair is done in a dramatic upsweep anchored by a clip covered in black sequins. She even glued on false eyelashes. "Lonnie's coming," she whispers; "I want him to regret everything. His affairs, the divorce, the secret bank account he set up in his dead mother's name to hide marital assets from me. All of it. I want him to look at me and get a lump in his throat." Toot swirls her hand from her bust down to her left hip. "Look what he gave up."

"What possessed you to invite him?"

"He's family." Toot plucks a mini-cannoli from a four-tiered silver tazza on the Venetian table. "People aren't paper plates, B. You can't just throw them out when you're done with them."

Or when they're done with you, I'd like to remind my sister, but I don't want to ruin her upbeat mood. "Good point." I grab a mini-cannoli and toss it back. What the hell, it's my birthday and it's gonna be a long night. What's an extra nine hundred calories when I'll be hitting the dance floor later? I wave at Cousin Iggy With The Asthma as he waits on the buffet line with his wife, Moochie.

"Can you believe it? Iggy and Mooch drove all the way from Vegas. It took them a week. Of course, you can't get decent calamari out there."

Two hands his mother a whiskey sour.

"You done good," she tells him.

"Uncle B didn't suspect a thing." Two winks at me.

Toot smooths Two's curls, then cups her hands around his chin tenderly. "I wish you'd cut your hair, honey. It's too long. You look like the second guy from the left on the cigar box."

Cousin Amalia squeezes her way across the dance floor. She looks adorable in a pink Empire-waist peasant dress, with a matching yarn bow in her high ponytail. "Happy birthday, cousin B." She gives me a beautifully wrapped box. "It's not a wallet."

"That's okay. It turns out my fortieth is going to be the Year of the Dobb Kit. By the end of the evening I'll have a pair of toenail clippers for each toe."

"Don't you mean **Dopp**?" Toot says.

"I say **Dobb**."

"Huh," she grunts. I unwrap Amalia's present and lift out a round disk with a flat bottom.

"It's a paperweight. I sunk a picture of you and Mom into this plastic goopy stuff and let it dry. It's not supposed to have any bubbles in it, but some got in."

"I love it, and I can't believe you made me something. That means more to me than any other present." I give Amalia a big hug. Christina joins us wearing a turquoise mini dress in chiffon with matching kitten heels. "You dyed your shoes," I compliment her.

"I know how you like things to match."

"You're beautiful!" I tell her.

"Aunt Edith just gave me the eye. She doesn't like my dress. Evidently I'm supposed to wear black for the rest of my life, but I couldn't take it another day." Christina gives me a kiss.

"In her day they also saved up their stray hairs in tin cups, matted them into balls, and attached them to their heads with straight pins and called it a coiffure. Forget Aunt Edith's Victorian nonsense."

"I'm doing the best I can. But everybody has an opinion." Christina forces a smile.

My nephew Nicky works his way through the crowd to join us, yanking Ondine by the hand like she's a pull toy on a string.

"Here comes Sir Nicky with Lady Lubricant."

"That's her?" Christina whispers.

Nicky looks exactly like my father did in his youth—big head, broad shoulders, black hair, and stubby yet sturdy legs. He even walks like Daddy, with his head cocked to the side and his eyes in a squint. "Hey, Unc!" He throws his arms around me and pats my back hard, like

I'm a horse and he expects me to giddyup. "Happy birthday. Hey, cousin Chrissy." Nicky gives Christina a kiss, then introduces Ondine as his "girl." Christina and I look at each other and cringe. Toot joins us with a plate of stuffed mushrooms.

"Hi, Uncle B," Ondine says with a smile. "Do you like the balloons?"

"Don't tell me you blew them up yourself," I say, remembering that Toot overcame her animosity long enough to assign Ondine some chores for the party.

"Uh-huh." Ondine looks all around. "You know so many people. My family is teensy. You could fit the whole Doyle family on the riding lawn mower." Ondine's lush blond hair cascades around her shoulders; her sunglasses, perched on her head like a tiara, hold the wisps off her forehead neatly. (Why the sunglasses at eight o'clock at night is anyone's guess.) Ondine wears a pale blue denim miniskirt, a short matching jacket with gold-trim epaulets, a denim shoulder bag with a patch on it that says DON'T EAT YELLOW SNOW, and short denim boots with a spike heel. It's a genuine chuck-wagon ensemble—the only thing missing is a holster and a Smith & Wesson revolver. I compliment her. "That's quite an outfit. You look like a million bucks once removed."

Toot inspects Ondine from head to toe. "It's chilly tonight. No stockings?"

"I don't need 'em. I cream up. It's better for my tan." Ondine sticks her leg straight out and draws a circle in the air with her toe. "Sometimes I get as far as Thanksgiving before I have to put on nylons."

"Lovely." Toot nudges me as if to say, "See—proof positive she doesn't wear underwear." There is an awkward silence. Toot takes a piece of prosciutto and melon off a passing hors d'oeuvres tray. She eats the melon, then rolls the prosciutto into a thin pink-and-white cigarette and takes a dainty bite. She turns to Two. "Where's your brother Anthony?"

"He's coming with Pop. It's nice of you to invite Pop . . . and his . . . and Doris."

"He has a new wife and I accept that. Look." Toot checks each button on Two's crisp white shirt. "Your father gave me my sons. And the least I can do is open up my home to him during times of celebration and grief."

"I'm proud of you, Ma." Two gives her a hug.

"It's a lovely theory, sis, but let's see how you do in real life." I nod toward the door. "Forgive me if I find your sudden largess suspicious."

Lonnie, for whatever reason, comes into the garage through the kitchen. For a guy on his third marriage, he looks pretty good. Lonnie is five feet nine, with a small head and thick salt-and-pepper curls. He has handlebar sideburns, and it has been said that in profile he looks like an Italian Engelbert Humperdinck. I don't see the resemblance, though he has full lips and a small nose and eyes so black and deep they look like two raisins sunk in a wet waffle. I've never known Lonnie to wear anything but a suit; tonight it's a three-piece Johnny Carson gray serge with a lavender shirt and a wide black-and-white striped tie. Pretty dapper.

"That's his new wife," Two whispers in my ear.

"I thought it was the caterer," I whisper back.

"What caterer?" my sister thunders. "Every bite at this party from the hors d'oeuvres to the steam table with the pasta rondelet was made by family!" Several of our Farino cousins from the Poconos turn and look at her.

Lonnie's second wife, Sylvia Bonboni, was a lot like my sister—an Italian girl with lush black hair and a big black car. Evidently Lonnie had as hard time being true to her as he had to Toot. Marriage Number Two had the shelf life of a stuffed pepper.

I haven't been introduced to his current wife, Doris Falcone, née Cassidy. She doesn't look like Lonnie's type at all. First of all, she's not younger than Lonnie, seeming to be in her upper fifties. She's tall and willowy. At this party, she's a good foot taller than any of the other guests. Her shoulder-length hair is a soft dove gray, offset perfectly by a shirtwaist party dress in a mild pink Pucci print, which she wears with pink Pappagallo flats. "She's a dead ringer for Lady Sylvia Ashley," I say to no one in particular, thinking of Clark Gable's fourth wife, the zipper-thin British royal-by-marriage who came to the States and charmed Hollywood and its leading men after the war.

"I heard of her." Toot straightens her dress and pulls in her tummy.

"Have you met Doris?"

"I'm on my way." Toot goes to greet Lonnie and Lady Sylvia. I turn to Two. "We may not have to restrain her with this one."

Two shrugs. "Pop's a changed man now. He and Doris have a quiet life. She sits in the boat and knits while he fishes. Her kids are grown. She has her own money."

From across the garage, Capri motions for me to join her and Aurelia at a table marked "Reserved."

"B, you look divine!" Aurelia puts out a cheek for me to kiss, then the other.

"You're looking pretty sharp yourself, Aurelia." She wears a Bill Blass palazzo-pant jumpsuit with a Kenneth Lane brooch that can only be described as an emerald fly caught in a pink diamond spiderweb.

"Dance with Capri," she barks.

Cousin Dom, a few feet away at the electric keyboard, hears the order and complies with a jazzy "In the Still of the Night." No one ignores the mandate of the richest woman in New Jersey. I take Capri in my arms.

"I'm moving out," Capri whispers in my ear as we glide across the dance floor to a smattering of applause.

"What?" I'm stunned. "What did your mother say?"

"She doesn't know. It's bad enough to turn forty. I can't turn forty and still live at home." Capri exhales and I smell the crisp perfume of a double Manhattan on her breath.

"Your mother is not going to like this at all."

"Too bad. I want a life, B. I want to be independent, to come and go as I please. Like you. Like everyone I know. Of course, everyone I know is married and miserable with four kids. I don't want **that,** but I want **something.**"

Capri leans on me, and the deadweight of her almost makes my spine snap in two.

"She's always checking on me. I can't go anywhere without her waiting by the door until I return. She checks to see if I'm wearing the rubber support stockings I'm supposed to wear for my poor circulation. It's madness." I can see tears through Capri's thick lenses. "My life is not worth living if I'm a prisoner."

"Then you **should** move out. You're a grown woman, and your mother needs to accept that."

"Will you help me?"

"Of course." Instantly I regret my promise. Capri should stand on her own two feet, but when a girl is wearing orthotics, she might need someone to lean on.

"I don't want to be a bother," Capri whispers.

"You're not a bother. You're my friend, and there isn't anything I wouldn't do for you."

"Thanks." Capri goes to rest her head on my shoulder for the saxophone solo but instead points to the center of the dance floor. "Oh my gosh!" she says with hot breath in my ear. "Look at your sister! Isn't that her ex-husband?"

The couples on the dance floor have fallen away and formed a circle on the periphery. I scoot Capri to the edge to join them. Lonnie holds Toot's hand in the air, her fingers wrapped around the palm of his hand, and he leads with his pinky. They are holding each other entirely too closely for divorced people.

The bandleader looks at Lonnie and my sister with their arched backs and faces nose to nose and lifts his sax, blowing low and sexy. A few wolf whistles are heard. The crowd hears the musical call of the wild and holds its breath. I look over at Ondine, who has the glow of a woman who just ovulated. She stands behind Nicky and puts her hands in his front pockets.

As the opening chords of "Blame It on the Bossa Nova" wash over the crowd, Lonnie and Toot lock eyes like Rudolph Valentino and Mae Murray; even Sister Theresa and the nuns stop on their way out and feel the heat.

Lonnie pulls Toot even closer, his arm anchoring her waist. (I wonder if she can breathe.) He lifts her slightly, dragging her to the center of the dance floor under the blowup of Deanna Durbin doing a double axel at the Ice Capades. As he drags her, her dress sidles up. Thank goodness she's wearing opaque support hose à la Ann Miller. In a quick dip, Lonnie flips Toot onto the floor like a Sea World dolphin. He catches her, spins her, and snaps her back up to eye level. The crowd cheers.

"My goodness, where is her slip?" our great-aunt Edith Romano says loudly. "I can see her—" Before she can finish her thought, cousin Cathy Martinelli stuffs a mozzarella ball into Edith's mouth. ". . . coolie," Aunt Edith mumbles through the cheese.

It's as if a mating call was issued with that sax blast, and my sister and her ex-husband came to the edge of the woods like a couple of wild dogs, gave each other a quick sniff, and commenced rolling down the happy trail of memory lane, only this time it's to music and they've got a captive audience.

Their bodies seem young and supple, and with her dress raised thigh-high, everyone can see Toot has great legs. I look over at Lady Sylvia. She's sitting on a folding chair cutting her food into bite-sized pieces, unaware of the smoldering pas de deux happening on the dance floor. Maybe this is what it takes to stay married to Lonnie Falcone—sit in a corner, cut up his meat, and wait for him to return without complaining.

A gasp goes up from the crowd when Lonnie slides his hands down my sister's back. When he gets to her waist, he pulls her closer still with a quick yank, then glides his hands south and squeezes the cushiony rounds of her derriere as though he's wringing out a sopping wet **moppeen**. Not since the Folies Bergère floor show at the Tropicana in Vegas on the UNICO bus tour have we seen such private acts gone public. And I thought they hated each other! Clearly Lonnie had a few sips of the Manhattans Capri's been swilling, because I've never seen him this passionate about anything that didn't have an automatic engine, leather seats, and fins.

A round of cheers and applause follows the Folies de Filth. Lonnie leans over and kisses Toot on the cheek, then she grabs his face and plants a kiss on his lips. The crowd goes wild as Toot takes her thumb and forefinger and cleans up the lipstick smear around her mouth. Lonnie takes out his hanky and tenderly wipes away Toot's streaks of Cherries in the Snow.

Toot climbs up on the band riser and takes the microphone. "Lonnie Falcone, now the world knows why I had three babies in thirty-eight months with you." The crowd cheers as Lonnie makes a slight bow from the waist.

"Ma, please. People are eatin' here." Anthony, a compact version of his mother, gets a rolling laugh from the crowd as he enters the garage.

"Anthony, wish your uncle a happy birthday, please."

Anthony worms through the crowd and gives me a big hug. "Sorry I'm late. I had to send out a shipment for the holidays. Stampato bracelets, eighteen karats."

"Please, everyone, pick up your drinks. It's time to toast my baby brother." Toot holds her Fuzzy Navel cocktail high. With her free hand, she adjusts her dress so the peekaboo lace inserts resume their proper places. "B, come down here."

I move to the band riser and look up at my sister.

"Oh, the things I remember about my brother," she declares. "Forty years ago this day, I prayed to Saint Gerard to send me a baby sister. I wanted a girl because I had just learned to sew and wanted to make the baby frilly dresses and bonnets."

"That hardly stopped you," I shout. "Remember the sailor pants with the Austrian crystal buttons?" The crowd laughs and applauds.

Toot waves me off. There's no stopping her now. "Any-hoo, my mother, may she rest in peace, had Bartolomeo late in life. There was never any shame about this, mind you, because my mother believed that if God sent you, he had a job for you to do down here. B's first task was completing our family and making our parents proud. His second was to keep me company. I remember taking Bartolomeo to the movies. He loved melodramas, anything with Kay Francis. He was six years old when I took him to see her in **The White Angel.** He leaned across after a big tearjerker scene in the hospital and said, 'Sis, that was so hammy-sammy.' Can you believe it? He was **six**! That's my brother. He can tell a real from a fake anytime. B is honest and straightforward and true . . . and talented. Talent is not given out liberally by God. In fact, it's such a rare thing that most people just pretend to have it. But not my brother. He's got it—in **here**." Toot raps on her chest.

"Tell 'em about **The Wizard of Oz,** Ma!" Two shouts from the crowd.

Toot smiles. "Well, we were at the Rialto in Spring Lake, two shows plus the newsreel for a nickel. There was supposed to be this great new movie for kids starring Judy Garland. It was called **The Wizard of Oz.** So I took him. When B laid eyes on Margaret Hamilton on that bicycle, he started screaming and I couldn't get him to stop. Then all the other kids started screaming, and B took off running up the aisle and it caused a stampede."

"I like my monkeys without wings, thank you!" I shout.

"Well, we never went back to the Rialto," Toot says. "Of course, it wasn't our choice. We were banned for life."

"And I've never seen the whole movie!" I take another swig of my cocktail.

"When the flying monkeys scared him, I knew that, while he was a tough little boy, he had his own movie playing inside his head. But the movie in his head was pretty. As a child, he was so easy, you could entertain him with just about anything. He would stare at a silk throw pillow for hours, studying it, taking it apart in his mind's eye thread by thread. Little did I know that in those moments he was becoming a decorator. He was paying attention. I'm so proud of you, B. And I'm sick that you got the slim hips in the family, but for that small thing, I can forgive you. You are the best brother any girl could ever hope to have, and every night when I say my prayers, I beg God to forgive me for wishing he had sent a little sister instead of you. No girl would have been better." Toot raises her glass. **"Cent'anni."**

Nellie Fanelli, in a black rayon chemise (she's been a widow for seventeen years and still wears black—clearly she takes her cues from Aunt Edith's Widow Etiquette book), motions to Toot from the dance floor. Toot leans down as Nellie whispers in her ear.

"Uh . . ." Toot looks puzzled. Nellie prompts her. After a couple of awkward moments, finally, Toot speaks into the microphone. "I now am going to turn the microphone over to Father Porporino, who I guess is gonna do the invocation—though I should say no one asked him—but here you are, Father, so come on up." Toot makes a face and clonks the microphone onto the piano like it's a rotten banana. Nicky helps her off the riser as Father Porp climbs onto the stage.

A low moan of disgust rumbles through the crowd like a waft of gasoline from the spare cans hidden behind the balloons. Father picks up the microphone and turns to face us. He is wearing his weekend priest ensemble: black trousers, a white shirt with a Roman collar, and a black V-neck sweater. "Happy birthday, Bartolomeo."

The crowd is so quiet, I can hear the squeaks of the plastic knife as Lady Sylvia saws away at her veal parm.

"I came tonight without invitation." Father shifts uneasily from one foot to the other. "The good people of Our Lady of Fatima have been a little upset with me over the past couple of weeks. I went outside our community to find a decorator to renovate the church. I had no idea the firestorm this decision would cause. The phone at the rectory has not stopped ringing since I made the announcement. There is a depth of feeling for the House of B in this town that I was not aware of."

"You got **that** right, Padre!" cousin Tiki Matera yells, holding up her bottle of beer like it's a sword.

"And so I came here tonight to make things right. If you'll consider it, Bartolomeo, I would like to appoint you to renovate our church. I informed the firm of Patton and Persky this morning that we were no longer in need of their services. What say you?" Father extends his hand toward me, awaiting my answer. I sip my cocktail, which has made me feel fuzzy enough to love the world, Father Porporino included.

When I feel like I've made him squirm long enough, I shout, "Are you just trying to get out of buying me a gift?" The crowd cheers.

"I did bring a Saint Bartholomew medal for you as well," he jokes.

Maybe it's because I told Father off in the confessional—or maybe because I've always felt sorry for priests who have to live in a rectory, cannot have bank accounts, and live loveless lives—or maybe it's the extra shot of sweet vermouth in my Manhattan—but, I feel a rush of pity for him. I want to put a smile on his face, replacing the glum set of his mouth that seems to show genuine remorse for the biggest miscalculation of his clerical career. On the other hand, I'll have few opportunities as perfect as this for making sure he never sandbags me again. So I say loudly, "I'll take the job, Father—on one condition."

"And what is that?"

"No interference from anyone. That includes you, the parish council, the diocese at large, Bishop Kilcullen, his staff of evil trolls, and the Pope himself."

There is a long silence. Perhaps "evil trolls" was extreme. Too late to worry about that now.

Cousin Christina slips up beside me and takes my hand in support. Father Porporino looks out into the eyes of the faithful (the di Crespi version, at least) and makes his decision. "There will be no interference. The Church of Our Lady of Fatima is yours to do with as you will."

Christina squeezes my hand, but before the crowd can erupt into another cheer, Father Porp drops the other shoe. "There's one thing you need to know. Cardinal Angelini of the Golfo de Genoa in Italy will be here on the feast day of our church, October 13, 1971. You must be finished by then."

"You have my word, Father."

The crowd applauds as Dom Ruggiero takes his cue and plays "When the Saints Go Marching In." Toot forms a conga line, and I fall behind her and grab the grommets of her black stretch belt to follow. Christina latches on to me, Amalia on to her, and so it goes until all the cousins in my bloodline are hooked together like one of Aunt Carmella's crocheted car blankets. As we cha-cha in celebration, Toot leads the way outside and under the stars as the band plays. There are worse ways to turn forty.

CHAPTER FOUR

Matelasse in Manhattan

I'm no fool. The first thing I do the Monday morning after my birthday party is call my cousin the lawyer Carmine Mastrangelo, in Avon-by-the-Sea. He flits around from firm to firm with such regularity, I have to call his mother for his latest work number. It's as if he's an office temp, Juris Doctor, of course.

Although Carmine is not the finest legal mind in New Jersey, he works for a flat fee if you're a blood relative. (Luckily he's a second cousin once removed, so I qualify.) For a hundred bucks he'll do a will or a divorce, or sue the pants off anyone who has crossed you. I put in a call to him at the new office, the firm of Peter, Paul & Mary (no kidding, it's Pietro,

Paulo & di Maria), and have him draw up an agreement with Father Porporino and the diocese for my services in the church renovation. Carmine promises to have it ready by the afternoon, which tells me I'm not the first client who has needed a binding contract with RC Incorporated.

Toot calls and chews me out about Two's temporary defection from Villanova. I calm her down, assuring her that he'll return to get his degree in due course, but that he needs time to recharge his creative battery.

That afternoon I sit in the front pew of the church and let my imagination run wild. What to do with this Gothic masterpiece? I feel like Bernini confronting the empty space under the dome at St. Peter's. I have so many ideas to sort through. It's not going to be easy. All the ideas I had for the church seem too simple now. The deadline, while it's a year and a half away, looms large. I have to come up with a design and find the artisans to execute it almost immediately.

"I'm thrilled that Father came to his senses and gave the right man the job!" Zetta Montagna, in a simple navy blue suit, slides into the pew next to me. Rail-thin and chic, she is truly the Jackie Kennedy Onassis of Fatima Church.

"Thank you for going to bat for me." I'm no

fool. As president of the sodality, she is Father Porp's pet.

"You deserve it. The entire sodality is in full support of you. Whatever we can do to help, just let us know." She pats my hand.

I almost welcome their help until I remember when I renovated the church basement and asked the sodality for suggestions. They got in an eight-month war over what color enamel the stove should be. "Maybe you could say a novena for me?"

"Are you nervous?"

"I'm in that funny place of having gotten what I wished for."

"Are you having designer's remorse?"

"I'm feeling the pressure. There's a lot of work to be done in a short amount of time. And then, of course, it has to be perfect. Churches are renovated every hundred years or so. Imagine that. It will be 2070 when my work gets an overhaul."

"I'm sure you'll do just fine." Zetta gets up and genuflects before the altar. "Who did the flowers?"

"Me. Oreste Castellucci asked me to do them in honor of his mother's special birthday Mass tomorrow. I hope they hold until Sunday."

"They're gorgeous."

She goes into the sacristy.

I get up and genuflect at the altar. Then, I get to work. As I lift the flower arrangements out of their boxes, I say a quick prayer of thanksgiving.

I missed my church life immensely during the past month, and while I did head over to St. Catharine's in the interim, Father Porp's slight certainly shook my belief in the clergy, representatives of Jesus himself here on earth. (This is what I was taught and I'm sticking to it!) Now I see Father Porp as just another human being running a business. He, too, is Italian and not all that different from many men in my family who feel entitled to do whatever they want just because they're **men.** But Vatican II was eight years ago, and it's time for a little democracy here in Our Lady of Fatima. The people have spoken.

The door in the back of the church creaks open. "Okay, I'm here. What do you want?" Christina folds her arms and stands near the back pew. She's back in black, in a pair of black chinos and matching windbreaker. Evidently her turquoise blue party dress was a blip in her mourning attire.

"The first thing you can do is help me with the flowers," I chirp.

"Is this a setup?" She walks down the aisle toward me.

"Whatever do you mean?" I give her a spray of blue asters with yellow dahlias scattered through the greens, and she follows me up to the altar.

"I haven't set foot in this joint since Charlie's funeral. Do you think asking me to meet you here is going to inspire me to come back to church?"

"It would be nice."

"Oh, B. You'll be waiting a long time for those clouds to part so you can hear God's big booming voice: 'Come back, Christina. Your black heart needs redemption, and by the way, we need you to help us raise money to reseed the football field at Our Lady of Fatima High School.' "

"Oh, ha ha. That's the first thing you fallen away Catholics throw at us diehards. The church only wants your money. Well, I assure you, we want more than your money. We also want your soul. Now"—I give Christina the garland woven with fresh greens and point her toward the altar—"careful, it's delicate."

"So, what are you going to do to this barn?" she asks, laying the garland down carefully.

"It won't be a barn when I'm done with it," I promise her. "But I can't do it alone. I need your help. In fact, I called you here on a mission not to save your soul but to save my"—I point to my rear end.

"I knew it! My mother sent me a Maryknoll newsletter inviting widows to upstate New York for a retreat. Unless they're putting a carton of cigarettes and a fifth of Scotch on our pillows, I'm not going."

"Do you think that's funny?" I try not to be put off by Christina's sarcasm. "You're young. You have a lot ahead of you."

"It doesn't feel that way."

"Not in this moment, no. But it will come back."

"What?"

"Hope."

"You're dreaming." Christina turns to the white marble altar where the priest used to say Mass in Latin with his back to us. She opens the small gold tabernacle door and peers in.

"Don't touch that!"

"I always wanted to see what was inside."

"Now you know." I push the door shut. "Behave yourself. Only the select few who went through the rigorous altar-boy instructions are allowed to touch the tabernacle."

"When I was little and read **Alice in Wonderland,** I wanted to find a magic potion that would shrink me enough that I could go inside that door."

"It's just a box." I pick up a dusting cloth and wipe away our fingerprints. "Nothing exciting.

There is only a supply of stale consecrated hosts in a small gold canister to administer to the sick and dying."

"And Father Defede's pack of cigarettes."

"Who told you that?"

"Richie Sammarco, my eighth-grade boy-friend. He was an altar boy too."

"I can't believe he gave away a trade secret." I pull the marble urns to the foot of the altar and fill them with fresh greens. "I really need you. I'd like you to come and work with me."

"Come on."

"I'm serious. You can't live on Charlie's life insurance forever."

"Honestly, B, you get right to it, don't you?" Christina lines up the crisp creases of the cloth with the edges of the altar underneath.

"I only speak from concern," I remind her gently.

"Charlie had that life insurance from the Knights of Columbus, and I didn't even know about it. When the check came, I almost tore it up, I was so angry. As if money could bring him back."

"What stopped you?"

"Amalia. She yanked it out of my hands and said, 'This is a gift from Daddy.' "

"Smart kid."

"You'll never know." Christina sits on the

step in front of the Communion railing. I sit down next to her, after a quick genuflection in front of the altar.

"So you're going to live your life in that gorgeous Tudor that I decorated and be miserable?"

"For now."

"If you came to work for me, it would help. I promise you."

"I don't know a thing about churches. Really, even through twelve years of Catholic school, I didn't pay much attention. I just followed instructions. I wouldn't know a cruet from a crucifix."

"Which is why you're perfect for the job. I need someone who will pull me back from the safe choices. I want people to walk into this church, whether they're Catholic or not, and fall to their knees at its grandeur, have a mystical experience because the place is so beautiful it makes their eyes sting."

"How are you gonna do that?" Christina gets up and extends her hand to pull me up. "It's a church. It's supposed to scare you into being good. How do you decorate that?" She looks around and I know what she's thinking. My beloved church is a disaster. The place even smells old. "It's not bad if you like gargoyles and stations of the cross that look like scenes from **The Birdman of Alcatraz.**"

"Oh, all that's going to go. I'm going to reinvent the House of God. And who better to help me than the one person in the world who needs Him the most at this moment?"

"You sound like a kook, B." She sighs. "Count me in. But only because you're more fun than my addiction to the **Edge of Night** every afternoon at four. Let's face it. I need a job."

I might have been the most sought-after decorator in New York City and been in all the magazines like that chintz nut Mario Buatta, but I would have had to give up OLOF, Toot, and the boys. Duty is more important than self-advancement for a di Crespi. With that in mind, hiring family is always a bad idea, especially if you're Italian. I believe the problem began with the mezzadri system in Italy, where a padrone ruled over workers who took care of his land and lived on his property. A resentment of authority runs deep in our veins. So what have I done? In short order, I've hired two family members: Christina, who will assist me with the church, and Two, who will function as a gofer so I can keep my private-client business on track while I do the church.

Christina's first task as design associate (her new title) of the House of B is research. I send her to the divinity library at Seton Hall to find out everything she can about the miracle at Fatima. I grew up with a pretty good knowledge of saints and miracles, but I never studied them in depth. My mother's martyrdom gave me enough firsthand experience with suffering, so I didn't see a need to conduct further research. I leave the hard-core analysis of mystical experiences to Vatican tribunals, novitiates, and seminarians.

Four times a year I attend workshops in Manhattan sponsored by ASID, in which Members meet for high tea in the Blue Room of the Plaza Hotel (don't get me started on how much I love this hotel, right down to the Eloise painting in the lobby) to listen to various guest speakers. Today I feel like a Vanderbilt sipping tea while overlooking the summer foliage of Central Park. It's an afternoon of socializing, education, and tasty gossip.

"Thank you for the flowers." Mary Kate Fitzsimmons leans over, her soft hair brushing my temple as she whispers in my ear. "Peonies are my favorite."

"You're welcome."

"I came with my colleagues, so I can't sit with you." She smiles apologetically. "But I wish I could."

I stand up and kiss her hand. "Next time."

"I'll see you . . . sometime?"

"Of course, darling."

Mary Kate weaves through the tables to get to her seat. She sits down next to leggy Gloria Zalaznick, an up-and-coming decorator from Great Neck, and Bunny Williams, the spunky assistant at Parrish-Hadley.

I chat with the folks at my table. I always love seeing Helen McNeill, who knows more about rugs than anyone in town, and Norbert Ratliff, who first recommended Helen to me. Eventually I turn my attention to the agenda for the high tea.

On each table there's a cup of sharpened golf pencils in a silver cup. I take one to jot down notes. There's also a folder filled with vendors' invitations to lunch or showroom cocktail parties where they pitch new products (cabinet-front refrigerators, nontoxic paints, Orlon wall-to-wall carpeting). I find these seminars incredibly interesting, but throw in fresh scones, clotted cream, and jam, and it's just so civilized!

"Ladies and gentlemen," Barbara D'Arcy of Bloomingdale's says as she takes the podium, smiling out over the crowd. Her eyes match her sapphire blue blouse perfectly. I wonder if she chose this room because she knew her coloring would look best here.

Everyone loves Barbara, and the first stop for

any good decorator is her jammed-to-the-ceiling Interiors Department on the fourth floor at Bloomie's. If you can't find what you're looking for there, she gets on the horn and connects you to a purveyor who can. She is a walking, talking textbook for the interior decorator. There's a rumor going around that she's writing a book. I can't wait to read it.

"Thank you for joining us this afternoon," Barbara continues. "I've been trying to get our guest speaker to come and talk to us for several years now, but she's hard to pin down. Last year she was studying mosaic wall treatments in Eastern Orthodox churches in Moscow. This spring she was in China learning how to double-back embroidered silk, and last past summer she was in London learning about medieval marble inlay in cathedral settings. There is nothing in our trade this gal doesn't know, hasn't seen or attempted to master. You never know what sort of room she'll create next. She did the foyer at the Frick Museum, and the English club room at the Carlyle Hotel—and, let me tell you, it is British down to the sugar cubes! Most recently, she designed the Fifth Avenue penthouse for the ambassador to Indonesia. She's the magician behind the exotic-bird room in the glass solarium on the roof of Number Ten Park Avenue. But of

course you all read about that in the **Times.**
When it comes to interior decoration, she has
no peer. Please join me in welcoming our own
ASID member Eydie Von Gunne of VG Designs of Park Avenue."

Eydie takes the stage to enthusiastic applause. She wears a Mary Quant pink tweed
miniskirt, a cream-colored blouse, and knee-
high boots in tan suede with pink grosgrain-
ribbon laces. Leaning into the microphone, she
says, "My only hope is that I don't bore you.
I'm much better at doing things than I am at
talking about them." She catches my eye and
throws me a wink. She remembers me!

"Do you know her?" Helen whispers.

"We met at Gino's," I whisper back.

I sit in awe as she speaks. Afterward, the decorators surround her like poppies around a
rose. Finally I squeeze my way through.

"Bartolomeo!"

"You remember?"

"You never called. Are there that many
Gothic church experts out there?"

"No, no, it's not that. I just don't know what I'm
going to do yet. I'm still thinking. Forgive me."

"You sound a little overwhelmed. If you need
a sounding board . . ."

"Now more than ever. When you were talking about tile restoration, I couldn't help but think about the sacristy. I'd like to preserve the original materials as much as possible."

Eydie surveys the long line behind me. "Are you staying in town?"

"No, I was going to stop at the D&D Building and then go home."

"Can you stay? I'm free for dinner."

"I'd love it."

"Top of the Sixes? Eight o'clock?"

"Sounds great."

"I'll see you there." She squeezes my hand and then turns to a couple of decorators with a list of questions.

I have a ball for the rest of the afternoon. It's one of those blustery spring days in New York when the sky is so blue the buildings turn to polished silver in the light. I savor a cup of coffee and an apple tart at Rumpelmayer's and read the ASID newsletter. Then I walk through Central Park to the boathouse. I head back toward the Plaza Hotel, cross the carriage stop, and walk down Fifth Avenue past Gene Moore's sparkling windows at Tiffany's.

At Pierre Frey on First Avenue, I pick up swatches for Aurelia's summer furniture, then stop at Stroheim & Roman to return samples I borrowed for the Baronagan job. I jump on a downtown bus and stop in at the little smoke shop on Bleecker that is the only place that sells black beeswax taper candles for my candelabra.

As I look around at the bell-bottoms and crocheted ponchos of Greenwich Village, I remember how much I loved living here as an art student. The city was my muse. Its fractured sunlight and hard angles inspired me to create metallic-and-burlap tapestries that won me the prestigious Parsons Award for originality. I have nothing but happy memories of that time. Sometimes I want to chuck everything and move back into the city. The idea of an apartment with a view, a terrace, and a doorman is at times almost irresistible. Then I think of my Villa di Crespi, and how much I love spacious rooms, my garden, my garage, and my ocean, and I realize that I have the best of both worlds—a great life in the suburbs and fabulous times in the city. **Glass half full, B,** I remind myself. **Glass half full!**

I take the bus back uptown and buy a bright red silk tie at Bergdorf's. My subdued navy tie will not do at the Top of the Sixes—I need some oomph. A red tie on a man is like red lipstick on a woman—it gives instant sex appeal.

The elevator to the Top of the Sixes, crowded with well-heeled New Yorkers, opens onto a dining room so beautiful it takes my breath away. The rich hues of cranberry red and midnight blue and the low, twinkling red votives on the tables are downright Russian, and the smell of leather and smoke mixes with the occasional whiff of freesia.

Eydie waves at me from a table at the far end of the room. I don't know what sparkles more, this lovely lady in blue chiffon enveloped in a tufted red leather chair, or the city that twinkles behind her like a private kingdom. She extends her hand and I kiss it. "I hope you don't mind. I started without you." She lifts her martini to toast me.

"For you." I give her a box of Godiva chocolates, tied with a gold mesh ribbon and a silk rose, and take my seat.

"I love you for this!" She smiles. "But you shouldn't have." She motions to the waiter, who takes my drink order. "Now, before I hear all about your church project, I need to know a little more about **you.** What made you become a decorator?"

"I don't like ugly. That, and I come from a family that believes it's criminal to remove the clear protective wrapping from a lamp shade."

She laughs. "So you became a decorator to save the world from protective wrapping?"

"Partly. My father thought my career choice was frivolous. But I've learned that people who don't use interior decorators are the same people who cut their own hair to save money. But you, young lady, you're a true expert. Your presentation this afternoon made me proud to be a decorator. Did you notice the hush that fell on the crowd as they drank you in? We're used to those prim blue-haired Sis Parrish types who come in and talk about welting on polished cotton as though it's erotic. We aren't used to being held captive by an expert who is also a great beauty."

"Thank you." Eydie squeezes my hand. "I just broke up with an international financier, and he had enough of my beauty and my brains, thank you very much."

"Mr. Dimple Chin?"

"Oh, that's right! You met him at Gino's!"

"Not officially. Where's he from? Idiot Town?"

"Connecticut. He went back to his wife."

"Oh, no."

"I didn't know he was married. You know, you hear about this sort of thing and you always think, 'How could she **not** know? Is she some sort of a dunce?' But I travel so much that I really didn't notice that we never went to his house. I live on Fifty-third Street, so why schlep out to the farm when we could have a bite, take a walk, and go to my apartment? I guess I wasn't picking up the clues. I'm not good at clues."

"Well, good-bye to him and all of that. You deserve a full-time man."

"Maybe someday. I like the unavailable, evidently. My first boyfriend, whom I adored, ended up with a man."

"Oh dear." I take a sip of my drink. "You see that a lot in our business."

Eydie eats the olive from her martini, just as the waiter brings her a second. From the sound of things, Eydie is about five years older than me, although she doesn't look it. I think about my sister's friends and how they are beginning to resemble Eleanor Roosevelt (the later years) no matter how pretty they were as girls. New York City women, however, manage to stay youthful. Maybe it's all the walking that keeps them young. Or living in a place where trends are set. How can you grow old in a place that is constantly changing?

"Now, let's talk about that church of yours," Eydie says after the waiter takes our order.

I fill her in. Eydie knows the business side of church renovation, so she isn't surprised that the job took time to secure. She wants to come and see the church, especially the Menecola fresco of the Blessed Mother, as she has a particular fondness for amateur artists.

"I have a whole file back at my apartment about the renovation of Gothic churches. After dinner we'll head over, and I'll be happy to give it to you."

The meal is delicious—a medium-rare steak so lean I don't need a knife, al dente asparagus, and a glass of red wine, followed by a compote of stewed strawberries and apricots on a sweet biscuit drenched in a rum sauce. Over coffee, Eydie and I find even more common ground, since it turns out she grew up Catholic, in Chicago.

We take a cab to her apartment, and in the lobby, she opens her arms wide to envelop the chic Deco space decorated in ebony and silver with etched floor-length mirrors on either side of the elevator. "Love these mirrors," she says. "This is how I know when my seamstress sews my hem unevenly. You can check an outfit from five angles."

She presses Penthouse. As we ride up in the elevator, I am full of anticipation. I can't wait to see what she did with her space. "Don't get too excited," she says. "It's small." She unlocks the door and hits the light switch, revealing a long, wide main room. The far wall is all windows. She hits another switch, which raises the automatic window shades to reveal the East River, a wide ribbon of black velvet surrounded by tiny white lights that look like seed pearls.

"It's like you live in a jewel box!" I go to the windows and look out.

"I had a garden apartment on Perry Street for years, and then one day I said, 'I want sky and light and views,' so I found this."

"I love it." Her color scheme is soft camel and white, which must look amazing in daylight. Her sectional sofa is arranged in a half-moon, covered in a soft moleskin fabric. No coffee table! Instead, a low English boot bench is placed about a foot from the couch. An antique rocker and a floor lamp are angled in the corner. A series of paintings—long, wide canvases of white with small green leaves floating across them—are staggered on the wall. Modern and abstract, they make a real statement. Her kitchen, with sleek cherrywood cabinetry and a beige tile floor, can be glimpsed from behind galley doors on the southernmost point of the room. Next to it is a powder room, the door marked LOO. I can see its gold-foil wallpaper and black enamel fixtures.

"Come and see the bedroom," Eydie says casually.

I begin to sweat and decide to maintain my professionalism. I follow her into her bedroom. The east wall has sliding glass doors that lead to a charming terrace, which she has filled with wild plants. I follow her out the sliding doors to where two French café chairs and a small table are arranged. Thankfully, a cool breeze lowers my body temperature instantly. I take a deep breath as Eydie points out the bridges and Roosevelt Island. After the aerial tour, I follow Eydie back inside.

She has a king-sized platform bed with a thin velvet duvet in a leopard print (the perfect Diana Vreeland touch), a chaise longue covered in white damask, and in the corner, a small Shaker writing desk lacquered in white with a straight-backed chair. The opposite wall is a floor-to-ceiling closet with mirrored doors. "Very simple," she says.

I nod. "Very Elsie de Wolfe."

Eydie agrees. "You can never go wrong if you follow **The House in Good Taste**. It's my bible. Now I'll show you the best room in the apartment. Are you ready?"

I follow her through a dressing area with an inlay of terra-cotta tile on the floor, a vanity and covered tuffet (in sturdy beige corduroy) in front of a large mirror with full theatrical lights. "This is where I apply my war paint," she jokes, and continues through to another room. She flips on the lights. "My bathroom."

"Dear God," I say aloud. I don't think I've ever seen anything like it. It's a Cathedral of the Soak. White ceramic tiles cover the floor and walls. From the center of the vaulted-glass ceiling, a multicolored Venetian chandelier dangles like a pendant. At the far end of the large room is a white claw-foot antique tub with all the original fixtures in gold plate. There is a sofa covered in white terry cloth (sewn patchwork-style from lush Egyptian pima-cotton towels—genius move!) along the wall opposite the double sink and cabinetry. The toilet is behind a door a few feet from the tub. "Most women want closets. But I like a large bathroom, so I took the original bathroom, part of the terrace, and the second bedroom and turned it into this. I had friends who thought I was nuts. I still have outdoor space, just not as much as before."

"It's gorgeous."

"Well, it's me. I know what I need and I know what I like."

I follow Eydie back into the living room. She offers me a seat as she goes into the kitchen. Moments later she comes out, pushing an adorable bar cart. "Would you please fix me a drink?"

"Of course." I get up and lift the lid on the top compartment. Every liquor in captivity is in this cabinet. "How about Amaretto?"

"On the rocks, please." Eydie goes to a book-case near the kitchen entrance and takes a leather file box from the top shelf. She opens it and shuffles through, pulling out a file on the

San Siro Cathedral in San Remo, Italy. Eydie
tells me San Siro is situated on the Mediterranean, not far from where my people lived.
She explains how the twelfth-century Roman
Gothic cathedral went to ruin and was altered in
a baroque style. Then the town came to its senses
and restored it back to the original Gothic.

"You must see the statue of the Virgin Mary
there."

"Who's the artist?"

"My favorite." She pauses. "Unknown." Eydie sits cross-legged on the couch. "There is
something so pure about an artist creating
something for the sheer joy of it, then sharing
it with people and claiming no credit. To me
that's the height of romance."

All my life I've searched for someone with
the same level of passion that I have for things.
I have found it in Eydie. I could talk to her all
night. Maybe I will!

"You said an amateur did the fresco at your
church," she says.

"Yes, it was painted by a man who made the
signs for the roadside vegetable stands. Our
Virgin looks like she's hawking Jersey corn. The
stained glass needs restoration too."

"You need a team, then. I'll make you a list."
Eydie pulls a pad out of her purse. "I wrote an
article for **Life** magazine about frescoes a cou-

ple of years ago." Eydie chews on the tip of her pencil for a while, then says, "There are three people who I would meet with if this were my project."

"Three? In the whole world?"

"In my opinion. There's Gian Angelo Ruttolo of San Remo, Asher Anderson of London, and Rufus McSherry of Brooklyn." Eydie hands me the list. "I'll send you their particulars from my office on Monday."

"Rufus McSherry. Irish Catholic?" I ask her.

"We've never talked about it. Rufus is a brilliant painter of frescoes; he also restores them. He works with a guy from Mexico who does stained-glass windows."

"He sounds perfect!"

"Oh, he's perfect, all right. A perfect pain in the ass." Eydie smiles. "But he's worth it."

"Sounds like you know him well." I feel a pang of jealousy. Clearly this Rufus character has a history with Eydie. Romantic or professional—I can't tell.

"Oh, he's something." Eydie looks away. The lights are low, but I'm certain she's blushing. "Gian Angelo is in New York a lot, so you can probably see him here. He's an architect, mainly, so he can tell you if your building is structurally sound and what to do if it isn't. Asher rarely travels anymore, but he keeps up with correspondence, and he can be very helpful. He's the master of the treasure hunt. He can find anything anywhere—the right fixture, the perfect door, vintage molding no one else can get their hands on—that sort of thing."

"I figure if I design it this summer, and we get it under way in October, we should be ready a year later for the rededication. I like the sound of this Rufus."

"We'll see if he's available. I know he was offered the cathedral in Providence to restore but he wouldn't take the job. He doesn't want a bunch of clerics with Ph.D.'s in art history telling him where to put his paintbrush." Eydie stands and stretches. "Now, I hate to do this, but I have to throw you out. I have a big day tomorrow, and I'm starting early."

I don't want to leave, but I spring to my feet. "And so do I. Thank you for a wonderful evening. I had a lot of fun."

Eydie walks me to the door, giving me the file of research on Gothic churches. "Thank you for that lovely dinner."

We smile at each other and say nothing. It's that strange moment between two people that feels as delicate as a silvery spiderweb. It's a little presumptuous of me to expect a kiss, so I pull away just enough to break the spell. After all, she is getting over a bad breakup, and I still haven't cut Capri Mandelbaum loose. Eydie Von Gunne doesn't need another unavailable man in her life; not yet, anyway.

"Good night, Bartolomeo." She gives me a little wave before closing the door behind me.

"Good night, Eydie," I say softly as I go.

"Okay, B. What do you remember about the miracle at Fatima?" Christina opens her notebook in a bright red vinyl booth at the Tic Tock Diner as I lower the shade to block the bright morning sun. Route 35 buzzes with rush hour traffic outside as Christina and I have our first official staff meeting of the House of B.

"Three kids saw the Virgin Mary up in the sky in a farm field in Portugal," I tell her. "Pass the syrup."

"Right. In the spring of 1917, Lucia dos Santos, Francisco Marcos, and Jacinta Maro saw the Blessed Lady while they were tending sheep. She appeared to them several more times. The kids told their families and the local priest what they had seen. Soon, the story spread throughout Portugal. The Blessed Lady promised Lucia that she would return on May 13. Seventy thousand people showed up that day to see her."

"And then what happened?" I douse my French toast in enough syrup to float a tennis ball.

"It was wild. The Blessed Mother promised them a miracle, so she spun the sun out of the sky and sent a storm."

"Okay, that sounds like a bout of bad weather rather than a miracle."

"Well, that's sort of what it was. The Blessed Lady stopped the storm, though, and everyone who was soaking wet and everything that was flooded was dry in an instant."

As miracles go, Fatima has none of the glamour of Lourdes, where there was a mystical spring and saintly Jennifer Jones as Bernadette. But first things first. I need to begin with a clean slate. Everything in Fatima Church must go. "How are you with a camera?"

"Pretty good."

"I want you to go to the church and take pictures of everything inside. I don't need wide shots or anything general. I want an accounting of what's there; every chair, every table, every offering basket. Then I want you to type up a full inventory. Come fall, everything will be put in storage so we'll have nothing but a blank canvas to work on."

"I'll take care of it." Christina snaps her notebook shut. "Is that all?"

"For now."

"B?" Christina stuffs the notebook into her purse.

"Yes?"

She looks down at the table. "Thanks for the job."

"You're a smart girl with a marginal personality; why shouldn't you have a great career?" We laugh.

"You know"—tears fill Christina's eyes as she looks at me—"I think I had almost given up."

"No, you didn't. You're still in the middle of it. Grief doesn't hit and run; it stays. And sometimes for a very long time. Anyone with a heart knows that. I just want to help. I don't expect you to be the Christina you were before Charlie died, I just want to see you smile again. That's all. And if it's a few years away, that's fine too."

Christina takes her purse and goes. I watch her walk to her car as I wait for the bill. **Why her?** I wonder. It doesn't make any sense, but I guess nothing does. Why those three little sheepherders in Fatima? They were probably playing stickball when a divine revelation knocked them on their tushies and changed the course of their lives forever. Who knows what's in store for any of us?

Route 3 is jammed, so I take the service road to Toot's house. I have a slab of Reggiano Parmesan cheese from Little Italy to drop off. As I come around the corner of Corinne Way, I catch a rear glimpse of a woman wearing hot pink track pants and a matching sweatshirt chuffing up the hill. Poor dear. How are her bones taking that incessant pounding? I carefully navigate around her, then glance in my rearview mirror. It's Toot! I stop the car and she jogs slowly up to my window.

"What in God's name are you doing out here?"

"I have a date!" she says, panting.

"Where is he?"

"Not here. Not this minute. On Saturday night."

"With who?"

"Aren't you going to congratulate me? I haven't had sex in thirteen years. Eleven since the divorce, and the two before that Lonnie complained of sciatica, so it's a total of thirteen I've been living like a nun. Toward the end of my marriage, I had to beg for any slight remembrance of human companionship, believe me."

"Resemblance, Toot. Resemblance of human . . ." I give up. "Please, this is none of my business."

"I know. It's gotta be tough to hear that your only sister was chaste even while in the married state. But it's true." Toot pulls a handkerchief from under her bra strap and wipes her face. "Do you know Sal Concarni?" She stuffs the handkerchief back where she got it.

"From Belmar?"

"Yeah. The plumber. He's divorced too. Sixty-one years old. Is that too old for me?"

"I don't think so."

"It sounds old. I mean, I don't want to date a guy and then end up having to crush his pills, give him baths, and help put him back in his chair."

"Sixty-one isn't what it used to be."

"That's what I'm thinking. Women age so much better than men, though. I mean, I'm dyeing my hair, but at least I **have** hair. You know what I'm saying?"

"Sis, get in the car."

"Oh, I'll jog it. Meet you at the house."

I drive ahead and watch my sister put one foot in front of the other as though her sneakers are made of cast iron. I don't know if jogging is the right sport for her; something involving flotation might be a wiser choice. I pull into her driveway and grab the sack of cheese. As she jogs into the driveway, Toot raises her arms in victory as if she's just won an Olympic gold medal for track and field. "One mile!" she shouts. "Whoo-hoo!"

"Wonderful." I follow her into the house.

"I don't know what I'm gonna wear. The last time I was on a date was with Lonnie, and when was that? Truman was president. Sweet

God. I can't eat a thing tomorrow. If I lose another couple of pounds, I can fit into a lightweight Pendleton wool chemise I got for Lucy Caruso's wedding. It's pink plaid. Is plaid all right on a date?"

"Is he taking you clog dancing in the Scottish Highlands?"

Toot rolls her eyes.

"Skip the wool. You need something soft and touchable. Like Qiana. Have you got anything made with Qiana?"

"Some panties." Toot cackles and pours herself a glass of water.

"If you're not going to take this seriously—"

"Oh, B. Come on. All I've done is take things seriously for the past thirteen years. Thirteen? What the hell, **all** my life. I want to laugh again. I want to giggle like those girls in braces on the boardwalk who travel in packs and think everything is funny. I want to be silly. Romantic. I want to hold hands in the park and kiss under the moon. I need some . . . touch."

"Okay. I get it. Here's what you need to do. Go to Bamberger's and get yourself some new lingerie. And then—don't laugh—go to the men's department and buy a pair of black satin pajamas."

"I don't know Sal that well yet."

"They're not for him. They're for you. You're

going to wear a pair of simple black slacks with a satin pajama top."

"Out in public?"

"No one will know it's pajamas but you. It will fit with a little blousing, which you need. It will be very alluring."

"Wow, I never thought of that." Toot looks off in the distance, imagining herself in a sexy pajama top.

"And throw on some pearls and your diamond earrings. Black with cool white accents. You'll look like a Thin Mint. One of those Girl Scout cookies."

Toot's eyes fill with tears. "It's almost as if you want this for me more than I want it for myself."

"Your happiness means the world to me, sis. It's time for you to be a girl again."

CHAPTER FIVE

Monica Vitti's Chandelier

Sunday dinner at Toot's with the boys has been a continuation of a family tradition since our parents were alive. Occasionally one or two of us is missing, but the open seat is quickly taken by a cousin or some great-aunt who's visiting from out of town. Stragglers are welcome, and Toot makes enough stuffed artichokes, manicotti, bracciole, and tiramisu for the College of Cardinals and their secretaries. Even Two would make the drive from Villanova to join us. Everyone leaves with enough food for lunches the following week.

Toot has yet to invite Ondine to our family dinner, and for the past several weeks Nicky has made an excuse and stayed away. So, after much negotiation and many phone calls back and forth, Ondine has been included at last. While Toot and I arrange the food in the kitchen, Ondine is serving cocktails to the boys in the living room, which harkens back to her boffo career in Atlantic City waiting on the craps tables in hot pants.

"I almost invited Sal to dinner," Toot says as she moves a Corningware dish of Clams Casino from the oven to the table. "It's our seven-week anniversary this Saturday. But I thought it was too much, too soon."

"You shouldn't hide Sal from the boys. You're dating, and you should sit them down and be a grown-up and tell them that this is what adults do. They date and they have friends. I wouldn't worry. They'll be happy for you." I follow Toot into the dining room with a basket of hot garlic bread. She places the clams on the buffet.

"You think?" Toot knits her brow into a small checkerboard. "I don't know. When Natalie Covella started dating after her divorce, her sons almost killed the guy."

"That's because she'd been seeing him for the last ten years of her marriage. Yours is a completely different situation."

"What situation?" Two comes into the dining room carrying the crystal side dishes of celery hearts, black olives, and carrot curls artfully arranged.

"Oh, Two, I don't want to hurt you," Toot wails, beginning to cry.

"Oh, for godsakes." I hand my sister a clean **moppeen.**

"What is it, Ma? Are you sick?"

She shakes her head. "I don't want you to think I'm a **puttana.**"

"**What?**" Two is aghast.

"I'm seeing Sal Concarni. You know, the plumber from Belmar. There's nothing wrong with my pipes, it's strictly social. Anyhow, I'm so lonely, Two, and he's a nice companion." Toot is sobbing uncontrollably now.

Two takes her by the shoulders. "Ma, that's fantastic."

"It is?" Toot dries up.

"Yeah. I mean, you should be with someone. You're a beautiful woman with a lot to offer. Any guy would be lucky to have you."

"I've lived like Bernadette of Lourdes for thirteen years. I've sacrificed in order to enjoy whatever small morsel of happiness is in store for me. Whatever God has in mind—"

"Toot," I say, warning in my voice. "He's on your side. Don't pile it on."

"Sorry. But it's true." Toot wipes away her tears by giving a quick swipe under each eye with a clean **moppeen,** careful not to smudge her mascara.

"Two, please call the boys and Ondine to dinner."

Two goes into the living room. "How did I do?" She checks her lipstick in the butter knife.

"Sensational!" I say. "I don't know what I liked better, the wailing or the gnashing of the teeth."

"Hey, Unc." Anthony ambles into the dining room and gives me a hug.

"Hello, Anthony." My nephew slides into his chair and slumps low. Maybe his posture is so poor because he's hunched over working on tiny gold chain links all day, but I wish he had some manners.

"Where do you want us, Ma?"

"Nicky, you go there." She points. "And Ondine, you go there." Toot points to the seat farthest from Nicky.

"Can't I sit next to Nicky?" Ondine says softly.

"Oh, I guess so. B, you sit there instead." Toot switches my place card (from Lillian Vernon, small china flower baskets that you write on with a washable marker) with Ondine's. "You know, Ondine"—from my sister's tone I can tell an insult is coming; it's like the gurgle before the pipe bursts—"many hostesses—the Duchess of Windsor comes to mind—split up the couples at their dinner parties so the individuals can talk to people they don't see on a daily basis, thus giving the party some pizzazz and fresh conversation."

"But"—Ondine looks around—"there's only the six of us here."

"Right, but you do get my point, don't you?"

Ondine nods, but I'm certain she doesn't. Neither do I or any of my nephews who've never heard their mother invoke the Duchess of Windsor before.

"Okay, sis, shall we eat?"

We form a line at the buffet; the serving dishes cover the table like a completed puzzle. We load up our plates. When we've taken our seats, Toot says, "B, will you say grace?"

"In the name of the Father and of the Son and of the Holy Spirit . . ." I look at Ondine, who is not Catholic, and drop the traditional "Bless Us Oh Lord" in favor of a more ecumenical choice. "Thank you, God, for this beautiful meal made with loving hands by my sister. Amen."

"Everything's gone to hell since Vatican II," Toot says.

"Ma?"

"Yes, Nicky?"

"I hope you don't mind. I invited Pop over for dessert."

Toot puts down the Parmesan. "Is he bringing Doris?"

"She's his wife."

"That wasn't the question. I asked if he was bringing her."

"They go everywhere together."

"Well, there's nothing we can do about it now, is there?" Toot leans over and whispers into my ear. "Thank God I didn't invite Sal."

"You were nice to Doris at Unc's birthday party," Nicky says meekly.

"For the record, I can't be **nice** this close together. It's a strain for me to be friendly this close together, okay? When it comes to ex-husbands and their current wives I'm, at the **most,** a once-a-year girl."

"Two, tell us about your work at the studio." I change the subject swiftly, like Mario Andretti changes lanes at the NASCAR finals.

"I'm learning a lot from Hattie, the upholsterer. She showed me how to pipe a slipcover in grosgrain trim this week."

"Are you going back to college?" Nicky asks.

Toot interrupts. "He is taking off a while. That's all. Then he's going back to get his degree. Three sons, I want one with a diploma that's not from driving school."

"I plan to go back eventually."

"I'm sure the theater department misses you terribly," I tell Two as I pass him the hot bread.

"You're not going to end up like one of those theater fairies, are you?" Anthony grumbles.

"What's a theater fairy?" Two asks evenly.

"You know."

"I don't know." Two puts down his fork.

"Well, it's your basic she-male. Ballerinas, dancers, actors—you know—any guy that would wear tights." Anthony and Nicky laugh.

"So you're including professional wrestlers?" Two asks.

"They're different," Anthony counters. "They're all-male. If a guy does sports, he's automatically a man."

"What is a man to you, Anthony?" I interrupt. Everyone looks at me except Anthony, who looks down at his stuffed mushrooms.

"A guy who does guy stuff," he offers finally.

"What a relief." I throw my hands in the air.

"What?" Anthony looks confused.

"There are lots of people who think men who sit around on stools with tweezers and make ankle bracelets and toe rings are light in the loafers," I say. "You know, jewelry fairies." I saw my ravioli in half with my fork so hard I almost chip the plate. Two laughs, then Nicky and Anthony join in. Ondine looks relieved that an argument has not occured.

"I've been seeing Sal Concarni," Toot blurts.

"What?" Nicky says. "The plumber?"

"From Belmar," Two clarifies, as if there's more than one Sal Concarni.

"**Seeing** him?" Anthony is confused.

"I think Ma is dating," Nicky explains to Anthony.

"Yes, boys, it's true. I'm seeing Sal socially. There, I've said it. I've had romantic evenings out with a man who thinks your mother is cute. I'm sorry. I know this is an adjustment for you boys, but I'm not giving him up because I'm having a wonderful time."

"Good for you, Ma," Nicky says quietly.

"Maybe we'll get some free work on the boiler," Two offers.

"I will not accept this!" Anthony thunders.

"And why not?" Toot throws down her napkin.

"Because you're my mother and you're not supposed to go around town with a man."

"Well, get used to it, because I'm going. I've waited on men my entire life, starting with my father, then my husband, and ending with my sons. It's time for a man to take care of me." Toot looks around the table. I don't believe I've ever heard her so vehement on any subject. A few moments pass in utter silence.

"I think it's nice," Ondine peeps.

"I have a carbuncle on the left cheek of my posterior," I announce. Everyone stares at me. "Well, it just seems like everybody is digging deep into their bag of unmentionables, so let me drag mine out too."

"We're married," Ondine blurts.

"**What?**" Toot raises her hips up off of her chair. "You're **what?**"

"Married."

"Nicky?" Toot looks as though she might toss a serving spoon at him.

"We got married in Atlantic City yesterday." Nicky takes Ondine's hand in a sign of solidarity.

"**Atlantic City?** The spiritual capital of the world. The site of many an official sacrament. I like my weddings in a church, not in a seaside hotel where money is laundered more often than the sheets. What would the Holy Father say? What will **your** father say?"

"Look, Ma. I don't go in for all that jazz, I never have, and you know it. So don't start. I love Ondine and she loves me and that's the end of it. We're happy." Nicky doesn't look happy.

"Congratulations," Toot says softly, tears welling in her eyes. "May God bless you, Nicky, and you, Ondine."

"And the baby." Ondine squeezes Nicky's hand.

"Jesus, Mary, and Joseph." Anthony shakes his head in disbelief.

"You have a child?" Toot shouts.

"No, no child. Just the bun in the oven." Ondine pats her stomach.

Toot looks at me.

"You're having a baby?" Anthony asks. I'm beginning to believe that Anthony has a lobe of his brain missing.

"Uh-huh." Ondine smiles.

"Excuse me." Toot tries to get up but her legs fail her. "I need some air. Pardon me." She pushes herself out of her chair and goes to the kitchen. I make an excuse and follow her.

Toot paces in front of the window seat like a trapped rat. "I'm fifty-one years old, and I'm going to be a grandmother. I can't believe it! This doesn't happen in places where there are telephones! I'm a granny! And no church wedding! They probably won't baptize the baby, they'll throw some seeds on him and make a hippie ceremony while they smoke grass! What have I raised here?"

"Listen to me." I take Toot by the shoulders. "Stop this now. It's done. There is no changing it. There is a baby on the way with the di Crespi label on it. Your grandchild. Besides, you are hardly a card-carrying Catholic—you won't even spring for an annulment—so don't beat up on them. You have to march back in there, give Ondine a warm hug, and tell them that you are here for them no matter what. You are very happy for them. Got it?"

"I'm not. I can't. I'm dizzy. I'm gonna faint. I'm seeing stars." Toot holds her head.

"Toot. Remember when Pop died and none of his brothers came to the funeral? We were devastated. And then we found out that Pop's mother left our mother a cocktail ring, and Uncle Bones took it for his wife instead of giving it to Pop to give to Mom? Do you remember this?"

"I may throw up." Toot grabs her gut.

"You cannot, you must not, destroy your family over Nicky's situation. Nothing is as important as family. Nothing. No country, no church, no cocktail ring. You have to accept this marriage and baby and embrace them. All of them."

"It was a gorgeous whiskey diamond with sapphire baguettes." Toot pushes me away. I give her a look. "All right, all right, back off."

The doorbell rings in three gongs that sound like the opening bars of "Panis Angelicus."

"That's Lonnie and Lady Sylvia." Toot throws her hands in the air. "Now what do we do?"

"Invite them in."

"Oy oy oy." Shaking her hands around her head like she's thrashing at a mob of bees, Toot trundles down the hall to the front door and opens it. I hear her warmly welcome Lonnie and his wife and watch them go into the dining room together. I enter the dining room through the kitchen.

"Sy . . . I mean Doris, darling, may I see you in the kitchen, please?"

"Of course."

I open the galley doors and invite Doris through, shooting Toot a look. As I chat with Doris in the kitchen (she admires the wallpaper), I hear the low tones of the news being delivered to Lonnie. "Are you all right?" Doris asks me. "You look a little pale. Let me get you some water. Here. Sit down."

I sit as Doris goes through every cupboard looking for a glass. Finally she finds one.

"I asked Lonnie if he called Nicolina before dropping by, and he said everything was fine."

"You know how men are—they never call."

"When I get on better terms with Nicolina, I will call in advance. It's not nice to drop in unannounced."

"Doris, can you come in here, please?" Lonnie says from the doorway. Doris follows him out after placing a gentle hand on my shoulder.

Through the top half of the galley door, I see Toot sitting next to Ondine and holding her hand as Nicky stands behind her talking to Lonnie. Lonnie tells Doris that Nicky and Ondine have married and are having a baby. Doris embraces the young couple warmly. Then the strangest thing happens. Lonnie kisses Toot on one cheek and then the other. He smiles at her and takes her chin in his hands, giving her a look of reassurance. Then he takes his fist and gives her a sweet punch on the chin like he used to do when they were young.

"What do you think?" Capri cleans her glasses as I walk around the empty two-bedroom apartment in the nice section of West Long Branch. It's on the third floor of a modern ten-floor building, with a parking garage underneath.

"I think it's terrific."

"I'm going to sign the lease."

"Good girl."

"I'm so scared."

"Your mother will be fine."

"How do you know?"

"She's not an idiot. You need your own life."

"She said I could only ever move out if I got married."

"Capri."

"I'm not saying it so **you'll** marry me. Although we could get married, you could pretend to move in here, and then we divorce really fast."

"No thank you," I say firmly. "The last thing I need on my docket is a quickie marriage and instant divorce. My heart is not a glass of Tang."

"You're right. I sound desperate and silly."

"Capri, it's not wrong to want your own life. It's natural."

"I know! I want to work and come home to a cat. I want boyfriends. I want to travel with them, cook for them, exchange ideas in the forms of books and literature, and make love to them."

"Oh dear."

"Well, it's all I think about. I'm this . . . this . . . ripe plum. Everything inside me is aching to be loved. Suddenly I can really see myself."

Coming from a woman with 20/200 vision in both eyes, this is truly a revelation. "Go on," I say.

"Turning forty is freeing me. If I'm not going to change now, I never will. And it doesn't matter if it hurts my mother, because she's lived her life. She's had her true love, and now it's my turn. I'm a lover who has not yet found my thing to love! Who said that?"

"Bob Dylan?"

"I don't know," Capri moans. "I think about sex in church. I sit up there in the choir loft and watch the men as they go up to Communion and imagine being in warm places like Hawaii with them. I do! In church! Can you imagine? If I ever went to confession, I'd be excommunicated."

"Capri," I say in a tone I hope will shut off this valve of soul baring. "It's not all it's cracked up to be."

"Maybe not. But I'd like to find out for myself."

"You're saying what, exactly?"

"It would have been nice to be a couple. But the only two people in this world who knew we were wrong for each other were you and me. I only played along because I didn't have anyone else in mind. Now I know a girl has to look for it. We never had that spark." She shrugs.

"Not even the time your breast brushed my thigh in the den when I was hanging the valance?"

"That was an accident. I tripped on the rug."

"Oh." I don't know why, but I'm a little hurt. I wanted to be rejected all these years, and now that I am, my ego is bruised.

Capri continues, "I've been using you all these years, and I feel terrible about it. You've schlepped me all over the Eastern Seaboard on sightseeing tours, and then there was that trip to Florida where I got stung by a bee and had to be hospitalized and you sat in the waiting room for six days until the swelling went down. What I've put you through!"

"It's all forgiven and forgotten," I promise her.

"It's Mom who won't accept our true feelings. She thinks we have bad timing."

"We've known each other since kindergarten. How much time do you give something unless it's a slab of carbon that you're praying will become a diamond?"

"She thinks forever. You're like a son to her."

"I'm sure she'll like all your . . . boyfriends."

"I'm not Jezebel, for godsakes. I want to see lots of men at first, but then eventually whittle it down to one."

Capri walks into the empty bedroom to inspect it. I watch her go. My goodness, what a difference a potential pied-à-terre can make for a girl's self-confidence. The green banana has turned into a golden apple.

"Over here, Bartolomeo!" Eydie waves to me from the Pan Am ticket desk at John F. Kennedy Airport. I wave back.

"So glad you could make it on such short notice." She kisses me on the cheek. "Thank you for doing this."

"Are you crazy? Thank **you**. I like nothing better than getting a phone call from a beautiful woman begging me to run off to Europe with her."

"I need your passport, sir," the wizened lady behind the counter says, extending her hand. I pull it out of my sport coat pocket. "Destination Heathrow. Correct?"

"Correct."

"We're sitting together, right?" Eydie asks.

"Yes, ma'am." The attendant hands us our tickets as a gentleman takes our bags and snaps tags on them before placing them on the conveyor belt. "Have a wonderful trip," she says politely.

"It's going to be short and sweet." Eydie threads her arm through mine as we walk to the gate. "I called Asher Anderson and he's expecting you."

"Fantastic. What would have happened to me had I never met you?"

"Oh, please. When ASID said I could bring a guest on this trip, you were the only possible choice. I need London to revive, and you need it to get your church plans off the ground."

"What's this King's College speech you're giving?"

"Mica Ertegun of the MAC II firm dropped out at the last minute, so I got a call. I never mind being sloppy seconds, not when it's free tickets to my second-favorite city in the world."

We pass a concession stand. I grab a carton of Lucky Strikes and put them on the cashier's checkout. "It's a long jump across the pond."

After a smooth flight with seventeen meals, a pack of delicious cigarettes, and more laughs than I've had in a long time, a representative from King's College meets us at the airport, takes our bags, and directs us into a lovely Citroën with so much leg room we could stretch out and nap if we wanted.

Though this is my first trip to the United Kingdom, I am a proud Anglophile. I admire the practical temperament of the people. I love the artful details of daily life: a hand-stitched tea cozy in the shape of a Victorian mansion, the Wellie boots, the sheep's wool stockings, and the best tailors in the world. Thankfully, the Brits have a love affair with Italians, and if anyone asks me, the feeling is entirely mutual.

We are dropped at Claridge's in the heart of the city. The architecture is suavely Art Deco, with polished marble columns (Corinthian) and small square gardens spilling over with orange marigolds, neat sidewalks, and Palladian windows so sparkling they look like mirrors.

"Maintenance," Eydie says approvingly, pointing to the bright brass railing outside the hotel that leads to the revolving entrance door (not a single fingerprint on the glass!). "They know what they're doing."

My room is small and toasty. The queen-sized canopy bed is made up with a polished chintz coverlet in shades of peach and dark purple. A cherrywood highboy is buffed to a sheen. There's a rolltop desk with a small brass lamp and a fauteuil chair covered in a lavender velvet. I wouldn't choose it for my own home, yet it's exactly right. Even the pencil sketches of eighteenth-century Carnaby Street are the perfect accent to this traditional setting. It's probably noisy in this part of London, but I don't hear a thing. I sleep solidly for ten hours and wake up to the sound of the phone ringing.

"Meet me for breakfast in the Surrey Room!" Eydie commands. After a quick shower and shave, I throw on my sport coat and meet her downstairs, where we find a table and order coffee.

Eydie opens a file folder and hands me what looks like a report. "This is a little background information on my friend Asher. He's expecting you around eleven, but he's never been prompt, so don't worry if you're late. He can be a little prickly, but he's truly one of the smartest people I know, and he can definitely give you some ideas for the church."

Eydie gives me a quick kiss on the cheek and heads off to King's College for the day. I watch her disappear into the lobby, and for a moment it seems like she's not of this world, rather like an angel who appears when needed and then—**poof!**—is gone when she's made her point. I can't imagine why a hundred men aren't in love with her.

I pull her chair over with my feet, prop them on the seat, and I begin reading about Asher Anderson. He began his career as an artist forty years ago, which makes him roughly of my parents' generation. He studied art in Milan, apprenticed at the Palazzo Gregorio in Venice under Gian Angelo Rutolo (a name I remember from Eydie's list), then returned to London to run the Geffrye Museum. Now he's the manager of Antiquarius, London's esteemed antiques center on Kings Road.

I help myself to the breakfast buffet, with cut-glass bowls of stewed berries, hot toast lined up in triangle wedges on a ceramic bread server, and silver Victorian coffee and tea urns with brass hardware and carved ivory handles. Butter and jam are displayed in small white pots on a polished cherrywood lazy Susan. I wish Toot were here to see all the serving pieces. There are things on this buffet she has only dreamed of.

___

The cab lets me off in front of Antiquarius on Kings Road, a street so crowded with pedestrians that the cars can hardly get through. I make my way to the maroon-and-white awning and into the shop, which is more like a barn, with many vendors. Strolling through the first floor, I become depressed about having only three days in London—I could take a week on this floor alone. The vendors have decorated their booths like rooms to showcase their wares, featuring lighting, wallpaper, rugs. In one booth an antique dish offers jellies to shoppers in need of a sugar boost. Like an attic full of treasures, the place smells of wood polish, starch, cedar, and lavender.

I notice a booth done completely in white—white walls, a white vinyl floor, and an enormous chandelier hanging from the ceiling. Its center post is faceted crystal, surrounded by a circular tube of sparkling glass. Dangling from the tube are layers of glittering crystal daggers on half-moon hoops. From the interior bobeches hang a series of small blown-glass angels. Hanging from one of the crystals is a card that says: MONICA VITTI'S CHANDELIER. INQUIRE WITHIN.

"May I help you?" asks a petite white-haired woman wearing a brown apron.

"I'm interested in this chandelier. How much?"

"Four hundred pounds, dear."

"Can you do better?"

"Don't want to. It's her chandelier, you know."

"Monica Vitti, the movie star?"

"Yes. I can show you." The lady disappears briefly and returns with a **Look** magazine from April 1966. She opens to a spread about Monica Vitti's apartment in Rome. There she is, the classic blond Italian movie actress, standing in a white silk caftan, photographed through the glittering crystal angels of this enormous chandelier. "I also have a letter from the broker I bought it from in Rome. Here." She produces a letter from a file box and hands it to me. "It's included with the purchase, of course."

"I'll take it. Can you ship it?"

"Yes, sir. You pay over there. Give them this slip to validate. It takes a few months to ship by boat. Don't fret, nothing will be broken. I wrap each piece by hand, then we box it in a wooden crate the size of your house. I do it all myself so I know it will make the trip in perfect condition."

I drop off the slip to be validated, they hand me a packet of information, I pay the cashier with traveler's checks and thank her.

I check the paper Eydie gave me and see that

I am to report directly to Anderson's office on the second floor. I take the staircase to the second level, which is filled with purveyors of antique china and glassware. The fluorescent lights overhead illuminate the rows of glass, which sparkle like gems in an endless velvet case.

Outside Anderson's office, I introduce myself to the receptionist. She motions me into what looks like a junk-filled attic—hardly what you'd expect for the office of the manager. Anderson sits at a desk buried behind stacks of books, bent lamp shades, random chair legs, ripped cushions, bolts of water-stained damask, broken picture frames, a wagon wheel, and a Chesterfield lounger that is propped, half cocked, against a file cabinet overflowing with yellowed paper.

"Mr. di Crespi! It's a pleasure." Asher Anderson rises from his creaky seat and extends his hand. It's rubbery and cold to the touch, like a grandfather's. He is very tall, very thin, and very old. His white hair is combed neatly to the side, and his blue eyes are clear and intelligent. Asher's thin white mustache makes him look of another era entirely, a sort of beleaguered Douglas Fairbanks, Sr. He wears baggy brown wool slacks and a lumpy gold hand-knit wool sweater.

"It's a pleasure to meet you too, sir." I look for a place to sit. There is none.

"Now now, don't get comfortable," Asher says. "We're off straightaway. Eydie asked me to take you to the Geffrye."

"You used to work there."

"Correct. And then I needed to make some money to send my parents to the seashore in the summer, and that's how I ended up here."

"Are they still alive?" Once I say it aloud, I don't like the way it sounds.

"No, no. My God, they would be centenarians. No, now I work here to send **myself** to the seashore." He laughs. "My wife is already there. Follow me, please."

So far my trip has been like a crazy carnival ride, offbeat operator included. I'm surprised when we climb into his car, which itself looks antique. Its interior makes his office look organized. I sit on a pile of newspapers in the passenger seat. The backseat is filled with books and papers and what appears to be either a cracked ceramic basin or a large spaghetti bowl, depending upon where you're from. Asher jams the key into the ignition and stomps on the gas like he's killing a beetle; we lurch into the traffic of Kings Road. Certain I'm going through the windshield any minute, I grab the seat between my knees like I'm on a teeter-totter.

"We shall be there momentarily," Asher announces like some kooky British pilot in a World War II movie.

"No kidding," I tell him. This is faster than flying.

Maybe old people drive fast because they have nothing to lose. I close my eyes, say a quick decade of the rosary, and throw in a plea to Saint Christopher to get us there in one piece. At least Asher doesn't jabber while he's driving, and he keeps those steely blue eyes on the road.

"Ah, the Geffrye." Asher slams on the brakes. I climb out of the car and take a moment to get my bearings. The museum is Georgian, red brick (now faded to a dull orange), with large half-moon windows on either side of the entrance. The gardens are manicured, with low meatball bushes, spindly trees, and waxy ivy that climbs up to the roof.

"Right this way," Asher says peppily as I follow him to the entrance. "Allow me to explain what you are about to experience. This museum is set up like a private residence. But there's a twist, you see. Each room is from a different era in British history. We begin on the main floor with rooms from the seventeenth century. By the time you reach the top, you're in the present. When the museum was designed, we wanted visitors to feel time pass as they walk through. You can tell me, once you've made it to the top, if we were successful. Follow me, please."

If ever there was a dream house for the interior decorator, this is it. Every detail of daily life is considered in the room design. Coal stoves, rotisserie pits, and deep hearths are prominent in kitchens before electricity and gas. In pre-bathroom rooms, ornate ceramic pitchers, nestled in deep bowls, are situated in alcoves for privacy. It's interesting to note that there are elements to room design that haven't changed in hundreds of years: every home needs a well-lit chair for sewing, a table and chairs for meals, and a comfortable bed.

The museum celebrates every era of décor: a Stuart-style wood-carved desk, a Queen Anne washbasin, a Georgian rococo armchair with a crewel-embroidered wool seat, a Regency rosewood-inlaid game table, and, my favorite, an Edwardian chandelier with six tulip-shaped glass shades. "Makes you giddy, doesn't it?" Asher says from behind me.

"I have a weakness for chandeliers."

"My wife thinks I'm dotty, I love the old things so much." Asher smiles. "Come, I want to show you something for your church."

I follow him down a dark, narrow hallway to

the back of the Almshouse, the main building of the complex.

"Most estates in England have a chapel in the house. In the days when it was a far ride to the church, a family wanted a room to gather for services. It was used for everything from prayer meetings to funerals." He pulls back a velvet curtain at the entrance of a room and invites me in.

The room is circular (I'm sure this inspired the current British fad of building glass solariums on the back of houses). Small lead-glass windows line one wall, with an ornate marble-topped refectory table in front of them. A single candle is centered on the table, next to an open book with a leather marker holding the page open. There is a straight-backed bench at the foot of the windows behind the table. Six polished wood benches face the table on the other side like pews.

"This is what I wanted you to see." I follow Asher to the section of wall opposite the windows. Imbedded in the wall is a glass case about three feet tall and two feet wide. Inside the case is an angel, carved of Italian gesso. The pink cherub is suspended in midair by a clear wire so that it appears to be in flight. The back wall of the case is painted Tiepolo style with a flurry of white puffy clouds against a blue background.

Asher turns on a pin light. In the light the angel becomes a hologram. "Enchanting, isn't it? I have only ever seen this technique in Italian churches. It never caught on here. But when I took over the museum, I felt it belonged. I bought the case in a small town in northern Italy and kept it for a long time until I found the perfect spot for it. It turns out that it's one of the visitors' favorite pieces in the whole place."

The angel is such a small thing, maybe only eight inches tall, but it's the focal point of this chapel. "I was looking for a way to do the stations of the cross at my church. I think you just gave me an idea. Thank you, Asher."

"I knew you'd appreciate her." He points to the angel. "After all, you're Italian."

Asher screeches to a halt in front of the hotel when he sees Eydie waiting for us on the sidewalk. I almost go through the windshield again. The doorman helps Eydie into the backseat. She has barely settled in before he presses the gas pedal. When we get up to the comfortable speed of one hundred miles an hour, Eydie gives me a message from the hotel desk:

B: CALL ME. I MOVED OUT. MA IS SUICIDAL. C.

"Everything all right?" Eydie asks.

"Capri Mandelbaum's mother is about to jump out a window."

"Who's Capri?" Eydie asks.

"My fiancée. It was an arrangement made by our mothers before either of us could walk. Because neither of us ever married anyone else, it was assumed that we were a couple."

"Sounds like a mess," Eydie says with understanding.

"It is. I've learned that if you leave something go long enough, it will bite you on the behind. It's ironic, though—Capri broke it off with **me** before this trip. She told me that she wasn't attracted to me, and now that she's turning forty, she wants to find someone who warms her burners."

"Should we go back to the hotel so you can call her?"

"Absolutely not. Her mother has been waiting twenty years for me to marry her daughter. They can wait two hours for a return call." No amount of drama from home is going to ruin this trip.

I show Eydie the **Look** magazine photo of the chandelier I bought at Antiquarius. "What do you think? It belonged to Monica Vitti."

Eydie looks at the picture closely. "This is a knockout. How much did you pay for it?"

"Four hundred pounds."

"A steal with the strong dollar."

"I thought so. I hope I wasn't conned."

"What if you were? Will you ever really know for sure? Of course not. So just enjoy it and believe it belonged to Monica Vitti. What more do you want from an antique? From anything?" Eydie grins and watches the road ahead. She doesn't seem to mind the speed. She takes out a pack of cigarettes, offers one to Asher, who accepts, and to me. I decline. She lights her cigarette and declares, "I love England. No pesky speed limits." Suddenly Asher pulls up onto the sidewalk and slams on the brakes. "Here we are." He yanks the gear into Park.

"Is this legal?" Pedestrians walk around the car as though cars park on the sidewalks every day.

"It is when you own the building," Asher replies.

"Where are we?" I ask, helping Eydie out of the car.

"This is Pimlico Road."

"Come on, step lively." Asher waves us into a doorway next to a storefront with a metal guard gate locked to the ground. We follow him through a small dark hallway, where he opens three locks with three different keys, then hits a light switch and motions for us to enter. I almost run out the door when I see what's inside. It's a roomful of giants.

An army of saints—in marble, painted plaster, and bronze, some twenty feet tall, on pedestals that make them appear larger still—is arranged in neat rows, as though they are lining up for drill-team practice. They fill the enormous garret from end to end.

"How delicious and macabre!" Eydie squeals.

It seems the entire host of heaven is here. I walk along a row of Marys: Our Lady of Sorrows, Our Lady of the Lake, Our Lady of Mount Carmel, Our Lady of the Snows, Our Lady of Fatima. "Here's Fatima!" I call out.

Once I get past the feeling of being watched, I can see the statues are magnificent. Some—like Saint Michael, valiant on horseback and wielding a sword, Saint Theresa of the Little Flower with a cascading bouquet of roses, Saint Lucy with her eyeballs on a platter, and Saint Joseph holding the baby Jesus—look so authentic, I feel as though I'm reviewing the troops. "Where did you get these?" I ask Asher.

"They're from Italy."

"Made there?"

"Made there and then shipped here for safekeeping. During World War II the churches in Italy were bombed with such regularity that a group of priests came up with a plan to save their contents. They loaded these onto boats at night and sent them to England. Of course, many of the statues were destroyed by water, or the boats were hit and didn't make it. These are the survivors."

"Amazing." I turn and look at the side walls where the saints mingle with the Gloria angel and her trumpet, various kneeling angels, and a series of putti toddler cherubs dangling on wires from the ceiling.

"These are mostly from the north of Italy," Asher explains, "though the series in costume is from Naples. I have two hundred and seventeen saints and fifteen Marys. Years ago I wrote to the Vatican and told them, and they sent someone to look at them. They decided that they didn't want them back. They'd already rebuilt a lot of the churches, or like you, they were renovating after centuries so they'd commissioned new statues."

"Fools." I walk down another aisle.

"If they didn't take them back, they're not valuable," Eydie says.

"It depends upon how you define valuable," Asher says. "A lot of these were made by local craftsmen, unknowns if you will. I like them because they're different. It doesn't matter to me who made them."

"It shouldn't," I tell him. "I'm very impressed."

"I have the children of Fatima." Asher points to the back. "I'll show you."

I follow him to the back with Eydie close behind. "Here they are."

I stop in my tracks. Eydie gasps. "They're so real!" The life-sized Fatima children, while made of plaster and crudely painted, are dressed in actual clothes, which makes them seem eerily lifelike. Lucia dos Santos, around ten years old, wears a cotton skirt and blouse and a black veil. Francisco, eight, wears trousers and a hat, which is really a durable scarf wrapped around his head. The youngest, Jacinta, wears a version of Lucia's costume with a blue veil.

"Look at the eyes," Eydie says.

"It was the custom to use glass eyes at the turn of this century," Asher tells us.

"I want these," I tell him.

"Are you sure?" Eydie asks, stepping back. "They're awfully lifelike."

"Oh, yes, I'm sure." My eyes fill with tears. Maybe it's the story of these statues surviving the trip from Italy during the war. Maybe it's this room, filled with relics no one wants, that makes me want to take them home. Or maybe it's the first time the story of Fatima has seemed real to me. No matter where I go in the world, I am reminded in small ways that I need faith. I haven't prayed for the inspiration to renovate our church, it hadn't even occured to me, but I am going to start now.

"Oh for . . ." Eydie says, digging in her purse for a tissue. I see that she's weeping. "There's something about these kids, they look like terrified refugees. You can't buy these, B. They'll scare people in New Jersey. Those people like pretty." She blows her nose.

"I am going to buy them." The way the three statues look at me fills me with a longing to tell the story of Fatima. For the first time since Father gave me the job, I feel the stirrings of something truly creative. Maybe these three strange creatures are my swatches upon which to build the church.

"Now, now," Asher says quietly, "take some time and think about it. There are no returns."

My suitcases are filled with souveniers from our trip: an antique Dresden teapot with accoutrements, a cashmere scarf for Toot, ties for Nicky and Anthony, and a kilt for Two (maybe he'll wear it on Halloween). As I yank my suitcases off the conveyor belt, I realize that, as much fun as I had with Eydie, I'm ready to be home and to get to work on Our Lady of Fatima Church.

At JFK Airport I put Eydie in a cab and go to the parking lot to pick up my car. I found a pay phone and called Capri, promising that I would go directly to the Castle Mandelbaum.

As soon as I begin the drive, I'm sorry I said I'd come. I'm exhausted. I hardly slept on the trip home. Eydie and I couldn't stop talking, smoking, and drinking the free port from Madagascar. I told her about Capri and me, which she found fascinating.

I pull up the drive at the Mandelbaums'. The gardens are bursting with red-and-white impatiens while laurel spills its pink blossoms as far as my eye can see. I fish out the Queen Mum tea towels I bought them in London and ring the bell. Capri opens the door. She looks as though she's been crying for days. "Where is she?" I ask.

Capri points to the kitchen. I go to the back of the house with Capri on my heels.

"Aurelia?"

Aurelia is standing at the sink, snapping beans. She doesn't turn to look at me. "I'm not speaking to you," she says. "You knew all about this move."

I'm insulted by her rudeness, and so hungover from the plane that I lose my patience. "You can't possibly be angry about this."

She spins and faces me. "Capri went behind my back and signed a lease."

"She's forty years old," I remind her.

"I don't care if she's eighty! She's sneaking around!"

"This is hardly a rebellion. In fact, this can be filed under the category 'It's about damn time.' Your daughter is an adult who wants her own life."

"You have no idea what I've been going through here." Aurelia wipes her eyes with a handkerchief.

"And you have no idea how you hurt me with your control!" Capri pipes up.

"Stop it. Both of you." Aurelia and Capri look at me. "I mean it." I turn to Capri. "I'm not coming over here to defend you anymore. I'm sorry things got hairy when you decided to assert yourself, but you should have prepared your mother before you packed your bags."

"I needed—"

"You need to grow up!"

"Don't speak to her in that tone!" Aurelia barks.

"And you need to learn to let go." I steady myself on the kitchen table. Aurelia puts her hand over her heart. "I am sick of being in the middle." I look at Aurelia. "I am not your son." I turn to Capri. "Or your future husband. I am your lifelong friend. I love you both very much. But I'm too old to take your crap anymore. So, let's get it straight. Aurelia, your daughter doesn't want me. We have no sparks. There have never been any sparks. In fact, we are two sopping wet logs on a Girl Scout camping trip. Do you understand?"

"I do now," she says quietly.

"If you're smart, you'll help Capri pack and you'll give her some of the lovely modern pieces from Sy's old den that are stored in the attic. West Long Branch is no place for French anything. Now I must go. I just got off a plane, and my head feels like it's going to snap off, roll onto the curb, and burst into flames."

As I climb into my car, I realize that Aurelia is a decent lady, but I am seeing a side of her that I don't like. She never gives without strings, even though she's the first person to say she does. Capri put her needs after her mother's because she never had much of a choice. The family ties that bind can choke you. It's a lesson I would do well to learn from her.

I arrive home like a wrung-out dish rag and find a letter from Gian Angelo Ruttolo, to whom I wrote before zipping off to London with Eydie. He's coming to New York in late July and has agreed to take a day trip down to OLOF to see the church.

The English, with their rich colonial history, poached wonderful decorating ideas from around the world. My brief trip gave me more inspiration than I know what to do with. England is an endless resource for decorators. I admired the scrumptious silks, handcrafted wool rugs, and metal accents of India. The Far Eastern influences, like the use of fibers in rattan, straw, and hemp amid the faded chintz, really dazzle me. They say the Brits like bold color because it rains so much there, but I believe they simply took the most artful elements of every place they colonized and incorporated them into their own national palette.

Perhaps it betrays my Roman Catholic roots, but I love the Protestant cathedrals. They are simple, spare, and full of light. A medieval tapestry behind an altar might be the only adornment. When just one object of art is displayed, it has a deep impact. I flipped over the black-and-white marble harlequin-patterned floor at Westminster Cathedral, so I plan to copy it in the church foyer. It reminded me of a chessboard, and how that exquisite game is much like salvation—do a little good, move forward; sin, go back; ignore the needs of others, stay in the same square.

The doorbell rings, and I hear the door open with a key. "B, it's me, Toot. Don't shoot!"

"I'm in the kitchen," I call out.

Toot appears in the doorway carrying a red-and-white enamel pot balanced on a Tupperware cake saver. "Soup," she says. "I never

heard of anyone going on an international airplane who didn't get a cold."

"It's four hundred degrees outside. I may fry
to death, but I'm not getting a cold. Trust me."

"Now, B," she says sternly. "It'll flush out the
European impunities."

"Might you mean impurities?" I snap.

She ignores the comment. "How was your
trip?"

"Too fast. I could've used a month over there."

Toot gets out a place mat, a napkin, a bowl,
and a spoon. She ladles her world-class chicken
soup into the bowl and indicates I should eat. I
sit down as she takes a seat across from me. I
put my napkin on my lap and taste the soup.

"Good?"

"Delish."

"I strain the chicken stock through cheese-
cloth. Takes the fat out."

"I have a feeling you didn't pop in just to tell
me how you make broth."

Toot sighs. "Sal and I have gotten to third
base. I'm not going too fast, am I?"

"Sounds like you're right on schedule. Although . . ."

"What?"

"When your man is over sixty, I think you
should feel free to escalate the proceedings.
After all, the clock is ticking."

"Good point. Do I look thinner?"

"Stand up."

Toot stands up straight and lifts her neck like a chicken about to lay an egg.

"You definitely do."

"I'm jogging my ass off." She sits back down. "Oh, B. Someday I hope you fall in love."

"Are you in love with Sal?"

"Not at all. But at least I've bought a ticket to the game. I'm not on the field yet, I'm in the parking lot, but who knows? It could happen. And soon. I'm so tired of being alone." She raps her fingers on the table.

"What's so terrible about it, really?" I get up and find a box of crackers in the cabinet.

"Oh, it's awful. Being alone is a state of waiting. In my life I was waiting for a man to come along, and then when he did, I was stuck in a marriage that died a little more each day. When we got divorced, I became a woman with everything behind her and nothing in front."

"That's not true at all. You have a very full life."

"As a person, yes. As a woman . . ." Toot turns both her thumbs down. "Let me tell you about being a desirable woman, because it's the shortest career on earth. By the time you figure men out, it's too late to use the knowledge. Look at me. Fifty-one years old and I'm regrouping. Who does this?"

"Don't look back."

"Well, B, you have to. Because I don't want to spend Act Two of my life making another mistake and then having to bounce back from it. What elasticity I have left, I want to savor, okay? I don't know how people like Liz Taylor do it. I haven't got the stamina to deal with the breakups. Lonnie nearly ruined me. And I'm not blaming him. It was me. I saw the signs and I was busy with the boys, so I ignored them."

"What signs?"

"Well, after a few years in a marriage, let's say around . . ."

"Year eight?" How could I forget? That was the year we found a size-five blue patent-leather pump in Lonnie's trunk. (Toot is a size nine.) It was the first in a series of clothing items recovered from his car. I never understood it—didn't these women notice a shoe missing? Or their underwear?

"That's when he went out on me for the first time. Lonnie always liked a good-looking girl. He'd look one up and down like a greased pole. And I stupidly took that as a compliment, thinking, 'Out of all those girls, he chose me.' I should have realized I was totally expandable."

"Expendable."

"Right. He needed variety. A couple of times I tried to spice things up, like I wore a blond wig

and met him at the Steak and Shake, but someone saw me there and said, 'I didn't know you
had cancer,' and it killed the mood entirely."

"That must've crushed you."

"You'll never know. But Sal, he's not like
that. He looks at me like I'm a hot pie fresh out
of the oven. He practically saturates—"

"Salivates," I correct her.

"And if I make him a dish of spaghetti—even
schway schway, it takes me five minutes with a
can of tuna—he is so grateful. Lonnie used to
come home, look in the pot, and if he didn't
like what was cooking, he'd take the keys and
go right out to a restaurant—without us! I can't
see Sal doing that."

"I'm happy for you, Toot."

"There's just one problem."

"What?"

"He wants . . . you know."

"What?"

"You know."

"No, I really don't."

"He wants a . . . **particular** thing." Toot puts
both hands on the table and rubs the wood like
she's hand-ironing a tablecloth.

"What do you mean?"

"Let's put it this way. Ma taught me if a man
ever asked for **that,** he wasn't fit to eat on our
china."

"Oh . . . **that.**" Our mother had many rules. Thank goodness she spared me this one. "Toot, this is not an area I am comfortable discussing with you."

"I figured."

"Thank you." I take four saltines and crush them in my fist, then sprinkle them into my soup.

"So I went to Father Wiffnell. Not direct, I asked him in the confessional."

"You went to a priest? About **that**?"

"Why, naturally. What are we paying them for? I needed some guidance. Who the hell else can I ask when you're traipsing all over Europe?"

"Oh, I don't know. Maybe one of your **girl-friends**?"

"My crowd is very sedate sexually. In kinder-garten, Sister Mary Purification told the girls in my class to take baths with our clothes on. I learned to be ashamed of my body the same year I learned the Palmer Perfect Method."

I cannot even pursue the logic of that, so I ask, "What did Father Wiffnell say?"

"He was quiet for a long time. Then he said, 'Do you love this man?' So, I answered him truthfully. I said, 'I'm not sure.' He said, 'Why don't you wait until you're sure?' "

"Good answer."

"I don't know. I miss when they used to say, 'Don't do it! Go say ten Hail Marys, and the next time you think a thought like this, think of the oozing stigmata of Saint Rose of Lima.' Now, anything goes. I brought pound cake. You want a piece?"

"Make it a double."

CHAPTER SIX

The Bernini of Bay Ridge

We locals accept the crowds of summer in our beachfront town without complaint. Main Street in OLOF is always busy during August. There's a portable Italian ice cart that draws the crowd in the heat. The vendor parks it on the church plaza, where folks buy their ice and then sit on the church steps and eat it—our version of Italy's La Passegiata. I wait inside the church until I absolutely need a cigarette. Everywhere I go, I'm bombarded with questions about renovating the church. I'm tired of explaining that I'm still in the research phase.

Christina waits in the sacristy at Our Lady of Fatima with her typed inventory of the church contents. I go outside and light a cigarette.

Since this project began I've been smoking quite a lot, but I promise myself that as soon as the design is complete, I will quit. A good smoke is soothing, and for now I need it.

I see a town car from the city turning the corner onto our town square, and I wave. True to form, Eydie is right on time. The black town car pulls up to the curb, and Eydie jumps out of the backseat in her best ensemble yet: orange paisley stovepipe pants, pumpkin suede platform boots, a hot-pink blouse with flowing sleeves, and a wide-weave crocheted sleeveless bolero in orange, green, and white stripes. She **is** 1970.

"B!" She waves excitedly. The driver emerges from the front seat and joins Eydie at the back door of the car. It takes a moment, but Gian Angelo Ruttolo emerges with her help. He's small, around five feet two, and trim. He's dressed in black with a straw boater on his head, and when he turns his back to me, I see a long white braid down his back. I didn't think hippies came in senior-citizen packages. As I hurry to meet them, he is eyeing the church up and down. "Nice stonework," he murmurs before Eydie has even made the introductions.

"We're honored to have you here," I say as I shake his hand.

"Do you speak Italian?" he asks.

"**Poco.**" I make the sign for "little" with my thumb and forefinger.

He grimaces and pushes me out of the way. He climbs the steps, holding the brass banister.

"What's his problem?" I whisper.

"He's a handful. No patience," Eydie whispers back.

We follow him into the church, where Christina greets him in Italian. He beams, kisses her on both cheeks, and caresses her hands warmly. Christina doesn't seem to mind, even though she is a couple of inches taller than he. I never thought I'd see someone more petite than Christina, but here he is.

"**Cominceremmo?**" Gian Angelo turns and looks at me without letting go of Christina.

"**Vorrebbe che io le mostrassi la chiesa?**" Christina asks him.

"**Vorrei che mi mostrasse tutto il mondo,**" he says with a twinkle.

"Do you understand?" Eydie asks me.

I understand a come-on in any language. "He wants to show her the world," I whisper to Eydie. "Is he here to help me or to get laid?"

"Both." She smiles.

We take Gian Angelo through the church: up to the choir loft, over the catwalks, down the small staircase from the belfry, through the nave, to the side altars, back into the sacristy, the storerooms, the offices, and the hallway with access to the cemetery. He taps walls, looks under statues (for cash perhaps, or secret letters? Letters under statues have long been the postal service of choice for clandestine lovers), checks names and dates of construction, scratches any metal surface with his fingernail, and feels the marble for cracks and fissures. He spends several minutes assessing the Menecola fresco of the children of Fatima looking up at the Blessed Lady. Surprisingly, he doesn't seem to hate it. He seems very interested in the paint used and the technique of the artist. I feel like I'm on tour with an archaeologist instead of an architect.

Christina and Gian Angelo now have what appears to be a secret language. Eydie speaks Italian, but they aren't letting her in on their sotto voce sessions. I'm slightly irritated with Chris, but really, it isn't her fault. He is our guest, and she is only being polite. She turns to me and says, "Gian Angelo wants to give me his assessment in Italian, and then I will translate."

"Fine." I shrug and look at Eydie. We sit down in the front pew.

Christina, taking notes, and Gian Angelo, giving his impassioned sermon, walk in circles around the altar. He points, he gestures, he

shouts. Christina scribbles, occasionally interrupting him and repeating what he has said, or
asking a question. After fifteen minutes of diatribe, he sits down in the priest's chair, crosses
his legs, and looks at us.

"Gian Angelo says that the original construction of the church is excellent," Christina reports. "Good bones, he says. The statues are
junk, from molds instead of carvings. The only
thing he would keep is the rough-hewn cross
over the statue of Mary. He says it is Sicilian
and hand-carved. He likes the fresco. While it
was painted by an amateur, he feels that it was
done with heart, and that counts for more than
technique. His final recommendation is to
modernize the church, making it more accessible. Dispose of the Communion railing, the
confessionals, and the baptistery. Replace the
pews. The pitch of the pews is uncomfortable,
so he says we should get new ones. These are
monuments to another time in history, when
secrets and shame were part of the doctrine. A
church, he says, should serve the people instead
of appearing grand and isolating, and he sug-
gests we look to the Jewish synagogues and
Quaker meetinghouses, where the rooms are
multipurpose and not solely for religious services, for inspiration."

"Interesting," Eydie says.

"Ask Gian Angelo what he would do to make this place stand out from all the other traditional churches in New Jersey."

Christina asks Gian Angelo. He listens and then rolls his eyes.

"He says you should hire Rufus McSherry."

Eydie pats my hand. "It's time to go and see Rufus."

After I said good-bye to Gian Angelo, Eydie, and Christina, I came home to a light supper of sardines on toast, a holdover from my trip to England. It's a balmy summer night with a cool breeze, so I decide to take a walk on the beach. The beach behind the Villa di Crespi is public, but it's a thin stretch of rocky shore with coarse sand, so I only get passersby, never any sunbathers. In the distance, looking south, I can see people on the beach where it widens out and the sand is soft, but from here they are as small as bright confetti. Occasionally the wind brings the sound of a radio or laughter my way, but mostly it's quiet, except for the lapping of the waves.

As a matter of habit, I stop and pick up seashells that interest me, and I always put the ones I really like in a lovely Baccarat bowl in my living room. It's my way of remembering that I once was young and carefree.

In a way, the worst thing that can happen to an artist is to get what he wants. I dreamed of renovating the church, and was elated when I got the job. But it didn't take long for me to realize that I might not have it in me to deliver what I know the place can be.

It must be how a soprano feels when she can see the notes on the page—she can hear them in her head, but when the moment comes and she opens her mouth, she can't hit them. There she is, paralyzed in front of the orchestra, knowing she can't do justice to the aria. This is how I feel about Fatima Church. I have the ideas, but will I find the artisans to fulfill my design?

This job is not like decorating a home or a business. It isn't about suiting one client, it's about providing a place for all kinds of people to find inspiration and peace. A church is a host to the highest dreams, deepest fears, and greatest sorrows of the believer. One building has to be all things to all people who gather there. Perhaps this is why I can't crack it. I can't feel what it is I am supposed to be doing. I desperately need inspiration.

The sun is setting, leaving behind a trail of white clouds that looks like a window shade raised to let in the last of the light. As the sun melts into the black horizon like a scoop of orange sherbet, dusk settles around me, and I feel truly alone. This is one of those moments when I wish I had a lover to share my life. It would be nice to be supported and quell this self-doubt in the eyes of someone who believes in me. This must be why people get married. They're afraid of the dark.

Driving through the streets of Bay Ridge with Christina, I realize the neighborhood is a lot like OLOF, except our kids swim in the town pool instead of cooling off in the spray of fire hydrants, and there are more Irish people. Here we see that great American mix of the working-class Irish and Italians, which yields one of the most striking color combinations in all of humanity: raven-haired brunettes with blue eyes. The emotional combination is equally compelling—explosive tempers and quiet shame.

Rufus McSherry works in a warehouse on Seventy-second Street off of Third Avenue on a dead-end street called Bennett Court. Our Martinelli cousins live a couple of blocks over and invited us for a barbeque later, which translates to a bacchanalia of roasted lamb on a spit, a twenty-pound turkey, and several side dishes featuring eggplant, rigatoni, and artichokes. And that's before the tub of homemade ice cream.

"Do you have the photographs?" I ask Christina as we stand at the entrance door of the warehouse.

"Everything, including Gian Angelo's recommendations."

"I'm surprised he didn't take you back to Italy with him."

"He wanted to."

"How old is that man?" I press the buzzer marked McSherry.

"I don't know. Eighty?"

"Good God. When is it **enough**?" I ask.

"When is what enough?" a voice booms out of the intercom. Christina and I are startled.

I press the button on the intercom and answer, "I was speaking about an eighty-year-old man who still chases women."

"My kind of guy," the voice replies.

"I am Bartolomeo di Crespi."

"Come on up."

The buzzer is loud. I push the heavy steel door open and hold it for Christina, who looks at me as though we're on a fool's run. There is a long, narrow stairwell with no railing that goes up one floor and reaches a landing with a bare lightbulb dangling from the ceiling. We ascend in the August heat without complaint, but I am about two seconds away from turning down these rickety stairs and jumping back into our air-conditioned car.

"Rufus McSherry?" I ask the man hovering at the top of the stairs.

"No, I am Pedro Alarcon, his apprentice," the man says. He reaches out to shake my hand. Pedro is around thirty-five, with black hair, golden-brown skin, and a pleasant face. He is about five feet seven, with a square jaw, black eyes, and a small nose with a wide bridge. He shakes my hand and then Christina's. "Follow me, please."

Christina and I follow him through a small room filled with paint cans, sacks of concrete, boxes of marble rubble, skeins of small wires, flats of wood, and bags of dry plaster. Then we step inside the workroom. I inhale the smell of oil paint and varnish, a delicious combination that says art is being created.

The warehouse is a massive floor-through room that has been broken down into several work areas. The ceiling, over thirty feet high, is a series of old slanted skylights with steel casings. Some are propped open, letting direct sunlight and a welcome breeze peel through. The floorboards, wide planks of pine, warped from wear, creak loudly when we walk on them.

There is a row of worktables with recessed tops along one wall. This is where the stained-glass windows are made. Christina and I observe Pedro as he pours epoxy resin into the mold trays lined up on the table. He pours the clear liquid, lets it set for a few seconds, then gently shakes the mold, allowing it to settle. We peer over his shoulder, mesmerized by the process.

"This is an ancient technique," Pedro explains. "I don't make windows like the Italians. They are beautiful but too sleek. I like the Mexican way. We use sand and heat to make glass. No tubes for blowing the glass, we use our hands. The results are thick blocks of glass, layered in the molds to give them heft and texture. So my windows are primitive."

"They're very sturdy," Christina comments.

"A good window should last a hundred years. And it does"—he smiles—"if I do my job."

I look down into the mold where a series of geometric shapes emerges beneath the resin, like bamboo pushing through the surface of a pond. The mold is filled with square chunks of emerald-green glass anchored by a thick hem of clay.

"That's beautiful," Christina says.

"I hope my windows are like poems. I don't want to tell you what they mean. You should decide for yourself." Pedro points to the mold. "See the shapes? Some might see an angel, and others a butterfly. It's up to you."

Pedro goes back to work as we turn to a canvas stretched over forty feet in width and about twenty feet in height. The mural of a vivid blue sky with crisp white clouds could be the backdrop of any scene in a Tiepolo painting, but there is a twist. A shard of pink sunlight breaks through the clouds like an unfurled satin ribbon. The sky could have been painted by an old master, but the ribbon is strictly modern. The combination makes me smile.

"Imagine waking up to that every morning," Christina says approvingly. "Now, that's inspiring."

"Where would you hang it? You'd have to live in a gym," I tell her, not wanting to take my eyes off of it.

"Like it?" the intercom voice says from behind us.

I nearly jump out of my skin; Christina takes my arm. We turn around. "You like startling people, don't you?" I tell him.

He throws his head back and laughs. "Love it. I'm Rufus McSherry." He extends his hand first to Christina. She looks positively doll-like next to this strapping Irishman. He's around forty, over six feet tall, with broad shoulders and massive arms (from all that climbing around on scaffolds, I'm sure). He has the biggest hands I've ever seen; Christina's hand disappears inside his paw. His wavy hair has some red in it (hence his name!), but some gray too, which makes it seem more brown than rusty. He could use a haircut since it grazes his shoulders in that young Abraham Lincoln way. A shave wouldn't be a bad idea either. His face is big like the rest of him, with a pronounced jaw, a good straight nose with a bulbous tip, and a nice mouth with strong white teeth.

His deepset brown eyes sparkle with mischief. He squints most of the time, then his eyes snap open when he's interested in something. When he looks at Christina, it's as if his eyeballs are on springs. He tilts his head and studies her. From the way she is standing on her toes and smiling up at him as she tells him about herself, I deduce that there is more going on in this room than an artistic consultation.

I point to the mural in progress. "At first I thought Botticelli. But when I study it, I see Tiepolo. You like him?"

"A lot." Rufus smiles.

"There isn't a better blue in all of art, I don't think. What's it for?"

"It's a backdrop for the opera."

"Which one?"

"**The Barber of Baghdad.**"

"I never heard of it."

"Peter Cornelius. It's lousy. German. This is the sky outside his room, where the general lies dying. I wanted to give him something to live for. Are you hungry?"

I don't know why everything this man says gives me a shot of adrenaline, so I take a deep breath to calm myself.

"Actually, I am." I look at my cousin.

"Christina?" Rufus smiles at her. She nods that she's hungry, but I think she would agree to be painted green and hung from her feet on Fourth Avenue if this man asked her to. "Well, come on back."

"What about Pedro?" I ask.

"I'll call him when the food is ready."

As we follow Rufus, which is a little like the Lilliputians when they followed the Giant to the edge of the world and fell off to their deaths, Christina turns around and looks at me; she smiles. It's the old Christina suddenly—she seems happy for the first time in months. Rufus pulls aside some old velvet drapes to reveal a kitchen. After Christina passes through, I see that his eyes are studying her fine figure. When I finally catch his gaze, I give him an icy look, which makes him laugh.

The kitchen is clean but sparsely furnished. There's a Formica-topped table and matching silver chairs, diner-style, a stove, a sink, and a refrigerator. The pots and utensils are top-of-the-line. "Here, sit." He pulls a chair out for

Christina and then shows me where to sit. "Here, Bart, uncork this wine." He goes to the stove, where steam rises from a large pot of boiling water.

Christina laughs but then stifles it. "Bartolomeo hates to be called Bart."

"Why?"

"Tom Mix movies," I explain. "Black Bart and all that."

"What should I call you?" Rufus asks.

"B."

"Okay, B." He puts mismatched wineglasses on the table. "I'm going to make us spaghetti carbonara, okay?"

"Sure." Christina looks at me like my mother used to—with a big smile that means **Be nice.**

Rufus throws a pound of linguini into the water and stirs. Then he takes down a large cast-iron frying pan from the shelf and puts it on the stove over a low flame. He goes to the refrigerator, takes out a stick of butter, and throws it into the pan. He grabs an onion from a wire basket on the windowsill, hacks off the edges, pulls off the skin, and slices it thinly right into the pan (without crying). He takes four eggs and a carton of cream out of the fridge, cracks the eggs into a bowl, and beats them lightly, slowly adding the cream. He sets the mixture aside, pulls a package of bacon from the fridge, and cuts it open with a steak knife. Removing six slices of bacon, he cuts them into small pieces over the butter and onions in the pan. They sizzle and smell divine. He stirs the pasta again, scooping one strand out and sucking it into his mouth. (I could do without the slurp.) "Al dente."

Rufus dumps the vat of pasta into a colander in the sink. He gives the colander a good shake, then plops the noodles into the frying pan with the butter and bacon. He carefully folds in the eggs and cream, stirring constantly. The pasta turns a lovely golden color. He reaches into the fridge again and pulls out a wedge of fresh Parmesan. Turning off the heat, he grates the luscious cheese onto the hot linguini.

"That smells great," Pedro says from the door. As he washes his hands at the sink, Rufus pulls plates from the shelf and places them in front of us. Pedro brings paper napkins, large spoons, and forks. Rufus grates fresh black pepper over the pasta and transfers the pan to the center of the table.

"B, why don't you serve that up?" Rufus gives me a large spoon and fork.

He goes back to the refrigerator and pulls out a casserole dish and places it on the table. He has stuffed long, thin peppers with shards of anchovy and doused them with olive oil.

"Rufus, stuffed peppers are one of my favorite dishes," I say. "My grandmother used to make them."

"Mine, too."

"An Irish grammy made stuffed peppers?"

"My mother's people are Italian. Altezza. From Puglia."

"Pedro, where are your people from?" I ask.

"It's a small town in Mexico. La Paz."

"**Buon appetito!**" Rufus raises his glass, and we toast.

I have never eaten linguini served straight from the pan. My mother was so persnickety about the way a table was set she never even allowed a milk carton on the table when we ate breakfast. Everything had to be in a proper receptacle: bread in a basket, milk in a pitcher, pasta in a serving bowl. But here, straight from the skillet, each buttery bite is more delicious than the last. I wonder if it has to do with the olive oil that glazes the iron pan. It seems to give the sauce more flavor. Or maybe it's just Rufus. I can already see that he's the man who invented robust, from his stature to his art to his pasta. I want to know everything about him. The wine is a hearty Chianti, a perfect complement to the bacon and onions.

"Are you married, Rufus?" I ask.

"No. Are you?"

"No."

"The last bachelors in America," Christina says. "Who knew you'd find them eating linguini in a Brooklyn warehouse?"

"I'm not married either," Pedro offers.

"Congratulations," I say.

"How about you?" Rufus asks Christina.

For a split second I think, **If you thought she was married, why were you flirting with her like she was the last girl you'd ever lay eyes on?** But I keep this to myself. After all, we're guests.

"I was married. Happily married for thirteen years. My husband died a little over a year ago. His name was Charlie. Our daughter, Amalia, is twelve."

I can't know for sure, but I believe this is the first time Christina has mentioned Charlie without crying. "She's a pip, that Amalia," I say cheerily, hoping to change the subject.

"That's tough." Rufus looks at Christina. "How are you doing with it?"

Christina shrugs. "I don't know how to answer that." Pedro and I look down at our plates and roll the pasta on our forks.

"Try," Rufus urges gently.

"Well, it's very strange." Christina sits back in her chair. "When I was married, I used to wonder what would happen if my husband left me."

"You said you were happy," Rufus says.

"Very happy. That's probably why I worried about the worst thing happening. I couldn't imagine life without him. We had our fights, of course, and our tough times, but mostly it was great. A peaceful life. We really treasured that, and we knew if something bad happened, we would stick it out."

"We come from very resilient people," I say proudly.

"The biggest problem is that I don't know what to do." Christina takes a sip of wine. Rufus stares at her intently, willing her to go on. "I mean literally," she continues. "When Charlie was alive, there was a routine in our home. There were expectations, and they were met. There was fun. Sometimes the three of us would go out all day, and we'd come home and collapse on the couch and offer each other money to go get things because we were so tired. Charlie would offer, you know, a dollar to Amalia to get him a beer; if the phone rang, I'd offer Charlie fifty cents to answer it. That sort of thing. Our own weird family dynamic. And now it's gone. And I don't know how to invent something new. It seems impossible."

"How's Amalia?" Rufus asks. "Besides being a pip."

"That's the worst part. I can't give her what I

had. Two parents in a loving home. I know how important my father was in my life. For a girl, it's protection, a feeling that nothing can harm you. For a son . . ." She trails off.

"It's the same," Rufus says. "My father died when I was nine."

✳"And I lived in fear that mine would die because they were so old when I was born," I blurt out. "They were over forty. My father was almost fifty!" I don't know why I'm saying this. "I'm sorry. It's not the same. They died when they were in their eighties."

"No, no, that's okay." Rufus smiles at me.

"Since you lost your father so young, is there anything you know of that I can do for my daughter?" Christina asks.

Rufus sits back and thinks. "No one ever asked me that." He picks up the serving spoon and fork and, despite our protestations, gives all three of us second helpings.

"This is your best yet, boss," Pedro says appreciatively.

"Thanks." Rufus gets up and puts the pan in the sink. He turns, crossing his arms over his chest. "Christina, the only thing I can tell you is to talk about your husband. A lot. Don't think you're going to ruin the mood by bringing him up, because when you've lost your father so young, you want to remember every detail, and it seems the entire world is trying to make you forget." Christina looks at Rufus gratefully.

After we clean up, Rufus takes us on a tour of the warehouse. Christina and I are amazed at the scope of their work. Besides the green windows he showed us earlier, Pedro is also restoring a rose window for St. Francis Xavier Church in Chelsea while Rufus finishes a series of backdrops for a touring opera company. At the moment they are also restoring a small chapel in Connecticut. Their company takes on only projects that interest them, Rufus explains, and that use their various skills in glasswork, painting, and woodworking.

Rufus walks us out to the car, opens the door, and helps Christina in, giving her a friendly peck on the cheek. Then he turns to me and shakes my hand. I get into the car. "We really didn't get to talk business," he says through the window.

"Doesn't matter," I tell him. "What we did talk about was more important."

"I thought so." His face breaks into a wide grin. "But what about your project?"

I give Rufus the file on Fatima Church. "It would be wonderful if you could paint the frescoes, and Pedro could redo our stained-glass windows. We need a shrine for the Blessed

Mother. A new altar. There's so much to do. When can you come and see our church?"

"December."

"December! That's five months away!"

"You need time to do your research and design, don't you?"

"Yes, but—"

"It's fine," Christina says. "Father won't let us begin the actual work until after the Fatima feast day, and that's October thirteenth."

"See there? We're right on schedule." Rufus smiles.

I watch him go back into the warehouse. As the door closes behind him, I remember a story my mother used to read me about a giant who roamed the earth—his feet were so big that when he walked, his footsteps made valleys in the dirt. Some people are bigger than life. Rufus McSherry is one of them.

"So, what did Rufus think?" I ask Eydie, having called her the moment I pull in the driveway after dropping off Christina.

"He was intrigued. He thought you were funny."

"Do you think he'll take the job?" I press.

"He said he wants to see your design. Then he'll come and see the church. So get started. And it had better be good. He likes a challenge."

I feel my heart sink. "Eydie, listen," I confess, "I've been having some trouble."

"What do you mean?"

"I'm having some sort of artistic crisis. I can't seem to decide which way to go or what to do."

"Well, that's the easiest problem in the world to solve!" she says.

"How?" I sound like a pitiful sap.

"Go to Italy," she commands. "It's what we all do when we're stumped. Go to Italy, look around, and steal, steal, steal! Steal everything from the molding to the marble to the layout. If you're going to succeed, go to the source. You'll find the answer there."

I look over at Capri, fast asleep in seat 5A on TWA Flight 17 from JFK to Milan. How different it is to cross the Atlantic with Capri instead of Eydie. With Capri, I feel like a brother, making sure we're at the right gate, and that she has magazines and a book for the long flight. With Eydie, all I needed were cigarettes and the liquor cart. Time flew as we discussed art. This flight feels like a stint on a Conestoga wagon going west. Too long and too bumpy.

A great artist, I can't remember who, said that when you are blocked, you should return to your point of origin. Luckily, my artistic and spiritual origin is the Golfo di Genova, the vast sapphire-blue gulf that feeds into the Ligurian Sea. Eydie was right. As soon as we landed, I began to feel inspired. I had promised Aurelia that Capri and I would celebrate our fortieth birthdays in Italy, so while Capri shops for shoes, I'll shop for ideas to renovate the Fatima church.

I mapped out the trip with Capri. She wants to go to the beach during the day and out for dinner and dancing at night. I'm not looking for a tan or rumba lesson. I want to be hit over the head with inspiration.

Capri and I have always known we share Italian lineage from Santa Margherita. But she recently discovered that both of our families, the Castones and the di Crespis, were thrown out of La Spezia, a city south of our Santa Margherita, in some political brouhaha involving a harbor tax. The Castones were in the boat business, and the di Crespis were fishermen, so they banded together to fight city hall. Alas, they lost the fight and migrated north to this quaint, small cove and started over.

"I'm in heaven," Capri says as she greets me in her room. Her terrace faces the ocean while mine looks down the cliffs of Santa Margherita. "I don't feel forty at all. Happy birthday to me."

I notice that she isn't wearing her glasses. Her eyes are a beguiling chestnut brown with green flecks. "What happened to your glasses?"

Capri blushes. "You noticed. They came out with a new thing—soft contact lenses. They don't scratch the cornea like the hard ones. My ophthalmologist said to wait until we landed here to put them in, because they could dry up on the airplane."

"Wow." Capri is really attractive without her glasses, or maybe she's more relaxed because she can see clearly. Whatever it is, the results are a sizable improvement.

"I know. Big difference, right?" Capri beams.

We ordered up a light supper on the balcony outside her room. Capri ordered ravioli stuffed with fresh peas and mint drizzled in olive oil, grilled shrimp rubbed with garlic, and a cassis gelato. We have a cold, crisp white wine from the local vineyard. She toasts me, I toast her. We don't do much talking, just a lot of eating. There is a knock at the door. The minute I open it, three waiters in tuxedoes blow past me with a whipped-cream cake topped with red roses and sparklers. "**Buon compleanno!**" they shout. Capri is delighted as I snap pictures of her grinning from behind the dazzling sparklers. One of the waiters gives Capri a card: "Happy birthday. I love you, Mom."

"Nobody loves you like your mother," I say.

"And nobody can suffocate you like your mother." Capri yanks the sparklers from the cake. "I know she means well. But oy vey. I'm sorry, I don't mean to complain. Thank you for taking this trip with me, and helping me celebrate my birthday."

"It's my pleasure."

"We've always been close."

"Yes, we have. Your family had the money and mine had the taste."

"I should warn you. Even though we told her there wasn't a chance in hell, Ma still hopes we'll get married. As I was leaving for the airport, she said, 'I wouldn't mind it a bit if you and B eloped over there.'"

"Did you tell her to mind her own business?"

"What would be the point? Besides, she's starting to accept some changes. I showed her the apartment, and she liked it. As much as she'd like anyplace I move into that wasn't the Villa di Crespi."

The air is filled with the sweet scent of night-blooming jasmine that shimmies down the outside wall on tangling vines so dense you can't see the stone wall underneath. If I learn one new thing on this trip, it will be draping. In Santa Margherita, the flowers seem to grow to accommodate the shapes underneath, nothing blooms in neat rows; no gardens look manicured. It's wild, messy, and Italian, and I love it.

"I don't miss New Jersey one bit," Capri says

as she leans over the balcony and looks out onto the gulf. She wraps her pink silk shawl with the pale blue fringe around her shoulders. The doorbell rings.

"They must be here for the dishes," I say, walking over to answer the door a second time. When I open the door, a slim, fortyish Italian around five feet six with black curls and thick eyebrows extends his hand. "**Ciao.** You are Bartolomeo di Crespi."

I've never heard my name pronounced so perfectly. "Yes, I am. And you are?"

"Eduardo Pinetti."

"Eddie Pinetti?"

"Oh, don't make jokes." Capri breezes past me and pulls Eduardo into the room. "He's making a joke," she explains to him.

"Oh, I see." Eduardo smiles.

"Do you two know each other?" I ask.

"Kind of. Florence, who does the books at the Parsippany branch of the bank, met Eduardo when she was here on vacation. So we wrote to each other and decided to meet when I visited."

"Oh, you have a . . . date?"

"Yep." Capri smiles. "You don't mind, do you, B? You told me you wanted to turn in early."

"I don't mind." But I sound annoyed.

"Eduardo's going to take me dancing."

"Wonderful."

"You are welcome to come too." Eduardo looks at me. I can tell he doesn't mean it.

"No, no, you two go. Have fun. I have lots to do tomorrow."

"Oh, good, because tomorrow Eduardo's going to take me out on his boat. He's going to show me the homes along the gulf."

Capri grabs her purse and takes Eddie's hand. "Sleep tight, B. Have some cake!"

They practically prance out the door. I pull my chair up to the table and stick my fork into the word **buon**. I taste it. The icing is light and sweet. I pour myself a glass of cold wine and toast the moon overhead, which happens to be the perfect shade of powder blue. This is obviously the land of lucky love, so of course the spinster with dry eyes is going dancing while the bachelor with stomach muscles tighter than the springs on a trampoline sits in a hotel room and eats cake.

I finally call Capri at noon, having waited an hour for her to show up at the restaurant for brunch. I feel bad when I call, but I don't want to fritter the day away waiting for Ginger Rogers to come to. When she answers the phone, I hear Eduardo in the background. Moral standards fly out the window in Italy. It's as if the perfume in the air, the hot sun, and the wine conspire to turn a rational person into a wanton sex kitten. Capri, obviously, is no exception.

I leave the hotel and head for the small winding street that leads to town. The houses are painted pale blue and tangerine with white trim, looking like marzipan fruit set in whipped cream. In the distance, at the end of the main street, I can see the church of Santa Margherita. Eydie told me that I would find inspiration there, and I'm hoping she's right.

I pass the cemetery, which looks more like a real estate development than a place of final rest. The ornate mausoleums are built closely together, like fancy townhouses. The people of this town have enormous egos, especially when they are dead. The marble and gold-leaf accents give the burial site the look of a small kingdom loaded with miniature palaces. While some are large enough to include gardens, others have their own breezeways with altars. Most boast shrines, busts of family members carved in relief in doors and on gates. Some are stucco and painted Mediterranean hues of butter yellow, periwinkle blue, and moss green. Some of the doors are carved wood, some include panes of stained glass. Some of the mausoleums have simple wrought-iron gates that lead to a statuary where the dearly departed reside in style on either side of a flowing fountain. I wish I could read all the messages carved outside the crypts. There are blessings and warnings and paintings of the departed. The pharaohs of Egypt have nothing on the Ligurian Italians when it comes to opulent burial.

I climb the steps to the entrance of the cathedral, which makes our church in OLOF look like a Christian Science reading room. The Greco-Roman exterior is stucco painted a ripe peach that shimmers in the Mediterranean sun; the ornate trim is painted a shimmery pearl. Stately Tuscan columns anchor the main entrance under a wedding-cake pediment, while tall pilasters surround the smaller doors. Overhead, a second story looms with a glorious statue of Saint Peter with two obelisks. When I look up, I see vivid shades of coral and white against the blue sky, reminding me of an open seashell.

Inside, I feel as though I've been rolled in luscious Florentine paper, a mosaic of ruby red and dark green with flecks of metallic gold. The frescoes, filled with scenes of noble saints being followed by a flock of Italians (must be the Crusades), are painted in authentic detail in a palette tinged with soft orange, heather blue, and faded purple. Every inch of the walls and vaulted ceiling is filled with images of heaven and earth and angels and sinners. It's as if the artists ran out of space to say what they were feeling, so they painted their message from the baseboards to the vaulted ceiling.

At the far end of the cathedral I can see the Blessed Lady in an indoor grotto. She wears a flowing blue robe, and a gold halo—a ribbon of stars—is suspended over her head. The rough stones beneath her feet dance in the light of votive candles. I am so drawn to her that I blow right past the altar to the shrine. The artist took natural gray and black fieldstones in varying sizes and mounted them on the wall haphazardly to look like the wall of a cave. Shards of stone jut out from the wall, their edges coated in shimmering sand.

The statue itself is propped on a stone ledge about twenty feet high. Behind her the wall is painted in gold leaf, which gives the illusion that she is suspended in midair like an angel.

Below her, kneeling in prayer, is a carved stone statue of Santa Margherita around the age of eleven. I reach up and touch the hem of her garment. I must not be the first to do this, as there's a worn-away spot in the marble where I imagine many others have reached to touch the young saint. It gives me great comfort to know that others have had the same need, to somehow get close to this scene, to be part of it.

Did they come seeking intercession? Healing? Inspiration? The majesty of a grand church like this one can be off-putting, when it's good old **connection** that a sinner really needs. The groove in the stone feels like the palm of a hand extended in comfort.

As I push my hands away from the wall, I feel something cool. I look down at my hands and then closely at the wall. Water trickles from the high rocks like a glassy ribbon, then disappears into a crevice behind the statue of Santa Margherita.

I kneel at her feet and begin to pray. I don't even know what this small girl with the tiny nose is famous for. A tall metal candelabra loaded with long white taper candles that burn at different heights looks like a picket fence in disrepair. I get up and light a candle that has gone out and make the sign of the cross. "Show me the way," I ask. But it's funny, in this moment I think I may have found it. Eydie was right. All the answers are in Italy. I have found mine in the Cathedral of Santa Margherita, while Capri has found hers in a speedboat tooling around the Gulf of Genoa.

I don't bother to unpack when I return home. I am filled with inspiration and can't wait to get to work. I call Two and Christina and tell them that I need them in my office as soon as possible. I am a man possessed by Gothic architecture, baroque statues, and the smiling faces of the rococo putti. I have the picture of the Cathedral of Santa Margherita in my mind, and I don't want to lose it before I can apply what I saw to our church. I don't want a single impulse to slip away. Christina takes notes while I sketch. The final days of August give way to the first crisp breezes of fall as we toil with our research.

Two types up notes and makes us lunch and, sometimes, when we work late, dinner. Amalia comes over after school as I thrash around the office thinking, creating, and sketching what I hope will become the greatest church in New Jersey. The Villa di Crespi has become a creative factory of ideas and possibilities. I'm operating at full tilt, and I love it.

Christina and I take a day trip to the stonemason's for samples of indigenous New Jersey rock. I want to use local materials in the renovation, so we spend a lot of time collecting wood samples, marble, and fieldstone.

"Look at these!" Two comes through the door with a large, open cardboard box.

"What have we got?"

"Fieldstone from Wainscott. Look at the color."

I hold up a sample. "Hmm. Dentyne." The stone is the exact shade of chewing gum.

"Too pink." Christina looks up from her notepad.

"Not as an accent in the grotto. Especially if we're going gold behind the Blessed Mother. I might be able to use this in the foyer, though, as a backdrop for the holy-water fonts."

"Nice," Christina approves.

"Unc, I dropped off the wingback chair at the Shumans'."

"Did you put it in place for her?"

"Oh, yeah. She loved it. Raved about it. I was wondering . . ."

"What?" I look up at my nephew.

"Could I do some sketches for you on Lina Aldo's house? You're so busy with the church, I thought maybe I could try out some ideas on you."

I think about it for a moment. I want to lecture him on how long it took me to become a decorator, education included, but I think better of it. "That's a great idea. Why don't you do a design board and room plan, and I'll look it over."

"Thanks, Unc." Two grabs the mail and goes to the post office.

"Are you sure you want the competition?" Christina smiles.

"It's all in the family. Wouldn't it be something if Two actually took an interest in the House of B? It's an Italian uncle's dream come true. I want to pass along more than my cuff-link collection. To see the House of B continue with the next generation would please me."

CHAPTER SEVEN

A Mural in Manasquan

Mother Nature sent a dusting of white glitter just in time for my annual Christmas party on December 3. The night sky is a lush navy blue and loaded with silver stars, giving the Villa di Crespi a Currier & Ives glow. I hear the creak of my kitchen door as I put the last bit of parsley garnish on a tray of mushroom puffs.

"This is the first time I've dared to wear strapless since 1951," Toot announces, "and what better place to reveal my décolletage than your living room." She steps inside, drops a mink shrug to the floor, and reveals a tasteful black strapless chemise.

"You look gorgeous, sis."

"I know. Have I got a story for you. Wait until you hear the latest about my sex life. Are you listening?"

"No," I say flatly, giving her a platter of mozzarella balls to take to the buffet.

"Well, I'll tell you anyway. I feel like I'm one of those pups-in-skirts acts in the circus. You know how the clown opens a box and one by one these toy poodles jump out in pink tutus and jump through gold rings? That's what it's like with Sal. We get through one hoop, and then there's another."

"He's a challenge?"

"Like you wouldn't believe. It's tough when they're sixty-plus. Stamina is definitely an issue." Toot picks up an iced snowman cookie, thinks better of it, and puts it back near the reindeer with the cinnamon-drop nose. "We were going along just fine, and then we had a little problem. The plumbing took a hiatus, you know what I mean?"

"Uh-huh."

"So now Sal gets very nervous when we get close to the deed. He gets himself so rattled we have to stop. He's afraid of another infraction—"

"Malfunction."

She ignores me and continues. "And I don't

know how to soothe him. I've tried rum and Coke, rum and coffee, rum cake, massage, Cuban cigars, and oysters. We get near the goal posts and he peters out. Maybe I'm too much for him. Maybe that's it."

"Toot, as devoted to you as I am, I'm begging you: Please don't tell me another thing about your sex life." I pick up a platter of potato wedges with sour cream and caviar. "Come on." Toot follows me to the dining room. "This is a very important night. It's not just my annual holiday party. It's the first visit from the artisans who are hopefully going to work with me on the church. Rufus and Pedro are finally coming to Jersey. I'm half sick to my stomach, because I've finished the design and now I have to show them. What if they hate what I've done?"

"Since when have you ever been nervous about a job?"

"The minute Father gave me the go-ahead."

"But you **wanted** it."

"That doesn't mean I'm not terrified."

Toot puts the platter of cheese on the table and turns to me. "Now, listen to me. Buck up. You're the best. You're a di Crespi, for godsakes. You're a damn good decorator. Look at your Christmas tree. Who has the guts to decorate a tree in red only? It's like the flames of holiday hell over here! Who thinks red lights, red ribbons, and red popcorn? I'll tell you who—a man with balls. It takes courage to march to the beat of your own drummer. So march!"

Toot's pep talk only makes me feel worse. The doorbell rings. Toot and I look at each other. "Aunt Edith," we say in unison. Toot follows me to the door.

I throw it open. "Merry Christmas, Aunt Edith!" I lean down and kiss her on both cheeks. She tastes like lilac and mothballs.

"I almost broke a hip on the ice. Where are the crabbies?" I point to the dining room and a large tray of Auntie's favorite English muffins baked with crab salad and cheddar cheese. I give cousin Marlene, Edith's daughter, a quick kiss as she helps Aunt Edith to the buffet. Marlene is a long, lean woman with wide hips. From the rear she resembles a bass fiddle. The cummerbund on her palazzo pants only emphasizes the shape. Aunt Edith throws the crabbies back like a handful of pain pills. Pia, who gave me the crabbie recipe, is cousin Carmine's sister. She has a way with all dishes made with mayo.

PIA'S CRABBIES
Yield: 48 Crabbies

½ cup butter, softened
1 cup shredded mozzarella
1 cup soft pimento cheese spread
2 tablespoons mayonnaise
1 clove garlic, minced
8 oz. crabmeat
8 English muffins, split
Paprika
Salt
1 cup shredded cheddar cheese

In a large bowl, blend the butter, the mozzarella, and the cheese spread. Add the mayonnaise, garlic, and crabmeat. Mix well. Spread on the muffin halves, and sprinkle with paprika. Salt to taste. Sprinkle the cheddar cheese on top. Place the muffins on a cookie sheet and broil until tops are golden. Cut each muffin half into 6 wedges, and serve.

"The house looks gorge," cousin Marlene says, drinking in my winter wonderland. "It's a lot of red, but I don't feel engulfed."

"Good." **Oh, shut it, Marlene, I think. You have the worst taste in the family. You did your living room in black and white. It's like sitting on the inside of a sock.**

The doorbell rings again. Toot answers it. The party started at 8:00 P.M., which means every cousin I have (fifty-seven confirmed) will arrive within three seconds of one another for the next ten minutes, making the house look like the last round-up in a Joel McCrea western. The di Crespis are nothing if not prompt.

"B! City people!" Toot calls from the door. I excuse myself from a conversation with cousin Marlene about eczema and head for the door.

"Eydie, darling!" I shout.

Eydie is swathed head to toe in ruby-red velvet. "Pa rum pum pum pum!" I say approvingly as I kiss her on both cheeks.

Eydie is accompanied by four handsome men in tuxedoes. "Thank goodness you have the originality to throw your bash on a Monday night. These are the lead dancers from **Hello, Dolly!**, and this is their dark night. This is Mark, Averell, and Sam. And this is the dance captain, Ronnie."

"We also sing," Sam says with a grin.

"Well, you'd better. My aunt Edith didn't schlep three blocks to watch you eat ring baloney on rye toast," I tell them.

The quartet bursts into "Jolly Old Saint Nicholas" in perfect four-part harmony.

"Oh, sing another, please!" Toot begs.

"After some vodka," Averell (I think) agrees.

"Get these chan-toozies some drinks!" Toot yells helpfully.

I mix four vodka collinses at the self-serve bar. On cue, my cousins pour into the house, chattering like wind-up Halloween teeth. I load the Hello Dollies' drinks on a tray. As I worm my way through the crowd, I hear my cousin Frannie give Marlene a quick holiday recipe. "All you do is get a block of Philadelphia cream cheese."

"Okay," Marlene says, concentrating.

"Take it out of the foil and put it on a plate. Then you bathe it in cocktail sauce, you know, ketchup, horseradish, and a shot of fresh lemon juice."

"You put that over the cream cheese?"

"Uh-huh. **Bathe** it. Make sure you use a big enough plate—you don't want the cocktail sauce runnin' all over the table. You know what? Use a platter and fan a box of Triscuits around it. Dip them in the cream cheese and cocktail sauce, and honest to God, you don't even miss the shrimp."

I shoot them a look. To bring up a cut-rate hors d'oeuvre recipe at my top-shelf party is not cricket.

Eydie has commandeered a drink from Uncle Petey, who had a few before the party (who are we kidding, he had a few before lunch), so he's

genuflecting on the ottoman, whispering something into her ear. She smiles politely, and then
I see him unfurl his purplish tongue into her ear
canal. "Uncle Petey, really!" I thunder. "Go into
the kitchen and have a cup of coffee immediately!" He scoots out quickly. "Sorry about that,
Eydie."

"It's okay. It was just a little tongue."

"It starts with a little tongue, and then you
know what happens."

"What?"

"Pretty soon he's playing horsie." She looks
at me. "You weren't here last year. After a couple of highballs, he almost rode Aunt Georgie
into the sunset."

"B! The door!" Toot hollers from corner of
the dining room where she is holding court
about how to jog over the age of fifty without
giving yourself a heart attack.

I tear myself away from Eydie and go to the
front door. "Rufus. Pedro." I shake their hands.
"Welcome to the Villa di Crespi, where the wine
is flowing and the women . . . well, you pick."

Rufus gives me a bottle of wine in a chic silver sack. Pedro hands me a carved wooden box.
"It's from Mexico," he says.

"Thank you," I say. "Rufus, the haircut is a
winner." From the neck up he looks like a
Roman soldier, with his thick hair brushed

back. From the neck down he is Princeton (on work study), natty in charcoal-gray wool trousers, a blue shirt, and a navy blue blazer. Pedro wears black slacks, a white shirt, and a black jacket.

"I didn't know you hired a valet," cousin Marlene says from behind me.

I spin around and whisper, "It's not a uniform. He's a guest."

Marlene shrugs. "I couldn't tell. Sorry."

I make a mental note to scratch her off my guest list permanently. Marlene is positively backward.

"Hi, cousin." Christina, looking like a goddess, gives me a kiss on the cheek.

"B, I made an ornament," Amalia says, handing me a glittering red construction-paper bird. "Don't worry. It's red."

"Go put it on the tree." Before she turns to go, I pull her aside. "You look very pretty," I tell her.

"I do not." She blushes.

"Your father would be very proud of you." She smiles at me. "Now, go hang that bird."

Rufus and Pedro are at the buffet table, where Christina joins them. In a simple black sleeveless shift and white pearls, her hair in an elegant upsweep, she is a real lady. I look over at Toot, who walks toward me hiking up the heart-shaped bodice of her strapless with both hands.

"B, say hello to Sal," she says gaily.

"Merry Christmas, Sal." I find myself looking away quickly, because now I don't see the face of my sister's boyfriend but a walking plumbing problem.

"Isn't he a peach?" Toot drapes herself across Sal like a car tarp. Sal has a round face and a square body, reminding me of the first clown I ever drew. He is bald with long sideburns and not very tall (it doesn't matter, Toot is five feet four). He wears a dark blue suit with a red tie. Toot points to my face and makes a circle around it. "B looks like Mama." She points to herself. "And I look like Daddy. Go figure." Sal laughs. He seems genuinely entertained by my sister.

"Who are you?" Toot takes one look at Rufus McSherry and sashays over to him, extending her gloved hand.

"Rufus McSherry."

"May I call you Sir Scrumptious? B, you didn't tell me Mr. McSherry was so ruggedly handsome," Toot says, practically purring. The strapless has really brought out her wild side. I'm mortified.

"I wanted you to see for yourself." I make my way around the sofa and yank open the windows, now that Toot is throwing more heat than a coal stove. "The buffet is in the dining room. The bar is in the den. If you go home hungry or sober, it's your own damn fault," I tell Sal. "Try the punch. It's Aunt Vi's recipe. She lived to be ninety-nine and swore it was the punch."

SANTA'S HELPERS
Aunt Vi's K.O. Christmas Punch

Two 6-ounce cans frozen pink lemonade
concentrate
1 cup fresh blueberries
16 maraschino cherries
1 quart raspberry ice or sherbet
2 bottles rosé (or any pink table wine)
Sugar
1 bottle sparkling rosé wine, chilled

Make one can pink lemonade from directions on the can. Fill 4 ice-cube trays with the lemonade. Drop one blueberry or maraschino cherry in each square. Freeze. In a punch bowl combine the sherbet, rosé wine, and the other can of lemonade concentrate, and stir until blended. Add sugar to taste. Right before serving, pour in the sparkling rosé, drop in Santa's presents—the lemonade ice cubes—and serve at once.

✳"Hello, Tootsie." Lonnie and Doris kiss Toot.

"Oh, I had no idea you were coming," Toot says, looking at me.

"I saw Doris at the A&P and we were fighting over the last tube of fig paste," I explain. "What can I say? They're family."

"Thanks, B." Lonnie says, smiling. Doris squeezes my hand.

"Well, since we're having a love-in, Lonnie, Doris, I'd like you to meet my . . . boyfriend, Sal Concarni."

"Of Belmar?" Doris asks.

"That's me."

"I think you fixed the pipes at my townhouse once."

"Oh yeah, yeah," Sal remembers. "You had that bilevel number in the Sea Girt Estates."

"Oh, I love a man who can roll up his sleeves and fix a clog," Toot says. "Sal is very talented." There is a long silence.

"Where would we be without sewage?" Lonnie makes an attempt at party chitchat. "Really, think about it. What kind of a stinkin' world would this be without pipes and drains and septic tanks and what have you?"

No one knows what to say. After what seems like an hour, I manage, "Why don't you have something from the buffet? I made veal parm, Doris. I know you like it."

Happy to be released, Doris leads Lonnie to the food.

"Look," Toot whispers.

At first I don't recognize the woman, then I realize it's my niece, Ondine. She is so puffy her face looks like a pancake with two chocolate chips for eyes. "What happened?" I ask Toot.

"Water weight. It's gotta be a girl."

"How do you know?"

"It's stealing her beauty."

I go to Ondine and give her a Christmas hug. "I'm enormous, B," she whines. "Look at my hands. They look like catcher's mitts." She holds them up. They do. "I can't wear my rings anymore, and Nicky has to shave my legs."

"Oh, dear." What is it about the women in my family? Have they no discernment?

Ondine continues, "It's horrible. Nobody told me."

"It will all be worth it when the baby gets here," I say.

"That's what everyone keeps saying. I hope they're right. What if the little slugger has hooves like that kid in **Rosemary's Baby**?"

"Now, now, only think nice thoughts. And remember, only see happy movies. The baby must be surrounded by pretty—even now. So, you go and have a meatball hero and relax. Where's your husband?"

"They started a card game in the kitchen."

I holler to my sister, who is showing off her boyfriend to the sodality ladies. "Toot, your sons are in my kitchen playing cards. Please go and remind them that the three wise men didn't stop for a game of five-card stud before they visited the manger. I want their asses in here. Now. Thank you!"

"Oh, B!" Capri gives me a quick kiss on the cheek. "I've got so much to tell you." She looks like an adorable elf in her green velvet pants and a red sweater with a wreath brooch.

"Where's your mother?" I ask.

"She wasn't feeling well because I moved out the last of my stuff today."

"For crying out loud, you've been moving out since August."

"I'm trying to ease Mom into it. But it's not working. It's always something. First it was her birthday. Then it was Dad's tree ceremony at B'nai B'rith. Then it was the anniversary of Daddy's death. Then she got a kidney stone. I thought my luck was changing when she passed it, but then she got slight anemia, and now they've come for the final boxes. I'm sorry."

"It's all right. Come with me. I want you to meet some genuine New Yorkers."

Eydie, Rufus, and Pedro have formed a little club with Christina, who seems to be giving them the lowdown on all things OLOF. "Say hello to Capri Mandelbaum," I say.

"What a beautiful name," Pedro says, rising to shake Capri's hand. He drinks her in like cousin Marlene did my Christmas tree.

"It's after the island. My parents went there on their honeymoon, and here I am. Something happened in the Blue Grotto, and it wasn't a night swim." Capri holds on to Pedro's hand a little too tightly, then moves on to Rufus, then Eydie.

"May I get you a drink?" Pedro asks Capri.

"I'll go with you." Capri smiles. I haven't seen this smile on Capri since she climbed aboard Eddie Pinetti's speedboat in the Gulf of Genoa.

"Do you know where the bar is?" I hear Pedro ask her.

"I know my way around the villa," she tells him. He puts his hand on Capri's back and follows her through the crowd.

"This is quite a party." Father Porporino greets me and hands me a Mass card.

"Glad you could make it." I am warm with Father, but I still feel a slight distrust. I don't ever want him to think he can push me around. "The artisans I hope to work with on the renovation are here. I'd like you to meet them."

"Of course, I'd be happy to."

"B, you've outdone yourself!" Zetta Montagna says as she joins us. She wears a white blouse and a plaid skirt, made festive with Christmas-tree earrings and a matching pin.

"Father?" One of the Broadway dancers charges up. "I'm Mark Aquilino."

"He's in **Hello, Dolly!**, Father," I explain.

"I've seen it twice!" Father beams, which I've never seen him do. "I'm sick it's closing."

"So are we," Mark tells him. "But that's showbiz. The boys and I were hoping you could do that Saint Blaise blessing on us—you know, the one for singers, where you crisscross the candles under our throats?"

"Now?" Father Porporino asks.

"We don't want to be a bother, but we live and die by our pipes, so any extra something you could throw our way to keep us on the boards would be great. Sam is Jewish, but he's willing to go for it too."

"I'll be happy to bless you," Father says. "All of you."

Mark turns around and throws his arms high in the air. "Windshield wipers up!" The other dancers follow suit.

I am temporarily mortified, but Father Porp seems to take no offense. In fact, who knew Father Porp liked American musicals? I took him for an Agatha Christie fan. "Padre's gonna send up a flare to Saint Blaise!" Mark declares. "I think that calls for a song."

They sing "Hello, Dolly!" a cappella. My living room and dining room are filled wall to wall with family and friends riveted by the performance. As the boys hold the final note, Toot's voice sails over the crowd, "Cripes, Sal. If there's a problem, fix it. I gotta lotta life left in me yet! Get yourself to the doctor." There is an awkward silence until I shout, "How about something Christmasy!" The boys launch into an upbeat "Jingle Bells," and I hope it helps everyone forget that Sal Concarni has a little problem down south.

A few guests remain in the living room, chatting around the fire. The last of the relatives have left, and with them, the last of the cookies. My family never leaves a crumb of dessert behind. This includes the chocolate Kisses that decorate the cookie trays. They each take a napkin and stuff it full of fig bars, almond biscotti, brownies dusted with powdered sugar, and coconut balls for snacking on the ride home or for dunking in **gabbagule** (espresso and hot milk in a bowl) for breakfast. Every family party concludes this way. You never get a good-bye hug, only a kiss on the cheek, because the guests are juggling their booty of sweets. My mother used to take leftover cake too, which required stealing a plate. When she died, we found a full set of mismatched dessert plates in her server. Instead of photographs in a scrapbook, my mother remembered people through the china she stole from them. Every once in a while she would hold up a plate: "Look, Zia Ola's Pfaltzgraff!"

I take the enormous ceramic conch full of melted ice where the shrimp cocktail was (all that's left are the rosettes carved out of lemon peels) into the kitchen. Toot has on rubber gloves and is washing dishes. "Don't do that," I tell her. "I'll take care of it in the morning."

"You don't want to wake up to party dishes. I'm almost done."

"Where's Sal?"

"I made him drive Aunt Edith and Marlene home. Marlene made a fool out of herself with the show people."

"What did she do?"

"Lifted her skirt and showed them her legs. She told them the story of Uncle Noog pulling her off the bus to New York City when she was seventeen and going in to audition for the Rockettes."

"No."

"Oh, yes, she even told them how he locked her in her room and called the priest. And how no one thought it strange when the priest didn't come out of her room for twelve hours. They were riveted." Toot snaps off the Playtex gloves. "I'm going home."

"Isn't Sal coming to get you?"

"I told him to go on home after he did shuttle duty. I drove myself over anyhow."

"But what about . . ."

"Some holiday nooky? I know, look at me in a strapless. What a waste. Well, he was tired. So there's no sense going back to my place and hearing him snore all night long. It dawned on me when I was helping him read the dosage on his blood-pressure medication that I may have to find somebody younger. This is too hard."

"I'm sorry, Toot."

"When's it gonna be about me? When?"

"In the new year. We hope."

Toot gives me a kiss on the cheek, anchors her fur shrug over her shoulders with a yank, and goes out the back door. I turn on the porch lights and follow her out until she's safely in her car.

Rufus and Pedro have pulled two of my dining room chairs over to the loveseat in the living room where Capri and Christina sit. They laugh under a hazy cloud of cigarette smoke that hangs over them like a canopy. I blow out the candelabra on the dining table (two tapers are missing—Father Porp must've blessed the dancers' throats after all) and join them.

"I'm starving," I announce. "I never eat at my own parties. Anyone for pancakes at the Tic-Tock?"

My favorite thing about my Festa di Crespi is when it's over. I seize a moment to breathe and reflect on the fun. As I watch Capri and Christina dig into their pancakes, it dawns on me that I have never seen Capri so happy or Christina so animated since Charlie died. Boy oh boy, nothing like a couple of swinging bachelors from the big city to get the local girls' blood pumping. Can it be that I'm the man they tell their troubles to, so I never see them at their flirtatious best?

"Where's Amalia?" I ask Christina.

"She went home with cousin Cathy. Her kids love when Amalia stays over. My daughter would give anything to live in New York."

"Wouldn't we all?" I say wistfully.

"There's nothing wrong with your spread," Rufus says.

"B was smart," Christina says. "He bought that house when no one was living over by water. And now look."

"No, don't get me wrong, I love my house. But I do feel a little tug of regret when I see Eydie get into her town car and head back to

Manhattan for a bar crawl and all-night dancing."

"I'd move into the city, but it would kill my mother." Capri lights a cigarette, then passes the pack around.

"Then you shouldn't do it," Pedro says solemnly.

"The stress of upsetting her always outweighed my desire for personal freedom. But not anymore. I have to move on. At least to West Long Branch. Right, B?"

"One stick of furniture at a time. By 1980 you should be moved out completely."

"I met your priest," Rufus says, smiling.

"What did you think?"

"He's a cleric." Rufus shrugs.

"What the hell does **that** mean?" The way I ask this question makes everyone laugh.

"It means he toes the company line. He asked what my role was in the renovation. And I told him I just met you and I hadn't seen the church yet. He looked at me and said, 'Don't touch the choir loft.' "

"You see what I have to deal with? Small minds!" I throw my hands in the air.

"I was hoping I'd get to see the church. If you tell us where it is, Pedro and I can swing by and see the exterior tonight."

"I have a key. Let's go."

I feel like a high school kid again as I sneak Rufus, Christina, and Capri through the side door of Our Lady of Fatima and lock it behind us.

I turn on the lights. Rufus begins to look around. Pedro walks up the side aisle and genuflects before going behind the altar to look at the fresco. I forgot that Mexico is 90 percent Catholic. The girls and I join him. "What do you think?" I ask Pedro.

"It's very nice," he says quietly.

"There's a lot of potential here," Rufus says from behind us. "I like the height, the arcades, and the rib vaulting. Very nice."

"How about the mural?" I point.

"It was painted by my great-uncle by marriage, Michael Menecola," Christina tells Rufus.

"He painted all the signs in the town. And he painted company logos on trucks and things." I don't want to give Rufus the impression that we think Michael Menecola was Michelangelo. He was a painter who could copy from other pictures, not a true artist. Rufus touches the wall. Pedro joins him.

"It doesn't tell the whole story," Pedro says, flicking a bit of the paint with his fingernail.

"The story of Fatima is so much more than this." He points to the Blessed Mother floating overhead and the three children looking up at her.

"But what happened, exactly? I remember the kids had visions." Rufus looks at Pedro.

"Well, Fatima was actually a Muslim princess who lived in Portugal when it was occupied by her people. She died young, but after she converted to Catholicism."

"I didn't know that," I say. "Twelve years of nuns browbeating me with useless information, and I never learned that. Go on."

"In 1917, during the First World War, three little children, Lucia, Francisco, and Jacinta, were tending sheep, and they saw what they called 'the Angel of Peace' in the sky. They returned to the field many times, and sometimes the angel would appear to them. Months later, they saw an apparition they called 'the Lady of the Rosary.' She gave them Communion. So the kids told everyone they knew about what they saw and what she had done. The word spread, and on the day the Lady promised to appear again, thousands of people gathered to see her."

"And," Christina continues, "that's when the miracle of the sun happened. The people were praying, and then the sun turned black and seemed to spin out of the sky like a top. People were screaming, and then it started to pour rain. The field, according to reports, turned to mud, and they couldn't move. Then suddenly the sun returned overhead, bright as ever, and she appeared again, the Lady of the Rosary. And the people were dry instantly, and the earth was dry. No one could believe it. And then she spoke to them."

"This is giving me the creeps," Capri says, tightening the belt of her coat. "Remember, folks, I'm half Jewish. We don't do miracles." Capri sits on Father's chair. "If you're gonna tell scary stories, I need a drink. Rumor has it there's wine around here somewhere."

"The Blessed Mother had three secrets," Pedro continues.

"I'm warning you all," Capri whines. "I'm getting chills."

"What were they?" Rufus asks as he checks the supports to the vaulted ceiling.

"World War I would end, but if people didn't repent, there would be a worse war on the way," Christina says.

"Well, that certainly turned out to be true," I say.

"And the second secret was that believers needed to pray to convert Russia away from communism. And then there's a third secret that was supposed to be revealed in the last decade, but the Pope decided to wait until the year 2000." Pedro quietly finishes the story.

A shiver runs through me. Father Porp has always been cheap with the heat. We stand in silence looking at the mural. The face of the Blessed Lady, which I have prayed to without fail all of my life, suddenly seems bored by the whole scene. I used to believe that expression was one of quiet intelligence, but now it seems like she's saying, "Oh, get on with it." We hear footsteps. We look at one another and freeze.

"Someone's here," Christina whispers to me.

The sounds are coming from the sacristy. Father Porporino emerges from the door. "What's going on here?"

"Father! Whew. I thought it was a ghost."

"Or the Lady of Fatima making a Jersey appearance," Capri says wryly. Father does not find this funny.

From my place closest to the door, I see a shadowy figure slip out of the sacristy, through the door that leads to a hallway, then to the cemetery. Father doesn't notice that I saw anything. He casually closes the sacristy door behind him and joins us.

"I wanted Mr. McSherry and Mr. Alarcon to see the church while they're here." I chirp just like I did when I was a boy caught making figurines with the candle wax after Mass.

"Oh." Father Porporino seems nervous.

"I'm finished with my plans for the renovation, and I wanted to toss around some ideas with Mr. McSherry."

"It's a beautiful church." Rufus's compliment seems to go a long way with Father Porp.

"Thank you." Father smiles. "Let me show you around." Capri looks at me as though she'd rather gnaw on a pipe than get another tour, but I shoot her a "keep quiet" look.

"Any idea about that third secret of Fatima, Father?" I ask as he walks us to the side door after the tour.

"There are a lot of rumors, but no one knows for sure."

"Nobody can keep secrets like the Catholic Church," Capri mumbles.

We bid Father Porporino good night, and once we're outside, we laugh like a pack of teenagers caught with a six-pack and a **Playboy** after school. Capri and Christina say good night and get into my car. I walk Rufus and Pedro to theirs.

"So, what do you think?" I ask Rufus, pointing to the church.

"What do you have in mind?" he says as he lights a cigarette.

"I want to blow it wide open. New fresco, stained-glass windows, grotto, and floor plan."

"Let's figure out a time when you can show me the plans."

"Absolutely. So can I count you in?" I ask him hopefully.

"Count me in," he says and smiles.

As they drive away, I can't help but look up at the night sky and holler, "Thank you, thank you, thank you!" The Bernini of Bay Ridge, Brooklyn, is on board, so anything is possible.

The last bit of wisdom my professor Maeve Schlondorf imparted to me prior to my graduation from Parsons was "Never, never, never give anything away for free. Not advice, not a throw pillow, and not an ashtray. Nothing! We must train the public to hire interior decorators." I should have listened. Instead, I find myself driving to Manasquan to install a wall mural for Toot's college roommate, Booboo Miglio (one of the gregarious bobby-soxers from the all-girl St. Elizabeth's College, Convent Station, New Jersey, Class of 1940), for free.

I park in front of her Victorian on Hammer Avenue (Victorians, as a general rule, don't have driveways or garages, which is the first reason not to live in one). Booboo's yard is loaded with Christmas claptrap, life-sized plastic choir boys, and enormous candy canes, stuck in the ground like striped stakes. On the roof, Santa and his sled pulled by the reindeer are anchored on the gutter. Christmas in Squan is always decorative. I pull the mural out of my trunk, along with a tub of wallpaper paste and my tools. She greets me on the porch.

"Bartolomeo, hun-nee!" Booboo is still a girl, despite five children in quick succession and a husband who drinks. She has kept the ready-kilowatt smile and trim figure of her youth. An adorable brunette with a cap of curls and sparkling brown eyes, she likes beautiful things but cannot afford them, which I find endearing. People who like nice things should have them. Booboo holds the door open as I wedge past.

"Merry Christmas! Get rid of that screen door," I chide her. "It's winter."

"I know. By the time I get around to it, it's spring, so I just leave it."

"Remember what Aristotle said: 'Good style must be clear, it must be appropriate.' A screen door on a house in winter is like a sled in the swimming pool in summer."

Per my instruction, Booboo decorated her house in soft yellow and white. The furniture is covered in a sturdy, tufted cotton check—simple, clean, and cheery. When there's a gang of kids in a house, everything should be washable, so she used a clear lacquer sheen over the paint on her walls so she can wash them down like the family dog.

Booboo has cleared the wall in her living room and prepped it as I asked, so all I need to do is hang the mural. I spread the wallpaper paste evenly over a quarter of the wall. She helps me unroll the first of four panels and place it on the paste. "This is going to be stunning!" she squeals, clapping her hands. "You know, I need a little Italy in my life. A Venetian carnival. A seaside holiday. A little Rome, a little rococo."

"What you're getting is the harbor at Portofino." She doesn't need to know that they had a showroom final sale at D&D and I picked it up for a song.

"I love it already. I'll have a destination on my wall, and I don't have to actually go there."

"That's the idea." I step back after smoothing down the panel and see a few boats bobbing in bright blue water at the foot of the stone cliffs on the glittering Mediterranean.

"It will brighten up the whole house," Booboo says. "Did you know your sister is sleeping with her ex-husband?"

"**What?**"

"Toot is sleeping with Lonnie. They got together the Tuesday after your party. That strapless she wore drove him nuts. So they made a date. They went to Voltaco's in Ocean City for hoagies and then grabbed a hotel room."

"I don't need to know this."

"Somebody has to talk to her. She'll listen to you."

"I'm her brother. I don't want to know this stuff. Besides, she's dating Sal Concarni."

"He's impotent."

"Dear God. She told you **that**?"

"Your sister got tired of Sal's excuses—all to avoid . . . you know. Plus, he refuses to go to a doctor. What do men think, anyhow? That a lump goes away on its own? That a peter rises to every occasion without medical intervention? Anyhow, Toot has needs and Sal wasn't meeting them. He said he was tired all the time. He also drinks." Booboo motions toward the kitchen.

"Is your husband home?"

"No, he's at work. I just point to the kitchen because that's where the beer is kept."

"Oh."

"At a certain point, when a man drinks, it affects the apparatus." Booboo makes a sweeping gesture toward her thighs.

"Say no more."

"I have the same problem over here, but the difference is, I don't want to have sex with my husband. If it never happens again in my natural lifetime, that will be absolutely fine with me."

"Booboo, really. This is none of my business."

"I'm telling you, a man hits, let's say fifty-seven or so, my Vinnie is fifty-eight, and it goes away."

"I don't want to hear this."

"It's difficult for a man. You know, all your equipment is outside, and it has to work to be effective. Women can pretend to enjoy it or really enjoy it or not, it's all the same to your partner. But a man has to perform. It must feel like a burden. It can't be easy."

"No, it isn't."

"It's also the age. I mean, in a perfect world, I'd like to have a younger man. I didn't count on winding up with Grandpa over here. But what's a girl supposed to do?"

I feel myself getting claustrophobic, so I make fast work of the final panel, which features a couple in a rowboat reading to each other at the base of the mural.

"Oh look, young love." Booboo sighs. "You know what I tell my children?"

"What?" In all honesty, I am afraid to find out.

"Make love while you're young, while you're brisk and supple and interested in it. Because someday it will leave you just as it came—in an instant." She snaps her fingers.

I look her right in the eye. "Did **anything** the nuns at Convent Station drilled into you girls stick? My sister is gallivanting around in fleabag motels with a man from whom she was bitterly divorced. And you are instructing your children to enroll in Free Love Camp. Tell me, is this what the Holy Roman Church had in mind when they inculcated us with their dogma? What the hell is going on?"

"Life."

I present my final plans for the church renovation on December 13 at the last scheduled parish council meeting of the year, with Rufus and Pedro in attendance. Father Porporino is very curious, as is the council, whose members have called me individually at home. We gather in the church basement, surrounded by the unfurled flags of the Knights of Columbus, which are displayed on poles around the room like an indoor United Nations Plaza.

Rufus and Pedro are good sports. They drove out to meet everyone and hear my ideas. The council members sit at a long bingo table with their notes in front of them. Rufus and Pedro sit at the head of the table with me. I've laid out fresh doughnuts and a pot of coffee, and Zetta made a plate of fudge, which she passes around the room.

The entire leadership of our church is in attendance. Sister Mary Michael, principal of our parish-operated grade school; Zetta Montagna, president of the sodality; Aurelia Mandelbaum, chair of the Ways and Means Committee; Zeke Nero, Exterior Grounds and Fountains; Tulio Savastanno, Cemetery Maintenance; Father Porp, RC Incorporated. And recently elected to four-year terms on the council: Artie Rego, Gus Lascola, Finola Franco, and Palmie Barrone. Christina takes notes. Perky Marie Cascario, recording secretary, takes the minutes.

Father Porp calls the meeting to order and turns the meeting over to me.

"Thank you, Father. I've dreamed all my life of renovating our church. I'm not going to kid you, it needs it. Besides the aesthetics, we have some structural issues. Our engineer, Norman Thresher, came in and surveyed the building." I hand a stack of mimeographed reports to Christina, who gets up and distributes them around the table. "There is work to be done on the foundation, the stonework needs repointing, and there are issues with the roof."

"Slow down, B, I'm getting a corn on my middle finger," Marie complains.

"Don't press so hard on your pencil," advises

Sister Mary Michael, who taught everybody in OLOF under the age of fifty to write.

For the life of me, I have never understood why the slowest woman in the parish is the recording secretary. I continue, upbeat yet speaking slowly and deliberately so poor Marie can keep up. "And then, once the building is secure, we will begin our renovation. My plans will go to the architect Severino Carosso, who will turn them around for the engineer. We will need to close the church at least until next summer."

"Where will we have Mass?" Finola asks.

"The gym at OLOF High," Father answers.

"You can't hear a thing in there," Finola complains. "You might as well have Mass on the turnpike."

"What's the budget for this thing?" Palmie asks as he dumps a carload of sugar into his black coffee. Never mind that he's a diabetic.

"Aurelia Mandelbaum has graciously financed the renovation. A working budget can be found on page three of your report. Please note that not a penny of the church coffers will be used. Beyond that, I don't like to talk money."

"I don't either," Aurelia seconds me. "It takes the starch out of giving, my Sy used to say."

"What's the church gonna look like when you're done with it?" Tulio asks.

"It will be majestic and inspirational. You

can see some of my sketches on pages eight through twelve of the report. These are not set in stone. I'll be consulting with Rufus McSherry before we make any final decisions." I cut Tulio off because he is a malcontent who never has anything good to say about any project we undertake. He waited so long to make a decision about fixing the gutters in the church plaza that we had a flood on Easter Sunday 1969 that required half the congregation to skip the Mass of the Resurrection because they could not navigate the rushing water. Then I drive my point home. "I would like to introduce Rufus McSherry, the artist who will implement the design, paint the fresco, and, with the help of Pedro Alarcon, his talented apprentice, refurbish the stained-glass windows. Rufus and Pedro stand to a round of applause, then sit. "Any questions?"

"We gotta top St. Catharine's in Spring Lake," Finola says, pulling a hot-pink emery board out of her purse and commencing to file her thumbnail. "It's a replica of Santa Maria del Popolo in Vatican City." She points her file at me. "Three of my cousins were married there. I don't think we can beat its majestic grandeur, if you know what I mean."

"I think I do. Look at my drawings," I tell her bluntly. "We aren't trying to **beat** Spring

Lake, folks. We want our church to make its own statement and reflect the faithful of **our** community."

Gus Lacola says, "Yeah, okay, but be careful. Don't go off half-cocked and change everything. We worship in this church here, and we don't want some newfangled thing like they got over in Lambertville, where people are sitting on the floor singing to a yippie-dippie with a guitar and there's a modern dance during the Offertory and the priest half the time don't wear a collar. I don't want to see a buncha kids in leotards doing backflips when I'm taking my sacraments. We want what we're used to. Good ole' meat and potatoes Catholicism. Smells and bells. Just like they got over in Rome."

"Aurelia?" I look pleadingly toward The Benefactor for support.

"I trust Bartolomeo," she says simply.

I try not to sound terse when I address the skeptics on the council. "Gus, I'm going to be honest with you. Forget about Rome. The Pope doesn't really give a fig about Our Lady of Fatima. Aurelia has financed this renovation. The Diocese of Trenton could care even less— they told us to fend for ourselves financially because our congregation has always been self-supporting."

"The good people who pull their weight are

always punished," Marie clucks as she puts down her pencil and rubs her middle finger.

I ignore her. "For example," I continue, "we built our own schools and we finance them. And luckily, we were able to have the good sisters come and teach for free." Sister Mary Michael nods and smiles and moves her giant cross necklace to the center of her habit and pats it.

"Father?" I look to him for support.

"You're the expert." Father shrugs. I shoot him a look that says, **Thanks for the support, Padre.**

Aurelia raises her hand. "I gave the money for this renovation because Father asked me for it, and because when the full choir is in the loft we're afraid we're going to break through to the main floor and be killed in one of those trampling deaths. The church needs fixing and it needs it now. I trust Bartolomeo to deliver us a sanctuary in good taste."

"Thank you, Aurelia."

"I only ask for one thing in return. A cry room for the little ones. I can't hear myself think in Mass. People don't control their children worth a damn anymore."

The council nods in agreement, passing Aurelia's proposal with a unanimous vote.

As I climb the steps from the church basement to the nave, I hear Rufus and Pedro talking. They sit on the steps in front of the main altar, surrounded by blueprints of the church structure. The interior has been completely stripped; the statues, pews, and altar are in storage. There are paint shadows on the walls where the stations of the cross hung. I practically skip down the main aisle to join them. "Sorry that took so long, guys. I had to do a little post-meeting massaging."

Rufus studies my sketches. "This is it, huh?"

"That's it," I tell him.

"There's definitely something here."

"Something?" I hope I don't sound defensive.

"It's a start." He doesn't take his eyes off the sketches.

"I was hoping you'd say it was inspired and new and my sketches surprised you."

"Well, they're none of those things," he says flatly.

I feel my stomach flutter. "What do you mean?"

"This is a standard redo of what was here. It's just another church. There are some new elements, like the shrine to Mary, but other than that, it's pretty dull."

"What do you recommend?" My voice breaks.

"We need a focal point. A statement. Something that makes Fatima Church stand out from the rest."

"Okay." I've been self-employed all my life, and so I'm used to criticism. But his dismissive attitude hurts my feelings. After all, I worked for months on this renovation. Doesn't he realize this?

Rufus scatters my sketches on the floor like pages from an old newspaper. "What have we got to lose? You've got the dough and the cleric over a barrel. He'd agree to anything, so why don't you go with **something**? Let's think big." He gets up and looks around. "You want to blow out the ceiling with skylights, but for what?"

"Light!" My voice echoes in the vast emptiness.

"It should illuminate something besides a traditional altar. I'd like to make a suggestion."

"Go ahead."

"A moving wall of water."

"Where?"

"Behind the altar. Look, you have a wall there that is fifty feet high. Let's use it. We do a full mosaic wall of indigenous stone. And then we add water streaming down the wall in a way that makes it look like glass. You could have a pool, a trough basically, that recycles the water but also can be used to baptize your babies. Water is the fundamental element of your religion. It's also the fundamental element of life. You get the picture."

"Well, I was thinking water for the grotto." I point to the shrine to Mary.

"Why put your focal point in a corner? Let's get it out front and center," Rufus says impatiently.

"I want a fresco and I want stained-glass windows."

"You'll get them. But first you need to show us on paper exactly what your dream is. I don't see anything here that really soars above the expected and the ordinary, B. I don't think you've cracked this yet. Think about the miracle at Fatima. There are real clues in that story that could help you reinvent this place in a most original way."

"I don't want a moving wall of water," I say petulantly.

"Okay." Rufus shrugs. "Why?"

"Because I . . . I just don't like it."

"You told the folks in the meeting that you didn't want their input. Now I see why. You don't like to hear new ideas. You won't even consider them. You're threatened by them."

"I am not!" I sound like a child, but I don't care. This is **my** church. No one is going to tell me how to do my job!

"Okay." Rufus fishes in his pockets for his cigarettes.

"Are you comfortable following instructions?" I ask him pointedly.

Rufus leans against the altar, puts the cigarette in his mouth, but does not light it. "Not really."

"Then we have a problem."

Rufus puts his hands on the altar. "Look. I have a lot of notions. Some are kind of wild and others are fairly traditional. I'm not right all the time, but I think I can push you to take some chances. You need a worldview here. Your design is stale. I've restored a lot of churches, and I don't think you should do the same old thing. You have the money and you have the time and you have the support of the priest. You should really shake it down."

"Skylights and fabric and a marble floor treatment and a new altar and fresco and windows are what the place requires," I say firmly.

"Why?"

"Because it's a house of God and there are stipulations."

"Why?"

"It's the way it's been done since Jerusalem!"

"I thought this job was about breaking rules and reinventing the wheel. The people of this town could use that. They need a jolt of something. If that parish council is any indication, they aren't feeling the rapture."

"We need a church that looks like a church," I reply. "It has to be a house of worship. Look." I pick up my sketches. "The nave, the baptistery, the altar, the shrine to Mary, all of it is here. I went to Italy and I found a church that inspired my design. I need artisans who understand history and have the expertise to refurbish this church."

"No, it sounds like you're looking for a couple of foot soldiers to follow orders. That's not what we do."

"What do you do?" I ask him impatiently.

Rufus takes a deep breath. "We find the magic." He looks at Pedro. Pedro nods.

"That's all well and good, but I need craftsmen to deliver my design. You should know that I've sat in this church for thirty years and reimagined this place a million times. I know what I'm talking about."

"That's what you keep telling everybody. But I don't see your imagination at work, B."

"I'm sorry you feel that way."

"There's nothing to be sorry about. I have a different idea about what kind of house God might like. But you're a company man, you want to deliver what makes everybody comfortable. Look at your drawings. Except for some new windows and some color, it's the same place it was before. I think the people will dig it, but you can sell people anything."

"What's that supposed to mean? That we're a bunch of sheep? You heard Gus Lascola; he doesn't want anything new."

Rufus shrugs. "Why listen to him? Is he an artist?"

"No, but—"

"B, why don't you trust your own voice? You're letting these folks tell you how to think. You're snuffing your creative spark before it's even lit."

"I'm offended by that." I hear myself whine, so I take a breath. "I am honoring the spark."

"No, you're not. You're pandering. You say you want to fly, but you're falling back on the tried and true. You've probably got a brilliant concept in you, but it's totally bogged down in rules, dogma, and the past. There is no right or wrong in art. And when it comes to churches, it's an expression of a spiritual longing. You are not hearing it, man."

"I am completely flabbergasted!" My voice thunders.

"Good! It's the first sign of juice you've

demonstrated," Rufus says evenly. "You are stuck. Stuck in the mud of mediocrity." He looks at Pedro, then back at me. "You don't really want what we do."

"If that's how you feel . . ." I raise my voice.

"That's how it is," Rufus replies.

Without saying good-bye, Rufus and Pedro walk down the aisle and out the front door. I almost call them back when I remember the glorious clouds Rufus painted, Pedro's shimmering shards of stained glass, and how much fun the two of them were the night of my party. But I'm too proud to run after them. This job means too much to me. How dare Rufus Mc-Sherry tell me I lack the magic to reinvent Fatima Church? How dare he judge my talent and vision! I hear his truck drive off, and not for a single second do I wish to stop him.

CHAPTER EIGHT

Mrs. Mandelbaum Regrets

It pours cold rain all Christmas Day. My red tree twinkles and blinks like a big ruby ring on an old lady's finger, but even that can't cheer me up. I canceled Christmas dinner here. Ondine offered to make duck in Freehold, so Toot and the boys will go there. I've never had a Christmas alone, and while it's painful, I want to wallow in my misery. I am hurt by Rufus's assault, and I'm not sure how long it will take me to get over it.

I stack my records on the stereo, careful not to scratch them. I have all the Firestone Christmas albums, from Bing Crosby to the Ray Coniff Singers. I flip the ejector when I hear the violins prelude to "Angels We Have Heard on High." I kick off my loafers, lie down on the sofa, and look at the tree, getting lost in the red of it all.

The doorbell rings, which should irritate me; after all, I am falling deep into my depression like an olive in oil, but instead, I spring to my feet in hopeful anticipation and open the door.

"Merry Christmas!" Amalia and Christina say in unison.

"We heard you were home." Christina peels off her gloves, while Amalia kicks off her boots. "Is Ondine's cooking that bad?"

"That baby is going to starve, that's all I'm going to say."

"She's due any day now, you know. Fix me a drink, please." Christina sits down on the couch.

"Why aren't you at the Menecolas'?"

"We did Christmas Eve with them. Night of the seven fishes and the seventeen arguments."

"They fight a lot, B," Amalia says.

"Well, that's just part of a holiday celebration. Remember our cousin Renata?"

"Iggy With The Asthma's daughter?"

"The very one. She used to come for Christmas, we could seat thirty-two in the basement of Ma's house. Within forty-eight hours of her arrival, Renata would have a complete nervous breakdown and tantrum after God-knows-who said God-knows-what to her. She'd grab her suitcase and storm out in the middle of dinner

in a huff. She'd be out on Route 35 in tears trying to hail a cab to Newark Airport."

"She was a little nutty," Christina agrees.

"She didn't want to do the dishes," I tell
them. "We'd all get up, go after her, beg her forgiveness, and she'd return for dessert."

"Well, she provided the usual drama at the
Menecolas' this year. She left during the bac-
cala. Iggy put out a search party and brought
her back by the tiramisu."

"Great. Glad **her** holiday turned out well."

"How are you holding up?" Christina puts
her feet on the ottoman and looks at me.

"I'm fine for someone who has been person-
ally attacked, had his professionalism questioned, his integrity violated, and his vision
trivialized. Other than that, I'm great."

"What are you going to do?"

"I met with some people. They call themselves artisans, but they're really just contractors
who drywall churches. The bishop has a list. I
wasn't very impressed. I called Eydie before she
left for France—she does Christmas in Paris
every year—and she was very sympathetic. She
said Rufus is a genius. The problem with ge-
niuses is they tend to be temperamental."

"That wasn't his temper talking. He just
didn't like your ideas."

"Don't pile on."

"Don't get defensive. He thought you could do better."

"Did he tell you that?"

"No. You did."

"Well, that was a very cruel thing to say!" I sound like a two-year-old.

"He wasn't being mean. He was being honest. And nobody in OLOF is ever honest, so when the truth is spoken, it stings."

"My God, cousin, did you intend to come over here on Christmas Day and make everything worse? You know I poured myself into the design. I have nothing left to give. Whose side are you on, anyway?"

"I'm on the side of people saying what they mean. I don't know anything about what you do. I work for you, but usually I'm just in awe of how you come up with your ideas, and the big picture is not something I understand. I know what I like, but I wouldn't know how to go about putting it together. You're the artist. That's what you do."

"You wouldn't know it by talking to Rufus. He wanted nothing to do with my ideas."

"Sounds like he was pushing you to be great, not putting you down."

"Well, that might be his version." I pout.

"You waited months to get him here. Why don't you pick up the phone and call him?"

"And say what? 'You're right, Rufus. I stink!' "

"Arrange a meeting. Talk things through."

Amalia comes from the kitchen with Christmas cookies she's arranged on a plate. "Can I make hot chocolate?"

"No!" Christina and I shout in unison.

"Why not?"

"Because I make the best hot chocolate in New Jersey," I reply, gently this time.

"So, you make it." Amalia rolls her eyes. "I hope you guys realize that you just yelled at me on Christmas. I don't think I need that in my holiday memory book."

"Follow me," I tell them.

BARTOLOMEO'S HOT CHOCOLATE
Yield: 4 cups

½ cup cocoa
1 tablespoon flour
½ cup dark brown sugar, packed
2 tablespoons confectioner's sugar
1½ teaspoons vanilla extract
1½ teaspoons coconut flavoring
4 cups whole milk

FRESH WHIPPED CREAM
1 cup heavy cream
¼ cup confectioner's sugar
1 teaspoon vanilla extract
4 cinnamon sticks

Mix the cocoa, flour, brown sugar, confectioner's sugar, vanilla extract, coconut flavoring, and milk in a saucepan. Cook over low heat until all the dry ingredients dissolve. Using a whisk, blend well until it steams. In a bowl, whip the heavy cream, confectioner's sugar, and vanilla extract until stiff. Pour the mixture into 4 mugs, and top with a dollop of whipped cream. Use one cinnamon stick per mug as a stirrer.

Amalia and Christina sit at the kitchen table while I pour the steaming hot chocolate into big, white ceramic mugs. I ladle lots of fresh whipped cream on top, then drop a bourbon ball into my mug and Christina's.

BOOBOO MIGLIO'S BOURBON BALLS
1 cup finely chopped walnuts
1 cup confectioner's sugar
2 tablespoons cocoa
1 cup vanilla wafers, crushed
1½ tablespoons corn syrup
¼ cup bourbon
Confectioner's sugar for dusting

In a bowl, mix the walnuts, confectioner's sugar, cocoa, and vanilla-wafer crumbs. Add the corn syrup and bourbon, and knead to a doughy consistency. Use a melon baller and roll into small balls. Roll in the confectioner's sugar to coat. Makes about 45 balls. Store in an airtight container in the fridge until serving time.

"Come on," Amalia whines. "I'm going to be thirteen in January. Give me a bourbon ball too." I look at Christina, who nods. After all, it's Christmas, and I know of very few grown-up rum hounds who went down the wrong path because they ate one bourbon ball during the holidays. I drop one in Amalia's mug.

"Thanks, B." She smiles.

"Merry Christmas," I tell her.

"I want your honest opinion," I tell Two. "Look at these drawings and tell me if you think they're . . . good." I spent the Christmas holiday drawing a new group of sketches for the church.

Two carefully, flips through the spiral-bound notebook, stopping to study details. Finally, after a few minutes and a trip to the kitchen to pour a cup of coffee, I return to my study to hear what he has to say. "Nobody has eye for color and symmetry like you do."

"Thank you. So you think they're good?"

"It was built in 1899. This is the first renovation. Of course, there's annual maintenance. Painting, new roof, that sort of thing. So it's unlikely that there will be another renovation for a hundred years or so."

"Right, right," I say impatiently.

"The reason I'm asking, what do you envision the church to be a hundred years from now?"

Two's words ring in my ears, and suddenly he morphs from my favorite nephew to the giant Rufus McSherry, both of whom now have criticized my design.

"Unc, you're designing a house of salvation," Two says quietly. "What should a person feel like when they enter such a place? That's all I'm asking."

I pace around the study, then grab my jacket, hat, and gloves and head for the front door.

"Sorry!" Two calls after me.

"I'll be back later," I snap at him without looking back.

I slam the door behind me and cross the yard to the beach. My feet crunch on the sand, which is covered in patches of ice and frost, as I stride angrily to the water's edge. The ocean in winter is an endless gray blur, a giant well of sadness and despair. There is no sun today, just a cold final day of the year 1970. How promising this year began, and how sick I am that it is ending on such a sour note.

I don't like being this way, yet I believe an artist must protect his vision. But, God forbid, what if the naysayers are right? How many more people are going to tell me that I haven't delivered? Maybe I **am** just an egotistical small-town decorator who thinks he knows everything about everything. But I love what I do, and if I didn't think I knew best, I would step aside and let someone else do it. No one has the love affair with paint, fabric, and paper that I do. But somehow, the church has me thrown. I have never been in this situation before. I'm used to clients kneeling before me in gratitude. Did I overreach with this job?

"Unc?" Two calls out softly, so as not to scare me. I wave to him, and he joins me.

"I'm having a little snit," I admit, and, somehow, that makes me feel better.

"I know. I have snits myself." Two laughs.

"I'm a walking ego. Two legs and a temper. That's me."

"You just want what's best."

"No, I want things my way, and I want to be right, and I want everybody to know it. That makes me loaded with pride. Now, I grant you, that's better than being full of cancer, but I'm learning it's almost as dangerous."

Two buries his hands in his pockets. "I understand how you feel. But you shouldn't give up. You know what you're doing. I said I took a year off because I didn't fit in, but the truth is, I really came home because I wanted to work with you. You're the only artist in our family. And that's what I want to be. Who better than you to show me how?"

I feel myself tear up. "Really?"

"Yes. You've brought elegance and style into our lives. Mom would still have plaid café curtains on those spring rods from Sears if it wasn't for you. And at church, the altar would look like a wrinkled junk pile on Sundays if you didn't dress it; and our cousins would only see chandeliers in books if you didn't insist they buy them for their homes. You're the touch of class in the di Crespi family."

I take a deep breath and look out to the sea, feeling small and yet suddenly significant. "I am, aren't I?"

"Without you, we'd be a bunch of **gavones.** You lead us. We need you."

"All I want to do is make things nice."

"You do."

"Why, then, is there so much acrimony around this church project? I'm begging you, tell me what I'm doing wrong."

"That's easy. Church means something different to everyone. When you decorate a home, you can see how people live and do a version of them in wallpaper and paint. But a church is different. It represents the souls of people, whatever that means. For some, it's a private place to confess their sins. For others, it's a choir loft filled with light and music. For children, it has incense and men in dresses, so it's a little scary. What is it to you?"

I think about my church. It has kept me in line, and provided a framework for my beliefs, which I desperately need. It gives me boundaries and rules and perimeters. I believe in the afterlife, and I want a place there; I want to be told exactly how to get to heaven, and my church does that for me. I revere it, but I also try to live by the rules. I don't think my young nephew will understand that. Nowadays, the kids believe that everyone should have their own church. I like that thousands of souls came before me, reciting the same prayers in the same way. "My church is a place where I feel rebirth. I go, I pray, I confess, and I leave with a clean slate and start over again."

"Hmmm." Two thinks about this.

"I feel connected there," I say simply.

"Well, that's not what your sketches say. Those sketches show a place that's been redecorated with a nice floor and good paint and some gold leafing. It might as well be a fancy hotel. It doesn't show renewal."

"I don't know how to do that." I have never said those words in my life.

"Then your job"—Two looks at me—"is to find someone who does."

I feel my feet sink into the sand, and I realize that the water has rushed to the ankles of my Wellies. If I stand here much longer, I'll be washed away like the top half of an old clamshell. How do I find a way to dramatize rebirth against the backdrop of eternity for the people of Our Lady of Fatima Church? Is there a way? The sun makes a tear in the lining of this grim day, and while I should feel a little hope, what I really feel is sadness. Maybe I'm not the right man for the job.

"It's a masterpiece!" Toot whispers as she helps me lift Monica Vitti's chandelier from the packing crate. The entire staff at the OLOF post office tingled when the man-sized wooden crate arrived stamped BY AUTHORITY OF THE QUEEN. Maybe they thought I had shipped home a guard from Buckingham Palace.

This has to be my favorite purchase of all time. I like mementoes from trips. I have shipped home a ceramic birdbath on a pedestal from Deruta, Italy (a kitschy touch in my powder room), a statue from Málaga, Spain (it's in the garden), and a TV table from Provence (perfect in my study), and I have been thrilled with all of them. But nothing can compare to Monica Vitti's chandelier.

"What are you going to do with it?" Toot asks.

"I don't know. For now it's getting hung in my attic so the bobeches can breathe. It's not good to keep a chandelier in storage."

"Are you going to clean it?"

"Later. With a damp sponge of hot water and ammonia, crystal by crystal. Never use water on the wires, you know; it will weaken them, and then you've got problems." Toot helps me up the stairs to the second floor, the chandelier in tow.

"Imagine Monica Vitti and her paramours clinking champagne glasses and pitching woo under this."

This gives me the opening I've been waiting for. "When were you going to tell me that you're sleeping with Lonnie?"

Toot takes a deep breath. "It's not a big deal," she squeaks.

"You're dating your ex-husband behind his wife's back! May I remind you you're committing adultery?"

Toot mulls this over as we guide the chandelier up the attic steps. When we reach the top, I hang it on a hook usually reserved for the

Christmas garlands currently festooning my garage doors. I leave everything up through the Feast of the Epiphany.

"Doris won't sleep with him. She's too up-tight."

"Maybe she wants a faithful husband!"

"She doesn't know about us."

"Well, it won't be long. She'll see your cars parked outside the Asbury Park Motor Lodge one night, and that will be it."

"We're careful."

"What is it with you?"

"I can't help it. I'm just like Daddy. I have a secret life."

"Toot! Please don't use our parents as an excuse for your bad behavior. Take responsibility for yourself!"

"If you want to know the truth, thirteen years of celibacy made me realize how much I missed sex. That's right, B. I missed making love. And now I'm in this shit age bracket where I can't go younger—'cause they're married or have some infinity—"

"Infirmity," I correct her.

"Infirmity that prevents them from delivering satisfactory performance. And older men, forget 'em. Sal cured me of the over-sixties. They're like used cars—they look damn good on the lot, but you get 'em home and the wheels fall off and you're stranded. With all of Sal's aches and pains and pills, I figured out something: I can't stand taking care of a man."

"But that is the essence of love!"

"To you. Not to me. To me love is supposed to be fun. Fun and sexy and a little dirty. Okay? I like sneaking around. I like motels with the waxy paper strip across the commode and the hermetically sealed plastic cups on the sink and wearing a new bra and lacy little tap pants and slinking around like a kitten on a mattress with more lumps than the mashed potatoes at the Tic-Tock. Call me a tramp, because being a good girl made me miserable. Being a good girl got me a pile of poo, okay? It did nothing for me except make me feel bad about myself. I did everything like I was supposed to, and when it all went south, my perfect moral code only made me more lonely. Being a mistress has been good for me. I'm standing on my own. I'm a lover again. I'm a prize. I'm a tasty morsel. I've finally broken the shackles of my bad marriage. I'm free!"

"What broken shackles? You're sleeping with the same man you divorced, which means you're right back in the same shackles. Don't you remember when Lonnie left you for that fry cook, but when he dislocated his shoulder you took pity on him and you took him back and bathed him every night? Then he'd go off on a business trip to meet up with some **co-mare** on the road and give her the spry, healed Lonnie while you stayed home and wondered how he'd get through the airport with his arm in a sling? Do you just erase the past like a bad dream and paint in a lie?"

"No."

"Then what are you doing, Toot?"

"I'm not going to marry him again."

"It doesn't matter. You **sleep** with him."

"Okay, okay. On the surface it seems sick. But, I don't know, we **talk** now. He listens. He touches me! He rubs my back, he wants to know what I'm thinking, he kisses me like I'm Ann-Margret and he's Elvis Presley. Don't you see . . . he loves me like I matter!" Toot bangs her fists on her thighs. "Our foreplay used to consist of 'Lower the volume.' Now the TV isn't even on. Now he's watching **me**! The Toot channel! I promise you, Lonnie has changed. He looks at me like I know something—with respect, not like I'm a dummy dumdum. I don't know, B. Marriage almost killed us, but an affair has reviled us."

"Revived. You mean revived."

"Whatever. All I know is we're crazy about each other."

I hold my head in my hands and can actually

feel the network of blood vessels in my brain filling with fluid and commence throbbing. "All right. All right. Have your whatever-it-is with Lonnie, but I don't want to know about it."

"Fine."

"Thank you." I straighten the crystals on the chandelier before turning to go down the stairs.

"I'm finally fulfilled a little, and you don't want to hear about it. I think you're jealous."

"Oh, come on."

"You don't want me to be happy."

"Of course I do. But I would like it to be moral and legal and maybe psychologically healthy. What's happened to you? How could you do this to yourself? And what about Doris?"

"Oh, Doris, Doris. She's just a fascist who wants to run Lonnie's life with rules and regulations. The man has a curfew! She might as well be his nurse or his mother. She puts his juice out in the morning, his Metamucil at night, and in between she sorts the mail. Lonnie misses my passion. He values me. I mean the world to him."

"You're talking about Lonnie Falcone like he's a prince. May I remind you? He's **not**. He cheated on you, he hid money when you divorced him, and he tried to take your car away. Have you forgotten all of that?"

"I forgive him."

"Why?"

Toot raises her voice. "Because that's love, baby. No matter what he did, or does, or didn't do, I am able to step outside of the pain and say, 'Hey, you know what? Maybe you aren't the man I dreamed of, and maybe we've disappointed each other, and maybe we agree on nothing, but by God, we have this **thing,** this lock on each other, this special clicky bond that rachets a man and a woman together like a screw to a lug nut. We have glue!' I used to resent that glue. But when I think about him now, wild dogs couldn't keep me away! Just speaking his name makes me want to jump in my car and go over there and throw him up against the retaining wall of his backyard pool and have my way with him." Toot fixes the spit curl on her cheek. "You know what I want for you?"

"Toot," I warn her.

"I want you to taste life like I'm tasting it with Lonnie. I want you to lick the whipped cream right off the sundae and taste what's underneath."

"You've lost your mind."

Toot shrugs. "Maybe. Or maybe I've finally found what makes me truly happy. And it doesn't fit in any box, but I don't care. Mama, may she rest in peace, can kiss my heinie. Papa, who cares? And the Catholic Church can bite my shorts. I've lived by the rules and look what it got me. I was a good Catholic girl who hung on to her virginity like a savings bond, and when the marker came due, I found out there was no interest. What was the matter with me? Who was I trying to please? And for what? B, I'm alive again—on my own terms. You're the one who always wanted that for me, don't forget. And now I've got it, and I'm not going to apologize to you, or the church, or my kids, or anybody. I've finally found what works for me. And I'm not turning back."

I should have guessed that the news of Rufus McSherry leaving the church project would burn a trail straight to Father Porp's door. I pull up in front of the rectory, feeling very much like the thirteen-year-old boy who accidently dropped a lit baptismal candle during Mass and set the priest's robe on fire. I'm about to be punished.

Marie Cascario offers me a cup of coffee as I wait for Father in his office. It's like a dentist's office in here. There are no personal photographs, just a desk, a chair, a phone, and two seats for visitors who need counseling. As I sit and wait, I redo the bland space in my mind with a sofa covered in chocolate-brown tweed, low lamps, mahogany bookshelves, and a mirror on the wall opposite the windows to bring in more light.

"Bartolomeo?" Father Porp breezes past me and takes a seat behind his desk. I stand, as I was trained to do, whenever a priest or nun enters a room. He motions for me to sit down.

"Father, I'd like to explain—"

"Look. I don't have time for this. I have a shell of a church over there. I'm saying Mass in a gym, and, believe me, the parishioners are complaining already. They let their displeasure be known during the Offertory. The truth is, you are not only costing me time, you're costing me money. I want to fire you—" My stomach flips, and I clench my fists—"but I can't. Patton and Persky are not available, so I can't get them. And Aurelia Mandelbaum told me that she wants you to finish what you started. So I'm stuck."

"If you're not firing me, what is this meeting about? You just want to scare me?"

"Yes!"

"Well, Father, it's too late for that. I **am** scared. Plenty scared. I am so scared I haven't had time to pray about it. So here's what I'm going to say to you. I will get the job done, and if you're so worried about it, why don't **you** pray for me?"

Father sits back in his chair, his eyes widened in surprise. "I'll do that. But don't screw around, Bartolomeo. This church is not your playground. And I want the job done."

With the moral fiber of my family collapsed around my ankles like a pair of shorts with the elastic shot, and Father Porp threatening to take the project away from me entirely, I decide a change of scenery might help me think things through.

The D&D Building in Manhattan is practically empty. January is a dead month in decorating circles, probably because the clients with deep pockets head south where it's warm. I wander silently from showroom to showroom, and except for the ding of the security bell when I enter, it's like a tomb. I look back over my nineteen-year career as I peruse the stock, a bergere chair here and a refectory table there. It think of the homes I've decorated.

I don't have it in me to stop by and visit Mary Kate Fitzsimmons (she would want a belated Christmas gift from me, and that's the last thing I'm interested in today), or call Eydie, who is in Paris and hard at work on a Dorothy Draper retrospective at the Sorbonne. I don't want to bore my industry pals Helen and Norbert—lackluster January sales have them in a funk anyway. I don't feel like taking the bus to the Village for a manicure and a cocktail. If New York City can't cheer me up, I might as well go home.

On the drive back to Jersey it begins to snow, those funny, drunken snowflakes that fall in fits and starts and twirl around before hitting the ground. I take it slowly on the turnpike, remembering when my cousin Bongie Vietro drove his Le Mans coupe too fast in a snowstorm and slid under a semi truck and was dragged a mile and a half underneath. He crawled out unscathed when the semi pulled into a rest stop. My aunt said his Saint Christopher medal saved him. Others believe it was the beer buzz he got at the Cotton Bowl party at the American Legion Hall in Allenhurst.

Instead of driving home, I go to Toot's. The lights are always on and someone is always home, and in my state of mind that's a priceless gift.

I climb the steps to the back porch. I see Toot in the window, putting saran wrap on a pan of lasagna. If we're not cooking food, we're eating it, and if we're not eating it, we're freezing it. I rap on the door. Toot turns around and looks surprised to see me. "Come on in," she says when she opens the door. "I was just freezing some lasagna."

"I saw."

"I'm doing a whole round of meals for Nicky and Ondine for when the baby comes. Have you eaten?"

"I'm not hungry." Toot proceeds to make me a salami, provolone, and turkey hero. "How is Ondine?" I ask.

"She's a falloon."

"What's that?"

"A combination of a float and a balloon. Poor thing. I went over and helped her with the layette today."

"Wasn't the baby due around Christmas?"

"Oh please! There's more mystery surrounding this baby's due date than there was for the Annunciation. Ondine wasn't diligent about dates. Would she have gotten herself in trouble if she were familiar with her personal calendar?"

"I guess not."

"But you know, she's not half bad. She's scared to death, which is endearing in a girl who was the most popular date in the county."

I hear footsteps on the porch. "Are you expecting someone?" I ask, getting up and peering out the back door. Lonnie, wearing a ski jacket and hunter's cap, is carrying two paper cups of coffee toward the house. "It's your boyfriend."

Lonnie almost turns to go back to his car when he sees me. I wave and open the door.

"Hey, B," he says, shaking the snow off his boots. "I thought I'd better check Toot's boiler, with the bad storm and all."

"Uh-huh," I say.

"I brought you coffee," Lonnie says to Toot. "I'll check the boiler and get on my way."

"He knows about us, Lon," Toot says quietly.

"Knows what?" Lonnie asks innocently.

"You know, that we're . . . friends."

"Oh." Lonnie sits down and takes the cap off his cup. He removes his coat and hat and puts them on the chair.

"Lonnie, what the hell is going on?" Eleven years as his brother-in-law entitles me to be terse.

"What do you mean?" Lonnie's bushy eyebrows snap up like window shades.

"What are you doing?" I hope he doesn't answer "your sister," but with these two you never know.

"Don't start with him, B." It's like the old days when we'd find a pair of panties in Lonnie's new Lincoln and Toot would jump to his defense, saying they must've been left by Chrysler when it was on the conveyor belt in the plant in Detroit. Oh, how we can delude ourselves.

"No, no, I'm not looking for a fight. I just want to know your intentions."

"Intentions?" Lonnie peels the plastic top off of Toot's coffee cup and hands it to her gently.

"Why are you seeing my sister when you have a third wife at home?"

Toot pours half the coffee he brought her into a mug and gives it to me. Lonnie sits back in the chair and holds his cup between his hands like a chalice. "Well, I think about it a lot."

"And?"

"And I'm not sure."

"I'm not sure I like that answer," Toot says with some indignation.

"No, no, don't get bent out of shape. I'm not unsure about you, honey." Toot smiles at the endearment. Lonnie looks at me. "When I get what I want, I mess it up. So I make things complicated to make happiness stay." Lonnie sips his coffee. "Does that make sense?"

"It's sick."

Lonnie smiles and shakes his head. "You wouldn't understand, B. You haven't been married. When you're married, you're under contract. And I'm the kind of guy who doesn't like to be under contract. It brings out the worst in me."

"It didn't do a thing for me either," Toot says, patting Lonnie's hand.

"So you two are just going to have an affair?"

They look at each other and nod. "We ain't hurting nobody." Lonnie shrugs. "Long as nobody finds out."

"You'll have to be very discreet," I insist, realizing nothing I say will burst the bubble of their adulterous bliss.

"Oh, he knows how to do that," Toot says with a smile. "He had me buffaloed for fifteen years. I think we can make this work."

Eydie and I hail a cab on Fifty-seventh and Third, where the snow is piled in black mounds to our waists. I could hardly wait for Eydie to return from Paris. She has become my guru—professional and spiritual. Since Rufus walked away from Fatima Church, I've met with every artisan in New York, New Jersey, and Pennsylvania to help renovate the church, and not one has impressed me. I called Eydie in a panic and she ordered me into the city.

"Here's what you're going to do." Eydie closes her eyes and concentrates as the cab races toward Bay Ridge. She wears a black mink swing coat and pink velvet gloves, and she smells like peppermint and cocoa, which makes me want to curl up in her lap. "You're going to tell him that you want to collaborate.

That you've come to a place in your life where that is more important than your singular vision."

"Do you think I can get him back?"

"I don't know what his schedule is. Pedro was abrupt with me on the phone, which is why I think we should just go out there in person and beg."

Brooklyn seems depressed, like a steel town in the dead of winter; the murky slush on the ground against the gray buildings makes the place seem like a prison hemmed by a black moat, the East River. The only shots of color are the occasional bright coats and hats in the herds of pedestrians. Despite the rust-belt ambience, a backdrop of gray splashed with primary colors is exciting. I'll remember this when I do the new rec room for the Cartegnas in Wall Township.

We weave through the streets of Bay Ridge, and the driver leaves us in the middle of the street outside Rufus's building, since the curbs are piled with snow. I lift Eydie over the drifts, and she laughs as I set her down on the sidewalk. There's a handwritten note on the door: **Buzzer broken. Come on up.** At the top of the stairs, I push the door open, guiding Eydie inside. My heart is thumping in my chest. I'm terrible at apologies and worse at groveling, so I'm afraid I will blow this meeting.

"Hi!" Eydie calls out, her voice echoing through the vast warehouse. I see a woman across the room with her back to us. When she turns slightly to answer Eydie, my heart stops. I know that profile.

Capri Mandelbaum is sitting cross-legged on a broken-down easy chair near the scaffolding, wearing a pair of men's flannel pajama bottoms and a sweatshirt. Her hair is tousled, and she looks like a teenager. When she sees us, she is stunned, then suddenly modest, pulling the sleeves of the sweatshirt down around her hands and folding her arms across her chest. "Capri, what are you doing here?" I ask.

Before she can answer, Pedro comes out of the kitchen with two mugs of coffee. He stops and looks at us. "Oh," he says.

A few terribly awkward moments pass until Eydie, God bless her, says something. "Any more coffee?"

"In the kitchen," Pedro mumbles. I follow Eydie into the kitchen without looking at Capri.

"What's that all about?" she whispers while I pour.

"I can't believe it."

"We can't hide in here." Eydie gives me a mug of coffee. "It will look strange."

"My ex-fiancée in another man's pajamas isn't strange?"

"Hello," a man's voice says from the door.

Rufus McSherry stands in the doorway, looking three feet taller than he did the last time I saw him. "How have you been, Eydie?" He kisses her on the cheek, then extends his hand to me. "Bartolomeo?" We shake hands. The warmth of his big paw does something to me, and I find I don't want to let go.

Forgoing my rehearsed speech, I blurt, "Rufus, I'm sorry and I wish you would reconsider doing the church. I've done a lot of thinking. I'm ready to put aside my ego and work with you."

Rufus looks at my face as though he is studying a map. "There's nothing wrong with your ego."

"There isn't?"

"No. It's your fear."

I have no idea what he's talking about. I'm not afraid of anything. I'm the guy who put an indoor pond in a Stanford White knockoff in Deal and did a fleur-de-lis design in cobblestone on the entry drive of the Salesian convent in North Haledon. I'm not afraid to color outside the lines.

Pedro joins us in the kitchen and looks at me. "Capri would like to speak to you."

"Sure." I give Eydie my coffee cup and go out into the warehouse. Capri has changed into her clothes and combed her hair.

"I'm sorry, B," she says quietly.

"For what?"

"For keeping this from you. After Christmas I took a ride with Christina to bring Amalia to the Martinellis', and we came over here and Pedro and I got to talking."

"Okay." I feel for Capri, she seems so vulnerable. I take her in my arms and hold her close. It's funny when you take a girl into your arms for old times' sake, but you realize you had no old times.

"It turns out we have a lot in common. So I came back. The past three weekends. Pedro is a wonderful person."

"The fiancé is always the last to know," I joke.

"No, you're not. I haven't told anyone."

"Your secret is safe with me."

"I think this could be something for me. I think it's true love."

"Well, don't rush."

"I knew it when I met him at your house the first time," she explains. "I had a feeling."

Capri has the calm countenance of a woman

who is certain of her heart's desire. Gone is the dry eye-blinking and self-doubt. In their wake is a new Capri, quietly content.

"Whatever makes you happy, Capri," I tell her sincerely. "That's all I care about."

She takes my hand and gives it a squeeze. "I want you to find someone too."

"Let's take things one step at a time. I have a church to rebuild, then I can address my love life."

Capri laughs. I take a look inside Pedro's room. It's like a monk's cell, with a bed, a chair, a table, and a lamp. Neat but dreary.

"I know. It's rustic," Capri says.

"We can fix that," I promise her.

I am relieved to finally give up my status as the only "bachelor of a certain age" in OLOF. Rufus and Pedro each took a studio apartment in the Windsor Arms, one of Aurelia's investment properties. February 21 is our first official day of work in the church.

Rufus and I have spent time discussing our goals for the new church and then implementing those ideas into a design. Over the course of the last month we met with the architect and planned the steps. My team, Christina and Two, and Rufus's crew, led by Pedro and including a group of local construction workers he found through the parish council, have met and set the work schedule. Occasionally Father Porp comes by the empty church and glares at me. Obviously we are not going fast enough for him. I remind him that it's Aurelia's donation and **not** church dough financing the project, so he backs off.

"I have the notes from the last meeting," Christina says, reaching into her bag and pulling out a stack of papers.

"I'll set up the sketches." I place a large drawing pad on the easel.

"I'll pour the coffee," Two offers.

Rufus and Pedro enter from the back of the church. A crew follows them with a hand truck loaded with equipment, which they stack neatly near the side altar.

"The final load of supplies will arrive today," Pedro tells us. I ask everyone to take a seat. The crew sits on the floor and the altar steps, gathering in closely.

"Rufus, I'm going to turn the meeting over to you to explain our process in the coming weeks and months."

"We have a lot of work ahead of us," Rufus begins. "The engineer gave us some structural fixes that need to happen, mostly in the walls, as we plan on redoing the electrical wiring. Now, if you'll all look up, you'll see the vaulted ceiling and the catwalk beneath it. We're going to lift off the old roof and replace it with a series of broad skylights that can be opened from the catwalk level. If you don't mind, let's walk around and I'll show you the rest."

Rufus takes us on a tour of the church, showing us how he will implement our design to open up the seating and replace the stained-glass windows featuring eerie scenes from the lives of saints with designs depicting our local trades: scissors of the sewing trade, the hammer and nails of construction, books depicting education, the Greek symbols of the healing arts, and fishing boats.

We will create a grotto of local fieldstone for the Lady of Fatima shrine, like the one I saw in the Cathedral of Santa Margherita in Italy. I have written to Asher Anderson to send the statues of the children of Fatima.

Rufus thinks the altar should be oval, and that the tabernacle should have a clear glass door instead of brass, so that people can see the Blessed Sacrament. Rufus's eloquent explanation sold Father Porp on the idea.

As a backdrop, we are going to create Rufus's inspired Wall of Water. He assured us that we can have the wall dry when we wish it so, but that the water flowing over the rocks will be dynamic and fresh. This wall alone will take the crew two months to build.

Christina is in charge of ordering and delivering of supplies, as well as the business side of the renovation. She does the budgets, payments, and payroll. When he's not tending to my clients, Two will act as Pedro's apprentice as he designs the stained-glass windows and oversees the installation of the skylights. Rufus will paint the frescoes himself and supervise the construction of the Wall of Water. I will oversee each element of the project and provide help wherever I can.

Father Porporino enters from the sacristy, pushing back the canvas tarp where the door used to be. He carries a gold cup filled with holy water and the distribution wand, which rests in it like a spoon.

"Do you need something, Father?" I ask.

"It's customary on the day the ground is broken on a project for the priest to show up and give a blessing. Would you all like one?"

"Sure, Father," Rufus says, smiling. "It couldn't hurt, right?"

Father asks us to bow our heads. Pedro kneels. Father sprinkles us with the holy-water wand. Rufus gets pelted in the eye and smiles at me. Despite Father Porp's gruff demeanor and chronic impatience, all in all, it's an excellent start to the most ambitious undertaking of my career.

I've always enjoyed the solitary nature of my work. As a decorator, I've had plenty of human contact with the craftsmen I employ to cover furniture, build closets, and construct draperies. I spend time in the city at the D&D Building discussing selections and options with clients. But I've never enjoyed a project more than Fatima Church. I look forward to the morning and having a cup of coffee with Rufus as we go over the plans for the day. He's even become a part of the social fabric of OLOF, joining me for dinner at Aurelia's. When I asked Aurelia to include Pedro, she said, "Fine, if you insist." Evidently Capri hasn't bothered to tell her mother about her new **inamorata**. Maybe tonight, over dinner, Capri will share her news.

Rufus has had dinner out at least three nights a week since he arrived, all made with loving care by the women of OLOF. He's been wined and dined by the officers of the sodality and various parishioners who heard him speak after Mass about the renovation. When they're not hosting him for dinner, the ladies compete by leaving Rufus Tupperware containers of their best dishes on his doorstep. The cult of Rufus McSherry has replaced Roman Catholicism as the inspiration to love one another in our community.

"Do you have a girl, Rufus?" I ask as he's suspended overhead on a scaffold, stripping layers of paint from a section of rib vaulting.

"Do you?" he asks me.

"I asked you first."

He climbs down the scaffolding, and it reminds me of King Kong swinging off the Empire State Building. Anything this man touches seems smaller in proximity to him.

"No one in particular." He fishes a bandana from the back pocket of his jeans.

"You know you're the local catnip now."

He throws his head back and laughs. "I guess the parade of homemade pies is proof, right?"

"Let me tell you something. The women around here like tall and they like Irish. And in OLOF there are very few tall and just a couple of Irishmen, so you're now officially Mr. Delish."

"Thank you for boiling my attributes down to two characteristics that I have no control over. But what's your story, B? A good-looking Italian guy like you. Why aren't you with someone?"

"Who said I wasn't?"

"Good point. Maybe you're just discreet. Of course, I understand you were engaged once. For what, about twenty years?" He chuckles.

"Well, I wouldn't call **that** the real thing, Rufus. It was an arrangement made without my consent when I was a baby."

"Oh, I get it. Like royalty. You were promised."

"Exactly!"

Rufus replaces the lids on various cans of dry pigment that will make paint when he paints the fresco. Today he tested colors on the wall, making streaks of blue, from the palest aqua to the deepest azure. "I had it once, B."

"You were married?"

"No, in love."

"How did you know?"

"That's easy. I would have done anything for her." He fishes in his pocket for his cigarettes and hands me one. He lights his own and then throws me the matches while he steps back and squints at the stripes of color on the wall.

"What happened?" I ask gently.

"She died."

I take a breath. "How?"

"She got sick. And there was nothing they could do."

"What was her name?"

He takes a moment to answer. "Ann."

"What was she like?"

"You know, it's funny. I don't think of her face. I think of how I felt around her. But she was pretty. A brunette. Tall."

"Tall people should go together. The same with short. I don't like those Jack Sprat couples where the man is over six feet and he marries a four-foot door knocker. It's ridiculous."

Rufus laughs. "Man, you've got standards."

"Someone has to. This world has gone to hell. And if you haven't noticed that, then shame on you."

Rufus sits down on the steps of the altar.

"How long has it been?"

"Three years."

"Has there been anyone since?" I ask.

"Boy, B. You're a font of questions."

"I'm sorry."

"I like women, so yeah."

"But nothing has come close to Ann?"

"Nope." He smiles. "It helps though, to have a little female companionship."

"It does? I'd think it would be the opposite. You'd always be reminded of Ann and compare others to her." I usually don't play amateur psychologist, but there's something about Rufus that makes me want to ask the questions and hear his answers.

"It doesn't work like that. Well, maybe for women. But for a man, there's so much comfort to be found in the company of a woman. I would never turn away from that. I need it. It's not like anyone can replace Ann, but I need to live, to be present here and now. You know what I mean?"

"Being with a woman makes you feel alive?"

"No, to me it **is** life. I don't mean that in a cavalier way. I like how a good woman can make it all seem easy."

"How are we doing?" Christina calls out from the back of the church.

"Ring a bell or knock, would you?" I chide. "I'm having a private conversation here."

"Sorry, B." Amalia follows Christina, carrying a Tupperware container of brownies.

"Hi, Rufus," Amalia says, giving him the container. "I made you these. I put chocolate chips in the batter, so they're really good."

"That's sweet of you. Thank you."

"Even the thirteen-year-olds adore you, Rufus. Where's mine, Amalia?"

"You're always on a diet." She shrugs.

"So some celery sticks would have been nice."

"Okay, I'll remember that for next time." Amalia rolls her eyes.

I turn to Christina. "We're going to Aurelia's for dinner tonight. Want to come? She made that endless pot of sauce with enough meatballs for a potluck."

"We can't. We're going over to the Menecolas'."

"It's awful, B," Amalia complains. "They

play the TV too loud and put anchovies in the salad. I hate it."

"But they're family," Christina says kindly. "Well, let's go."

Christina smiles at Rufus, who looks back at her with something like flirty affection. I can't tell for sure. After all, Lonnie and Toot have been schtupping under my nose, and I didn't get so much as a whiff of it. So maybe I'm seeing something that isn't there. Amalia and Christina close the church door behind them. "Chris is a great girl," I say.

"She is."

"So?" I press.

"So what?"

"Is there something between you?"

"Now, B. Do I look like a guy who kisses and tells?"

"No."

"Then let's leave it," Rufus says, tactfully changing the subject. "You know, the painting of Our Lady of Fatima on the wall here isn't a fresco."

"It isn't? What is it?"

"It's a painting. The artist adhered a canvas to the wall and then did a treatment over it."

"Why would he do that?"

"I don't know. I haven't taken it down yet. I just peeled a corner at the top. That technique was used when churches changed the art around a lot."

"That's the only art that ever hung in this church," I say, wondering what Michael Menecola had up his sleeve.

That evening Rufus and Pedro drive over to Aurelia's and I follow in my station wagon. It's wonderful to spend time with the guys. It occurs to me that I've been surrounded by women all my life. At home it was Ma and Toot, at school Capri, on weekends Christina, and then when I became a decorator I mostly dealt with women clients. It feels good to have Rufus and Pedro around. I'm surprised Rufus and I have become so friendly, and relieved that there's finally another man in town who is as passionate about art as I am. I really enjoy our conversations, and I try not to think about how I'll miss him when he leaves.

I park behind Rufus in Aurelia's driveway. Rufus and Pedro follow me up the front steps and through the front door, which Aurelia always leaves open for me.

"This is a palazzo," Rufus says as he looks around.

"French Norman. And don't miss the Monet in the living room. All the art is real. There's more paintings hanging in here than there are at the Met." The guys follow me into the foyer, where they take a good look around. We hear shouting from the kitchen.

"Ma, I don't understand!" I hear Capri yelling.

"I won't have it!" I hear Aurelia shout back. "I simply won't have it!"

"Wait here," I tell Rufus and Pedro. Pedro looks lost as he holds his bottle of wine for the hostess. I walk past the dining room where the table is set with a tablecloth, flowers, china, and crystal, into the kitchen, where the argument between Capri and Aurelia has escalated.

"How could you do this to me!" Aurelia is sitting at the table, her face buried her hands. Capri stands behind a chair, holding it for strength.

"I haven't done anything wrong," Capri insists.

"What is the matter, ladies?" I ask from the doorway.

"Go away, B," Capri cries.

I turn to go. "No, stay," Aurelia orders.

"What's going on here?" I demand as I pivot to face them.

Aurelia points at her. "She took up with the spic!"

"Are you speaking of our friend Pedro?" I ask

evenly. I motion to Aurelia to lower her voice so Pedro won't hear the slur. She ignores me.

"And it's all **your** fault!" Aurelia directs her rage at me. "You brought these . . . these people here."

"He's a good man and a talented artist, Aurelia. Pedro is a stained-glass window expert, a true craftsman. He's brilliant."

"Don't start with me, B. I don't want my daughter with a Mexican."

I begin to speak when Pedro appears in the doorway. "Mrs. Mandelbaum?" he says.

"Pedro, please," Capri says to him softly. "Go."

"I want to talk to you, Mr. Alarcon!" Aurelia walks toward him.

"Mother!" Capri tries to stop her.

"This is my house and I will say whatever I please." Aurelia turns to Pedro. "I want you to stop seeing my daughter."

"I'm sorry you feel this way," Pedro says quietly.

"I didn't raise her to do this."

"To do what, ma'am?" Pedro says respectfully.

"You know exactly what I am talking about, young man!" she thunders.

"You raised me to be alone," Capri says. "It's like I've been pickled! I've been waiting forty years for someone to open the jar and let me out! You betrothed me to Bartolomeo, for godsakes. Talk about limbo."

She makes an engagement to me sound like a death-row sentence, but now is not the moment for my ego to be assuaged. "I'm sure we can work this out," I say diplomatically.

"It's too late." Aurelia turns to Pedro. "You're sleeping together! For shame!" She points her finger at Capri. "Your father would be so ashamed of you. I want you out. Both of you. Get out of my house!"

In an instant, Capri's body fills with strength. She seems a foot taller as she lifts her head high. Her spine, which is usually collapsed like an accordion, stretches long, giving her a look of fierce determination. She takes Pedro's hand and leads him out of the kitchen. She does not look back, merely shouting, "You'll be sorry!" before she slams the door behind them.

Aurelia collapses in tears as Rufus comes into the kitchen. I motion for him to go.

"Aurelia?"

"This is all your fault, B. You wouldn't marry my daughter, and now this happens. You did this!"

"Hey, wait a minute. I found the best artists in the country to come here and work on our church. This wasn't some scheme I hatched to find romance for Capri. This is her choice. Why can't you let her choose?"

"You gave her away." She cries.

"Aurelia, you are overreacting. She's not doing anything wrong." There's a part of me that can't believe that Aurelia would treat her adult daughter like she's a fifteen-year-old girl caught in the back of a car with a boy. Capri was right: Aurelia might as well have locked her in the attic like Rapunzel. I feel like a fool for letting her use me all these years to put Capri on ice. "You're going to lose your daughter," I warn her.

"She's gone already," Aurelia says, glaring at me. "She left me the night she went with him. Leave me alone." I try to soothe her, but she pulls away. I go outside. Rufus stands by my car. "Pedro took the truck," he says.

"Come on. I'll buy you dinner," I tell him.

The last time I was summoned to the rectory was the summer when I was fourteen and Father Dragonetto invited me in to discuss my potential future as a priest. He asked me if I had gotten "the calling." I hadn't, but that wasn't the answer he was looking for. I remember it was so hot in his office that I couldn't breathe. Finally, to break free of the meeting, I told him that I could never be a priest because insanity ran in my family and the church of Rome should not be saddled with a nut job. He never bothered me again.

"Bartolomeo, we've got a big problem," Father Porp says from behind his desk. It occurs to me that the office hasn't changed since the reign of Dragonetto, except that there is less clutter.

"What is it, Father?"

"Aurelia Mandelbaum is pulling her money out of the renovation."

"What?"

I feel as though I have been socked in the gut. My shock turns to anger.

"She said that the church could keep the initial one-hundred-thousand-dollar donation, but she is not giving another penny. Do you know what this is about?" He looks at me accusingly.

"Capri has been seeing Pedro. Evidently Aurelia—who married a Jewish man!—doesn't want a Mexican Catholic in her family." I throw my hands in the air. "Can you talk to her?"

"I tried. And then she had her lawyer call me."

"What are we going to do?" My heart races as I picture Rufus, Pedro, the church council, the congregation full of disappointment as they stand in the empty shell of Fatima Church.

"How much time before your money runs out?"

I do some rapid calculation in my head. "Another three weeks," I tell him.

"Keep working. I'll make some calls." Father Porporino looks at me. "Now you understand why I wanted Patton and Persky. This is a disaster."

I ignore his dig as I stand to go. "The diocese has deep pockets, Father. If there's money for a new football stadium at Our Lady of the Snows in Piscataway, surely they can cough up the rest of the dough we need for the church."

"I wish it worked that way, B. But it doesn't."

My heart feels like a lead anchor in my chest. My years of friendship with The Benefactor account for nothing. I am so angry I can hardly speak.

I cross the street to the church where the crew is hard at work. Two is helping Pedro remove the old stained-glass windows, to be replaced with temporary clear plastic as the molds are salvaged for the new windows. I go into the sacristy, where Christina is working on an order of supplies.

"Christina, we're in big trouble."

"What's the matter?"

I pace the floor. "Aurelia pulled the money. It's a little late in the game for bingo, car washes, and raffles. We'll ask the parishioners, but that will only cover a fraction of what we need. Can you rework the budget and see if we can cut corners anywhere?"

"Every penny is accounted for." Christina looks at me. "What happened?"

"She's angry about Pedro and Capri."

"Shame on her!" Christina raises her voice. "They're in love. Aurelia's a widow. She **knows** what it's like to be alone. To wish that on her own daughter is cruel."

"I've seen a side of Aurelia that I wish I hadn't."

"Come on, B. It was there all along. Everything she does out of the goodness of her heart—excuse me, bank account—has strings. She controls this parish and has for years. Everything from the landscaping at the cemetery to the foot pedals of the organs, she has bought and paid for, and it's done to her liking. There isn't a generous bone in her body."

"She's always been kind to me."

"Oh, B. You do things out of obligation—not because you want to. You've humored her all these years, and there's a little part of you that likes the big money because you know how to use it. I doubt very much that Aurelia's castle would be gorgeous without your touch. You're the one who always tells me that the people with money never know how to spend it."

"I've had a bad day, Chris, I don't need to hear about my shortcomings."

"I don't mean to insult you, I'm just trying to help you see what's going on here. She gave you the money to redo this church, but it came at a price to your integrity. If you think for one moment you were able to be free with the renovation of this church, you're crazy! She said she trusted you at the parish council meeting, but who do you think is pushing Father Porp to call you in and put the fear of God in you? It's her. It's always been her. Capri should run while there's an open door. No good will come of her trying to please her mother."

Two stands in the doorway. "I heard everything. I think we should talk to Dad."

"Your father hasn't set foot in a Catholic church since his first wedding day," I say.

"He's got the dough."

"Not if he goes through another expensive divorce," I say aloud, instantly regretting it. "Not that he's getting a divorce, but you know what I mean."

"I'll have Mom talk to him. They've been really friendly lately."

"Good idea," I say to my nephew as he goes. I turn to Christina. "A new teddy and some tap pants at the Freehold Inn just might buy us some time. I'll give Mata Hari a call and tell her to work her magic."

Christina looks confused.

"I'll explain later," I promise.

New York City has always been my refuge, so I escaped into the city as soon as I could after hearing the news. I called Eydie immediately about losing our funding. I can't face Rufus and Pedro yet. Besides, I have three weeks to come up with the money. As a Catholic I believe in miracles, which is exactly what we need to finish Fatima Church.

The bar at Gino's is empty except for Eydie and me. We share a plate of prosciutto and melon over cocktails.

"And it's so sad. Capri and Pedro look so happy together." I chase the maraschino cherry with a plastic sword around the bottom of my Manhattan like I'm spearing a fish in the South Pacific.

"They're a wonderful match," Eydie says, crossing her legs on the bar stool. "Mexican, Italian, and Jewish. Name one vegetable that won't be used in **that** kitchen."

"Capri is a mess. Pedro is full of guilt and offered to break up with her. There's some Mexican belief that any man who comes between a mother and a daughter winds up without a lung or something. It's crazy."

"Is your ex-brother-in-law going to give the rest of the money for the church?"

"I sent my sister into the trenches to finagle a donation. I hope she comes out with more than rug burns."

"How's Rufus?"

"Working like a dog. It's not just a job to him, it's a mission. He's the best."

"I know," Eydie says as she blushes.

"Don't tell me you fell under the spell?" I throw up my hands. "Who hasn't?"

"There's a reason. Rufus is magnificent. The problem is, only half his heart is available. The other half will always belong to the woman he lost."

"It's tragic."

"For any girl he meets."

"Were you two serious?"

"We had a whirlwind romance. When the storm died down . . . well."

"Don't leave me hanging! What happened? Start at the beginning. How did you meet?"

Eydie settles back in her chair, absolutely delighted to remember every detail. "It went like this. I met him in Queens at the Scalamandré factory. He was there to pick up some fabric for a theater curtain he designed for an off-Broadway house. We started talking shop, and he asked me out for coffee. One thing led to another. Isn't that the way it is when it happens to you? Like **this**." She snaps her fingers.

When I think of the women I've been with, I realize I spend a lot of time standing up, so it's unlikely that they or I am looking for anything too permanent. "Well, we're a lot alike, Eydie. It seems to happen in an instant. At first I can't tell if a woman is interested, and then suddenly I can't find my pants. I never know how I get where I'm going. It just happens."

Eydie laughs. "I knew when I met you, we had a lot in common."

"And it never ends badly," I continue. "They always want to be my friend. Is that how it is with you?"

"Always. And that's how it was with Rufus. We had our little delicious thing, we enjoyed each other, and then it was done. But I feel for the woman who really falls in love with him. I wouldn't want to be her."

"Are you Barty Crispy?" the bartender asks me.

"Close enough," I tell him. I look at Eydie. "See what I put up with?"

"Your sister called. Said for you to go straight to St. Ambrose Hospital in Freehold. Your niece is having the baby."

CHAPTER NINE

Brocade in Brielle

St. Ambrose Hospital is tucked in the middle of Freehold's main drag like a book on a library shelf. I am familiar with it because my father had a hernia repaired there. I park on the street and run through the entry doors.

I've been through three births with my sister, so I know she's a disaster when she's panicked (or when she's famished, which is another story). I can hear her loudly barking orders when I come off the elevator to the waiting area. "Nicky, Ondine wants you. You have to go in there!" Toot stands over her son, trying to yank him out of his seat by his collar.

Nicky is crumpled in a heap on a small green plastic chair. "I can't, Ma. I can't." Toot takes her son's face in her hands. It's the color of the chair.

"You must. You have to be strong and be a man and be there for your wife."

Toot lifts Nicky up from under the arms and pushes him into the hallway outside the labor room.

"Oh, B, thank God you're here," Toot says as she drags her son.

I follow them inside.

"How is Ondine?"

"She hasn't started pushing. She's screaming like a banshee in there, though. She even scared the other girls." Toot pushes Nicky through the doors.

After a moment a young nurse in small wire-rimmed glasses comes out. She is awfully young and looks like one of those girls who danced around the campfire at Woodstock. I'm worried. "Are you coming in, Mrs. Falcone?"

"I wasn't planning on it," Toot tells her.

"Maybe you should. Your son is a nervous wreck."

"This is my brother. Can he come too?"

"Let me check with the patient." She goes back inside.

"I don't want to go in," I tell Toot.

The nurse returns. "It's fine. As long as he stays out of the way."

Sure, I think. This is a hippie hospital where anything goes. Ondine will probably have strangers passing a bong while watching the birth.

"I'm not going," I protest.

"Yes you are!" Toot clamps down on my biceps so tight she pinches a nerve and my elbow goes limp. I follow her into Labor Room 4, where Nicky stands gripping the metal bars near Ondine's head. As soon as he sees Toot and me, he collapses on the floor in a chartreuse heap. A nurse picks him up and pulls him off to the side like she's carrying him off a battlefield and deposits him in a chair in the corner. Toot goes to Ondine's side. "Your mother is on the way, but it's gonna take a while. Just pretend I'm her."

Ondine takes Toot's hand and screams so loudly even the nurse takes a step back.

I liked it much better when Toot had babies. They knocked her out and I waited outside, except when Two was born. Toot had switched doctors and had a Hawaiian fellow who allowed me into the room and let me cut the cord. I don't think he worked in New Jersey after that.

Poor Ondine. She is so full of fluid that I cannot detect a single bone in her face. Her head is a beach ball. Her nose seems to have sunk, and her eyes are two blue dots. The only way I could pick her out of a lineup is the hair, which lies on her shoulders in soft blond curls.

The doctor—a middle-aged fellow with his curly mop in a hairnet—instructs Ondine to push. Toot won't look, and I try not to, but when the doctor tells her, "Again," I can't help but look, and out comes the baby, fists in the air, like he plowed through the defensive line of the Baltimore Colts and made a touchdown. When the nurse shouts, "It's a boy!" Nicky revives suddenly and rushes to Ondine's side. Evidently this was the news he wanted to hear.

The doctor asks Nicky if he wants to cut the cord. He shakes his head violently, but Toot smacks him lightly and says, "Cut the cord, it's the least you can do." The doctor hands him giant shears (the kind used to install carpet) and shows Nicky where to cut; Nicky clips the cord and the baby screams.

Ondine smiles at Nicky and he kisses her tenderly. I didn't think my nephew had the courage. Evidently neither did Ondine. As they coo and cuddle with their baby boy, Toot and I practically dance out of the delivery room when we're asked to leave.

"My first grandson!" she weeps. I put my arm around her and push through the doors into the outside waiting area. Anthony and

Two, the new uncles, and Lonnie and Doris wait for the news. Toot looks at me.

"I hope being an uncle brings you as much joy as it has brought me," I tell Two when I hug him. "And Anthony"—I give him a hug—"you must never put this boy on your motorcycle. Okay?"

"Okay, Unc," he says.

"Lonnie, congratulations!" I give my ex-brother-in-law a kiss on the cheek. "And Doris, you too!"

"It's so exciting," Lady Sylvia says. Poor thing. She's a classy woman, but there's just no way she fits in with this clan. It's like a platter of boiled potatoes and spaghetti.

I look over at Lonnie and Toot, who seem as happy as they did on their wedding day. Lonnie reaches down to kiss Toot, and I distract Doris while he slips his tongue into my sister's mouth. What a family.

Nicky comes out to join us. His skin tone has returned from green to his usual shade of oatmeal, and he beams with pride.

"What's his name?" Toot asks.

"Moonstone."

No one speaks. Finally I say, "Nicky, are you sure?"

"Say that name again," Toot growls.

"Moonstone," Nicky repeats.

"Moonstone Falcone. Now he and Nellie Fanelli can be song lyrics together," I offer.

"What does that mean?" Lonnie looks perplexed. According to tradition, the boy should be named Alonzo Vincent, after him, the paternal grandfather.

"Ondine likes it." Nicky shrugs.

"Did you tell her in Italian families we name babies after people, not rocks?"

"Don't start, Ma. Did you see him? I love him. If she wanted to call him Riptide Rex, it would be fine with me."

Toot opens her mouth to reply, then thinks better of it and embraces him instead. "Oh, who cares? He's perfect. And I'm so proud of you."

"But I didn't do anything," Nicky whispers.

"I know." Toot smiles. "But you gave me my first grandchild. Your daddy and I love you very much." Then, in a moment of largess, Toot looks at Doris. "And you're a step-grandmom now."

Lonnie gives Nicky a man hug, one of those awkward big kinds where the bodies don't touch but there's a lean-in and some mutual backslapping. Then Two and Anthony hug their brother. Only Doris and I are left out. We look at each other and smile. After all, we're family once removed.

Moonstone will arrive home to the most beautiful nursery in Freehold. With Ondine in the hospital for a few days, I zip over to the house and give the baby's room an upgrade with circus-themed wallpaper in bright primary colors, an apple-red changing table, a white crib with navy-blue-and-white polka-dot sheets, and café curtains with elephants parading across the hems. (I installed blackout shades underneath for the parents, who will thank me until Moonstone is in college. I've been told nap times are a cinch with the miracle shades.)

It's late and I'm hungry, but I stop by the church. It's interesting how life took precedence over work for one night with the arrival of the baby. But now that Moonstone is here and he's healthy, it's time to turn my attention back to the church. I am so angry at Aurelia for pulling the funds that I can't think. How will I tell Rufus and the crew we have no money to continue? And how will Pedro feel when he finds out he's the reason?

When I reach the foyer, I see that most of the church is dark, except for the fresco behind the side altar where Rufus is working. I hear voices, so instead of interrupting, I stay behind one of the pillars and listen.

"You're beautiful," I hear Rufus say.

I peer around and see my cousin Christina, legs dangling from the end of the scaffold, looking up at him. He leans down and kisses her tenderly. I look away. I know to honor a private moment when I see one. I've been so busy, but I have noticed that Christina seems better, less morose. Maybe still a little depressed, but not in the black, hopeless funk that has gripped her since Charlie died. I thought, selfishly, that it might be working for me that made her feel better, but I see now it's not the job with the House of B, it's the time spent with Rufus of Brooklyn. Rufus goes back to work as Chris watches him, and I realize I've just observed a small miracle. Christina has been so sad for so long that I didn't think it was possible for her to connect with someone again. Maybe it's the small miracles that make a difference. Maybe a kiss can be a step to salvation if it brings a grieving woman from despair to peace. Maybe being understood is what a widow misses when her husband is gone. Maybe she just needs to be heard.

I sneak back out the door and reenter, calling Rufus's name. If Christina wanted to tell me about Rufus, she would have. And so would he. But they didn't, so I'm going to respect that.

"Something interesting up here," Rufus says

as he extends his big paw to me and helps me climb up the scaffolding. I think of those rescue scenes on the news where a man in a uniform is pulling another man to safety over a churning pit of flood water. I could never imagine how it's done. It takes brute strength and determination on the part of the one man and complete trust on the part of the other. When Rufus practically lifts me from the ground to the scaffold, I understand how a person could be saved.

"Okay, what have we got?" I say peppily.

Rufus leans toward the face of the Blessed Mother on the fresco and tugs at the area around it. He pulls the edge of the fresco toward him, loosening the stucco.

"It's just as you thought. A canvas mounted on the wall."

"Yeah, but that's not what's interesting."

We watch as he pulls the peeling canvas all the way across the fresco, exposing the wall underneath. I can't believe what I see.

Painted on another canvas is a nude of a voluptuous raven-haired Italian girl with brown eyes you could fall into. She reclines, Rubenesque, on a blanket of red velvet. Her expression is pure contentment. There is nothing cheap or tawdry about her, yet her face and form are very come-hither. Underneath her body in repose, the word "**Credo**" is painted in gold leaf.

"I believe," I translate aloud. "I wonder who she is."

"She sure doesn't look like Nonna Menecola," Christina says softly.

"I love it." Rufus stands back. "There's my idea of faith."

"For now," I chide him. "But when you're old and sick and your sex drive is a distant memory, I will guarantee that you will pray to all the saints and God Himself to relieve you of your misery. You won't be thinking of her."

"I think you're wrong about that, B. I think God is in the details, the places you think He'd never be."

"In the arms of a sexy woman?" I ask incredulously.

"Especially there."

Rufus pulls the canvas up over the brunette bombshell, and I heave a sigh of relief. If Father Porporino were to see this, he'd throw the lot of us out for turning this sacred place into a nudie club.

"Ondine had a baby boy," I tell them, and to my own surprise, I begin to cry. Christina puts her arms around me, and Rufus climbs the scaffold and sits next to me.

"I know," Christina says. "It's overwhelming

when a baby is born. You were a mess when I had Amalia, remember?"

"I remember. This time, though, I saw it. The whole thing. And they named him . . . Moonstone." I sob.

"I'd like to help you, B, but gold is at a low," Lonnie says sadly. He sits across from me in a booth at the Tic-Tock, stirring his coffee extra-light.

"Lonnie, I'm desperate. I'm going have to let the crew go on Friday if we can't come up with twenty-five thousand dollars."

"What about the churchgoers? Did you ask them?"

"The most money I ever raised quickly in our parish was fifteen hundred dollars on Bingo Night, and that's only because the Knights of Columbus and sodality matched the take of the door. I need a big check **fast.**"

"I wish I could help you out."

"So do I." I'm starting to feel defeated.

"Look, I need to talk to you about something," Lonnie whispers. It's hard to hear him through the din of the diner. "I love your sister. And I'd like to get divorced."

"Lonnie, I don't want to get involved. Can I go twenty-four hours without hearing some detail about Toot's libido and your sex life?"

"It's something, what we got. That's why I'm thinking remarriage." He smiles.

"Don't do that. I'm begging you. Don't you get it? It's the thrill of the chase for you. If you and Toot remarried, you'd kill each other."

"I haven't asked her. But if I do give Doris the sayonara, then I have to give her the house."

"Why don't you just buy women houses instead of marrying them?" I snap.

"The thought has crossed my mind. I don't know, B, I'm a traditional guy. I believe in laws and all that. I believe when you bed, you wed."

"What about all those women you ran around with when you were married to Toot?"

"That's different."

"How?"

"That's just sex. Half the time you're not even on a mattress, for cripesakes. Trust me. Those dames weren't looking to get married. They just needed a little Lonnie."

That this man believes he has done the women of New Jersey a favor by servicing them sexually in their times of need makes me want to throw up. And they say I have a big ego. The decorating world has nothing on Lonnie Falcone. "Okay, okay, whatever, Lonnie. I just think as long as the current arrangement is working for you and Toot why change things?"

Lonnie looks away. At certain angles he looks

like Robert Taylor when he was young and married to Barbara Stanwyck; at other times he resembles a hairy baboon. "You're right. Status quo is working."

"I don't mean to get back to business, but can you think of anyone else I can ask for money to get this renovation done?"

"You know, B, to be perfectly honest, the church is not the place people put their money anymore. They give direct to old folks' homes and disabilities and such. The church seems to have enough dough, you know?"

I ring Aurelia's doorbell, which is a first—usually I'm expected and walk right in. I saw that her car was in the garage, so I know she's home. After a few moments, she opens the door. "Can we talk?" I say politely.

"I'm not giving you the money, B."

"What is your problem?" I demand. I'm empowered as soon as I realize she's not going to give me the money, so there's no reason to be less than perfectly honest with her. "You married a Jew in 1929. What's wrong with your daughter loving a Mexican in 1970?"

"I will not discuss my daughter with you. She is dead to me."

"You're a horse's ass!" Aurelia steps back, stunned. "Yes! A big fat horse's ass! Let me tell you about Pedro Alarcon, because all you see is a poor man from a foreign country. I could be describing our ancestors from the Gulf of Genoa, but that's too obvious. Pedro is one of the most devout people I have ever met—and remember, I served Mass for Cardinal Cushing on his visit to OLOF in 1954, so I know devout. Pedro is humble and quiet and talented. And he loves your daughter. This is something she wanted and wished for. Capri has lived under your shadow for forty years."

"My shadow? I knew she wasn't a party girl, so I pushed her out from my shadow. I didn't keep her there!"

"You tried to marry her off to me, knowing it would never happen." Aurelia tries to protest. I stop her. "Uh-huh! Yes! Even though you pretended to want us married, you were thrilled when it didn't happen, because she would be here to take care of you. That's not what Sy wanted for you or her. In fact, Sy wanted you to remarry—"

"Never! One God, one man, one life!"

"That's a nice sentiment to put on a coin, but it's a bitch to live."

"It's my truth!" Aurelia thumps her chest.

"You kept your daughter in this house like a prisoner. I really believe now, when I look back on things, you had me redecorate this joint so many times so Capri would think she had moved. You wanted her to have a sense that something was going on here when, in fact, it was just a way to trap her in your world. Maybe the wallpaper changed, but they were still the same four walls, and the same mother inside to care for."

"You're wrong!" Aurelia bellows.

"And now to the matter of your millions. What will become of them when you disinherit your daughter?"

"I have plans for my money."

"Sy always stood by his word. I think he would be very angry to know that you promised the money to the church and then pulled the plug. After all, you rebuilt the Temple Beth-El in Oakhurst. He would have wanted you to do the same for your own house of worship."

"Things changed."

"For the better! You loved your husband and he loved you—and it's astonishing to those of us who witnessed that love to watch you take that away from your own daughter."

"He's not right for her."

"You haven't given him a chance."

"He doesn't deserve a chance. They're sleeping together and they're not married!"

"Is that what you're upset about?"

"No, I'm more upset that he's a Mexican!"

"Okay, now we're getting somewhere." I take a deep breath.

"No, we're not. I'm home, Mom." We both look to see Capri standing in the doorway. "Pedro broke up with me." The vibrant girl with the soft contact lenses is gone, and back is the frump in Coke-bottle eyeglasses.

Aurelia takes a deep breath. She looks at her daughter first with relief, but within seconds the walls go up. "I knew you'd come to your senses," she says coldly.

"I'm really nervous about showing you this job," Two says as we drive to Lina Aldo's house in Brielle.

"Relax. She called me and told me that she was thrilled."

"I can't thank you enough for giving me a chance to design a room for one of your clients. A bedroom, no less. I really appreciate the vote of confidence."

Two is right. It was a vote of confidence to hand over the reins when it comes to a favorite client. But to be honest, I've been so worried about losing funding for the church that I never would have been able to give Lina the attention she deserves.

The charming Cape Cod sits back on Windsor Avenue like a gray bird. Inspired by the black-and-white birch trees in the backyard, I used a palette of lavender, silver, and deep maroon for the interior. The only adjustment I asked her to make on the exterior was to paint the casement portion of the windows deep burgundy instead of black, and the front door burgundy instead of white to give a hint of what's to come inside.

"Come in, come in!" Lina greets us at the door. "My gosh, when I see you together, you look like father and son."

"How is that possible?" I reply. "My hair is coal black and he's a brownette."

"It's the face," Lina insists.

"Everyone tells me I look just like you." Two punches my arm.

Lina wears a burgundy silk blouse and a deep navy blue skirt. Her white hair is done is a simple pageboy. A great decorator pays attention to the client's personal taste and appearance. One look and you know her favorite color. Her style will dictate the things she likes around her. If she's ornate and wears lots of jewelry, that bolt of flocked wallpaper you picked up for a song at the Pierre Frey sale has her name on it. If she's a simple girl, she'll love early American or Shaker and cozy fabrics in cotton and linen—forget damask and silk taffeta. In a sense, a home is the landscape of a person's style. The surroundings should enhance what is already true about them. When I first met Lina, she wore a lovely burgundy-and-dusty-grape bouclé coat. That fabric, with the cue from nature in the form of birch trees, provided the palette I used in her home.

I did the living room, den, and hallway walls in dove gray with white trim and installed wall-to-wall carpeting in a slightly deeper shade of gray to give the small rooms a feeling of spaciousness. Lina is a classic, so I used tone-on-tone plum (Brunschwig & Fils #54) matelasse on the furniture, and the occasional stripe on the throw pillows—no busy prints anywhere. I kept everything trim and classic: no ruffles, beading, fringe, or ruching—clean lines only.

I convinced Lina to blow out the wall between her bedroom and bathroom to make a true master suite, with a row of windows along the back of the house; I allowed Two to oversee the contractor, and instructed him to come up with the bedroom décor.

I follow my nephew back to the bedroom. The first thing I notice are the window treatments. Two designed floor-to-ceiling draperies in a white dupioni silk, which opens up the room with light. The bed faces the entrance door, with nightstands on either side. A writing desk sits in front of the windows, and a chaise peeks out from an alcove that connects the bedroom to the walk-in closet.

"This is magnificent. Tell me how you came up with the design."

"Well, now that Lina is alone, she spends a lot of time in her room, so we put in a small desk for correspondence and a chaise longue." Two points to a unit of open shelves on the wall opposite the bed, where books, photographs in silver frames, and a small Deco vanity mirror are arranged. He talks fast, clearly proud of his work. "Let me turn on the low lamps for you." He flips the switch on two matching pewter lamps on the nightstands. The custom-made duvet of lavender satin trimmed in white is old Hollywood. The chaise is covered in eggplant velvet. It's a plum fantasy.

"Oh, Bartolomeo, Two designed a room fit for Gloria Swanson. I actually drape myself on that chaise like a fading film star," Lina says happily.

"It has just enough Deco, doesn't it?" I agree.

"Here is my favorite feature." Two sounds professional. "I had to think of a way to hide the television set."

"I hate TVs out in the open," Lina says.

"So where is it?" I look around the room.

Two goes to the étagère and points to a large oil painting hung in the center of the unit. It's a pastoral scene of green fields and a farmhouse, very soothing. "Watch," Two says. "It opens like a book." He pulls the painting toward him, swinging it open. Behind the painting is a television set.

"Isn't that brilliant?" Lina marvels. "During the day I close the painting, and at night, when I want to watch television, I open it."

"Great idea!" I give my nephew a quick hug. "I love it!" I couldn't be more proud if Two and I were father and son.

On the drive home, Two says, "Unc, I really want to work for you full-time."

"I'd love to have you," I tell him. Who knew I would love this mentoring business. I thought I'd hate working with others, but Christina and Two have changed my mind.

"Really?"

"After you graduate from Parsons or whatever design school you wish. You need a degree, and then you must be ASID."

"If you promise me that I can work under you, I will absolutely go back to school," he promises.

"You'll always have a job with the House of B."

While I appear to be unflappable, the truth is I am absolutely sick to my stomach about Capri and Pedro's breakup and the events it has triggered. It's not easy to raise money quickly, but God knows I'm trying.

After I went to Lonnie, I called Zetta Montagna to coordinate fund-raisers with the K of C. I groveled and went back to Father Porp, throwing myself on his mercy. After much begging, he agreed to go to the bishop, although Father is so angry at me that he can barely speak. I told him to put his feelings about me aside and think about his parish.

I am not above raising the money myself. I know many wealthy people, but, by and large, they're Episcopalian and they give to their own church. Short-term, I need twenty-five thousand dollars to keep Rufus, Pedro, and the crew working. Long-term, we need an additional hundred thousand dollars to finish the job. The ambitious Wall of Water is almost as much again. It might as well be a million dollars. I've managed to keep my pleas for funds quiet, hoping I won't have to tell Rufus we will soon be broke.

Pedro, poor, dear Pedro, is sulking around the church like the Hunchback of Notre Dame with his beloved Esmeralda. If you need proof that his love for Capri was true, all you have to do is look at him. I worry he'll slip with the cutting blade while he's working on the windows just to put himself out of his misery. Rufus promises to keep an eye on him.

When I arrive home Toot is waiting for me by the garage. She has borrowed Anthony's pickup truck.

"What's up, sis? Dear God, you're thin."

"I know. First time I lost weight in my life without dieting. It's all this running around. Now I know why the mistresses are always thinner than the wives. A **comare** is always on the go: running to meet him here or there while the wives sit home eating cannolis and wait." She points to a large crate in the back of the truck, marked BY ORDER OF THE QUEEN. "My friend Dahlia at the post office called. I told her you were on a job, so I went over and picked this up for you. What is it?"

"The children of Fatima." Toot helps me lift it out of the back of the truck. "I'm so blue, Toot. Where did it all go wrong?"

"Come on. It's only money. You've come too far. Make those bishops and cardinals give you the dough."

"Father said he'd go to them, but he doesn't think they'll help. Father wants to see me fail."

"What an idiot. It's **his** parish. He could get the money. Father Porp is a caddy for the bishop. Everybody knows it."

"Well, he's not going to call in his chit for my project, believe me."

"Makes me sick. The money is there! Look at the Vatican! Art up the yinyang! Gold everywhere! If I stood still in Saint Peter's long enough, they'd gold-leaf my ass. Furthermore, Fatima has gotten the shaft financially. We don't get half of the stuff the other parishes get. I don't know why Porp doesn't grow a pair and go to the bishop and say, 'Hey, why does every other Catholic church in Jersey get buildings and gyms while we have to beg for a holy-water font? Where's the justice?' "

"I don't pretend to understand the financial dealings of RC Incorporated."

Toot and I gently place the crate in my kitchen. I get out a hammer and lift the staples off the planks. The four sides of the box fall away when I lift off the lid. The statues are packed in burlap and cotton batting. Toot helps me unwrap Lucia, then Jacinta, and finally Francisco. The statues are taller than I remember, around five feet. Toot and I line them up across the kitchen floor.

"This is a sad bunch," she clucks. "These outfits are from hunger."

"They were poor sheepherders in Portugal. You weren't expecting Bob Mackie, were you?"

"They need a scrub-down and new rags."

"I'll have Aunt Edith make them new outfits. Let's take them up to the attic."

Toot takes Francisco, while I take Jacinta. We climb up the stairs to the attic and place them near Monica Vitti's chandelier. I go back down the stairs and into the kitchen where Lucia has fallen over, even though we left her upright. I lift her up, noticing she's heavier than the other two statues. They're made of gesso, so they're sturdy, but not weighty like statues carved from marble. I pick Lucia up like a baby and head up the stairs.

"You know, these glass eyeballs give me the creeps," Toot says. "They're like escapees from the Holy House of Wax."

"They like authentic in Italy, what can I tell you?"

"Yeah, and they take pictures of their dead in caskets too, but that doesn't make it civilized. I don't like the statues to be so real, the eyes follow you around the room. There's so much stuff in our religion that scares me."

"That's the point," I remind her. "Keeps us in line."

As I place Lucia on the ground, her foot falls off.

"It's broken!" Toot exclaims.

I lay the statue down on its back and check the foot. The suede boot she was wearing has fallen off, and it looks as though her foot, inside a long stocking, is damaged. I carefully remove the stocking. There is a seam around the ankle, as though the foot has been repaired before.

"They sold you damaged goods," Toot says.

"Wait a minute. There's something in the leg." I gently shake the statue, and something rattles. I stand Lucia up and hear a soft bang against the floor. I lift her up gently, and out slides a thin, white marble sculpture.

"What the hell is that?" Toot comes closer to look.

I examine the small statue. It's a long flute of polished marble with faint gold veins and an orb in the center. There are no etchings or carvings. It's sleek and modern. "It's the Blessed Mother," I tell her. "See?" I point out the veil, the robe, the orb, which represents the baby Jesus.

"Well, it won't work in my house," Toot announces. "I have real rosary beads on my Saint Theresa. You keep it."

No one has seen Capri since she moved back home. Aurelia is not likely to allow me into the house, so I asked Christina, a neutral party, to take a run over there to see how she's doing. Rufus, Pedro, and I are having lunch at the Tic-Tock, waiting for Chris. She's late, which is not a good sign.

"Pedro, stop beating yourself up," I tell him. "You fell in love. That's not a crime."

"It wasn't right. At first, when Capri and I were together, it was bliss. Then, as the reality of her mother's hatred set in, she withdrew. It became too difficult. She started to question what she was feeling. And then it was over."

"It's crazy." Rufus shakes his head. "Provincial town. Italian control."

I bristle. "Oh, the Irish have no rough edges, I take it?"

"Rough edges, yes. But not a general prejudice toward others."

"You have to understand that Aurelia is not familiar with Mexico and its people, except for a brief pit stop in Cabo San Lucas on a day trip when she and Sy were vacationing in southern California. I think, in time, she would have come around."

"You're dreaming," Pedro says, looking away.

"The worst thing Capri did was go home. That made it look like she agreed with Aurelia. She should have stood her ground." I tap the table for emphasis.

"Was she this way when you were with her?"

"Pedro, I was never **with** Capri. We're platonic friends who pretended to be boyfriend and girlfriend. Kind of like Judy Garland and Mickey Rooney."

"Deep down, Aurelia knew that you weren't husband material." Rufus stirs his coffee and looks at me.

"Right." I agree with him, but I'm insulted. "It's not that I'm incapable of love, it's just that Capri is like a sister to me." I sound awfully defensive, so I take a breath.

"Nobody said you were incapable of love. We all know you're a passionate guy. I've seen you mix paint."

Christina pulls up in front of the diner. Rufus watches her get out of the car; he raises one eyebrow ever so slightly and doesn't take his eyes off of her until she's inside the diner. I wonder if Rufus told her about Ann. Maybe I should say something to Christina later. Christina squeezes into the booth next to me. "What happened?" I ask her.

"We had a cup of coffee and she gave me this." Christina gives Pedro an envelope. Pedro's eyes light up. He really is quite attractive when he's not depressed.

"Excuse me." Pedro takes the letter and goes outside. Through the window, we watch as he lights a cigarette, then opens the letter and reads.

"How is Capri, really?" I ask Christina.

"Aurelia is not budging. And Capri thinks if she follows her heart, it will kill her mother."

Rufus pats Christina's hand and goes outside to talk to Pedro.

"Have you told Rufus about the money?"

"No. I don't have the guts yet. I keep hoping somebody will come through."

"He's probably dealt with this sort of thing before."

The waitress freshens up my coffee. I pour some cream into the cup. "You like him a lot, don't you?"

"Who?"

"Mr. McSherry."

She smiles. "He's interesting."

"Be careful."

Christina takes a moment to watch Rufus and Pedro outside. Then she answers me. "I will."

"OLOF has turned into the Broken Hearts Club of central New Jersey. As far as I'm concerned, they already have two members too many."

Christina shakes her head and studies the menu like a complex theorem. I know her well enough not to say another word.

———

The morning light streams through the main doors of the church, which are propped open as we work inside. The scaffolding makes the empty church feel like a large train station; and without the flow of people, it seems to have no purpose.

Rufus has prepped the walls of the church to paint the frescoes. There are a series of stripes on the wall where he has tested his paints—a rainbow of soft gold, ruby red, magenta, and moss green, and a small white cloud. It looks lonely on the expanse of the dingy wall. I close my eyes and imagine the grandeur of what his fresco might have been.

Rufus has begun to sketch onto the finished, smooth plaster walls. I see the outline of the countryside of Portugal, and what look to be angels in the heavens.

Pedro returned to the warehouse in Brooklyn to pour the glass for the new windows. He uses actual silver in the molten glass to give a rippled, iridescent effect. Before he left, I almost asked him if there was a way to make the windows more cheaply but thought better of it. What would I do if a client told me I couldn't use fabric from Scalamandré?

We have two days until payday, when we will officially run out of money. I've prayed to Saint Anthony, Saint Theresa, and Saint Jude, who handles hopeless cases. So far, no magic money has appeared. I have a few meetings later today to try and raise the funds, but they are long shots.

To keep my mind off the inevitable, I re-upholster the altar chairs myself. I found a wonderful cut velvet that I'm lining with muslin. Rufus has gone out to the truck for more spackle for the grotto wall.

"Bartolomeo!" Aurelia stands at the back of the church. She spots me and marches angrily down the aisle. She throws a letter in my face. "She left with that Mexican."

"What are you talking about? Pedro is in Brooklyn working on the windows."

"No, he isn't. He's off getting married to my daughter somewhere. Read it." I scan the letter, written by Pedro. Carefully, briefly, and respectfully, he tells Aurelia that he can't live without Capri.

"I'm sorry, Aurelia."

"Not as sorry as I am."

"No, I'm sorry you're determined to ruin Capri's life. I wish you'd take a couple of minutes and hold up a mirror. You would see how ridiculous you are."

"How dare you?" Aurelia puts her hands on her hips. When I was a boy, she was so tall she scared me. Now she seems like just another little old Italian lady in low-heeled pumps.

I put my hands on **my** hips and look her straight in the eye. "I've known you all my life, and I had no idea what you were really made of. I thought you were a humble Catholic girl who married for love and got lucky when it came to money. But you're a controlling woman whose generosity comes at a price. You can't see how good and decent Pedro is because when you look at him, all you see is brown skin. He'll be a better husband than I'd ever be, than most men would ever be, not that you'll ever see it."

"This is not what I wanted for my daughter."

"Yeah, but it's what **she** wants." I give the letter back to her. "Sy would be ashamed of you."

"He trusted my judgment in all things," she thunders.

"Well, he'd be really disappointed now. You want Capri to give up a chance at happiness to stay home and watch **Bonanza** with you while you eat pot pie and complain about how the church is soaking you for funds. Guess what? Capri wants more from her life, and as far as this church goes, we don't need your money. For the first time in the history of Our Lady of Fatima, we won't rely on the Castone Mandelbaum fortune to get us through. We'll do just fine without The Benefactor." Aurelia puts her hands in the air and goes.

After a long day of fund-raising, I pull into my parking spot outside the church. The soft work lights spill out the front door of the church, making a path down the stairs to the sidewalk. I sit and look at it for a long time. All around me, the black sky nearly swallows our little town in darkness. In the distance, the street-lamps throw white light like small moons, but for the most part it is bleak. I went to my top four clients and came away with a whopping twenty thousand dollars, which will buy the baptismal trough at the base of the Wall of Water and not much more. It's almost midnight as I climb the steps into the church with a heavy heart. I've been shamelessly avoiding this painful conversation with Rufus, hoping he's so engrossed in his work that he hasn't noticed how distraught I've been. I halfway expected Pedro to find out what Aurelia did, but I guess The Benefactor knew her daughter wouldn't rush home to save the day. Capri was always generous, but never devout. At least some small good came of this renovation. Capri found true love with Pedro. It almost makes the whole mess worth it.

I stand in the nave and watch Rufus sitting on scaffolding as he sands the wall where the stations of the cross will hang. I've seen how much he loves what he does, and it's heartbreaking to think he won't be able to finish his masterpiece. I look around the empty church, imagining what might have been. The dust from the plaster makes me sneeze.

"God bless you." Rufus looks down at me.

"Rufus, I need to talk to you."

He climbs down the ladder and meets me on the floor. "Sounds serious."

"We're in trouble."

"What's the matter?" He wipes the sweat from his face with a bandana.

"The funds have been pulled."

"What do you mean?"

"Aurelia cut us off because she's furious about Capri and Pedro. I went to Father, who went to the diocese. The bishop said he wouldn't give us the money. He said the renovation was too ambitious. He told Father to paint the joint and put the pews back in and call it a day." I have to force the words out.

"Great. What if the popes during the Renaissance had said the same thing?"

"I went to four of my biggest clients today and raised twenty thousand dollars, which buys us the baptismal font. The windows are safe because we paid for those supplies up front. I want you to finish. But we'll have to forgo the

Wall of Water. I'm sick about it, but it's too labor-intensive. We need a big crew to pull it off, and we just can't afford it now. It's the most expensive item in the design."

Rufus digs into his pocket and finds his pack of cigarettes. He offers me one. I take it. He lights his cigarette, then mine. Rufus exhales a cloud of smoke that disappears into the darkness.

I look around at my beloved church, in shambles. There are slabs of wood where the stained-glass windows used to be. A pile of rubble sits in the altar's place. The sacristy is filled with Sheetrock, tubs of dry plaster, and cans of paint. "I'm sorry, Rufus."

"It would've been something. Hey, this isn't the first time commerce won over art, and it won't be the last."

Eydie's town car pulls up in front of the Villa di Crespi on the dot of seven. I've prepared a lovely supper of tortellini stuffed with mushrooms in a spicy arrabiata sauce followed by a roasted rosemary chicken and a fresh escarole salad. I've been thinking about Eydie a lot. The crushing disappointment over the church has really depressed me, and I need to replenish my spirits with an evening of good food, expensive wine, and the company of a beautiful woman.

I greet Eydie at the door. She kisses me on

both cheeks and hands me her mink. She wears winter-white wool trousers and a pink cashmere sweater. Her long black hair is separated into two pigtails, loosely braided on the ends. "My God, that's extraordinary," I say catching a whiff of her perfume.

"I know, I smell like cookies, don't I?" she says, laughing. "I make my own perfume, you know. Right in my apartment. I buy the pure essence oils in Chinatown from a vendor I know. I take a drop of this and a drop of that in a base of pure alcohol. Then one day I tried a spicy Oriental mist and added a few drops of crème de cacao. That's what you're going gaga over," she explains.

"I knew it!"

"And I can't keep the men away!" She laughs.

I invite her into the living room, where I've set up a small table for dinner. "This is lovely," she says, pointing to the table. I pour her a glass of wine.

"Where did you get this?" She points to the marble statue of the Blessed Mother on the mantel.

"You know the statues that Asher sent me from England? Well, one of them was defective, and inside was that little statue."

Eydie picks it up carefully and turns it over. "This is a Modigliani."

"What?"

"It is. Here's his marking." She points to it.

"How is that possible?"

"World War II, the bombings? Asher said they hid things—"

"But **inside** the statues?"

"Obviously." Eydie is so excited, she places the statue down on the mantel and peers at it closely. "There was a story that Modigliani got so angry once in Venice that he threw a bunch of sculptures into the canal. They're still searching the canals for them. This statue could be from that period."

"I'll have to return it to Asher."

"You'll do no such thing. You found it."

"By accident. I paid for Lucia dos Santos, not this."

"Don't be an idiot. It would be generous of you to give him a finder's fee, maybe fifteen percent of what you sell it for."

"I don't want to sell it. I like it."

"I don't blame you. Lots of people like having great art in their homes, but the museums would fight over this."

"Really? Do you think it's actually that valuable?"

"It's one of the few sculptures of his that remain. He was known as a great painter, mostly."

"How much do you think it's worth?"

"Two hundred thousand dollars, at least," Eydie says. "Or more."

"You're joking! I've never been lucky in my life. I've never won at bingo, or guessed the right amount of jelly beans in the jar, or been the one hundredth customer at the free shopping spree at the Ben Franklin's. This is crazy!"

"You're going to be rich, my friend." Eydie smiles.

I can hardly eat my dinner. Eydie chatters on about Modigliani's life—what a handsome, temperamental cad he was, how he became a legend in the Parisian art world and a fixture in that city's wild nightlife. All I can do is look at the statue of Little Mary and dream.

How did this stroke of luck happen to me? I always wondered what it would be like to be rich, how it would feel to know that you have so much money that work is a hobby, not a chore. I am giddy with the possibilities. There are so many things I would love to do with this money. A house on the Golfo di Genova, for starters, or a year in Hong Kong watching the local artisans make silk. Or design school in London, where I would learn how to design wall treatments to the trade. The list is endless!

"I have to get back to the city," Eydie says after we've talked until midnight.

"Don't go."

"I have to," she says sadly. "When do you want to bring"—she indicates the sculpture—"to town?"

"Monday morning?" I ask.

"Meet me at my apartment, and I'll take you to the best appraiser I know at Sotheby's."

We stand in the doorway for what seems like minutes but is only seconds. I take Eydie in my arms and kiss her. She kisses me back, and I fill up with all sorts of emotions. I want her. This isn't like it was with Mary Kate, who gobbled me up like an oatmeal cookie. This is grown-up stuff, complete with untapped desires and feelings.

She gently pushes me away. "Bartolomeo, this is a bad idea." She smiles.

"Why?"

"I'm not the right person for you."

"How do you know, if we don't give it a chance?" I kiss her again, and this time she reciprocates with the passion I had hoped for. Her lips and skin are softer than the silk charmeuse I used to line Toot's duvet.

"Trust me," she says, breaking away from me. "This is a bad idea." She opens the door and turns to me. "But I adore you," she says with a smile. I watch her go, wishing she'd stay, but a little relieved she isn't. I like happy endings. Always leave on a high note. How could we top that kiss?

I place the last of the clean dishes back in the cupboard. I go to the living room and put the stacking tables back in their corner. I empty the ashtrays and take them to the kitchen. As I turn out the lights and head off to bed, I think about Eydie and me. She's probably right. We aren't right for each other. Two artists in a romantic relationship is one too many. When we're together, I can't get enough of her. I'd be overbearing and smother her.

I open the window in my bedroom to let the night air swirl through. I take my pajamas out of the dresser and lay them on the bed. I wash my face, brush my teeth, and put on the night-light in the bathroom (a habit since I was a boy). As I undress, I fold my clothes neatly and put them away. I put on my pajamas and climb into bed. I lie back on the pillows and think about Eydie. I wonder if she's thinking about me. The phone rings loudly, nearly giving me a heart attack. I reach over to answer it.

"I had to call," Eydie says breathlessly into the phone.

"Are you all right?"

"I'm fine. Just a little stunned."

"What's wrong?"

"I looked up your Little Mary statue. Oh, B."

"Don't tell me, it's worth less than you thought."

"More. How does three hundred thousand dollars sound to you?"

I can't speak.

"B? Are you there?"

"Oh, Eydie."

"I know. This is some news, isn't it?"

When Aurelia went to the local police to file a missing-persons report on Capri, they gently explained that a forty-year-old woman who leaves a note saying she is running off to get married does not fall into the category of "missing." I encouraged Father Porp to go over and have a chat with her, but Aurelia threw him out of her house, just as she did anyone who tried to reason with her.

With the news from Eydie, I skip up the stairs of the church. I holler, "Rufus! Rufus?"

"I'm over here," he shouts. I run to him.

"You know, it's a real shame," he says, surveying the work in progress around us. "Pedro is almost done with the windows."

"How do you know? You've heard from him?"

"They're at the warehouse in Brooklyn."

Rufus's eyes twinkle with the news. "They got married yesterday. City hall in Manhattan."

"Good for them."

"So, what do you want us to do here? Wrap things up?"

"Not quite. I have a plan."

"A plan? Did you figure out a way to keep going?"

"Rufus, let's just say I've run into some money."

"Legal?"

"Oh yes. Legit."

He picks up a scraper and chips away at the wall, then stops. "I'm glad. I really wanted to finish. I've worked on a lot of places, but this one—well, let's just say I'm hooked on the idea of Fatima."

"Don't tell me RC Incorporated got under your skin?"

"Nope. Don't sign me up yet."

"What, then?"

"It's her." Rufus points to the old canvas painted by Michael Menecola. This time the Blessed Lady seems to wink at Rufus.

"You're kidding."

"Nope." He goes to his paint can and stirs. I watch him for a few moments.

"Why do you work in churches?"

He laughs. "I'm nuts. There's nothing worse than working for Defenders of the Faith. They're all like Aurelia. They want it majestic, but on their terms."

"It's so frustrating."

"Yeah, but there's a lot of history in these old barns."

"But you don't really buy the final product: salvation."

Rufus smiles. "Oh, I believe in **that.**"

"I've never once heard you speak of faith. You've told me that dogma is for idiots. So, what's your motivation?"

"Women."

"Oh, come on." I throw my head back and laugh.

"What's yours?"

"I don't know. Beauty, I guess."

"Maybe we're talking about the same thing. Any man who tells you he creates something for his own pleasure or his own ego is lying. He builds and creates and struggles for one reason and one reason only: to impress a woman."

"You would boil down two thousand plus years of Judeo-Christian religion and the art it has inspired to impressing one woman? You **are** crazy."

"What is more eternal than love between two

people? It's been my experience that true love never dies. How about you?"

I cough to avoid answering him.

Rufus lifts his thermos off the Communion rail and offers me a cup of coffee. He pours a cup for me. "You ever been in love?"

"I think I'm in love with Eydie!" It spills out of me like the hot coffee out of the thermos. The second it's out of my mouth, I want to take it back.

Rufus smiles. "We all are. Any guy who's ever met her falls a little bit in love with her."

"What **is** it about her?"

"Eydie's wearing the best perfume they make. It's called 'I don't need you.' That is irresistible, my friend."

"I'm glad it's not just me." I sigh. "She has me by the neck."

"No, no, you're in good company," Rufus assures me.

"And Christina has you. Right?"

He puts down his coffee and pauses before he speaks. "She's an angel."

"I think so too . . . you're not going to hurt her, are you?"

"No," Rufus promises.

"Good. Because she's been through a lot."

"I wouldn't worry about Christina."

"She **is** strong," I point out.

"I'd worry about me." He grins and takes his paintbrush, shoves it in his back pocket, and climbs the scaffolding, reminding me of Clark Gable when he climbed the ropes on the **Bounty** before declaring mutiny. How I'll miss my friend when he is gone.

Henry Baxter at Sotheby's recommended that Eydie and I see a gentleman at Spolti Ltd. on Park Avenue. Grayson Asquith is a Modigliani expert and would be able to give us an appraisal and a list of collectors, including museums, who might want to buy the piece. Eydie wisely told me to act as though I didn't want to sell Little Mary in order to get the most money I can. We sit in Mr. Asquith's office, a crowded professional lounge on the corner of East Seventy-third Street. From this second-floor window, the well-heeled Upper East Side crowd goes about their business.

Last night I could hardly sleep. After the commission to Asher Anderson, I will take the rest of the money and put it into the renovation of the church.

Eydie is stunned at my decision. She thinks I should give part to the church and keep the rest. But little Lucia dos Santos did not come this far so that I might have a second home on the Gulf of Genoa. She expects a little more of me than that. I do not want to disappoint her. Father Porp is over the moon. He can't believe anyone would give this kind of money to our church who wasn't swimming in it (like Aurelia).

I've been around people who have a lot of money, and I see how it corrupts. Rich people develop a feeling of invincibility, but none of us are exempted from the pain and suffering of life. A wealthy person thinks, **If I need a kidney, I'll buy one; If I lose my career, I'll coast;** or **When I'm old, I won't need to rely on the kindness of others, I can pay someone to take care of me.** Instead of building relationships that matter, the rich man nurtures his relationship with the accountant.

It's true, this kind of money could go a long way at Scalamandré, and no one likes gold lamé more than me. Believe me. I have a moment where I envision myself flying on a plane to Italy to buy the best silks at Fortuny. But I take a deep breath and remember that I've managed to design gorgeous rooms regardless of budget. Besides, money spent doesn't necessarily translate to good taste. A cheap can of paint can change the mood of your room and, thus, your attitude about life. I have found cotton velveteen for three dollars a yard that is as exquisite as the stuff that sells for seventy-five.

My favorite sofa, a Georgian with carved legs, picked out of a Dumpster, was free. And it's my favorite piece of furniture. But there are people who believe that the more they pay, the more something is worth.

When I walk along the edge of the ocean behind my house, I am the richest man in the world. I don't need an enormous bank account to own that knowledge. I've come forty years living well on my means. I don't desire to accumulate more than I can use. I don't want my nephews coming to see me when I'm old because they're afraid I might cut them out of their inheritance. I want them to seek me out of love, not obligation, and not because they're expecting a check.

So many people in my family have severed their relationships over money. I find this terribly sad. Greed is insidious; it seeps into the bones of good people when they are unaware. You might think that money doesn't matter—until you're left out of someone's will. I've seen branches of my family collapse when that happens. I've noticed that bitterness and anger around money give folks health problems down to their bones. No thanks. I'll take sleeping at night over counting pennies any day of the week.

"Bartolomeo?" Eydie nudges me and whispers. "Are you listening? I just heard Asquith on the phone. They'll give you three hundred and fifty thousand dollars for Little Mary."

My head spins. "I can give thirty-five thousand to Asher?"

"He'll weep at the news!" Eydie tells me. "He'll never be able to thank you."

"And the rest goes to Rufus to finish our church."

"It's your money, baby." Eydie puts her head in her hands. "But you're crazy."

CHAPTER TEN

The Real Miracle of Fatima

Eydie and I celebrate the sale of Little Mary Modigliani at Valdino's on Hudson Street in Greenwich Village with the best bottle of wine they have. Every once in a while I take the check out of my pocket to look at it. I wave to Capri and Pedro, who just came in the front door. When I knew I'd be in the city, I called to invite them to dinner to celebrate their town hall nuptials.

"It's the refugees!" I say gaily.

"Don't even kid. Mom sent a private investigator to talk to us," Capri says.

She kisses me and Eydie, Pedro shakes my hand and then Eydie's, they sit down, and I pour them each a glass of wine.

"So the P.I. hears the whole story and feels so sorry for us that he tells us he's going to call Mother and tell her he couldn't find us. Can you imagine?"

"Any sensible person is on the side of true love," I tell her.

"Thank you for keeping me off the market, B. You saved me for Pedro."

I try not to be insulted. "I'm happy for you."

"Wait until you see Pedro's windows," Capri gushes.

"I'm almost done. Your nephew has been a great help," Pedro says to me.

"I was happy to send him to you. He is talented, isn't he?"

"He has a good eye." Pedro smiles. "Like you."

"I hope he has a better business sense. B is going to give all the money he made on Little Mary to the church renovation. I think he's crazy!" Eydie pats me on the back.

"B is one of those people who will give you the shirt off his back. And if that's not enough, he will also give you his pants." Capri smiles.

"Enough about me and my pants," I say impatiently. "How is married life?"

Pedro and Capri look at each other. "I was born to be with Pedro," she says.

"Can you top that, Pedro?"

"I don't think so. I love her very much." Pedro takes Capri's hand and kisses it. "But I want to make things right with Mrs. Mandelbaum. I don't like that I came between a mother and daughter. It's wrong."

"She made it impossible for you to be happy. I think Aurelia is the one with the problem, and she's the one who has to make it right." I tap the table with a soup spoon for emphasis.

"It's hard for her, B. It's just been the two of us since Dad died."

"Oh, please, Capri. Please. Your mother knows better. She is a fine person who, in a panic, said things she shouldn't have. She owes you an apology, and you"—I look at Pedro—"a new car. She was totally out of line. Here's a woman who suffered discrimination over her marriage to your father, and she turns around and persecutes you? Nuh-uh."

"I would like to go and talk to her," Pedro says.

"Take the priest. And if you know any cardinals, that's even better."

I roll into my driveway around 2 A.M. Toot's car is parked by the garage. She is fast asleep in the front seat, wearing a kerchief on her head and sunglasses. I rap on the window, and she awakens with a start. Through the glass, I see her mouth "Jesus."

"Don't you have a key?" I help her out of the car.

"I couldn't find it. Why are you so late?"

I ignore her question. "What are you doing here?"

"Doris and Lonnie are getting a divorce. She thinks he's having an affair!"

"Well, he is."

"**I** know that, but **she** doesn't. I can't risk my happiness. We've got to get the two of them back together." Toot follows me into the house. I flip on the lights as we go back to the kitchen.

"This is insane! Why don't you just let them divorce? You keep your house, he keeps his, and you continue this hot thing you two have without the hatchet of marriage hanging over your heads."

"God, B, don't you understand? It's the thrill I'm after. It's sick, but I **like** the cheating! And believe me, it does a world of good for Lonnie too. He cuddles and he compliments and he buys me things—it's what I always dreamed of. Now she'll leave him and he'll be at loose ends and looking to me to entertain him. As long as he's married, he has to go home sometime, which leaves me the bulk of my week to do what I please. If he's free, he'll be hanging around here and the starch will go right out of our relationship."

"Calm down. You're almost hyperventilating."

"You would be too! I don't want Lonnie full-time, B! I don't want to do his laundry, set his doctor appointments, and wash his car! Help me!"

"Okay, here's what you have to do. You have to break up with him."

"What do you mean?"

"Cut him loose. If I know Lonnie, it will take him a month to replace Lady Sylvia with another pretty Irish lady who likes Italian men. He'll marry number four; you lurk around in your teddy and mules, and pretty soon your hot affair is resumed."

"Honest to God, you're a freakin' genius. Maybe I'll go and see Iggy With The Asthma for a month."

"Good idea. By the time you get back, Mr. Lonely will have a new woman, and you can make a fool of her behind her back."

"I like this. I like this a lot."

"Okay, do you feel better?"

"A hundred percent."

"Good. Call him up and break his heart—first thing in the morning. Now get out. I'm tired."

Toot gives me a quick kiss on the cheek. "You always know the right thing to do."

The first thing I do at 9 A.M. is go to the bank and deposit the check from Sotheby's. The poor cashier almost faints. When I used to work behind that counter, I wondered what it would be like to have more money than you could possibly spend. Now I know. And I can't wait to unload it for a cause I believe in.

When I drive over to the church, I notice that the streets around it are filled with cars, which is very odd since it's not a holy day of obligation and no one called to say there was a funeral.

I pull up in a free space near the cemetery. I see Rufus's truck parked in its usual spot. I can't wait to tell him that Modigliani saved the day. We won't have to let the crew go—we can finish the job.

When I walk into the church, I hear the murmur of voices. I enter the nave, and the chattering stops. There must be a hundred people here, the very same faces that filled Toot's garage for my birthday party. This time, however, nobody's dancing. They're working.

Lonnie leads a line of men, including his sons, Anthony, Nicky, and Two. They pass large fieldstones to Gus Lascola, Zeke Nero, and Tulio Savastanno, who pass them on to the men of the Knights of Columbus. They look like Egyptians building the pyramids. When the stones reach the altar wall, another group of men, headed by Rufus, place them in a configuration that will become the Wall of Water.

Norman, our engineer, with the help of more parishioners, is mixing concrete in a wheelbarrow to point the stones together. Uncle Petey helps Pedro remove the wooden slats from the holes where his stained-glass windows will go. Capri stacks the wood carefully off to the side. Aunt Edith, cousin Marlene, and Nellie Fanelli polish the new stained-glass windows under Pedro's supervision.

Christina is on the scaffolding, showing the ladies of the sodality how to paint the pillars with a striae of faux marble. Oh my God! And there is Eydie, suspended high in the air, applying gold leaf to the molding. (What is she doing here, and who called her?) Near the sacristy, Toot makes coffee and puts out Danish on a bingo table in the alcove where the Blessed Lady shrine will go. Zetta stacks cups and napkins for break time.

I feel like I'm in the middle of a dream, where everything around me is moving but my feet are rooted in the ground. My heart is bursting in my chest like the sun breaking through heavy black clouds. I am so filled with awe and love that I cannot speak. I thought renovating this church mattered only to me, that I was the only one who had the pure heart to make beautiful the place where I learned how to pray. But I see now that I was never alone.

After a few moments, Toot sees me. "Hey, everybody, he's here! B is here!" They stop their work and look to me. When they see that I am moved beyond words, they leave their posts and walk toward me, until I am surrounded by the faithful. Christina pushes through the crowd. "Don't be mad at me. I felt so badly for you. I didn't want to see your dream end before the job was finished."

"Screw the diocese!" Gus Lascola pipes up. "We don't need their money." Everyone cheers.

I wipe my tears on my sleeve. "What are you looking at? Get back to work!"

Laughter fills the church like music. As the teams return to their tasks, Rufus puts his arms around me and gives me a hug. "Come and help with the wall. I want to make sure we do it right." But it doesn't matter what I think. Everything is more than right.

———

Rufus has hung clean muslin drapes on rods in front of the frescoes so prying eyes will not see them until they are dry. It has been a week since everyone pitched in to finish construction. I agreed to give Rufus the church to himself so he could complete the frescoes.

Like me, Rufus has a streak of the temperamental artist in him, and **he** alone decided when he would unveil his work. Between the money from the sale of Little Mary and the help of the parishioners, we had enough funds left over to replace the front steps and renovate the church plaza, which we had not budgeted initially. I was able to extend the black-and-white checked marble floor from the foyer throughout the nave. As eager as I was to see the frescoes (I suppose I could pull rank as The Benefactor), I didn't ask, out of respect for a man who has become a good friend.

As I walk down the side aisles, I can see the vivid tones of the murals through the flimsy muslin. How marvelous these bright colors are against the black-and-white checked marble floor (à la Westminster Cathedral) in the nave and foyer.

Rufus has been working day and night. He

approached the frescoes like a Renaissance artist. He used traditional dry paint pigment and then painted every inch of the wall himself.

I go to the sacristy. There are three dress bags marked LUCIA, FRANCISCO, and JACINTA with a note attached.

CLOTHES FOR THE FATIMA KIDS.
FROM AUNT EDITH.

I open the bags. The outfits for the statues are the same design as the originals, except that instead of being made from burlap and cotton, they've been redone in velvet. Tiny Francisco now sports beading on his shepherd's cap. These poor Portuguese sheepherders have become Italian American icons.

"Okay, B," Rufus says when he meets me in the sacristy. "It's just us for the first official tour of the frescoes. Now, if you don't like something, you'll tell me, right?"

"Rufus." He turns and looks at me. "You're nervous."

His face bursts into a grin. "I guess I am."

"There's nothing wrong with that. It means you care. This is like when Michelangelo"—I point to Rufus—"sweated bullets when Pope Leo"—I put my hand on my chest—"came through Saint Pete's to see the Sistine Chapel for the first time. It was a genuine tension convention."

Rufus puts out his cigarette and opens the side door of the church. "Let's enter from the front." I follow him outside, and he doesn't say a word as we climb the steps. We enter the foyer. "Here we are," he says as he flings open the door. I go in first.

The first thing that strikes me is the intense butter-yellow morning light shining through glass ceiling; it fills the church like an open field in summer. I catch my breath. The pits and shadows and Gothic somberness of the old place is gone, replaced by this heavenly light. The new pews of polished cherrywood with gold velvet seats and matching kneelers add to the spacious feeling of the church. The clean, soft sound of water cascading down the rock wall brings nature indoors.

The craftsmanship is breathtaking. I have never seen anything like it.

"You have to see the altar," says Rufus.

I follow him up the main aisle, inhaling the sweet smells of oil paint and plaster—the smell of something new. The altar is a simple oval Quaker cherrywood table. Hanging from a piano wire, just a few feet above it, is Monica

Vitti's chandelier. I knew I would find the perfect place for this glittering jewel, and here it is.

"Look at the stained-glass windows. Pedro made them rustic on purpose. I wanted the feeling you have in the village churches of Mexico. See the shards of color baked into the glass? That's an old technique from Spain. It gives dimension, makes the images almost dance in the light." Rufus points out the symbols of local life: the fish, the boat, the hammer and nails.

"Wonderful. No one will miss Saint Rose of Lima, who used to stand there in her window and look at you like she wished you were dead."

"Oh no, the messages of guilt and shame are gone now," Rufus promises. "This is all about rebirth and renewal. Just like you envisioned."

I follow Rufus to the Wall of Water. I touch the water as it flows over the rock wall like a sheet of sparkling rain.

"Step back," Rufus instructs me. "Can you see what we carved on the rock under the water?"

I see the word "**Credo**" in simple script. "I believe," I say. Looking up at the Wall of Water, we are as small as the base stones that make the baptismal font. I feel like I'm at the foot of a mountain waterfall.

"I know," Rufus says, reading my mind. "It turned out better than I hoped. Now come and see the frescoes."

I follow Rufus to the back of the church and he begins to yank away the muslin curtains. The walls are awash with brilliant colors, such a change from the dusty hues that were there for years. Rufus has painted the scene of the miracle, a hillside with the three children kneeling in prayer. On the hill itself, we see the observers, the townspeople. I am astonished to see that their faces are familiar. It's us! All of us. In the crowd I see Lonnie, Toot, Gus, Anthony, Nicky, Zetta—face after face of the people of OLOF. Rufus used the faces of the parishioners in the frescoes. The Blessed Lady hovers overhead. She is far more sleek and modern in Rufus's rendition. Gone are the pencil-thin eyebrows and veil. In its place, a real woman in a blue flowing gown and a crown of stars. "It's Christina!" I gasp.

"Who better to show the sadness of the world?" Rufus points to the ceiling. "Did you find yourself?"

I look up at a flock of cherubs peeking down from the clouds of heaven. I see my face as a boy, smiling.

"Toot gave me your First Communion picture."

"I'm stunned, Rufus. This is beyond anything I dreamed of. It's truly the church of the people. They will be overwhelmed."

"Most painters in Italy during the Renaissance used real people from their families and villages. It's an old idea, but it seemed to fit here." Rufus indicates that I should follow him to the side altar. He pulls the muslin away from the wall. He has angled the statues of the children of Fatima (in their new clothes!) on a small grotto of stone. Instead of the usual votive-candle trays, he has candleholders nestled into the rocks, so that when they're lit, they'll give the effect of a real cave grotto. It looks just like the cathedral in Santa Margherita; Rufus brought my sketches to life! What a perfect touch for this Italian American parish.

"Did you see Father Porp?" Rufus smiles and points. His face is near the baseboard, looking up at the Blessed Lady. "I put him in the most southern corner."

"Closest to hell."

"Yoo-hoo?" A voice calls out from the sacristy. I am so overwhelmed that my eyes are full of tears and for a moment I can't focus. I dab my eyes with my handkerchief.

"Hello, Aurelia," I say after a moment, wondering why she has to ruin such a perfect moment by showing up.

"This is spectacular," she says quietly, looking all around.

"We aren't showing it to the public yet," I tell her. After all, she did give us a substantial gift to start the project. I don't mean to be unkind. "Rufus gave me the first tour."

We stand awkwardly for a moment. So many years of history between us. Capri and me, playmates since we were toddlers. I was just a boy when I went to work for Aurelia's husband. Her house was one of my first projects as a designer, and became the endless job, one I have to admit I thoroughly enjoyed. It's hard for me to hold a grudge against a woman who has been so good to me. Finally she says, "I want you to have this," and hands me an envelope.

"What is it?"

"It's the money I promised for the renovation."

"But we don't need it anymore." I give the envelope back.

"I heard about the statue and the money, and it's wrong, B. You shouldn't have to pay it."

"Why should you have all the fun?"

"Excuse me?" she says.

"No, really, Aurelia. Why should you have all the fun? In my life, with all the rooms and all the homes I've decorated, I've never been so moved by a place as I am by this church. It was worth every penny. It was even worth the hell you put us through."

"I'm sorry about that." She looks away.

"I'm sure you are. And since you're sincere, I forgive you."

"Thank you."

"But I'm not the person you need to ask for forgiveness. You need to talk to Pedro. Look at his work!" I point to the windows. "Only a great man could make such art."

"I miss my daughter." Aurelia begins to cry.

"There's only one way to fix that."

"I'll do anything. I thought giving you the money was a start."

"Oh, Aurelia, I don't care about money. It's just another way to keep score. Don't get me wrong. We needed it, but I learned a big lesson here. If you do your work, money follows. It shows up. But it doesn't have anything to do with the magnificence of a person. It doesn't. What matters is what you **make**. Whether it's a cake for bingo night or a costume for a saint or a wall of water—whatever you pour yourself into in this life is what makes you rich."

"I've made terrible mistakes."

"Everyone does."

"Capri won't have anything to do with me."

"You shouldn't jump to conclusions. Although she **is** half Italian, and you know how

Italians are. We love not speaking when we've been slighted. You know, there's nothing more effective than the deep freeze, or sending you to the island—that sort of thing. But her lucky break is that she's half Jewish, and in that respect, if **you're** lucky, she'll throw her arms around you and let bygones be bygones. But I can't be sure, because I haven't asked her."

"Do you think she'll talk to me? Will you help me, B?"

Rufus, Aurelia, and I are stuffed into the cab of his pickup truck, reminding me of that publicity still of the Marx Brothers when they were crammed into the peel of a banana to promote the movie **The Cocoanuts.**

There isn't much to say; it doesn't take a genius to realize that Rufus doesn't care for Aurelia. I'm stuck between them like cannoli filling. Aurelia bristles as we take the exit off the Brooklyn Bridge and onto the winding streets that lead to the warehouse. This is a place she wouldn't want her daughter to visit, much less live in.

Aurelia takes the hike up the stairs to the studio slowly. Rufus bounds up ahead of me. When I reach the top with Aurelia, he has propped the door open. Capri waits in the middle of the vast room. Rufus and Pedro are nowhere to be seen.

Aurelia steps inside the studio and looks around at the scaffolding, the floor covered in splotches of paint, the dirty windows propped open to let in some of that fresh Brooklyn air, and finally, her daughter. Aurelia holds back the tears, but I can see how happy she is to see that her daughter is well.

"I'm going to leave you two girls alone," I say.

"No, stay," Capri says softly. She goes to her mother and puts her arms around her. Aurelia begins to cry.

"Can you ever forgive me?" she asks her daughter.

"Of course."

"I didn't want anything to change," Aurelia says quietly. "I wanted it like it always was, with you and me and Daddy. How happy we were."

"We were happy, Ma. But that was before I wanted to make my own life. I just wanted what you had."

"I understand that now."

"I'm married."

"I know."

"Pedro is my life. I want you to know that too."

"My mother always got along with her in-laws. She used to say, 'If you love him, I love him.' She never questioned anyone's choices when it came to marriage. I'm so ashamed I didn't follow her example."

"It's okay, Ma."

"Where's Pedro?"

"He's in the kitchen."

"I would like to speak to him alone, if that's okay."

Capri and I watch as she goes into the kitchen.

"What happened, B?"

"The miracle of the new Fatima Church. She came to see me and she was transformed at the Wall of Water."

Capri laughs. "That's all it took?"

A few minutes later, Pedro and Aurelia come out of the kitchen together, holding hands.

"I just booked the first wedding in your new fancy church," Aurelia announces.

"I'd like a Mass," Pedro says to Capri, clearly relieved that the mother-daughter rift is over and ancient Mexican curses won't be visited on him.

"I guess I'm planning a wedding," I tell them.

"Unc, where do these garlands go?" Two calls out from the altar.

"Festoon the pillars!" I holler back. "Spin them around the columns like crepe paper! The longest one, with the daisies, goes across the water trough at the base of the wall." Two nods. I climb off the ladder and help Zetta and the sodality ladies place a candelabra on either side of the entrance.

"This is quite a decorating job," Father Porporino says, standing back and observing the garlands of fresh daisies, red roses, and white tulips draped across the base of the choir loft.

"Oh, you haven't seen anything yet, Father. The mariachi band is coming from Philly—Capri will enter the church to a trumpet blast—and wait till you see the traditional lasso."

He blanches but forces himself to smile. After all, I am The Benefactor, which means I get to do whatever I want! "The first wedding in our new church. Thank you, Bartolomeo. Every day I thank God for what you've done here."

"Father, it was my pleasure. All I've ever wanted is a glorious church for our people. And now we have it."

"Go home and get dressed, Unc. I have it all under control." Two gently pushes me toward the door.

"Don't forget, candles lit before the first guest is seated. Dimmer on Monica Vitti's chandelier over the altar. Mariachis in the loft."

"I got it, I got it. Go."

As I drive home, I am filled with happiness for Capri—and so happy that it's **her** wedding day and not **ours**. If Sy Mandelbaum were alive, he would be so proud to walk her down the aisle. He always worried about her—worried that Aurelia was too overbearing, that Capri's countless ailments would prevent her from getting out in the world and making friends, and that his money might be not an asset but a hindrance to her finding her way in the world. "Nothing to worry about, Sy!" I send up a friendly prayer. "Things worked out just the way you wanted."

I stand back from the three-way mirror in my bedroom and marvel at the sight. I wear tight wool toreador pants and a red velvet bolero with gold trim. The crisp white dress shirt against my tanned skin makes me look like an Italian Cary Grant.

All of the men in the wedding party, including Rufus, will wear traditional Mexican attire for the ceremony. Mexicans, like Italians, like a crowd up at the altar. It's not a real wedding unless there are so many attendants that it looks like the graduating class of a large high school. Pedro has twenty men in attendance, and Capri has matched him a woman for every man. Believe me, that proved a real challenge—Capri was so short on friends, she invited two girls from our kindergarten class to be bridesmaids, my second cousin once removed, the peppy Monica Spadoni, and Coco Ciabotto, who overcame polio to found her own dance studio, Tots in Tights.

The women wear white silk flamenco dresses and carry fans decorated with crystals and lace. Aunt Edith's fingers must have bled sewing miles of ruffles for the skirts.

I hear the toot of a horn; my ride is here. I practically skip outside. I stop at my rosebush and yank off a red rose to place in my lapel. A happy day deserves a fresh flower—and a day where I remain a bachelor deserves a bouquet! Relief is a wonderful emotion, highly underrated. In fact, I prefer it to elation or joy. Relief lets the air out of the Tire of Pain. And I am reveling in it today. Everyone I see I love, and everyone is my friend. I didn't ruin Capri's life by not marrying her. In fact, I made a way for her to find true happiness and, with that, secured my own.

I climb into Rufus's truck next to Christina, who wears a darling flamenco dress with a tasteful mantilla. I look over at Rufus in his bolero and pants. "You look like the Nutcracker."

"Whose idea was this?" he complains.

"Pedro's. And don't worry, Capri got her two cents in. He's doing the Jewish thing, breaking the glass, and Capri's doing the Italian thing with La Boost, and together we're a glorious pack of Aztecs, down to our white socks and shoe buckles!"

"You make an excellent Mexican." Christina kisses me on the cheek. She turns to Rufus. "And you . . . not so good."

There's a traffic jam outside the church. The plaza is filled with revelers—family, friends, even the governor of New Jersey and his lovely wife.

Aurelia is stunning in a pink gown and matching mantilla. Her brother escorts her down the aisle, and she cries the whole way.

I stand in the back of the church and watch as Father Porporino takes his place in front of the altar and Pedro comes out of the sacristy and stands next to him.

"**Pssst.** Bartolomeo!" Nellie Fanelli pokes me in the ribs. "I love the redo," she whispers.

"Thank you." I hardly think this is the moment for chitchat.

"I have something to tell you."

"Now?" I'm officially annoyed.

"You see Father up there? He remains behind that altar by the grace of God."

"What are you talking about?"

"I blackmailed him."

"You **what?**"

"I went to him and told him that he better fire Patton and Persky and hire you or I was going to the bishop with some information I had." She winks.

"What are you talking about?"

"He's got a girl."

"Who has a girl?"

"Father Porp. I caught him and Zetta Montagna in the rectory. You know, I used to do the ironing over there too."

I don't know what to say.

"The right man got the job." Nellie jabs me again and finds a seat in the church.

For a moment I feel I might need to lie down. This is like Toot's wedding all over again—the heat, the drama, the emotional overload, and my gut churning with shock. But when I look down the aisle as the sunlight bounces off the Wall of Water like tiny stars, I could care less how I got the job. I'm just happy I did.

Capri has opted, out of respect for her late father, to walk down the aisle solo as the mariachis play "The Isle of Capri."

The traditional Mexican lasso, a rosary made of silk tassels (thank you, Mary Kate Fitzsimmons and Scalamandré), is given to the priest by Amalia, who wears a tiara of rosebuds that match the bodice of her white peasant dress. Father drapes the lasso over Capri and Pedro like a figure eight. A prayer of love and fertility is offered by Pedro's father. Father Porporino administers the vows, while Pedro and Capri look at each other with enough love to fill the place several times over.

Then Pedro is given the glass in the velvet sack, and I remember Sy Mandelbaum as Pedro smashes it with his foot. "Mazel tov!" shout the Mandelbaums, who roll with the Catholic/Jewish/Mexican ceremony like it happens every day. When Capri and Pedro kiss, two doves are released. They head straight for the open skylight and out into the world.

If I have to pick my favorite season on the ocean, it would be autumn. The foliage is less vivid near the salt water, but beautiful nonetheless. Pale yellow, sandy brown, and soft maroon leaves cover my yard like velvet petals. As I rake them into small piles, I remember where I was a year ago, and how much has changed in this short time. I didn't think it was possible to reinvent yourself after forty, but here I am, a different artist with a new point of view.

The breeze underscores my thoughts like soft music. Suddenly I hear the crackle of car tires on my driveway. I look up to see Toot pulling up in her Cadillac, followed by three other cars. It's a caravan.

Toot jumps out of her car. "B! B! Where are you?"

I wave from the yard. I see Nicky and Ondine get out of one car and Anthony and Two get out of the next one. Finally, a few paces behind, comes Lonnie. Everyone's yelling, apparently resuming an argument in full swing.

"What is the matter?" I hold my rake up like a school crossing guard with a stop paddle.

"Why didn't you tell us?" Nicky points his finger at me.

"Tell you what?"

"That Mom and Dad are having an affair!"

Two and Anthony look at me expectantly. "Sorry, Unc," Two says, "I begged them not to bother you with this."

"Bother him?" Anthony says. "He's in on it!"

"I'm not in on anything. Your mother and father's . . . arrangement is their business. It is none of mine and it never has been."

"Oh no, you're not going to weasel out of this," Nicky says. "You practically raised us and we need you. You have to fix this."

"Count me out." I turn, place my rake across my wheelbarrow, and lift its handles to roll it toward the garage. They follow me.

"Where's the baby?" I ask Ondine.

"With my mother."

"I didn't want Moonstone to witness this!" Nicky shouts.

"Oh, come on," Toot shouts back. "So your dad and I still get together."

"We don't mind if you have lunch every once in a while. It's having sex that's upsetting us!" Anthony says.

"What difference does it make to you?" growls Lonnie. "How the hell do you think you got here?"

"Yeah!" Toot piles on.

"You're cheating on Doris!" Nicky points out.

"Oh, I wish you had rallied to my defense when he was cheating on **me!**"

"That's different," Anthony counters. "You were his wife. Now you're his **comare.**"

"Would it make any difference if I left Doris and got back together with your ma?" Lonnie asks. Nicky and Anthony grumble. Two looks at me and rolls his eyes.

"Lonnie, I don't want you back."

"Huh?"

"I don't. I like a little taste of honey once in a

while, but I don't need to suck back the whole jar. If it's all the same to you, I'll continue our arrangement as is or not at all."

"You're breaking up with me?"

"I don't want to, but if everybody is on their high horse about us having an affair, why would I continue? After all, I am a mother figure."

"Grandmother too," Ondine says seriously. Poor girl. With the birth of her baby, she has gone from a hot New Jersey version of Connie Stevens to Eleanor Roosevelt.

Nicky throws his hands up. "What kind of examples are you people? You're acting like teenagers."

"It is a little unsavory," I agree.

"Who are you to talk? What kind of example have you been for my boys in the romance department?" Toot demands.

"I didn't know that was part of my job as uncle."

"Of course it is. If you were married, I wouldn't have two single sons here as they crash and burn toward thirty years old."

"I got time, Ma," Anthony promises.

"I'm never getting married," Two announces.

"See? See? Your bachelor status has soaked through the fabric of our family like motor oil. Why don't you want to get married, Two? It's me, isn't it? And all that pain Daddy caused us so many years ago." Toot puts her arm around Two.

"No, no, that has nothing to do with it," Two says. "I wear the powder blue."

"What the hell does that mean?" Lonnie asks.

"I love a nice shade of powder blue," I say. They all look at me. "Well, I do."

"It means I like men," Two says simply.

"Jesus Christ, what are you saying?" Lonnie booms.

"I'm a homosexual," Two says quietly.

"I knew it," Anthony says, pleased with himself. "It's the theater."

"Are you sure?" Nicky asks Two.

"Why would he tell us if he wasn't?" Lonnie barks. "Just to give me a stroke?"

"I don't think you can be unsure about that," Ondine agrees.

"Everyone knows there are no Italian homosexuals!" Lonnie grabs at straws.

"Da Vinci, Michelangelo, Tiepolo—shall I go on?" Two looks at me.

"No!" Lonnie shouts. "Well, he didn't inherit this from my side!"

"No, I'll get hardening of the arteries, prostate cancer, and diabetes from your side, Dad," Two says diplomatically.

"I'm completely speechless," Toot says quietly.

"Ma, you knew all along."

"Maybe I did. But I didn't think you'd ever bring it up! I should have never let you wear Christina The Widow's Communion dress for your Halloween costume when you were seven. That was a mistake." Toot shakes her head.

"I told you so at the time!" Lonnie says critically. Then everyone looks at me.

"What are you looking at?" I ask. "You think I wear the powder blue?" No one answers. "Well, let me say this. Two, no matter what you are, you're my nephew and I love you. I put up with a philandering father and a mother who cried about it for fifty-some years, and I never judged them for it. Toot married your father, a good man but not without his weaknesses, and I never judged him either. For me, the definition of family is that group of people who love you for everything you are, regardless of what they think of it. So, if you wear the powder blue, that is absolutely fine with me."

"Well, sure," Lonnie says. "You're a decorator. Your profession's loaded with them."

"I have news for you, Lonnie. They're everywhere. Even in the jewelry business. Even in RC Incorporated."

"Dear God," Lonnie clucks.

"You know, I love being a bachelor. And I'm tired of explaining it. I love my family, but I don't want to make one." I point to them. "I never wanted . . . this. The great love of my life is my work. I've never found a person who thrilled me as much as a blank piece of paper in a sketch pad."

"Cheaper than women," Lonnie says.

"I didn't have a family because I don't like this." I indicate them as a group. "I don't like drama. Now, you need to get in your cars and go back to Toot's and sit down at the table and talk through your problems. If you don't like Dad schtupping Mom, tell them, not me. And Two, thank you for sharing your news. Now, if you will all leave me to rake my leaves in peace."

After some more bickering among themselves, Toot, Lonnie, Nicky, Ondine, Anthony, and Two take a hint, climb into their cars, and go. I take my wheelbarrow back out into the yard and go back to my raking. How funny. People wonder if I wear the powder blue. Doesn't everyone want to fall in love with a special person? It's almost a given at birth, isn't it? For me, I knew long ago that one person would never be enough for me. My dream companion would be half Eydie Von Gunne and half Rufus McSherry. Alas, it can never be, not in this world anyway, so I will wait until the next, where all mysteries are solved and all secrets are revealed.

The di Crespi/Falcones gather in the foyer of Our Lady of Fatima Church on a warm September day, wearing our Sunday finest. Baby Moonstone, who at seven months is too large to fit into our family christening gown, is in a little white tuxedo with a bow tie. He is so big, he could swim in the baptismal trough, not just get dunked.

"Look, Ondine, we're Catholic," Toot says patiently. "And Catholics, as a general rule, need a saint's name somewhere in the configuration. It's how it's done."

"There's no Saint Moonstone?"

"Not in any of the books we've consulted." Toot looks at me.

"I like the way it sounds." Ondine shrugs.

"Maybe Father Porp will give us a pass on the name," I offer. "I'll ask him." Ondine looks at me gratefully.

"We gotta get this kid baptized," Toot says nervously. "I'm at the point where I don't care **what** you call him. I'm terrified of limbo."

"I could turn Catholic," Ondine offers.

"It takes a year."

"Why?"

"Well, you have to learn all the rules and regulations. And you have to take classes and then
must undergo the sacraments: baptism, First
Communion, penance, and then confirmation.
And then you and Nicky need to get married in
the church, and then you can become
Catholic."

"They don't make it very easy for people."

"That's a common criticism."

"Cripes." Ondine shakes her head. "Why is
being Catholic so hard? If you want to be
Methodist, all you have to do is show up."

Father Porp meets us in the back of the
church to bring us up to the altar for the baptism. Moonstone Falcone is the first baby to be
christened in the new church. Father gave us
no trouble about the name, which means that
as The Benefactor, I now have some sway in
this province of Rome that I didn't have before.
The ceremony is quick and lovely. We pile into
our cars and head for the Villa di Crespi for the
celebration luncheon.

Christina and Amalia, good soldiers that they
are, stand in my kitchen and put garnish on the
platters. I give Amalia a basket of rolled linen
napkins to take outside. "Christina, come with
me," I tell her.

She follows back to my bedroom. "What is it, B?"

I show her a package propped against the bed, eight feet long and six feet high, wrapped in brown paper. "This came for you yesterday. There was a note." She opens it.

Dear Christina, Amalia should have this someday as part of her family legacy, but for now, enjoy it. Love, Rufus

I help her untie the string around the package. "Have you heard from him?"

"Once in a while. He's in Italy now. He sent us a postcard."

Christina carefully pushes away the brown paper. There, in a gilded gold rococo picture frame, is Michael Menecola's painting of the Italian bombshell. Christina puts her hand over her mouth and laughs. "I wondered what happened to her."

"Rufus restored it for you."

We stand and look at it for a moment, remembering the day we found her underneath the fresco. "I think Charlie would have liked him," I tell her.

"I think he would have liked her"—Christina points to the brunette—"more."

We hear the sound of our family out in the kitchen.

"Time for **la festa!**" I clap my hands together.

Once we're back in the kitchen, I give Toot the mozzarella-and-tomato salad. "I'll check on the table." Christina goes outside. I direct Toot to follow her. "Put this next to the antipasto. Thank you."

"It was nice of you to make this party."

"Could you see us cramming into Nicky's house?" I ask practically.

"Well, it was very generous of you." Toot turns and looks at me. "You know, I don't know what we'd do without you."

"You'd get along just fine. The napkins wouldn't match, and the china would have chips, and somebody, God knows, would burn the gravy. But other than that, you'd make do."

"No, I'm serious. You're always there for us. You make everything beautiful. I just want you to know that I notice."

"You're welcome, sis."

Doris comes into the kitchen carrying a Jell-O mold. "Where should I put this?"

"Take it right out to the table," I instruct her. "There's a bowl of ice in the center. Place it inside." She smiles and goes. "I like a girl who follows instructions. Hello, Lonnie."

Lonnie carries a beer tap. "Anthony's putting the keg out back."

"Excellent." I pick up a platter of chicken cutlets. "I'll see you outside." I turn to open the back door with my hip and see Lonnie put his hand on Toot's ass and give it a squeeze.

I decorated the yard for the party. The Moroccan tent of bold black-and-white canvas stripes, with a circus-tent top, notched Greek key accents, and draperies tied back on four poles, makes a dramatic canopy. How luscious it looks with the ocean in the background and a clear blue sky overhead.

Under the tent, Ondine hands the baby to Doris, Christina tosses the salad, Amalia gathers the salad bowls, Anthony shares a joke with Nicky, and Two serves the beer. Ondine's parents and sister seem right at home. Amalia rings my grandmother's crystal dinner bell as Toot and Lonnie join us under the tent. I give my sister a subtle sign to fix her lipstick smear.

As we gather around the rough-hewn farm table made by my grandfather, I am reminded that my family has come together for generations in this same way. Summers were always our favorite times; we would eat outdoors under the shade of a tree—hand-rolled pasta with a sauce of fresh tomatoes and basil from the garden, cheese from Aunt Carmella, olive oil sent by our cousin in Santa Margherita, and wine from our own jugs. After having our fill of food and laughter, we'd pluck ripe figs right off the trees, peel and eat them until the sun disappeared into the blue. I can still taste those summer days, and will always do everything in my power to re-create them. This is what it means to be a di Crespi.

There was a time when family meant more than just a common name on a document. We actually had a shared goal, something to make together. When Mom and Pop were alive, the aunts and uncles and cousins (whether you could stand them or not) would come for the harvesting of the grapes to make wine. And in between all the stomping, straining, siphoning, and pouring, we'd play bocce under the arbor, a gnarl of branches, old veins now plucked clean of fruit. I remember feeling safe and wishing it would last forever.

When my parents died, Toot was determined to hold it all together, so come holidays she would cook enough for an army, hoping that if she fixed the amounts that Mama did, made them with the same ingredients, and served them on her dishes, somehow, magically, those who had passed on would show up again and it would be as it once was.

What we've learned, of course, is that no one comes back; the grief becomes a part of us in the same way a new baby does. No matter what, we find out if we grow old enough, we go on. Italy and her influence upon us seem to fade as each generation rises, much like a stamp saturated with ink, used over and over again, until the message finally is so faint it can't be read.

So we gather on summer Sundays at noon after Mass for family dinner or on special occasions like this one. Each sister, aunt, and cousin still makes a dish and brings it. We argue about the recipe, who makes it better, and who will make it next time. We set a table, we come together, and we make a life.

For those of us who are new to the scene, like Ondine—whose family isn't sure of their origins, knowing only that they've been in America much longer than we have—to those folks this ritual must seem silly. Why not grab a meal at a restaurant and call it a day? Why not make it easy and call a caterer? Well, that's not our style.

We have a way of being as a family that is purely Italian, beginning with the food we eat and ending with the regalia of our funerals. The care we take with our recipes, the slow preparation of the food, the retelling of old stories with the same familiar punch lines, bring us joy. Of course, there's also the dark side—the arguments, the freeze-outs, the Evil Eye. But eventually forgiveness washes away bad memories like clean rain. To an outsider, this may seem hypocritical. So what? We are what we are.

We even find a way every now and again to rewrite our family history. A **comare** becomes a friend of the family. Forget that she slept with Grandpop behind Nonna's back—she was there for all the big events, so she's one of us, a beloved aunt of sorts. The business deal that went south when money changed hands between uncle and nephew, well, it was only money. The cocktail ring that Nonna left to her granddaughter wound up on the wrong hand after sister had a falling-out with brother, but what the hell? It's only a ring.

What makes us different is what helps us stick together. We're Italian first and foremost; we can be wily and inconsistent, and to the outside world we may appear temperamental, moody, and clannish, separating ourselves from the greater culture with a cup of arrogance and a dose of superiority. But the truth is, we are bonded by all of it, the best and worst of ourselves, by what we are, how we walk in the world, and the way we hold one another close.

We are the sum of all of it, the devotion, the blind faith, the disappointments, the slights, the hurts, the surprises, the insanity, and, yes, that passion that drives us to make love with careless abandon and hold a grudge with the same intensity. What would I be without them? Would I, given all I've seen and know, have picked up a brush to paint the picture differently? I wouldn't have. I wouldn't have it any other way.

Acknowledgments

As someone who sits alone and writes in a laundry room, I am always amazed at how many people work so hard to publish my books on time and beautifully. Each of the following folks are stellar at what they do, and without them, I would be nothing. So, my love and gratitude to Lee Boudreaux, my brilliant and graceful editor, and the team at Random House: Gina Centrello, a great publisher with an enviable bench that includes Libby McGuire, Laura Ford, Jennifer Hershey, Carol Schneider, Tom Perry, Karen Fink, Kate Blum, Jennifer Jones, London King, Jennifer Huwer, Cindy Murray, Rachel Bernstein, Allyson Pearl, Magee Finn, Christine Cabello, Avideh Bashirrad, Stacy Rockwood-Chen, Judy Emery, Vicki Wong, Beth Pearson,

Beth Thomas, and Anthony "Z" Ziccardi. Kim Hovey at Ballantine is one of the all-time greats and I adore her.

Allison Saltzman is the divinely talented artist who designs my book jackets. You know the old saw "You can't judge a book . . ."? Well, in this instance, I hope the words inside rise to the glorious covers she creates. The audiobook for **Rococo** was recorded by the delicious stage and screen star Mario Cantone. Wait until you hear him! The Random House audio team is first-rate: Scott Matthews, Amanda D'Acierno, Sara Schober, Susan Hecht, Carol Scatorchio, Aaron Blank, and the great Sherry Huber.

At William Morris: Thank you to the hard-working, ageless, and delightful powerhouse Suzanne Gluck and the equally ageless Jennifer Rudolph Walsh, along with Cara Stein, Eugenie Furniss, Leora Bloch Rosenberg, Erin Malone, Judith Berger, Raffaella DeAngelis, Andy McNichol, Tracy Fisher, Candace Finn, Michelle Feehan, Alicia Gordon, Bari Zibrak, and Rowan Lawton. And at ICM: my champion, the ageless beauty/brain Nancy Josephson and the adorable Jill Holwager.

My fellow writers, I remain in awe of your talent and thank you for your support and guidance: Jake Morrissey, Thomas Dyja, Ben Sherwood, Susan Fales-Hill (thank you for the

French translation!), John Searles, Rosanne Cash, Sister Karol Jackowski, Robert Hughes, Charles Randolph Wright, and Russ Woody.

Michael Patrick King, you mean the world to me. Thank you for your daily counsel.

My dad, the late Anthony J. Trigiani, would have loved this story, as he was the first man to introduce tasteful flocked wallpaper to Big Stone Gap, Virginia. And my mom, Ida Bonicelli Trigiani, who has the best taste of anyone I've ever met, is my hero in life and home décor.

I thank my mentors: the late Ruth Goetz; George Keathley; at the Italian American Playwrights Forum: Donna DeMatteo, Rosemary DeAngelis, Theo Barnes, and the late Vincent Gugleotti; my teachers, Reg Bain, Fred Syburg, Max Westler, Sister Jean Klene, Theresa Bledsoe, and the late Greg Cantrell; and those who gave me great jobs in television: Bill Persky, Janet Leahy, Alex Rockwell, Laurie Meadoff, and Gail Berman. How lucky I am to work with the great producer Larry Sanitsky of the Sanitsky Company, Susan Cartsonis and Roz Weinberg of Storefront Pix, independent producer/writer Julie Durk, and the tireless Lou Pitt.

Ann Godoff, thank you for opening the door to my literary career.

In the UK, thank you to my dazzling publisher, Ian Chapman; my editor, the stunning

Suzanne Baboneau; the darling Melissa Weatherill; and Nigel "Left to Carlisle" Stoneman.

Mary Testa, you're the best. Elena Nachmanoff and Dianne Festa, I adore you.

My thanks to Gina Miele, who provided Italian translations and a detailed knowledge of all things Jersey Shore; Helen McNeill of Saxony Carpets, the Queen of the D&D building; the eagle eyes of Randy Losapio and Jean Morrissey; Ellen Tierney and Jack Hodgins, for their vast knowledge of furniture and antiques; and Ralph Stampone, ASID, for taking me to Scalamandré's in the first place. Thank you, Debra McGuire, the dazzling designer who taught me about color and taking risks, and the megatalented B Michael, who taught me about shape and form. Father John Rausch, thank you for all Roman Catholic facts pre– and post–Vatican II.

My love and devotion to Ruth Pomerance, Wendy Luck, Craig Fissé, Stewart Wallace, Catherine "Shag" Brennan, Cate Magennis Wyatt, Dee Emmerson, Liza Persky, Jim Powers, Todd Steiner, Sharon Watroba Burns, Nancy Bolmeier Fisher, Kate Crowley, Emily Nurkin, Adina T. and Michael Pitt, Maureen O'Neal, Eydie Collins, Pamela Perrell, Carmen Elena Carrion, Jena Morreale, Jim and Jeri Birdsall, Dolores and Dr. Emil Pascarelli, Joanna Patton,

Danelle Black, Jeff Snyder, John Melfi, Andrew Egan, Grace Naughton, Gina Casella, Sharon Hall Kessler, Lorie Stoopack, Karen Gerwin, Constance Marks and James Miller, Denise Spatafora, Bill Testa, Sharon Gauvin, Beatrice Branco, Cynthia Rutledge Olson, Jasmine Guy, Jim Horvath, Jim and Kate Benton Doughan, Joanne Curley Kerner, Dana and Richard Kirshenbaum, Daphne and Tim Reid, Caroline Rhea, Kathleen Maccio Holman, Susan and Sam Frantzeskos, Beata and Steven Baker, Eleanor Jones, Mary Ehlinger, Drs. Dana and Adam Chidekel, Brownie and Connie Polly, Aaron Hill, Gayle Atkins, Christina Avis Krauss and Sonny Grosso, Susan Paolercio, Rachel and Vito DeSario, Irene Halmi, Hannah Strohl, Matt Williams and Angelina Fiordellisi, Karen Kehela, Sally Davies, Liz Welch Tirrell, Jenny Baldwin, Mary Murphy, Marisa Acocella Marchetto, Elaine Martinelli, Lorenzo Carcaterra and Susan Toepfer, David Nudo, Laura Sonnenfeld, Bill Goldstein, David Blackwell, Todd Doughty, Joe O'Brien, Greg D'Alessandro, Anne Slowey, Barry and Molly Berkowitz, Carol Fitzgerald, Deb Stowell, Eric and Denise Lamboley, Dona DeSanctis, George Dvorsky, Rhoda Dresken, Beth Hagan, Jim and Mary Hampton, Patrick Kienlan, Kathleen Sweeney and Bettye Dobkins, Mike Sieczkowski and Mark Yarnell,

Rick and Laurel Friedberg, Nancy and Chris Smith, Iva Lou Daugherty Johnson, Phil and Patsy Vanim, Tom and Barbara Sullivan, Veronica Kilcullen, Madge Bryan, Amy Chiaro, Joanne LaMarca, Doris Shaw Gluck, and Eleanor "Fitz" King and her daughters, Eileen, Ellen, and Patti.

To the Trigiani and Stephenson families, my love and thanks.

I remember and thank the late Margarita Torres Cartegna (and her girls, Wendy, Cyndi, and Laura). I will always miss Monsignor Don Andrea Spada, June Lawton, Helen Testa, Ernest "Poochie" Felder, and Wayne D. Rutledge. Jim Burns, please continue to leave a light on for us in heaven. And to my husband, who can fix anything, and to my daughter, who can break anything, may you be happy, healthy, and mine all the days of your long, long lives.